IN THE ARMS OF A KILLER

Ellie stumbled for the opening, the crumbling hole in the rock.

The voice from the opening stopped her cold.

"Come," it said. "Come, you must meet my lovelies."

"Nooo," Ellie screamed. She threw herself backward and flipped over, crawling away, scrabbling.

Powerful hands caught her and pulled her back.

She clawed at the rocks, panting, grunting, her hands becoming slimy with blood as her palms and finger pads shredded, sobbing, not feeling anything except the awful burning for survival and the knowledge that she failed.

She was pulled back, screaming . . .

She met the killer.

And, she met his lovelies.

"Fatal Flowers is a chillingly authentic look into the blackest depths of a psychopath's fantasies. Not for the faint-hearted . . . Smith's a cop who's been there, and a writer on his way straight up. Read this on a night when you don't need to sleep. You won't . . ."
-Ann Rule, bestselling author of *Small Sacrifices*

Also by Enes Smith

Dear Departed
Cold River Rising
Cold River Resurrection

FATAL FLOWERS

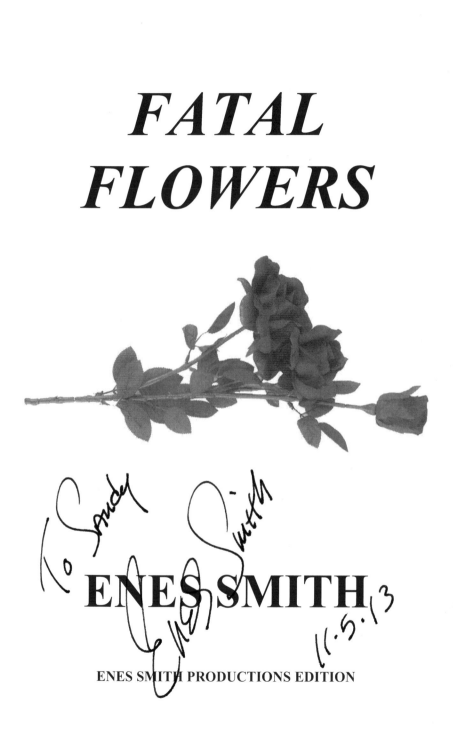

ENES SMITH

ENES SMITH PRODUCTIONS EDITION

FATAL FLOWERS

Printing History

The Berkley Publishing Group
Diamond Edition
May 1992

Enes Smith Productions Edition
June 2009

Cover design by Kent Wright

For additional copies, go to Amazon.com

ISBN-10: 1453832882
ISBN-13: 978-1453832882

Printed in the United States of America

AUTHOR'S NOTE

Fatal Flowers was my first novel, and there were many people who contributed to the novel seeing the light of day: Ann Rule, who believed in me and encouraged me when I needed it most; literary agents Joe and Joan Foley; and my editor at Berkley, Melinda Metz.

Fatal Flowers was first released in May of 1992 by the Berkley Publishing Group, with their Diamond imprint. The first printing had an embossed cover; the second printing, in June of 1992, had the same cover art but was not embossed.

This new edition reflects changes in society and technology since I wrote the story; other than that, the story remains unchanged.

FRIDAY
JUNE
30

Northwest Arizona
Sundown

The van showed the sand of the high desert as it slowed and pulled into the pump island of the service station. An hour after sundown, the night air was starting to cool from the heat of the day. The bell rang twice, bringing the attendant awake in the fishbowl of the office. The attendant, a kid barely out of his teens, shook his head and tried to focus on what rang the bell. It sure wasn't usual for it to ring at this hour. Not much business after dark.

The driver sat with his head resting on the seat back, letting his shoulders sag. He should have felt rested, having slept until noon, but he had a thousand miles ahead of him before he could stop. Before he would feel safe enough to stop.

The race up from Phoenix had drained him. He'd taken State Highway 93 northwest, through Sun City, up through the high desert country of Wickenburg and hit I-40 just 20 miles east of Kingman. The desert had resembled a solar landscape, lonely and forbidding in the twilight, eerie in the moonlight, and had not helped the feeling that someone was after him.

And maybe someone was.

It was always this way when he got tired. With a full night of rest, he knew that nothing could stop him.

The kid approached the van, rubbing sleep from his eyes. Good thing the damned van stopped after all, he thought. He needed this job, piece of shit that it was at minimum wage, and it wouldn't do to let the owner catch him sleeping.

"Help you, mister?" It was dark inside the van, with the roof blocking out most of the floodlights that lit up the lot.

"Fill it." The voice was tired, disinterested.

The kid started the pump. Be damned if I wash the windows, he thought, and then he heard the whimpering coming from inside the van. Some people just didn't take care of their animals, shouldn't be allowed to own a dog.

He shrugged and icily dug at a pimple with his fingernail. Wasn't his concern.

Jesus, this thing sure takes a lot. Be out here all night. Already over two hundred dollars worth and not stopping yet. He looked up from the pump and along the van, where he caught the eyes of the driver on him in the side mirror,

"Hey, mister, we just went over two hundred dollars. You want more?" He scratched at the pimple again, wanting to get back to his chair.

"Fill it."

When the hose clicked to the off position, the total was two hundred twenty-eight dollars. The attendant went forward to collect. He heard the whimpering again, louder this time, eerie, and it sent shivers down his legs. Something in the van wanted out.

"Hey, mister, that'll be two hundred twenty-eight dollars. How big a tank you say you got in this thing?"

The driver handed him two hundred thirty dollars, and still said nothing. The whimpering came again.

"Mister, we can let your dog out if you want. He must be pretty hot and tired now, and I heard him back there, and---."

"Where can I eat in Kingman?" the driver demanded. The attendant started to lean in the open window. There was something about this man, something that caused the hair to come up on his neck and arms as he got closer. The whimpering started again. He felt the van shift as something moved inside . . . something trembled . . . and he started to back away, shaky. "Really, you can let your—." The hand shot out and grabbed him by the neck so fast that all the air was shut off from his throat.

"Look, shitass," the driver growled in the kid's face. Tell me where the fucking restaurant is, and I'll take care of my own animals, okay?"

He pulled the attendant up from his already sagging knees. "Just nod your head if you really understand me."

The attendant was shaking so hard he couldn't tell if his head was nodding. The man's breath was in his face, cold. He was starting to gurgle. The fingers clamped to his throat loosened, and he sucked in a ragged breath. The fear came up again, and he could feel the fried egg sandwich he'd eaten just sitting there, right below the hand.

The whimpering was louder now, the dog or dogs in the van starting to shake it. The driver released the attendant's throat. The kid gasped and pulled some more air in, then remembered the command.

"One mile." He bent over in a fit of coughing.

10

"One . . . uh . . . one mile that way." He pointed north down the highway. The van pulled out, accelerating onto the highway, and the kid held onto the pumps, waiting for the sickness to pass. When he thought that the van was far enough away, he raised his hand and jabbed his middle finger at the darkened back window.

"Motherfucker," he croaked, rubbing his throat on his way back inside.

He thought later that the whimpering really didn't sound like a dog after all.

Enes Smith

Phoenix 11 a.m.
CHAPTER 1

Phoenix Sky Harbor International Airport baked in the late morning sun, the heat shimmering off its runways a visible, living thing. The temperature was 93 degrees Fahrenheit. In the shade. The hot part of the day was still hours away.

Inside the terminal, the temp was a cool, almost cold, 75 degrees. The concourses were surprisingly crowded for the start of summer, the off season for the sprawling desert community that would be a giant sauna for the next few months. The travelers were mostly women, retired, widowed by husbands who were planted somewhere in New York or New Jersey, victims of stress and cholesterol and gotta-have-enough-money-so-we-can-retire-in-Florida-or-Arizona. They came south with friends and tour groups, wondering why they didn't do this when Norwood or Bert or Harry was alive.

On her last day, Ellie Hartley had a drunk removed from one of her shops at the airport.

What a miserable jerk, Ellie thought. She stood in the doorway of her office and watched the customer hustling Donna, her new clerk, listening to his not very original line of boozy seduction. She was vaguely aware of the stream of travelers going by on the concourse that ran the length of her store.

The drunk was getting loud, insistent, his slurred speech dissonant, out of place among the morning travelers and shoppers at the airport. He staggered backward and caught his balance in a way that defied both the law of gravity and that of substance abuse, the stagger a strangely smooth roll on ball bearings, a curious kind of break dance, a dance in slow motion that only drunks can do. The customers and clerk watched.

The drunk didn't seem to notice.

This kind of thing didn't usually happen so early in the day, although Ellie knew that some people used a morning flight as an excuse to start drinking as soon as the stews could serve alcohol. She left her office and started through the store, her irritation growing as she listened.

"C'mon honey, you just slip out from behind that counter and I'll buy you a drink," the drunk said. His face was flushed, his eyes watery. He lurched forward this time, over the glass counter. He was wearing some kind of godawful yellow jacket, a reincarnation of an old leisure suit, with a black shirt open down his chest, complete with gold chains. His stomach pushed the bottom part of the shirt out and onto the glass display case. Christ, the guy must be all of fifty or fifty-five, Ellie thought, trying to hustle a nineteen-year-old college kid.

She could see his yellow, tobacco-stained teeth from across the store. Why me, and why today? She had too much to do on this particular Friday. The sour knot beginning to form in her stomach reminded Ellie how much she hated this kind of unpleasant confrontation. Maybe the guy would get discouraged and leave.

"Cmon, I said, le's go have a drink," he yelled, his face thrust closer yet to the new clerk.

"Sir . . . I, uh, I can't do that," Donna said, flustered and uncertain.

The drunk suddenly reached across the counter for the girl, hitting a display of Bic lighters in the process. The lighters scattered on the floor behind the counter, spreading out like a school of multicolored fish. Donna jumped back, scared, and threw a wild look in the direction of Ellie's office.

Ellie walked quickly through her store toward the counter, anger rising visibly to her face. She slipped around the clothing racks hung with Arizona State University sweatshirts, blouses, swimsuits, and evening wear. She was wearing a stylish beige linen suit with a pale blue silk blouse, and had the store been full of customers, several heads would have turned to watch the pretty, blond, thirty-year-old owner of Karen's, Inc., approach the counter.

There were only four other customers, three of them elderly ladies waiting several safe steps behind the drunk, each clutching her purchase to her like a well-worn purse, trying not to look at the scene at the counter. An Indian man, older yet than the ladies, stood behind them, his head appearing well above their blue hair, his face weathered into wrinkled parchment. Ellie thought that he looked something like the old Indian-turned-movie-actor, Chief Dan George.

He stood with his arms crossed, looking at the stupid drunk white man with the gray hair—hair that was slicked and swept forward like that rock and roller Elvis used to wear his.

13

"I'll take over, Donna," Ellie said, and got a grateful look as Donna stepped back to let her into the space behind the cash register. The drunk saw her for the first time.

"Hey, now, girlie, jus'a minute . . . I was talking to the guh—."

"She has other things to do," Ellie said evenly. "Now, may I help you, sir? I believe these ladies behind you would like to . . ."

"Hell with what they'd like," he said loudly, thrusting his blotched face within inches of Ellie's, the sour booze on his breath invading the small space.

Ellie's heart jumped up in her chest, and then began skipping along, fairly humming as she closed the fear down tight, letting her anger up through it. Take control, Ellie girl, she thought, willing her heart to slow down, wanting to tell the drunk to get the hell out of her store and leave them alone. Always the diplomat, she tried to appease him instead.

"Sir, if you would like to make a purchase—."

"I don't want to buy any of your shit, lady!" he yelled, cutting her off, his face even more flushed. The smell of his booze and anger jolted Ellie's stomach, and she took an involuntary step back. The ladies flinched at the yelling and recoiled in a wave, as if they were one person.

"I was just talking to the girl here, and you came along and—what the hell--!"

The drunk screamed.

He was suddenly yanked off his feet, legs twitching out of control. Ellie caught a glimpse of the Indian's weathered face above the drunk, expressionless as when he was waiting in line behind the ladies. He spun the drunk around and gave him a push. Ellie let out a slow breath, and then the jerk was gone, or at least out of the store, judging by the yelling out in the concourse.

The three ladies were still standing with the items they had picked out, hesitant. Poor dears are probably scared to death, Ellie thought. She smiled and called to them, seeming more cheerful than she felt. Her knees were still shaking. She hated that helpless, scared feeling.

"Ladies, can I help you?" They came to the counter and solemnly presented their purchases. Ellie laughed and said, "Too much tequila in the morning, what do you think?"

She soon had the ladies chattering and laughing, and they left the store, with promises to come back when their vacation trip ended. Donna came back behind the counter and began to pick up the lighters.

"I'm sorry, I guess I didn't handle him very well."

"I didn't do very well myself," Ellie said as she kneeled to help Donna. She threw her arm around the younger girl and gave her a hug, getting an appreciative look in return.

Ellie laughed again, feeling better, her anger dissipating.

"Bet that jerk will look around a little more carefully before he tries that again. Did you see the way his feet dangled?" she said, and they both gave way to laughter. Donna dropped her share of the lighters and leaned back against the display case.

"Did you see that asshole's face?" Donna shrieked, and then stopped, looking over at Ellie. "Sorry."

"He was an asshole," Ellie agreed. "No need to apologize." They laughed again, and bumped into each other on the floor, getting the last of the lighters. Ellie straightened, and looked into the weathered face of their savior, He gave her a hint of a smile and dropped a five on the counter for a sack of Bugle cigarette tobacco and some Top "roll your own" papers.

"Thanks for saving us from that . . . uh . . . unpleasant man," Ellie said. Donna started to giggle beside her. Ellie wanted to present him with a gift, or at least give him the tobacco, but thought, correctly, that he would refuse and insist on paying for it. She took the five and gave him his change.

The parchment-faced Indian winked at her and left the store, slipping into the crowded concourse.

CHAPTER 2

Meredith sat down across the desk from his boss and waited for the older man to speak, knowing full well that Jonathan Ward would not let signals of impatience hurry him. The Phoenix case was going to be the topic of discussion. He glanced at his watch and saw that it was only the lunch hour in Phoenix, 2:30 p.m. here in D.C., and already there was an exodus of government types out of the city. Most wanted to get a jump on the weekend, and with the Fourth of July on Tuesday, it would be a four-day party.

Meredith looked through the window at the boats on the Potomac, colorful sails tight with brisk early summer wind. He thought sailing boring, but watching the boats was better than looking at the office. It was the same kind of office given to most bureaucratic upper management types in Washington: plush carpet, solid wood desk, a floor-to-ceiling bookcase behind the desk, and the ubiquitous split-leaf philodendron hiding by the door.

Meredith pulled himself up in his chair and saw in the glass pane a shadow of his face looking back at him. He thought the sailboats more interesting. His curly brown hair was starting to go back at the edges and frown lines on his forehead seemed a little deeper. At age forty-two, he supposed that it could be worse.

Ward put the folder on his desk, and fiddled with an old greasy pipe, another badge of leadership, Meredith thought. Ward had been going over the file again, trying to find something that others had missed. The investigators invariably missed something, or so Ward said, and he usually brought these salient points to their attention.

As the head of the new Federal Violent Crime Investigation Administration, Ward was one of the best bureaucratic actors in town, smooth and respected. Meredith knew that Ward was fair, an unusual quality here. Ward's tailored suits, his oxford shirts and silk ties, his homicide investigation background, and his confident demeanor said to underlings and peers: I am a successful man in my profession— don't mess with me.

"How many in Phoenix so far?" Ward asked.

"Five, if you count the Pearson woman. Could be as high as seven. We're not sure about the two in Scottsdale, but the lab may tell us that it's the same man working there."

"All the women were taken from the scene of auto accidents. You seen this before?" Ward asked.

"No. Not as a strict M.O. Maybe as an opportunity, but not as a pre-planned serial abduction. This guy's slick. Crime scenes are neat, and with one exception there was no real evidence left. He gets in an accident with the victims, a female driving alone, and they disappear. No bodies have been found." Meredith rubbed his knee and waited.

"This guy in Phoenix they have working on these, he any good?"

Ward closed the file and looked up.

"Detective Sergeant Dennis Patterson. He's the one who found the blood in the second car, after the lab had gone over it. The blood was from the victim of the first abduction."

Ward picked through the file again, and played with it, seemingly disinterested, like a person bored with his food. It's because he knows every damned word in the thing, Meredith thought.

Five missing women.

None returned home.

No bodies found.

Meredith knew that the Phoenix police and Maricopa County deputies had walked the heels off their boots in the surrounding desert, and worn out a couple of methane probes in the process.

Nothing.

No trace of bodies.

Zip.

Ward looked at the lab reports and grunted, removing the pipe from his mouth. "I see that young Gardiner is doing our computer work again on this one. I can't believe that I've hired someone who takes his dates to work with him."

Meredith laughed. "That's because he's the best. Anyway, he spends his life at the shop; his social life just follows him to work in the evenings. He claims that the girls feel like they've met someone immortal, a person who peeks at death. He says it makes them horny."

Ward gave the file to Meredith.

"Stop in Phoenix on your way home. Look things over and offer our assistance. Tell Josh 'Hi' for me when you get back," Ward said as they shook hands. He held the door open for the younger man, sending a wreath of smoke out into the hall.

Meredith nodded and left the office, trying to walk without limping, holding the file as if it were a fragile thing that would shatter if he dropped it. Five missing in less than six months. He knew that they hadn't seen the last of their man—and the guy left blood.

Why was he leaving evidence? Did he want to .get caught? Meredith didn't think so. The killer's donation of evidence at the abduction sites told Meredith one thing: the killer was taunting them, he was upping the stakes. Meredith would go down and look at the next crime scene himself.

As it turned out, he didn't have to wait at all.

<u>**Phoenix**</u>
CHAPTER
3

Ellie waited until she was sure Donna had things under control, then returned to her office. She busied herself with the never-ending paperwork, and when she next looked up she saw she had worked through the lunch hour.

From her office in the back corner she could see most of the store and out into the concourse. Donna was talking to Frank Allman, another ASU student who worked for Ellie as a part-time clerk. Donna was re-telling the story of the drunk, waving her arms and laughing. They both looked in the direction of Ellie's office and Frank laughed with her.

Karen's, Inc., belonged to Ellie. At thirty, she was the owner and manager of two shops at Sky Harbor international Airport in Phoenix. The shops contained most of the usual necessities for travelers: magazines, paperbacks, souvenirs, candy, toilet articles. Since taking over the first shop three years ago, she had expanded her merchandise to a casual sportswear and swimsuit line, and was displaying original Southwest jewelry and pottery.

The store was starting to fill with shoppers, and both Donna and Frank were busy ringing up sales, their bright red ASU sweatshirts making them visible through the crowd. Ellie herself was an ASU alumna, and in fact had worked in the store as an undergraduate.

She fiddled with her pencil, watching the clerks. When she had worked here as a student, the business had been called Sky Harbor Gift Shop, and was owned by Julio "Herbie" Jararnillo. After graduation with a degree in business, she stayed on, looking for a corporate job or a small business to buy. During the years at ASU Ellie had developed a close relationship with Herbie, much closer than the other employees. Herbie and his wife had had Ellie over for dinner many times during those years, something that meant a lot to a girl from Pasadena, California, new to the state of Arizona.

After graduation, Ellie came to realize that she didn't want just any small business—she wanted to own Sky Harbor Gift Shop. Herbie knew of her love for the store, and eventually sold the store to Ellie with a deal she couldn't refuse. The gift shop was merely a cubicle then. But the airport was expanding constantly, a hub for the Southwest, with a large percentage of flights to Mexico connecting there. With the dollar gaining against the peso, the airport bustled, stretched, and expanded some more.

Ellie, whose full name was Karen Elizabeth Hartley, had changed the name of the shop to Karen's and expanded along with the airport. Last year she had opened a second shop at the opposite end of the airport, along a newly-constructed concourse.

She dropped her pencil and put the papers into the top desk drawer, papers for yet another expansion project to put Karen's, Inc., into the big time, a franchise business for regional shopping malls.

Ellie picked up her jacket and looked out over her store from the doorway. Frank gave her a wave and a smile as she walked out into the concourse.

She walked to the main counter area of the airport, moving with the flow of travelers, airline crews, and airport workers. She nodded occasionally at people she knew, but was preoccupied and in a hurry.

It was easy for the man to follow her in a crowd.

She had promised Stacey that she would come home early today, and nothing was going to get in the way of that promise. She carried a burden of guilt for the number of occasions that she'd had to call her four-year-old to tell her that she would be late because of the demands of running a business. She had no one with whom to share business responsibilities or child-rearing problems. She had no husband and Stacey had no father. Not a father that Stacey had ever known, or one that counted for much. Ellie slipped sunglasses from her purse as she stepped outside into the bright heat.

She didn't see the man follow her from the terminal.

She opened the door to her Camaro and began the familiar ritual: start the car, roll the windows down part way, turn the air conditioner on max, and step outside to wait for the interior to cool.

The next part of the ritual was something she had learned from Herbie Jaramillo. He had stood beside her car on a summer night, and had stopped her with a hand on the door.

"Watch the planes take off, Ellie," he said (it always came out "Eelie"). "Watch the planes take off and land from the white runways, and feel the life of the airport, and at the same time get the work from your head. That little girl of yours, she don't know work, all she knows is Mommy." He had put his arm around her, and looked directly into her eyes, this gentle Mexican man not much taller than Ellie, and said quietly, "I know what you are trying to do here, gal, and you will do it, Jaramillo knows. But don' forget, watch the planes take off, and think about Stacey." Then he had given her a hug and walked to his car.

Ellie smiled at the memory and put her folded suit jacket on the passenger seat. She backed out, thinking that she should stop and pick up another dozen fruity Popsicles. Stacey had probably invited every kid in the neighborhood to a swimming party while her mom was at work.

She drove through the aisle of palms that lined the airport road and caught Interstate 10, and then took the on-ramp to Interstate 17. Ellie put the white Camaro into the far left lane and kicked the speedometer up to seventy, heading north.

She didn't see the blue van follow her from the airport and slip into the fast lane behind her.

CHAPTER
4

Ellie had decided on two dozen Popsicles, thinking that her daughter's ability to make friends quickly might bring more kids over to the pool than they had planned. She'd picked up a bottle of California Chardonnay for the grownups, and carried the bag through the heat to her car.

She drove through the shopping center parking lot, the air conditioner sending out cool air that left a taste like old plastic in her mouth. She stopped at the McDonald's drive-through and got a large Diet Coke. The girl at the window thrust the Coke, the straw, and the change at her all at once.

She left the shopping center and turned onto Rampart Street. She was less than a half mile from her home, where she and Stacey lived with Maria, their friend, housekeeper, and nanny.

The light blue van followed her.

She sipped on the Coke as she braked for the four-way stop on Castle Rock. Just a few more blocks and she would be in her bathing suit and in the pool, almost before the Camaro came to a stop. Maria and Stacey always laughed at her entry; she would throw her clothes across her room in her haste to get them off and get into her suit and into the pool. It had been Stacey's idea to time her, and Ellie knew that they would be waiting with a stopwatch when she entered the house.

She looked both ways, mechanically.

No one coming.

She started into the intersection.

Ellie never did see the van approach. It slammed into the rear of her car, and the jolt jerked her head back into the headrest. The large Diet Coke splattered onto her chest, cold and sticky on her blouse.

The Camaro bounced through the intersection, and she instinctively jammed her foot on the brake pedal and brought the car to a stop just across the road. She looked up into the rearview mirror and saw the grille of some kind of truck.

Dammit! Ellie beat her hands on the steering wheel, flinging Coke and ice into the windshield. She picked up the empty Coke container and flung it onto the floor in front of the passenger seat. The cup and ice landed on the grocery sack. She couldn't smell wine, so the bottle probably wasn't broken. She jammed her finger on the power window button and thrust her head out against the heat. She glared at the other vehicle behind her. She couldn't see inside.

Ellie pushed the door open, shaking, the last of the soda and ice sloshing in her lap, and she came as close to losing control as she ever had.

She had worked too hard for her car to have it bashed in by someone who couldn't even stop for a damn sign! She jerked the parking brake up and kicked the door all the way open and got out, anger hard in her face, and walked back to look at the damage. The momentum had pushed her car a few feet away from what she now saw was a large van. The damage wasn't as bad as she'd thought, but it still looked terrible on her new car—bumper banged in and a crumpled left rear fender.

"Hey, sorry, lady," a voice called from within the van. A man's voice with rough edges. Ellie looked back and saw the driver leaning out the window by the large side mirror. She walked up to the door of the van and looked again at her car. There was some black paint from the bumper of the van on the white fender of her Camaro.

"Look, I'm sorry, it's . . . uh . . . my fault," the driver said quickly, "but let's pull off the road further and I'll give my insurance information to you. It was definitely my fault."

"You . . . why can't you watch for signs? And look at my suit!" she yelled. The heat from the pavement slammed into her, making her already queasy stomach roll in on itself. She was vaguely conscious of other cars going by. She looked down and pulled her sticky blouse away from her, and saw that the material was now transparent, clinging to her breasts. She abruptly spun around and walked quickly to her car, even more upset because she had yelled. She clutched her stomach in an attempt to keep the churning in control.

Her car was still running. Ellie popped it into gear and chirped the tires as she pulled off the road. She got out and walked back to the van as it was pulling up behind her. The heat from the pavement came up again, mixing sweat with the Diet Coke on her blouse. The glare from the sand on both sides of the road made it hard to see into the van.

Her anger had dissipated somewhat, and she was now more hot and irritated than mad. She was almost willing to be civil, but not before telling the idiot what she thought of his driving.

Another car went by, the driver looking over briefly. The passers-by had established a pattern now. When they decided that no one was hurt, they accelerated away. The Coke had probably rendered her blouse and bra invisible, but at this point, all she wanted to do was go home, put on her swimsuit, pour a large—huge actually—glass of cold wine, and watch Stacey with her friends.

The driver of the van hopped out, awkwardly holding his right arm up across his chest. He grimaced and gave Ellie a small wave as she approached.

Oh shit. Just what I need, she thought. *The guy is hurt, and now I don't even have someone I can be mad at.* By the time she got to him, she just wanted to get it over with. He was a large man, maybe 6'3", 220 lbs., with a full head of dark hair, perhaps thirty to thirty-five, with a rugged-looking but nice-appearing face. He was wearing a white dress shirt, blue jeans, and boots.

He winced and pointed to his arm. "Banged it on the steering wheel. You okay?"

Ellie nodded.

"Look, I'm terribly sorry 1 hit your car." He glanced at her blouse and skirt, shaking his head ruefully. "I'll buy a new suit for you, and uh, pay for any inconvenience." He stood there, smiling,

"I'll get my registration and a pen," she said finally, and walked back to her car. A few cars passed them, the drivers intent on their destinations and getting out of the unseasonably early heat.

They paid no attention to the fender bender. Most of the drivers who were later contacted did not remember the cars at the intersection, and those who did thought that there was maybe a truck, or motorcycle, or a sedan involved One witness was adamant. "It was a red '88 Corvette. I'm sure of it, and I'll swear to it."

When Ellie returned, she saw that the other driver—what did he say his name was?—was on the passenger side of his van, away from the road, trying to open the glove compartment with his arm held tight against his chest.

"Can I help?" Ellie asked, although she didn't feel that charitable. The man stepped back and out of the way of the door frame and smiled at her.

"Sure can, and look, I'm awfully sorry."

Ellie stepped in the area between the open door and the van. She couldn't reach the glove box from where she was standing, her five foot three inches not quite enough, so she stepped up into the van, and began looking for the registration.

"I'm really sorry about this," he repeated.

"Oh, no problem, I just want to get home." The driver quickly moved into the opening behind her, and Ellie was suddenly aware of her vulnerability, the quickened breathing behind her. She put the thought that something was wrong out of her mind. There were cars going by, weren't there? It was daylight. What could happen? She'd be out and home in a minute.

She punched the button on the glove box, determined to find his registration and get the hell away from here. The box fell open, the contents shouting up at her face. A grisly, mutated horror was only inches away.

Ellie brought her hand up and gagged.

Her knees started to give way, and the driver caught her and suddenly slammed her forward, her head striking the side of the seat. Her stomach churned, and, absurdly, she thought how nice it was that his arm wasn't broken after all.

She screamed, a mixture of surprise and fear, and the driver stepped up into the van and pushed his way in on top of her. He grabbed Ellie's hair, pulled her head back, and slammed her face down onto the engine cover. She felt her nose crunch, and the blood sprayed out on the seat. Her eyes watered and her breath was jerked away. She was too shocked to scream.

Not that it would have done any good.

The man was reaching for something under the seat. A knife?

She beat feebly at the arm that was around her neck, and the driver brought a smelly rag up to her face. Ellie struggled harder. She pulled her face down into the arm and sank her teeth into the muscle. She started to gag again, the thought of what she was doing nauseating her. She kicked backward, finding nothing to hit. This couldn't be happening! There must be cars passing. Why wouldn't someone help her?

The dark windows and the position of the van blocked the view from the road.

This . . . can't . . . be . . . hap . . . The smelly rag closed around her nose and upper lip, her teeth still working on the arm, something warm on her lips. Blood?

She gagged and kicked and kicked, and—*Don 't breathe, Ellie! Don't breathe! Can't br---! Can't!*

Her mouth was slipping, sliding on the man's arm now, and still he said nothing, just held her in his strong grasp, knowing he would win. She ripped with her teeth and lost her grip on his arm, blood now running down her chin to mix with the Coke stain on her blouse. She kicked something on the floor of the van, and it skittered out and fell to the pavement with a clatter.

The popsicles! The popsicles will melt!

The man pushed his heavy weight on her, and Ellie took a breath.

There was an odor in the van . . . a smell of . . . and for an instant she was a little girl again, when her father was her world.

Oh . . . Daddy . . . help me.

CHAPTER
5

Stacey sat on the lounge chair and watched the bright empty pool, not feeling the heat that was drying her suit or the wet towel she had on her shoulders. Mommy had brought the suit home from her store yesterday, a shiny blue one-piece Speedo, and she had put it on for her party. She sat quite still with her hands in her lap, looking at the water, occasionally glancing out toward the driveway through the iron gate.

Five kids came to swim, and she could remember their names: Scott, Carmen, Jennie, Mary, and Ben. At first it had been fun, and she forgot about Mommy. Scott and Jennie's mother talked with Maria; now they were all gone, and Maria was in the kitchen. That meant it was late!

Mommy wasn't here yet, and she had *promised*. She'd promised that this time she would come home early. She sometimes had to work late, had to go to things called meetings, and do other work called *payroll* and *ordering*. Sometimes Stacey got to go to the airport with Mommy, and see the work and have Cokes at the restaurant and talk with all the people there. She especially liked it when she got to see Herbie, 'cause he gave her cakes and took her around the airport, and once he bought her a stuffed giraffe.

A car approached and Stacey looked over at the gate. The car came closer and slowed. Mommy! Her disappointment forgotten, Stacey ran around the pool, her sandals slapping on the red tile. She got to the gate in time to see the car go on by their driveway and continue up the street. She waited there until the sounds of the engine faded. *Too loud anyway, you goofy kid. Mommy's car is a new one—you helped her pick it out, 'member?*

She stood looking out the gate, and started to cry.

Maria watched from the kitchen and wiped the counter, more for something to do than out of necessity. She was worried. It wasn't like Ellie to be so late, at least not without calling. Maria had been with Ellie since Stacey was a tiny baby, and she was part of the family, a mother to Stacey, and sister, friend, and confidante to Ellie.

When Ellie was a student, she had been living in a small apartment near the Arizona State University campus, in Tempe. Maria was a family friend of the Jaramillos, and she had met the bright young blond girl from California on several occasions. Then, when Ellie was pregnant with Stacey, and it looked as if her boyfriend was not going to be around, she'd asked Maria if .she would look after the child while Ellie ran her new business. *Never could figure that David out*, Maria had thought more than once. She had met Stacey's father and thought him a nice young man, and as it turned out, it was Ellie, not David, who had decided that they would not marry.

Maria had taken care of Stacey, commuting each day between the Hartley's place and her own apartment. Once, when her car was in the garage for repairs, she'd stayed at Ellie's house for a week, and they'd both gradually come to realize that Maria was a part of their lives and should live with them. She'd moved with Ellie to a larger house, and then, when the business and profits grew, she'd moved again, to this new, much bigger house with the pool.

The adobe ranch-style house was spacious, with a large living area opening to the kitchen. A large, kidney-shaped pool was at the back of the house, with a red tile deck and wrought-iron fence. A low veranda ran alongside the living room and kitchen so they could watch the pool and garden area from the shade.

Maria fidgeted with the towel. Come home, *hija*, my little daughter, she willed Ellie. She reached for the kitchen phone and dialed the number for Karen's, Inc., watching Stacey from the window.

"Karen's, may I help you?" Frank answered.

"Frank, this is Maria. Sorry to bother you again, but . . . ."

"No bother. She not home yet?" He sounded worried now, and that made Maria even more scared.

"No, not home, and you know that she promised Stacey. It just isn't like her . . . not in all the time I've known her."

"Well, let's see, as I said, she left here at one thirty, and even if she went shopping, she should have been home by two thirty or three at the latest, and it's now---."

"Seven twenty-five," Maria croaked, her mouth dry with fear."Do you think that we should call the police? I—uh, I'm afraid to call them," Maria told him softly, and began to cry.

Frank glanced at the concourse, hoping to see his boss stroll in. She should be on the arm of some handsome airline captain, with a martini or two on her breath. But Frank knew that this wouldn't happen with their Ellie. He was a graduate student in Econ at ASU, and had worked for Ellie for three years. He'd never seen her with a date. Not once.

Not that Ellie didn't get offers. His boss was a very attractive— *admit it, Frankie, she's a damn sexy lady*—petite woman, who didn't seem aware of her striking beauty or the effect that she had on others.

"Maria," Frank said, wishing she would stop crying. He was beginning to worry plenty by now. He knew how unusual it was for Ellie to not show up on time. "Maria," he repeated, "call Herbie and talk with him. Then if she doesn't show up, he will know what to do."

"Okay . . . and thanks." Maria's voice quavered. Her hand shook as she hung up.

The phone rang while she was looking on the refrigerator door for the number to the Jaramillo residence. It was someone from the police department wanting to know about Ellie's car. Had the owner been in an accident? Maria leaned over the sink and looked out at the lonely little figure standing by the gate, feeling a sickness come over her body. She could only manage to choke out a yes when they asked if she would be home to talk to an officer.

She wiped her eyes on the towel and went out into the heat to get the four-year-old who stood looking at the driveway.

CHAPTER
6

Detective Sergeant Dennis Patterson stood in the middle of the intersection at Castle Rock and Cottonwood. At almost midnight he could still feel the heat coming off the pavement. The Hartley woman's car had been towed to the police impound lot; the technicians and crime-scene cops were gone. He pivoted in a slow turn, his movement almost imperceptible, and took in the four corners of the intersection: the four stop signs, the sand beside the road, the rocks, the cactus. He had purposely parked his car about a hundred yards back on Cottonwood so it wouldn't interfere with his view of the area.

Patterson hitched up his belt; it didn't come up in front anymore—he had a fair-sized gut for a small man. Wearing a gun on his side didn't help. The damn belt sagged on the side and the front, too. He had left his jacket in his car when he arrived, removed his tie, and rolled the sleeves up on his white dress shirt.

Patterson was fifty, and it didn't bother him as much as he thought it would. His middle-age paunch didn't really bother him either. He had decided last year that he was never going to grow any taller than 5' 6". His hair was grey, and that didn't cause him much grief. In fact, he had come to terms with just about everything in his life except his receding hairline.

That bothered Sergeant Patterson so much, he'd been considering transplants. It wasn't that bad now, but he could envision himself bald, and he thought that he would rather be dead.

Even with that, his outlook was generally a positive one, and why shouldn't it be? He had already outlived all the victims he had come to know over the years.

This case, if he could call it that, was beginning to worry the shit out of him. It worried his boss as well. The press had been on them after the Wallace woman's disappearance. Too many people missing in a short period of time. He thought that the press would feel easier about what was happening if they had bodies to account for the disappearances.

He knew that he would.

Most of the cases that he had investigated during the past twenty years were what he called misdemeanor murders - husband/wife, boyfriend/girlfriend, bar fights—cases where the suspect knew the victim.

He stood in the road, turning, watching, as if he could see the events of the day. Lights came up behind him, fast. He stopped his evaluation, and walked to the sandy roadside. A Ford pickup with large tires and a row of lights above the cab slowed, three young males inside. The truck stopped at the intersection, then quickly accelerated. Patterson stood immobile, listening as the pitch of the exhaust rose and fell in response to the changing gears. He stood there for almost a minute after the silence chased the sound away.

They didn't even notice me, he thought. *Here I am, standing by myself on the corner of a deserted intersection, blocks from the nearest house, and those kids didn't even notice me. They should have seen my gun and the badge on my belt.*

Was this how it had been with the Hartley woman?

No one saw anything happen. Even if we found some potential witnesses who drove by when the abduction was taking place, they wouldn't be able to tell us a thing.

She had been here less than ten hours ago. Ordinarily, the police department didn't get too concerned about a missing person until some time had passed.

In this case, however, they were obliged to. Six women had been reported missing in the past two months. That in itself wasn't any cause for great alarm. People moved, ran away, went on vacation.

But the media had gotten their teeth into this one after the third woman disappeared. Leanne Wallace was an honors graduate of ASU with a B.A. in journalism, the wife of a local businessman who owned a chain of jewelry stores in Maricopa County. Patterson's partner suggested that maybe Leanne ran away, and was "spending her time on her knees polishin' someone's diamond cutter of a hard on," but Patterson didn't think so. She was twenty-eight, had a baby boy from whom she had never been away for longer than an evening, and her forty-year-old husband was, in Patterson's estimation, a decent family man who lived a pretty quiet life.

The press and Mr. Wallace went fairly berserk when they found out that this was the third case in less than a month where a Phoenix woman had been taken from a car following a minor traffic accident.

Now there had been three more. As with any case he was assigned, he could recall—sometimes for decades—all the intimate details. He sifted through the files again from memory, casually, hoping that in the association of cases in his head something would stand out, something would jump up and grab him.

He thought about what he knew of the victims. There had to be something, some common denominator that made them targets.

Georgia Bachman: Thirty-three years old, white female, married, with two kids and a black lab named Benny. Missing from her car on May 4, during a late-night trip to the store to get some Tylenol and Pepsi for a sick kid. Her Chevy Celebrity had been found two blocks from the Chris-Town Shopping Center, on a side street. The rear bumper had a dent in it that had not been there earlier.

Leticia Alvarez: Twenty-five years old, Mexican female, married, three kids. Missing since May 12. On her way home from work at the Desert View Care Center, where she worked as an R.N. She got off work at 11 P.M., and had not been seen since. Her husband found her new Ford minivan near the main entrance to the Phoenix Zoo. He'd told the police that she was so proud of the new van, the one she picked out, their first new car (it didn't even have plates on it yet), that she would have left him and the kids before she abandoned the van. When they considered victimology and profiling, it was considered by some that Mrs. Alvarez did not fit. But now they knew that she was part of the insanity that killed the others: the vial of blood found in her car was definitely from the Bachman woman. This killer was not going just by looks. He was doing something else.

Leanne Wallace: Her disappearance on May 27, fifteen days after Alvarez, got things rolling for Phoenix and Maricopa County. Her silver BMW 745 was found on Dobbins Road, about a mile east of the Phoenix Police Academy. She had just left the Thunderbird Golf Course after eighteen holes of golf with three girlfriends. This was the first disappearance in daylight—about 4 P.M. They had a couple of days without much pressure, except from the Wallace family. Then the press found out about the other two women being investigated as missing, and about the "accidents."

The Wallace BMW had been rear-ended, hard, the damage high up on the trunk . . . in the height of the damage similar to the other crashes, but much more severe. Did this person, this killer, not like the more obvious signs of wealth?

Lisa Pearson: Thirty-four years old, white female, married, no children. She left the Phoenix Public Library on the sixth of June, at two in the afternoon, and was never seen again. Her Toyota Corolla was found on June 8, up at Echo Canyon Park, her purse and library books missing. It looked as if the car was parked there sometime on the sixth. This was the only car that showed no damage. Was she taken by the same person? Some said no. Patterson thought at the time that she was. When they found the next victim's car, they were sure of it.

Carol Zibrowski: At twenty-three, the youngest of the missing women, and, up to this point, the only single woman. She was also the only missing woman with no children. A Maricopa County Sheriff's Deputy found her car on State Highway 89, at a wayside a few miles northwest of Phoenix. Her car, a two-year-old Caddy, owned by Carol's parents, was found on the 18th. They never would have made much of it if not for the other missing women. By the time the girl's parents were contacted, the county had notified Patterson, and he had the car processed by the crime lab.

They found the blood in a vial in the front seat. The techs kept a sample and sent the rest off to a federal lab in D.C.

He couldn't believe that a piece of masking tape wrapped around the vial had the name "Pearson" written on it.

The feds told him just today that it for sure belonged to the last victim.

Karen Hartley: Thirty years old, white female, with a four-year-old daughter. From what he could find out so far, she was the owner of some shops at the airport. The people at the airport told him that she used her first name, Karen, professionally; her family and friends called her "Ellie" for her middle name, Elizabeth. She had been on her way home, and was in fact a few blocks from her home when her car was hit. Patterson had visited the daughter and a housekeeper who had been waiting for him in tears.

No husband. Check the father of the kid, his experience told him, and they would. But he didn't believe there was a connection.

Patterson walked back along the shoulder of the road toward his car, the weariness after the day's events and the weight of his profession showing in his stride. He looked down at the hard-packed sand, not seeing, his mind covered with a blackness that wouldn't lift.

He wondered if the Hartley woman was dead yet. No, probably not. He felt certain that the women were not killed at the scene. They hadn't found any evidence to suggest it. It might take the killer too long to accomplish at the scene, and the son-of-a-bitch probably wouldn't want the women dead. At least not for a while.

Where the hell were the bodies? He knew that there were some places in the state where the killer could hide bodies and they would never be found. Maybe he buried them in the crawl space under his house like John Wayne Gacey did up in Illinois. He had been checking husbands, families. Maybe six were murdered to cover for one murder. But he really didn't buy that theory.

Why these particular women? Were they taken by chance? Maybe. The killer might not even know why he selected his victims. Patterson didn't give a shit for the why. He just wanted to stop the bastard.

He began to drive back to his office to prepare a national all-points bulletin regarding the Hartley woman, a bulletin that would be sent to every police agency in the U. S. and Canada. Hell, it was like waving a magic wand over a cancer patient, for all the good it would do, but it was procedure, and sometimes it worked out.

SATURDAY
JULY
1

CHAPTER 7

Gardiner pulled the all points bulletin from the printer and sat for a long time, not moving. Except for the corner where he sat hunched over his desk, the lab was dark. A girl was seated next to him, sleeping with her head down on his desk.

"Bingo," he said softly.

The girl stirred. She stretched her arms out on the desk and opened an eye, turning her head to look up at her lover. He was reading something.

"Another one . . . Jesus . . . another one," he muttered.

"What?"

He didn't answer. She could see the excitement work on his body, his movements becoming jerky and unnatural as he snatched the phone from the wall.

"Derrick, it's almost four a.m. Who in the world are you . . . ?"

Gardiner dialed the unlisted number and waited, drumming his fingers on the lab table.

The phone was answered on the second ring.

"Ward, you old degenerate," he drawled. "It's time for Meredith to earn his pay. We got another one.

"Phoenix."

Nevada

Blackness covered her. The smooth plastic cocoon that was her world vibrated and rocked with the movement of the van.

Ellie opened her eyes as the van jumped, hitting a break in the pavement. She blinked and raised her head in the dark, sightless . . . bewildered. It would soon be time to get up for work—but she could go back to sleep for a few minutes. The snooze alarm will wake me, she thought.

The vibration and the hum of the tires resumed; she carefully placed her head back down, as if it were fragile, something to be protected. She had the disturbing thought that something was wrong— that she wouldn't be able to go to work after all.

Her heartbeat was a shudder, a ragged thing that shook and trailed off, shook and trailed off. Shook and rattled. It stopped once in the dark, and she waited for the rattle to begin again. At times it would race toward defibrillation, and she would hold her breath, willing her heart to slow down. Her nose was swollen and clogged with blood. Her blouse and skirt stuck to her. A strong ammonia smell cut through her clogged nostrils.

She snuffled, tasting the blood and mucous. There was a sweet chemical taste (*odor?*) in her mouth. She couldn't remember what she might have eaten to cause it. It added to her growing unease. She whined, the sound loud and unnatural in the small space. Her stomach suddenly recoiled and cramped as she realized that she was not in her bed. She was somewhere . . . she was being taken somewhere in a van in a black plastic cocoon. She rolled on her side and retched, the vomit coming fast and warm, not getting her leg out of the way in time. She gagged, automatically holding her blond hair out away from her face with her right hand, using her left for support.

* * *

Her heartbeat and her breathing were the only sounds she could count on, sounds that belonged to her; the only sounds she trusted. She slept.

When she awakened an hour later, she thought that she had dozed for maybe five minutes. She had moments of lucid thought where she skipped up to the edge of her impending death and looked at it, raw and full of pain, a dark maw that stretched before her. That she would die soon, she was certain. Each time the van slowed, her body froze in panic—she knew that the small door that led to the driver's compartment would open and death would crawl through and perch on her shoulder. And she would turn her head, slowly (*dear God, I can't!!! I don't want to!*) and see the horribly blotched and rotted face, the breath warm and decaying, moist on her cheek.

The death's-head would sometimes turn into a bird with feathers that moved, moving, squirming with the promise of something dead inside. Something once buried.

(*Hey! Ho! It's off to dig we go!*)

Each time the van once again reached cruising speed, the head would disappear and—Ellie was certain of this—resume its vigil just outside the door.

She knew that she had been abducted by the man who had been taking the other women . . . and she knew from the newspapers that their bodies had never been found. It was the kind of story that she used to skip over. After glancing at the headline she would turn her eyes quickly to another story—she didn't want to read about things like that. Hell, she couldn't even watch a rerun of M*A*S*H on the tube when she was eating, for fear that Hawkeye or one of the other doctors would be cutting into someone and there would be some blood or something worse on a sheet, and once she saw it, she wouldn't be able to finish her meal.

And now look at me.

Although she had no way of knowing, she thought that they were traveling north. They had been on the road for how long? She wasn't sure of the passage of time, but she reasoned that they weren't going south into Mexico (*oh, dear God, I hope not*), because the roads were too smooth. Not California. So maybe north. They were, in fact, two hours north of Reno.

She was in some kind of a compartment in the rear of the van, a compartment that was the width of the van and maybe six feet in length. The compartment was covered with a thin plastic material; it rustled and crackled when she rolled on it in the darkness. There was no light in the chamber, and except for the movement and vibration of the van, the sensory deprivation was almost complete. Ellie thought that the van must have some ventilation. She could sometimes feel a slight breeze.

The smell of her body, her blood and vomit, cut across the sharp odor of plastic. It was as if she had crawled into a large black garbage bag and couldn't get out. Had she been in it for hours? Days?

She remembered leaving the airport to go home to Stacey, and . . . She drifted and couldn't remember the rest. Stacey! She moaned and drew herself up into a sitting position, rocking with the movement of the van, folding her arms across her chest, hugging herself. She moaned and cried for her little girl, who would grow up alone, without a mom or dad. Ellie's tears made clean paths through the grime on her cheeks; she rocked forward and back, her grief and tears increasing her dehydration.

"Stacey . . . oooohh my God . . . Stacey," she whispered low in her throat, harsh and guttural.

She also cried for Ellie. She grieved for her own death, with the awful knowledge that she wouldn't see Stacey grow up, wouldn't be there for her.

If only David had stayed. The guilt over his leaving hit her. She knew that Stacey's father would have stayed, if she hadn't driven him off. She had thought that it was best for all of them at the time. She had been so damned sure of herself.

Stacey had never met her father. Even if he took Stacey now, he would be a stranger.

Ellie drifted on a black cloud, her mind mercifully leaving the van and the slick, smelly, grisly reminder of her fate: the plastic killing ground.

Ellie met David during her junior year at ASU. It was an unlikely union from the first, he the iconoclast, she the student in business administration—the future yuppie.

Later, much later, when Ellie was pregnant, she knew that David didn't want to be a daddy.

She was a happy pregnant person. Ellie's father supported her throughout the months, as she'd known he would. When Stacey was born, Grandma was there and immediately fell in love with the little demanding bundle.

David saw his daughter once, when she was ten months old. He sat for a long time on Ellie's couch, watching Stacey crawl on the floor, watching her eat lunch, then go down for a nap. He saw much of what he was missing.

Ellie knew that David would stay if she asked him to; she also knew that it would destroy him—and them—to become a part of the life that was all she had ever wanted.

For the past few months, four-year-old Stacey had been asking her mom about her daddy, and Ellie had told her daughter as much as she could. At times, when Stacey thought no one was looking, Ellie would see her daughter searching the faces of men in crowds: at the store, at ball games, and especially at the airport, her serious intent giving her little face worry lines. *She's looking for her daddy*, Ellie thought, and at those times Ellie would be filled with a great sadness and self-doubt.

Self-loathing was more like it. Who do you think you are, Ellie old girl, she'd ask herself, to deny Stacey her daddy—to think that you can raise a child alone, to give her what she wants and needs? Are you giving her what she needs? Can you give her that? Can you be both daddy and mommy?

She always finished this critical introspection by telling herself that David would find a way to be there if he really wanted to. He had made his choice, as much as she had made hers,

After a while, Stacey would stop looking and bounce back to her mom. She was generally a very happy, well- adjusted child.

Ellie sat in a corner of the van, the left rear one, she judged from the occasional braking movement. The van was laboring under a climb, cornering. The transmission clunked down a gear, the engine revving higher. Automatic, she thought, filing this bit of information away. For all the good it would do.

She was breathing badly, the crust in her nose and mouth forcing her to take slow, easy breaths. She put both arms up on the slick plastic sides, pressing her palms outward. She sat there, her eyes watering in the blackness, thinking about her trip so far, wanting it to be over, wanting to reach the end, whatever it might be.

She was tired. Dead tired, she thought, and grinned weakly at the pun, her dehydrated lips cracking.

And, at least for the moment, Ellie was thinking quite clearly. The language of her thoughts would have bothered her, at one time. While she hadn't been a prude prior to all this, she had made a conscious effort to clean up her thoughts and language when Stacey came along, and she had succeeded. Well, fuck it, she thought. *Fuck it!* She would clean up her language if and when she ever got out of here alive.

She slid her hand slowly down the slick plastic wall, slightly wet from condensation, and knew that she wasn't the first one in here . . . the horror fairly oozed from the walls. *Bet he hoses it out after each one of us takes a ride, she thought. He just gets out the green 50-foot 5/8-inch garden hose and lets the old buggy have it. Right there in the driveway, next to the wife's Olds Cutlass.*

"Whatcha doin' honey?" the wife would ask.

"Oh, nothin'. You know how I like to keep things clean." He would twist the nozzle, forcing the water into the hard stream to remove the stubborn piece of—what? Flesh?

"Have a rough trip?"

"Yeah," he would say with a grin. "It's murder out there."

I'll bet he has everyone believing that he's normal.

Ellie pushed her grimy, once-blond hair back, and wrapped her arms around her sticky blouse, hugging herself. She tried to think of some way to trip the driver up, to let someone know that this van was used as a slaughterhouse . . . to leave a message after her death.

Her eyelids drooped. She wondered if Stacey would ever remember her mommy when she grew up. She was too tired to cry. Mercifully she fell asleep.

CHAPTER
8

On his last day in Washington, Patrick Meredith got up early and had a quick continental breakfast in the coffee shop of the Washington Hilton. He wanted to get home, but he had most of the day before his flight left for the west coast.

He walked up behind the Capitol to the residential area of Capitol Hill, one of his favorite places in Washington, with its parks, houses, tree-lined streets, and shops. He bought a cup of black coffee and a doughnut from a vendor, and found a park bench near the old Eastern Market.

This was a quiet place, cool and beautiful beneath the trees, with the grass shining with dew in the early morning sun. The rising humidity gave a hint of the heat to come.

He absently massaged his right knee, gently rubbing the scar tissue. He couldn't go as far now, the stops coming more frequently than the last time he walked on the hill. Two joggers went by him on the sidewalk, the man looking to be well into his fifties, the woman half that, with coltish athletic legs. The guy's daughter? He doubted it and felt a mild resentment. Is it because your knee is gone and you can't jog? He wondered. Or is it because the guy is making it with someone so young—and your last date said that you needed this job with its fine regular hours and its horror as an excuse to avoid a relationship?

The joggers started uphill, and he saw that the man was sweating hard, faltering a little. His companion slowed to match his stride as if nothing had changed. Meredith thought that he saw some cellulite there on the back of her thighs. He grinned a little and sipped his coffee, feeling better.

Josh, buddy, wish you were here, he thought.

He ate the doughnut, thinking that he would have to wait to call his boy. It was only 3:30 A.M. on the west coast. His boy. He liked the sound of that.

Two things had happened to Meredith in the past year and a half that changed his life: He was medically retired as a police detective, and he'd adopted a child.

After his forced retirement, he was hired by the feds as a homicide specialist for the northwest region. He thought of it as being picked up on waivers by another team. He was in Washington for training, and he yearned to get home.

With the adoption of twelve-year-old Joshua, he'd become a first-time parent as he was entering middle age—a single parent at that—at a time when most people are thinking of retirement.

The loss of his career with the Portland, Oregon Police Bureau was bittersweet. He had been a good homicide detective, who took professional pride in his work—work he'd often hated. Still, it was a job that he'd done well. Having Josh helped to compensate for the loss.

That September, almost two years ago now, he'd met Josh's mom, Angie. She was twenty-eight going on sixty-eight, and she and Josh were living in a run-down shithole of an apartment in northeast Portland. A warren of warehouses, decaying tenements, and old, converted motels, it was one step up from the street for the blacks, whites, Hispanics, Asians, and assorted transients who lived there.

Angie had quit school at fourteen, pregnant with Josh after a union with a married man. She started working as a waitress in a diner, then moved up to the better-paying job of cocktail waitress in a succession of increasingly nicer dives, raising Josh with the help of neighbors, teachers, and co-workers. When Josh was five, Children's Services Division removed him for a month while Angie tried to straighten out a problem with meth, and from what Meredith could learn, she didn't do too badly.

The year that Josh turned ten, Angie was running drinks in a small bar off Lombard, a dive called Dudley's Hunt Club. She left for work one Friday evening in September, wearing a black miniskirt, white blouse, and black stockings. She waited for cars to pass on the busy highway, with Joshua watching to make sure she made it across safely.

On weekends, Joshua walked the three blocks to the lounge and sat outside to wait for his mother, rain or not, because she usually put a load on after her shift. He worried that she would get run down trying to cross the street. He would walk his mom across, she tipsy and leaning on him, telling him about her night.

"I made twenty-two dollars in tips tonight, Joshie, whaddaya think?" she would say, showing him the money, their arms tight around each other, Josh grinning up at her, laughing with her when she tripped. Angie was a lot of things, Meredith learned, but she worked hard at being a mother. She was trim, a small woman with brown hair, and except for the haunted look in her face, Angie was attractive. She was mildly interested in finding someone to take her out of this shit, but most of the men she met at the Club were assholes, looking for a lady to trick for them, or looking for a meal ticket, and they were certainly not looking for a woman and a ten-year-old kid to support.

On his mother's last night at work, Joshua was waiting at 2 A.M. and was still there at 3 A.M., when Dudley shook him. "Hey, kid. Your mom left a coupla hours ago. Musta had a hot date. C'mon, I'll give you a ride."

Josh had waited in the apartment all day Saturday. Meredith found him there Saturday night.

Angie had been found, earlier in the day, by a crew cutting brush on the side of Valley Rest Cemetery. When Meredith met Angie, she was no longer wearing her miniskirt. It was torn and bloody, lying at her feet. She had been propped up against a small cedar tree, the tall grasses and brush hiding her from the cemetery. The lower branches of the tree created an umbrella, giving the attacker an area to work unobserved. Her blouse, red with blood and torn, lay under her; her bra was draped on a lower branch of the cedar, flung there in a killer's hurry. Flies had found her before the workers had. There was a smell of blood.

Of madness. Meredith recognized the pieces of clothing, and her shoes not far from her feet.

He didn't recognize Angie as a human being, and the hell of it was, he had to look at her. There was what looked like lung tissue where her head was, and her breasts were sliced, badly (*huh, don't shit yourself Patrick old kid—badly, my ass, they're cut right down to the rib cage*) . . . and . . .

After a few minutes, he continued, a part of him clinical now.

He had thought, months later, when the image of Angie continued to return, that there are some things fathers don't share with their children.

He remembered seeing Joshua that night, sitting in Angie's apartment in the dark, with the TV on. He was not watching it. Meredith knew at once that it was on for company. The kid was eerie - he knew somehow that his mother wasn't coming back. The kid looked up when Meredith entered, the rusty hinges on the screen door making the announcement. Although Meredith was wearing a suit, the kid knew who he was. Meredith still hadn't forgotten his walk across the room, dread rising with each step; he had never had to tell a kid before that his mom, his only parent, was dead.

Joshua didn't cry, not at first, he just sat there, rocking, hugging himself, with his 49'er T-shirt pulled over his knees.

When he finally did let loose, Meredith wept with him, holding him on the faded and cracked linoleum. He broke all convention and department rules, and took Josh home with him that night.

The next day, the Child ProtectiveServices Division placed Josh in a foster home.

When Meredith went in for surgery a month later, Josh showed up in his 49'er T-shirt. They both had a need.

Pulling himself back from his memories, Meredith finished his coffee, watching the rising sun put a glow on the east side of the capitol building. He got up, stretching, letting the sun warm him. He shrugged and started walking north toward the Hilton, the knee reminding him that he would never ski Squaw Valley or Mt. Bachelor again. He didn't see the joggers coming back down. Maybe the old guy went tits-up with a heart attack, he thought and smiled.

There was a terse message from Ward at the hotel desk. "Find Gardiner and meet at my office—ASAP!"

Meeting Ward at the office wasn't a problem; he was ready to check out. Finding Gardiner might take the CIA, and the FBI, and the *National Enquirer*.

CHAPTER
9

The coyote caught the scent of the rabbit and padded quietly through the sagebrush, his belly tight with hunger. He dropped down in the thick brush and waited for the movement, his breathing imperceptible.

There.

Just ahead.

The coyote leaped forward, a blur of grey. The rabbit jumped at the last second, sensing the charge, and instinctively ran, squeaking fear. He made quick cuts and lightning turns around the sagebrush, seeking a hole, refuge of any kind, with the coyote close behind, going around some of the sage and over some.

The rabbit left the sand and ran over the oily rocks and onto the blacktop, his fear of the coyote all consuming and more powerful than any fear of the road, the other death.

Twin circles of light bracketed the rabbit, and he hunched down, unable to move.

The light approached fast, a blinding wave, caused by thunder. The coyote made his attack; he swerved at the last possible second as the car roared past, exploding into the rabbit's hind legs, spraying the roadway with blood and bone.

The light was gone, an ugly apparition, an intruder on the desert drama.

The rabbit nerve-jumped on the center line, its eyes glazing over as the coyote approached.

The driver of the van grinned, baring his teeth at the quickness of death he caused. He saw the dark shadow make its run for the rabbit. He instinctively pulled his foot from the gas and held it above the brake pedal. At the last second, he didn't brake and felt the thump as the wheels hit the rabbit.

He cheated the coyote. This was *his* turn. And he didn't want to upset the lovely in the back of the van.

He held her Arizona driver's license with the thumb and forefinger of his left hand, and absently turned it over. He peered at the front of it, holding it down in front of the dim instrument lights. Karen Elizabeth Hartley, with an address in NW Phoenix. Manzan something. He squinted in the dim light. Manzanita Circle.

The picture didn't do her justice. He would have to tell her about it, how pretty she was. She wouldn't need her license anyway.

The van seemed to glide now, to roll effortlessly on the two-lane highway, as if fueled by the blood of the rabbit. He felt the power. He could steer the van without touching the wheel; he could guide it with his will. The sagebrush hills blurred past the van, a surreal landscape in the grey light of dawn.

He had a power that he never dreamed was possible. And it was building. The peripheral events surrounding his work pleased and excited him, particularly the media coverage.

He tracked his progress in the papers.

Brad Hogarth, the rotund owner of the Hogarth Bullseye Shop in Phoenix, was quoted as saying, "I've had my best month ever. This bastard who is takin' those women is gonna make some of us rich."

In Phoenix, a man shot his seventeen-year-old son as the kid came into his dad's bedroom to apologize for coming home late. Fortunately the old man didn't plug his son very well—he just broke his arm with a .38 special. In nearby Scottsdale, a fifty-six-year-old grandmother was driving home from her bridge club when her Cadillac was smacked in the left rear quarter panel by an Olds 98. The driver of the Olds, a thirty-two-year-old insurance salesman from Tempe, sat with his wife and kids and watched in astonishment as she suddenly ran over the curb, crushing a bicycle, as she tried to leave. Flooring the gas pedal, she smoked her tires and sped away, leaving twin black marks on the sidewalk, her face a mask of stark terror.

Oh, yes, these events excited him
He was coming
He wanted others to join him
Some of the best in the business
He was going to bring terror into the homes of 300 million
And no one knew it
Not yet, anyway.

CHAPTER
10

Meredith sat on the bed in his room and called Josh. His son was staying with Meredith's seventy-six-year-old mother while Meredith was in Washington.

"Hi, it's me. How're you doing?"

"Fine."

"Just fine? That's all?"

"Yeah. Just fine," Josh said, noncommittal.

Meredith hated phone calls, especially obligatory long-distance calls, and even though he missed Josh, they didn't do very well on the phone.

"Dad?"

He's never called me that before, Meredith thought. "Dad . . . when you coming home?"

"Ah, soon. In fact (it's been almost a year, and he's never called you that before), ah . . . in fact, I'm flying out tonight for Phoenix, and then on to Oregon. I should be there in two days. How's Grandma?"

"She's fine. You want to talk with her?"

"No, tell her I'll see her in a couple of days."

"I love you, Dad."

"I love you too, son."

Meredith left the room, whistling, and took his bag down to the front desk.

Two hours later he parked the rental car and walked inside the cool interior of the lab. Gardiner was somewhere in here, probably the only worker here on a Saturday. Meredith liked the strange forensic analyst. Gardiner was different. He read between the lines and saw things—no, he *looked* for things—that the rest didn't. He worked Saturdays, nights, or any time he had a project that intrigued him or evidence was needed.

Gardiner was hunched over a computer in the third lab Meredith tried.

"You get around pretty good for a crippled-up ex-cop," Gardiner said, concentrating on the screen.

""I'm okay," Meredith countered, "but you're about to undergo a rectal exam with a baseball bat."

"Ward pissed again, huh?" Gardiner fiddled with some keys, watching the new information spread on the screen, the green light giving his face a fiendish glow.

"If you don't stop bringing your dates in here and using this for your private bedroom suite, he'll have you scraping paint on a forty-year-old leaky destroyer in the Persian Gulf."

"But I'm not in the service." He turned to Meredith. "Ward could do that?" He grinned.

"He could do that," Meredith assured him.

Gardiner's grin faded. He stroked the keyboard. "Well, Meredith, my boy," he said, in his best imitation of Ward, sounding stern and official, "that's a whimsical charge, that I'm bringing young ladies into my place of work, especially with no evidence."

Meredith pulled up a stool, glancing warily at the seat cover. Gardiner continued to work at the keyboard and his defense.

"That's a spurious charge. Besides, it ain't against the rules to give tours."

"Tours!" Meredith snorted. "Tours, my ass. Ward overheard two of the secretaries talking about you and your `tours.' I'm telling you the boss is pissed." Meredith shook his head as the younger man grinned up at him. "I'm also here to tell you that we have a meeting in his office, A-sap, right now, immediately. It's about your phone call this a.m."

"So, why didn't he call me back?"

"He sent me here to collect you in person."

"I'm flattered, but I can find my way there."

"I know, 'cause I'm driving," Meredith said.

Gardiner pointed to the stool Meredith was perched on.

"That's evidence, you know," he said, with what Meredith's high-school buddies would have called a shiteatin' grin.

"Evidence?" Meredith slowly pulled his leg up and looked beneath it.

"Yeah," Gardiner said, somber, his hands clasped behind his back. He bowed forward slightly, as if he were a funeral director consoling the bereaved. "Do we have to take it to Ward? See, this girl, Eileen she was shy and—."

Meredith held up his hand.

"And we had to use the stool as a . . . well . . . as a sex-shu-al aid," Gardiner said, carefully enunciating each syllable.

"Stop!" Meredith cried, holding his hand up again. "I don't want to hear any more, nor do I want to be part of this—" He jumped up and looked at the stool, wondering what might be on the thing.

"I don't want to hear any more about this nightly 'tour' of the lab," Meredith said. "Do you have the results of the blood tests?"

"Yeah, here." Gardiner held up a manila folder. He walked toward the door of the lab, leaving Meredith standing by the computer.

"C'mon," Gardiner waved. "Let's not keep the old fart waiting for us. He might not have too much time left." He went out, laughing.

Meredith followed, shaking his head. Youth. Invincibility. Gardiner was maybe all of twenty-three. Meredith couldn't understand what so many girls saw in the kid, but still, there was something about him that he couldn't quite identify. And, he was the best forensic analyst they had.

Meredith watched Gardiner absently push his broken plastic frames up on his nose and thought that the kid looked like a nerd.

When they got to Ward's office, they slipped in quietly and waited for the head of the agency to speak. Meredith found a chair in front of Ward's desk and watched through the window, as he always did from here, the sailboats on the Potomac. Gardiner stood behind Meredith, holding charts and case files. He was, for once, quiet, as if he realized that his unorthodox working habits were a capital offense, and it would not do to piss off the boss too many times.

Ward fiddled with his pipe, which, Meredith suspected, was a gentle stalling tactic, one that gave Ward time to organize the meeting.

Ward pulled the flame from the lighter down into the bowl, sending out a wreath of smoke around his white hair. "Tell me about the blood," he said without looking up, a command more than a question.

"The killer or kidnapper, or whatever he is, left some blood in his last victim's car—a small vial of blood," Gardiner said. "The hell of it is, the blood belongs to the victim he took ten days before—it's a match on the Pearson woman. I've never heard of anything like this before. This person is telling us that he is responsible for more than one disappearance."

"It's been done before," Meredith said. "A killer in New York left the body of a victim in the same lot he'd left one in the night before. The detectives had just finished their crime-scene investigation on the first one." He turned and looked at Gardiner. "This guy is just playing with us now. I don't think he wants to get caught—he's just raising the stakes. More of a thrill if we show a constant interest."

"How can we be sure that the blood is from the Pearson girl, the one you say it is? DNA analysis?" Ward asked.

"Forensic DNA analysis," Gardiner said. "We don't know if the Pearson girl gave up her blood post mortem or not."

Ward walked around his desk to where Gardiner was standing, as if to size up the young lab technician. "I know what the process is called. How do we know that we have a sample from the girl?"

"Well, to begin with," Gardiner said, "we got lucky. The Pearson girl from Phoenix left some of her blood with the Red Cross in case she had an accident and needed some blood. She apparently was worried about AIDS and other blood diseases that are sometimes transmitted during transfusions. We got a sample of her donated blood and matched it with the blood in the vial left in the last victim's car. It was a perfect match." Gardiner looked over at Meredith, gave him a wink, and went on, as if his boss were in another room, not standing there in front of him, breathing fire.

"From a small sample of blood—one tenth of a milliliter or less—we can tell without question that one blood sample matches another. By isolating the cells, and purifying the DNA from the cells, we can use some chemical and X-ray methods that give us an end product of developed film. The film shows a series of 'bars' or 'bands,' each of which reveals the position of a DNA fragment. For purposes of illustration, the bands on the X-ray film are similar to the bar codes that are read by the machines at the checkout counters in the supermarkets."

Gardiner reached into his briefcase and withdrew a thick file. He removed a computer printout, and handed it to Ward. "This is the lab report on the blood samples."

"Why is he doing this?" Ward asked. "Think he knows we can match the blood?"

"We'd better figure that he knows exactly what we can and can't do," Meredith said.

"Who knows how this process works?" Ward asked Gardiner.

"Any advanced student of molecular biology, a few chemists, forensic specialists, and most homicide detectives."

"A rather chilling prospect," Ward said. "I believe that Mr. Meredith here will be forwarding any future evidence to you and your colleagues. He is going into the field for a few days. As for you, young man," Ward pointed his pipe at Gardiner, "you're not to give any of your 'tours' to my secretaries."

Meredith laughed. Gardiner nodded, grinning. They left the office, with Meredith promising Ward daily phone contact.

Gardiner paused to talk to Ward's secretary. Meredith grinned. The kid might be a whiz at computer work and forensic science, but his hormonal imbalance was destroying his good sense, if not his safety. Corning on to Ward's secretary was dumb. Real dumb.

Meredith finally pulled Gardiner away, and they made it out before their boss could catch the kid.

As they drove back to Meredith's hotel, he kept thinking, I gotta get out of this town. Get back to the Northwest. Spend some time with Josh.

He made it sooner than he thought.

Oregon
CHAPTER 11

The large bird caught the afternoon thermal coming off the bluff, and circled effortlessly. The green Douglas Fir Trees on the mountain continued to the horizon, where twenty miles to the west the rolling forest met with the ubiquitous fog bank of the coast.

The sharp eyes of the bird of prey caught movement on the bluff. The bluff was a column of basalt, formed when a volcanic eruption poured lava onto the slope, and earthquakes split the land and lifted the plateau from the surrounding forest. From the top of the plateau the trees continued in an unbroken line to the top of the mountain range.

The thermal carried with it the movement, the sounds, and the smells of the forest.

The uplifted air carried the decay of something on the plateau.

The bird turned the tip of its large left wing toward the trees, and begin a spiral that carried it to the source of the food.

Twenty miles east of the circling bird of prey, the Pacific Ocean thundered at the rugged coast, the high tide giving a spectacular display of energy. The waves swept into volcanic chutes, and in some places the spray covered the highway.

The blue van with its human cargo was almost at its destination, the dust of the desert washed off by the rains of the past few hours.

The wipers slapped at the windshield, setting up a metronomic cadence that was lulling the driver to sleep. The wheels of the van sent geysers of water into the southbound lane of Coast Highway 101 as they hit puddles in the road, a highway eroded by the constant stream of Winnebagos and log trucks. The van continued north, the driver oblivious to the spray of the surf on his left. It was a dreary day, one that isolated people in their cars and houses, keeping them in small, depressed capsules of privacy.

The driver liked the rain. It hid his van, and more importantly, hid his passenger from everyone, including the Oregon State Police assigned to patrol this lonely stretch of coastal highway.

He slowed for a family of tourists turning into the Sea Lion Cave visitor parking lot. He laughed at the rain, the glorious rain, the rain that was going to ruin the vacation for those suckers who wanted sun and a hot beach. If they wanted warmth, let them go to Mexico, or the Caribbean. He laughed at that. He didn't laugh often.

But they were laughing at him. They always had. Everyone always had. Except for one person, and she was dead.

Their laughter hit him now with such force that his eyes flicked down, shutting out scenes from another time The rattle of a compression brake and the blast of an air horn startled him. He snapped his head up and jerked the wheel to the right, swerving on the slick highway as a log truck loomed suddenly in his windshield like a huge grey monster. The truck roared past, and the contorted face of the bearded driver flashed at him.

"Jesus," he said aloud, shakily, fighting to control the van as it slid perilously toward the ditch, as if it were on a self-destruct mission of its own. "I was over the line." His voice came out harsh and guttural in the enclosed space, the sound leading him further out of the trance-like fog that the wipers had held him in.

He continued north, up 101, fighting the laughter that tried to seep in from the corners of the cab. He knew that the laughter would come again. It always did when he was tired or excited. But he could make it stop.

"Hey Thomas, Hey Thomas, stick it out man."

"Hey Thomas, show us your wanger."

The van swerved, imperceptibly at first. It would get worse.

He had to get off the road. The voices and the laughter were the invisible blows of an old enemy who punched him from hidden angles. He saw a sign that said "Oregon State Park 1/2 Mile." He had to stop. He pulled into the parking lot of the Devil's Churn State Park at Cape Perpetua, and drove down into the lower level. He parked the van so that it was hidden from the highway by a stand of trees that were shaped into a canopy by the constant battering of wind and rain. Below him, and to his right, the waves racing into the basalt chute were funneled higher and higher.

The spray from every third or fourth wave reached the highway. He could see the Pacific Ocean through breaks in the trees directly in front of him. He had the parking lot to himself. Almost to himself.

The lovely was with him.

She only had to stay alive a while longer.

Then he would set her free.

It had been the same for years, all of his early school years anyway. And the girls had been the worst. When he was in high school, Jane Poskell had been the worst.

In his mind he saw again the little girl (How old was she? They said seven. Maybe seven?) playing alone on the swings. He watched her and he began growing huge. Then he walked slowly from the street to the playground. He touched himself, reaching into his cutoff jeans, grabbing himself, and then she saw him.

She smiled at first, friendly and yet uncertain. He had to get it out to finish, and he jerked the buttons apart on the cutoffs, and then he exploded, spurting on the sand below the swing. The girl gripped the chain of the swing, watching, knowing that something was wrong—the big kid was angry or something—and then she put her thumb in her mouth and started to cry.

The urgency was gone now. He glanced quickly around, and saw no one. Talk to her, he thought.

"Don't cry. Look, don't . . . uh . . . I'm not really such a bad guy. Don't . . ."

She screamed. He jumped and looked around again. She jumped off the swing, and started to run. She caught her tennis shoe on the grass bordering the swing set and sprawled on the ground. Before Thomas could get to her, she was up and off, screaming.

"*Mommy!*"

He ran toward her, frightened now, with his cutoff jeans sliding down his hips, further exposing his crotch and his guilt.

"*Mommy, Mommmeee!*"

He ran toward her. He had to make her see that he really didn't mean any harm, that he wouldn't hurt her.

"Don't cry," he yelled, and slowed as he saw old Mrs. Donnelly come out on her porch. He ran. And of course everyone found out about it.

His mother said she didn't believe it. But the little girl's mommy certainly did. And Jane Poskell and the others at school did, after she told everyone. Even the cops didn't do that.

The jocks took it up in the school corridors.

"*Hey Thomas, flash your dick, man,*" they shrieked. Especially Gregg Budd and Jane. They always waited until the others were watching.

"*Hey Thomas, scare us, man. Make us scream,*" they howled.

"*Make us cry, scaaaare us!*"

The laughter would continue until he could find safety around a corner, or in another hallway. If it happened outside, he was at their mercy until he ran.

He looked at the windshield, not knowing right away where he was. Absently he turned off the wipers and the engine. The rain gathered on the windshield, blurring the view of the ocean, closing him in even more. Inside with the voices. The roar of the surf and his view of the fogged windshield dimmed as the laughter started up again.

"*Hey Thomas, wanna pet my puppy?*"

"*Hey Thomas, didja shine your wire today? Huh, didja Thomas?*"

Gregg slapped his friends on the back, yelling down the hall to Jane and her friends.

"*Look out, Jane. Thomas is gonna jack off in fronta little girls!*"

Hey Thomas, they called, and never let up. He had known then that his days at school were over.

"*Hey Thomas, choke your gopher, man. Hey Thomas . . .*"

The van was a darkened capsule. The windows up front were steamed. No windows in the cargo compartment, thank you very much; the lovelies like the darkness. Thomas heard a car door shut somewhere to the rear of the van, and shook himself from his dreams. The roar and hiss of the water in the chute came back to him. He wiped the side window with his sleeve and saw a small green Chevy out near the rock wall of the viewpoint. A woman and a man got out of the car, one from each side, and ran to change places, with the man now the passenger. The car left the lot and moved south, lost in the rain. Thomas was almost alone again.

He opened the partition that separated the cab of the van from the cargo area. As he ducked through the small doorway, the plastic covering rustled, giving a warning to his passenger. She moaned and scuttled crablike back into the rear corner, her eyes blinking against the sudden light, becoming round with fright and pain.

The expected smell of urine and vomit was strong.

He reached out to touch her, and she tried to melt back into the corner, as if she could shrink away from this madness. She whined from deep in her throat.

Thomas watched his lovely for another minute, and listened to the rain. He was calm now. Powerful.

He reached over to stroke her hair, and didn't care at all that she squirmed weakly.

"I'm glad you're awake," he said. "It's time to meet the other lovelies."

CHAPTER 12

Ellie had been sleeping.

Dreaming.

Her vomit and urine rolled with the movement of the van on the slick plastic covered floor, a slimy bilge that nudged her as she drifted in the safety of her dreams.

She was dreaming of her daddy, William Frederick Hartley, "Freddie" to his friends, who taught literature at the California Institute of Technology in Pasadena. He had been at Cal Tech since Ellie was six months old, and she always thought of him as a professor, a teacher, a kind father, and, since Stacey's birth, a wonderful grandpa. He used to complain to Ellie about his students and their complete and undeniable lack of interest in literature. He told Ellie, "They know as much about Dickens as I do about electricity—no, that's not entirely true. At least I know how to turn on a light switch." But Freddie loved it there, and he was well-respected by the faculty and students. He took science classes from his colleagues, and razzed them relentlessly for thirty years about their "illiteracy."

Ellie' s mom, Janice, was a stockbroker for Shearson Lehman. She was nine years younger than her husband, and Ellie often accused them of a student/professor love affair, which they both denied with silly grins. Ellie and her dad were close in a way that she and her mom didn't share, and in the strange way of relationships, it was he, the literary man, and not her mom, who led her to an appreciation of business.

She drifted in and out of her dream, a dream of her as a little girl, not much older than Stacey was now. When she was six, Ellie thought that she and her daddy should become beachcombers, or at least weekend beach bums. They would roam the beaches of Southern California together, leaving Janice home with her bridge and investment clubs.

She often thought in later years that Freddie was a perfect dad in every way. He had a gift for seeing things the way kids do, as if he were seeing them for the first time, and in a way he was, with Ellie. They shared the joy of new discoveries in the world about them like a pair of twins. Delighting especially in their expeditions to the seashore, they would come home with their booty of shells and driftwood, smelling vaguely of salt air and fish, faces burned by sun and wind, laughing, arms around each other. Janice would hug them, glad for her day alone or with friends, and examine their treasure.

During the summer of Ellie's sixth year, she and her daddy found the bird.

The day had started off like the other summer Saturdays; they'd parked on the beach just after dawn, early enough to have the beach to themselves for a couple of hours. The sun filtered over the water, making it shine and sparkle as the surf came in. The tide was low, and they walked along the water's edge, Ellie and her daddy wearing their usual beach costumes—floppy straw hats and sunglasses, T-shirts, jeans, and canvas shoes.

Ellie had her sand pail in her right hand, her dad's hand in her left. They were going to dig up some treasure and take it home, aided by a map that Ellie and her dad had constructed the evening before.

"Hey! Ho! It's off to dig we go!" Ellie sang, swinging her daddy's hand. He looked down at his daughter and winked, and added his baritone to her small voice.

"Hey! Ho! It's off to dig we go!"

They came to a dip in the sand, the lip of a tidal pool, and Ellie stopped, staring at the movement below her. "Hey! Ho! It's off . . ." Her tiny voice trailed off.

A sea gull was in the sand at her feet, making a crablike movement in a circle, dragging its left wing. It was a large coastal scavenger, almost as big as a dog, she thought. As the gull turned, it appeared to be looking right at her, its eyes full of pain. But the wing . .

"Daddy, what's wrong with its wing?" Ellie asked, and stood, unable to move, as the gull crabbed toward her. She was seized by a hideous terror; the gull was coming for her, and she couldn't move. A trickle of pee slipped down her leg, unnoticed in her fear. Her daddy picked her up and turned her around, away from the bird, but not before she saw the wing again. The bone was showing through where the skin and flesh had been torn away—maybe eaten, she thought, and shivered—the flesh rotted, pink and moving on the bone, with small white wormy things squirming.

"Daddy . . . is it . . . dead?" Ellie whispered huskily.

Her father put her down some distance away, and walked back toward the tidal pool. Ellie stood there holding her pail, her heart gripped by icy tendrils as she watched her daddy walk away.

Don't go, Daddy . . . it's not what you think it's . . .

The bird glared at Ellie, eyes small and sharp, filled not with pain but hatred, looking right at her.

Hey! Ho! It's off to dig we go . . .

The gull scuttled away from Daddy, and gave a sharp cry, dragging the decaying wing after it. *What are you going to do . . . Daddy . . . fix it?* He stopped and watched the bird work its way along the surf, running with the crabbing motion in front of them. He returned to Ellie and picked her up. They both watched the bird until it disappeared behind a ripple in the sand.

"Daddy?"

"What, Honey?"

"It is going to die?"

"Yes," he said, matter-of-factly, thinking that she already knew the answer to that one.

Her daddy put her down and they resumed their walk. He kept looking at her and she thought that maybe he knew that she had pee'd in her panties like a baby. Nah, if he knew, he would have them go back to the car for some dry clothes. Their pirate song kept running through her mind, but she couldn't sing it again. They didn't find much treasure either.

Ellie sat slumped over, her shoulders sticking to the plastic. She smiled at her daddy as he walked over to her and picked her up. She wondered why he was here.

And then her daddy was gone, replaced by the vibration of the van, and a sharp, thrumming sound. Where was she? She was older, bigger. She wanted to go back to her dream. She tried, as she sometimes did when she woke up with a pleasant, unfinished dream.

Her dream wasn't all bad, her daddy was there. She was somewhere, being taken somewhere.

She could feel the van sway and hit something, like it was running into . . .

Water?

And then she knew what it was—rain. They were driving in the rain, and when the van hit puddles, the spray hit the wheel wells with a thump. A thrumming sound.

She could see her dad, a small man, his grey hair covered by a European driving cap, with his gold-rimmed glasses perched on his nose. The thought of his face brought a quick smile, the pain in her lips worth the memory.

Had she really been dreaming?

Her body lurched slightly, as the forward motion of the van stopped. Her eyes blinked in the dark, useless; she tried to swallow and couldn't. Her lips were cracked and crusted with dried blood, her nasal passages were blocked, and her body raged with thirst.

The small door to the driver's compartment opened a few inches and the light exploded onto the plastic. Ellie caught a glimpse of green, and movement, before her hand blocked out the pain to her eyes.

Movement! Someone was coming in. Maybe something? She saw a bird's face then, the gull, and she whined, deep in her throat. *Oh, dear God . . . I don't want to die . . . I don't wanna know what happened to the others . . . let someone else do it.*

(Hey! Ho! It's off to dig we go!)

Death in the form of a man filled the doorway.

He said something. *Reaching for me! What's he saying? What's that sound?*

He backed out, enclosing her in darkness.

As she drifted away again, she thought it funny that he looked like a man she had met somewhere . . . maybe an accident?

The van started again.

CHAPTER
13

Ellie woke suddenly, going from sleep to wide awake in seconds. She blinked, unaccustomed to the light after more than twenty-four hours of blackness. It was grey in the van; a trickle of light came from the small door that separated her from the driver's compartment.

She could now make out her arms, her hands as she held them up in front of her face.

Her throat was swollen and breathing was difficult. Her dehydration was becoming advanced, but she was, for the moment, lucid, aware of her surroundings.

She stirred from her corner and pulled her legs around on the plastic, working her way around to bring her face up to the door. Terror gripped her as she suddenly realized that the van was really stopped and she had no idea for how long. She thought that she was alone in the van, although she couldn't say how she knew.

Her heart was thudding, competing with the ringing in her ears. She slowed her breathing, brought her hand up, and gently pushed against the door. The plastic baggie covering made a rustling sound, and she stopped, the door now open an inch. The direct light blinded her, but gave her a glimpse of a steering wheel before she shut her eyes against the pain.

Steering wheel. That means he's gone, she thought. Out of the van. She pushed the door open another inch and sat, scared enough to be incontinent, miserable with her blocked nose, her sense of death, her thirst, and worst of all, her fear of leaving her cell/sanctuary. Afraid of what she might find.

A collage of thoughts flooded her: Stacey, her dad, Herbie, her office at work. She was too weak to cry.

She pushed the door open another inch, and by looking out the driver's side window, saw the grey overcast sky and the rain.

She pushed the door open a foot, enough room for her to slide out *(Hey! Ho! It's off to dig we go!)*, then hesitated and leaned her cheek against the cool plastic, gathering strength.

For Stacey!

She pulled herself out to the floor of the van behind the driver's seat. This area was carpeted, with oak cabinets on each side of the van.

She looked back at the plastic prison, and saw the plastic was a dark green color, as if someone had taped a lawn and leaf bag on the door, ceiling, and floor.

Her skirt was wrinkled and rolled up to her crotch, the once beige linen now a filthy brown, smeared with her blood, urine, and vomit, her pantyhose in tatters, her blouse open and missing buttons. The strap to her bra had broken on the left side, and was hanging down the front of her blouse.

She crouched behind the seat, and listened to the rain, straining to hear. The steady mumbling noise the water made as it hit the roof of the van made this all but impossible; she couldn't tell if her kidnapper was waiting just outside, out of her view, or if he had gone somewhere, thinking that she would be unable to get out.

She tried to swallow, a reflex more than conscious effort, and was reminded by the crust in her mouth and nose that she couldn't; her breathing, dry and labored, served to dry out her mouth even more.

She raised her head to look through the windshield, her heart thudding in her ears. *What if he can see me?* She raised her head a little higher, cautiously, and saw that she was in some kind of forest, with the immediate view in front of the van blocked by a stand of fir trees that towered to perhaps 100 feet. The trees grew thick, the boughs touching, and in places the trunks were so close together that passage between them would be impossible. Thick brush littered the area.

She had to move.

She pulled herself up by the seat, determined now, regaining some anger at what had happened to her, all hope lost that this was a dream. She grasped the top of the high-backed bucket seat on the passenger side and pulled herself between the seats, and crouched there, panting through her mouth, willing her heart to be quiet. She first glanced out the driver's window—nothing!

She risked a quick glance out the passenger window. The brush was close on both sides. She reached out to steady herself on the instrument panel as she crawled across the seat, and her hand brushed the glove compartment. She froze, all of her anger and determination replaced by a mind-numbing fear, the coldness hitting her like a sudden fall into icy water.

The glove box! The thing that she saw . . . the thing with eyes that . . . was a sick Halloween joke that the driver had left there. Who would carry a Halloween mask in their car? She was sure now that death was waiting for her. That thing . . . that half-eaten? half-buried? thing in the glove box . . . a picture flashed in her mind, a picture that had been on the front cover of *Time* magazine a few years back—the picture of a human face half submerged in water. The top half was normal; the lower half was stripped of flesh, a skeleton. The feature article had to do with the effects of pollution on the human animal.

A grinning, horrible skull.

A Halloween mask.

(Hey! Ho! It's off to dig we go!)

Ellie jerked her hand off the dashboard and reached for the door handle. She pulled, and then yanked on it in a panic. The door popped open and she slid out across the seat and fell to the ground. She was staring at a carpet of pine needles and clumps of grass. Her right hand was in a puddle of water. She dropped her face in it, and sucked in the sweet cold water, not minding the fir needles that came with it or the slightly bitter taste. The water hit the cracks in her lips and burned, and that didn't matter either. She drank until she had to stop, until the pain in her face was greater than her thirst.

She rolled over into a bushy vine maple, and stared up at the low grey clouds, the coolness of the rain snapping into her mind and clearing away the sluggishness of the ride in the plastic horror.

She could get away. She had no idea where the hell she was, but she might be able to beat death yet.

The man watched from the edge of the timber, some fifty feet away from the van. He was standing beneath the boughs of a large fir tree, in an almost closed umbrella of green, concealed from Ellie's view.

She waited on the ground, gaining strength and determination from the wetness. She raised her head and took a quick look around, able to see only a few feet. She rose to her knees, and grabbed the sideview mirror with her hand to steady herself. She pulled herself up, caught a glimpse of a face in the mirror, and gave a terrified yelp before she realized that the face was hers. Her blond hair was stringy, twisted, matted; her eyes were sunken, a black mass of bruises surrounding them, and her nose was swollen and crusted with blood.

Fear had put deep furrows in her face.

She looked away from the mirror, walked to the rear of the van, using the side to steady herself, sliding her hand along the outside of her prison.

She shivered. *At least I didn't die in that place.*

She looked down the narrow track the van was on. It was bordered on both sides by brush and trees, and in some places the brush seemed impassable. The trail ended in a graveled road. She could see a small road sign, green with white numbers. She could hear running water now, something larger than a trickle—a stream? a river? She started down the trail and was about ten feet away from the back of the van when she caught some movement near a tree directly in front of her, where the trail turned.

She froze.

As Ellie watched, a man stepped from behind the tree. He appeared to be watching the trail. She backed up cautiously, holding her right hand behind her to feel for the van. When she reached it, she turned and ran. Just ahead of the van, she saw a break in the brush, on the right side of the trail. She stumbled forward, and turned into the trail, slipping as she ran. She landed in a seated position, facing back toward the track. She began to push herself backward digging in with her heels and palms of her hands. When she moved about fifteen feet further in, she stopped and listened.

She saw the movement again at the start of the new trail, and saw the head and neck of the man! The man who'd run into her Camaro. And he was coming toward her.

He had something in his hand.

A knife! Oh God, a knife, he has a knife—a big one I think . . . he's holding it out there in front of himself

She shook herself and moaned, then gave a low, eerie, guttural growl, an animal sound that scared her even more. She got up and ran, her legs shaking with cramps and fear. The trail led uphill through the trees.

She glanced over her shoulder when she had gone maybe two hundred yards, and saw nothing. But he was there. She was sure of it.

She would go until her body failed her.

The trail was used by small animals and deer, and not much of a path for humans. In places the trees grew so close together that she had to squeeze between them. Constantly turning her head to look down the trail behind her, she had an occasional view of a blacktop road below, the one that they must have taken to get here. If she could only make it back around to the highway, she thought, maybe she could flag down a motorist.

Yeah, if only.

Off to her left, the mountain fell away, and she saw what looked like tall, limbless trees poking up into the mist. They looked like masts on a fleet of ghost ships, sticking holes in the sky.

If she had turned then, and made her way down to the trees that had no branches, she would have found that they were logging yarder booms, remnants of a logging town that hadn't quite died yet.

She might have made it.

She stopped, and held onto a small tree the size of a fence post, and sucked in air, gasping. She saw movement down the trail from her, and she pushed off and up. The climb was much steeper now, and she used her hands to claw her way upward, heedless of torn fingernails and deep scratches and cuts in her hands as she grabbed sharp basalt rocks. Her feet were becoming numb with cold; they hadn't been cut much, even though she'd left her flats in the van. Suddenly the path leveled off, and came up against a basalt column, a vertical rock face.

She was trapped!

She began panting to the point of hyperventilation, searching both sides of the trail to see if it continued around the column, and then saw the small opening off to her left. The opening was just below her, screened by a large rhododendron bush. If she had been able to stand up then, she would have been able to see the road below, a ribbon in the grey mist, and down to her left, the logging camp.

Unconsciously she rubbed her bleeding palms on her skirt, her eyes darting from side to side to find another way of escape.

Nothing!

She started into the cave-like opening.

The hole in the rock was like a small pipe, running upward through the basalt for ten feet or so. Ellie crawled through on her hands and knees to the upper end. She came out on a small plateau, an area maybe two hundred by a hundred feet, on top of the basalt column that had stopped her below. A few tenacious fir trees struggled up through the rocks and patches of soil. She stumbled quickly over to the closest side of the plateau, looking for a trail down, and felt a momentary dizziness as she got too close to the edge. The drop was at least a hundred feet, but it was hard to tell in the rain.

Hide! Gotta hide.

Maybe he's missed the opening.

She looked around and found no place to hide in the small, limited area. She couldn't waste time looking. If the man had continued to track her, he would soon be here.

Maybe someone will come. She laughed bitterly at that, the sound a cawing in her throat. No. The killer had planned this carefully. This area was isolated; she knew that she was no longer in Arizona, and, judging from the rain, she was probably in Oregon or Washington or British Columbia.

She stumbled and fell hard on her way across the grassy top of the plateau.

"Shit!"

She put her hand out on a smooth rock to push herself into a sitting position (*maybe he won't find me, maybe I can walk to the road and get out of this mess*), and the moss and green gunk covering the rock came off in her hand. She looked dumbly at it, then saw movement above her. It's stopped raining, she thought, as she looked at a large eagle sliding out of the sky, toward the end of the plateau. As the bird came lower, she realized that what she had thought to be an eagle was something else.

A vulture!

The large bird, graceful in flight and often mistaken for an eagle, had an ugly, raw, wattled skin covering its head and neck.

Death, she thought, still holding the moss.

The bird made a pass within a few feet of the end of the plateau, then dropped from sight.

Ellie held the moss and looked down at the rock. It looked vaguely familiar, like something she had seen before, something she didn't want to see.

She pushed the rock, then jerked her hand back, as if she had been burned. She was staring into the empty eyes of a human skull, a skull turned green with constant dampness.

A moan left her throat as she got up fast, shaken.

"Settle down, girl, settle . . . down," she said aloud. The sound of her voice was reassuring. *Probably some climber. Someone dumb enough to climb alone . . . someone who didn't tell anyone where they were going.*

She wanted to believe that, oh boy, she wanted to . . .

She took a step, and saw before her many more green rocks (*some are brown – this is crazy*) in a circle that stretched to the edge of the cliff.

She saw now that the rocks had some other stuff next to them (*don't think about it kiddo . . . just don't*). Her hair bristled, even in the moist air. She was suddenly hit with what was the main attraction for the vulture – the sweet smell of decaying flesh.

She was dimly aware of the bird making another pass, of the other shapes that she didn't want to know about, and, making no effort to be quiet or to calm herself, she stumbled for the opening, the crumbling hole in the rock.

The voice from the opening stopped her cold.

"Come," it said. "Come, you must meet my lovelies."

"Nooo!" Ellie screamed. She threw herself backward and flipped over, crawling away, scrabbling.

Powerful hands caught her and pulled her back.

She clawed at rocks, panting, grunting, her hands becoming slimy with blood as her palms and finger pads shredded, sobbing, not feeling anything except the awful burning for survival and knowledge that she failed.

She was pulled back, screaming, blood splashing from her hands.

She met the killer.

And, she met his lovelies.

The large bird was gaining height again, rising with the warming air, waiting as it had done countless times, waiting for the movement on the ground to stop.

Thomas Brunson carried his load on a dark, winding trail. Wet fir boughs closed behind him as he walked, and the trail was silent. He left no memory with the forest. On his way down the mountain he paused on a rise, a dark figure with his gruesome burden, backlit against a sky that was losing light. He started down through the trees, hurrying now as the trail leveled out near the road.

He had much to do.

CHAPTER
14

Meredith reached down, grabbed his right knee, and gave it a squeeze. He massaged it absently while he waited for the plane to take off. The view from his window seat showed Dulles International as a myriad of flashing colored lights and jumbled activity that never ended.

He had planned to fly out at the end of the week, when his seminar was over. Finding a reservation at the last minute meant that his seat was confirmed only to Denver, and he might just have to spend the early morning on an airport bench before he could find a flight to Phoenix.

He would have had a much easier time of it if he'd waited for a morning flight, but he wanted to get out of this town and back to the west. He would stop in Phoenix and then it was home to Josh.

The captain gave them another progress report. Only three more planes in front of them and they could take off.

Meredith liked trains. At least he could walk around and even get off now and then if he didn't like the way things were going.

He stretched his knee out as far as he could and rubbed it harder. He'd been walking most of the day – Washington is a city for that – and his knee was telling him all about it. It gave him an obvious limp when he was tired. He told the curious that it "blew up," and if they thought it was the result of an old sports injury, they usually lost interest.

His knee didn't just "blow up." It was cut, sliced and diced one night in a supermarket in east Portland. He remembered thinking as he pulled into the parking lot that night how he liked to shop when no one was around. There was a lot less hassle and he was not as rushed.

Other people liked to shop at night, too . . . for other reasons.

He thought about it again now.

It had been ten-thirty when he pulled into the lot. He was on his way home and had almost driven past when he realized that he hadn't eaten since noon. The box of bite-sized Shredded Wheat and the orange of questionable age were all he could think of when he tried for a mental picture of what he had to eat at home.

The shopping center parking lot was well-lighted, with only a dozen or so cars parked in front of Safeway. To his right, where the building formed an L-shape back out toward the street, there was a Pizza Hut with the lights still on. He parked the Blazer in front of the store and removed his tie and jacket. The .38 revolver looked a little conspicuous with his jacket off, and so he slid the holster off his belt and locked the gun in the center console. *Might as well be comfortable while you shop, Patrick kiddo.*

There was only one checker on duty, stationed in the middle of the dozen checkout counters, a pretty woman of about thirty, bantering with a couple of teenaged kids as she rang up their order. A night manager sitting up in a glassed-in office near the counters was staring at a computer screen. He glanced down at Meredith for a brief moment as he heard the electric door open, his glance an evaluation, then went back to adding up receipts.

Meredith got a cart and pushed it slowly through the paperback book section alongside the cash registers, looking at the colorfully embossed covers, taking his time, waiting for an idea of what he would buy for his late dinner.

A bag lady pushed a cart by with a lonely dozen eggs, giving Meredith a hard look, her three layers of clothing flapping as she walked. She looked sixty but probably wasn't. He knew that living on the street could bring age on in double time.

The eggs made him decide on an omelet – quick and easy, and he fixed them reasonably well. Eggs, cheddar, some mushrooms, green onion, and a bell pepper should do it. He headed for the far corner of the store. On his way down the far left aisle, he picked up a six-pack of Guinness.

A skinny kid wearing gloves and a fatigue jacket passed him, and Meredith watched the boy until he turned the corner by the cottage cheese. The kid made him feel uneasy.

Cholesterol. That's what I need before bed, he thought. At the least the Guinness will counter some of the fat running up and down my arteries.

He picked up a bunch of green onions, and the kid went by again. This time the alarm bells went off. Several things came to Meredith all at once now. Wrong things. The kid had seen joint time, that he was sure of. The way he walked, the hint of a jail tattoo on the back of his hand.

Jesus, Meredith, he said to himself, any rookie with ten months experience would have made the kid the first time he went by. He's wandering around a Safeway store in a suburban shopping center at eleven at night, with no cart, looking for people, not radishes.

The kid ducked into an aisle and headed for the checkout counters. Meredith felt the familiar cold knot forming in his stomach. Sure, he worked robbery/homicide investigations, but he didn't take people off while they were busy working their trade. The real cops did that, the ones wearing the blue suits, the cops who made high-risk arrests every night.

He walked to the end of the aisle, and peeked around the corner. The kid was talking to his partner, and Meredith realized that the kid was the apprentice. The partner was the journeyman.

The partner was short, about five foot six inches, and would go about two twenty, with huge arms and a gut spilling over his greasy belt. Biker. The guy had no jacket, no shirt, just a leather vest, with tattoos and stomach prominently displayed.

Meredith thought that he was overreacting, that nothing was going to happen, and he started to turn away. His stomach was already calming down, and then the biker put on a ski mask and tossed one to the kid. The biker pulled a gun from under his belt; the kid held a survival knife of some kind. Hope the manager gave these two a look when they came in, Meredith thought, and I hope that he's made of something, 'cause we're about to find out. The biker has a goddamn .45 Colt, and the kid has the look of a killer.

Maybe they'll get out clean. No problems – just take the money and run. Be a witness, Meredith my man, don't be a cheap hero.

He'd left his gun in the Blazer, and his stomach would sure as hell feel better with the reassuring weight on his hip. *Oh shit, ain't this grand!*

He breathed slowly, and moved up the aisle toward the front. He stopped by a table piled high with oranges, thinking that they would make a terrible weapon, and would be worse cover from fire from a .45 caliber handgun. He heard yelling.

The flat blast of the .45 echoed through the store, the concussion making his ears ring. He jumped, and his stomach started an honest-to-God hurt now. He walked cautiously to the corner of the aisle and peeked around at the front. The fat biker and the kid had their backs to him, maybe twenty feet away and down in front of the office, the kid holding his knife out in front, the biker yelling something at the manager.

Meredith inched away and then ran for the back, trying to be quiet. As he reached for his cell phone he realized that he had left it in his jacket, in the car. He checked the signs above the aisles as he ran, looking for the kitchen appliance section. He found what he wanted in the middle aisle.

He glanced quickly down the wide, empty aisle toward the front of the store, and selected a large butcher knife from the rack. He removed a small paring knife from its plastic wrapping, and slipped it up his left sleeve. He put the larger knife under his belt at the small of his back, and was pulling his shirt over it when someone jerked his arm.

"Young man, you put that back *right* now!"

Meredith turned to face the bag lady. Her eyes were scrunched up, accusing, her mouth twisted in a thin grimace.

"Lady you don't understand, we're being robbed," he whispered urgently.

"You're right, I've never understood a thief. Now get -."

The .45 went off again, making them both jump.

Meredith grabbed the woman, his face inches away from hers. "Call the police," he whispered hoarsely, then shoved her toward the back.

With both knives concealed, he walked to the front, his legs and stomach trembling. The customers were lined up in the bright wide aisle in front of the checkout counters. The fat biker had the girl pulling money from her register; she was shaking as she jerked the bills out.

"Hurry up, hurry up, hurry up!" the biker yelled at the scared clerk, his voice gravelly and hard. *He's looking for a reason to use the gun on someone,* Meredith thought. *He's pulled the trigger two times, and he wants to see some blood. The kid isn't much better—he's strung out on meth, extremely dangerous and unpredictable.*

The kid held his knife on the night manager, who was trying to open the safe in the cubicle. He was too slow.

"Open it up, asshole!" The kid screamed, his high-pitched voice cracking. He slugged the manager, a vicious, quick blow to the head with the butt of the knife, the blood spraying the glass and office walls as if a red fountain were suddenly turned on, out of control.

72

Meredith tensed, and his hand went to the knife at the small of his back. He pushed his cart up to the line of people trapped in the front aisle.

"Don't be a fool," a voice behind him whispered. He turned and saw the bag lady.

"Let them go with the money, and maybe nobody will get hurt," she whispered, her face up close behind Meredith.

"Yeah, I hope so," he whispered back, "but these two . . . I think they like this." He turned toward her and asked, "You make the call?"

He looked at the register where the biker had the girl, then bent his knees, flexing, getting some blood to his leg muscles so he could move when he had to.

Things began to happen fast.

The biker grabbed the girl and shoved her toward the next register, the one directly in front of Meredith and the bag lady.

"Open it!"

"I . . . I cuh . . . cuh . . . can't—."

The biker brought his gun up to her face.

"I don't have the kuh . . . keys," she said, crying and shaking with fear. The biker hit her with a backhand, and she crumpled below the register.

The phone in the office began to ring over the pounding in Meredith's ears, and he wondered if the manager had hit the panic button. That was probably a police dispatcher, calling the store to check on the alarm. The kid looked up wildly at the biker. Then he stabbed the manager twice. Meredith and the bag lady watched; they twitched in unison with each thrust of the knife. The bag lady was crying. The other customers stood frozen in place, trying to avoid eye contact with the robbers. The two teenagers who had been talking to the checker when Meredith came in seemed to be in shock. They were standing next to the check stand, holding their bags, staring, frozen in place.

"Let's go!" the fat biker yelled. The kid hopped through the open doorway, and ran for the front doors with his partner. The biker stopped as if he had hit an invisible wall just inside the door; the kid ran into him. They both started to back away, slowly.

Meredith knew that the deputies must have arrived.

He moved toward the biker, crouching as he ran. *Take the gun first. Take the biggest threat first, old son. Go for the gun.*

The biker ran back to the counter, grabbed the checker, and put the barrel of the gun up to her head. He began to yell, and Meredith launched himself at the man, looking at his throat, looking at it like a wide receiver looks at the football with pain coming fast from all around. He slammed the big knife into the biker's throat. Meredith's fingers slipped off the handle, and he saw the quizzical look in the biker's eyes as both of them and the cashier went down in a spray of blood, with Meredith's mind screaming *watch out for the skinny kid! watchout! watchout watchoutwatchout!*

The old woman, the bag lady, slowed the skinny kid up somewhat.

But not enough.

Meredith could feel the kid coming, like a wide receiver can feel the presence of the linebackers when he has to go up for the ball over the middle, and he tried to push himself up, to untangle himself from the dying biker and the girl, the smell of blood and gunpowder and body odor making him sick, the screaming coming from the customers a counterpoint to his fear.

The .45 auto was on the floor, partially under a forty- pound bag of puppy chow, and Meredith lunged for it, pulling the girl with him. He swiped at it, and missed, and the knife caught him just below the right knee. He screamed, grabbing for the gun. The kid stabbed him again and the old lady came up behind them and hit the kid in the side of the head with a magnum of Sebastiani Zinfandel. It sounded as if she had hit a flying cantaloupe with a baseball bat. What a sweet fucking sound, Meredith thought.

The kid fell face down on Meredith.

The deputies came in slow, one after the other, leapfrogging high and low for cover. One grim-faced officer covered Meredith and the cons with his Glock while the other tried to sort out the bag of shit that the robbery had turned into.

"Hold it right there, lady!" the deputy commanded the bag lady. She dismissed him with a wave, and pulled a rag from her clothes and put it on Meredith's knee.

"Boy, you got sliced up good," she clucked. He tried to get up. "Be still." She held the rag on his knee.

Meredith waited impatiently for the ambulance. What the hell am I going to do during the ski season? he wondered through the pain. Guess I could always go to Timberline Lodge and drink.

Josh came to visit him in the hospital.
They both had a need.

Meredith jerked awake and looked around the quiet cabin of the plane, his hand absently straying to the damaged knee as he pulled himself upright. The lighting was muted as he made his way to the restroom, limping, the hum from the engines the only sound accompanying his walk. The plane landed in Denver in time for breakfast.

<u>SUNDAY</u>
JULY
2

Coast Range of the Cascade Mountains, Oregon
CHAPTER
15

Ellie was cold. She shivered and tried to draw her arms up around herself, but for some reason they didn't work. She was tired. So tired.

It was dark, a world of shadows.

If this is a dream, why am I so cold? Her thoughts were vague, diffused. She was half asleep. In her dream, she was lying on some fir needles and cones, under a tree whose branches spread over a large area. A transient, gusting wind brought goose bumps to her skin. The brush around the tree rustled, moved by the wind, shifting into shadowy shapes which Ellie saw for a second before they were gone, replaced by others.

The wind brought the smell to her, and took it away.

It came back with each new gust, sweet, terrible, a smell so overpowering that only when it went away did she dare to breathe, to whimper.

Dead stuff.

Yucky stuff.

She was a little girl again. She was playing in the dark, digging in the sand with her shovel, digging and singing happily to herself.

"Hey! Ho! It's off to dig we go!" Her voice was high-pitched, the voice of a six-year-old, with a singsong quality.

She was cold.

Daddy?

Her shovel hit something hard, harder than the wet sand, and the smell came floating up to her then. She tried to get away, but couldn't move. *Something has my arms . . . my arms are . . . where's Daddy?*

Make it go away.

It was still cold, and starting to rain, and she cried.

"Daddy . . . help me! Come find me!"

She lay down in the sand, and waited for her daddy.

She was laying down now, but the sand was gone, and in its place was a mountainside with trees, rocks . . . dead things.

Ellie whimpered, a sound not unlike the cries of the six-year-old in the dream.

"Take the dead stuff away, Daddy. Make it go away."

The wind brushed through the tree, bringing rain with it. Ellie snuggled against the tree and pulled her knees up. She pulled her right arm, trying to bring it to her chest. Something was on it. She couldn't see it in the dark, and didn't want to look that way. She tugged once more, and the weight fell away. She put her arm around her chest, and hugged herself.

The horrible, rotting smell struck her with such force that she gagged. Nothing would come up.

She sat up slowly, pulling her left arm free, and came suddenly and fully awake. She heaved once more, her stomach cramping with nothing left to give.

She became aware of a presence beside her, touching her on her left side. She wasn't going to look. It was dark, and she didn't have to, she thought petulantly.

She tried to push herself away, and her hand slid on something wet. Finally she looked at the horrible thing lying next to her, the shadowy thing with flesh that was beginning to slide away.

She scrambled over on her hands and knees, her shredded palms sending jolts of pain up her arms, and she pushed herself backwards out from under the branches of the fir tree, moving away from the horror.

She backed away, moving down into a ravine, scraping her knees and hands on rough gravel. She continued down, a scared, wounded animal. The rain came stronger now, windblown.

Her movements slowed, the night on the hill taking its toll where the killer had not. She backed up the other side of the ravine, and was in the middle of an asphalt road before she realized that the rocks and brush were no longer clutching her.

She moaned, wrapping her arms around her chest, and sat in the middle of the road, rocking slightly.

She looked at the fir tree.

"Hey . . . Ho . . . It's off to dig we go," she muttered.

In some places, the higher boughs of the evergreens touched thirty or forty feet above the ground, giving the small blacktopped road the appearance of a dark tunnel, with light from the dawning day filtering down through the canopy.

Ellie stared at the fir tree, peering into the dark with the cold rain on her, making sure nothing had followed her from the place where the dead stuff was.

Light came streaking toward her from down the road, fast, behind her back. She didn't realize that it was a car driving toward her until she heard the tires squeal and slide on the rain-slicked pavement. The car hurtled past, sluing onto the gravel shoulder then spun around, coming to a stop facing her, the headlights blinding her.

What if it's him?

She was too tired to care anymore. She sat rocking as the sounds of running steps on the pavement reached her.

"Holy jumped-up Christ, lady, I almost squashed you deader'n a shitbug . . ." The voice trailed off as the feet stopped beside her.

She rocked. Forwards and backwards.

"Hey . . . Ho . . . It's off to dig we go." She didn't know where she had heard the song before, but it made her feel better to sing.

She watched the fir trees.

Nothing moved.

Cassville, Oregon
CHAPTER 16

When Sheriff John Robinson was eight years old, he caught the neighbor's Labrador retriever in one of his gopher traps. He was out tending the traps on a morning much like this one—some rain and some fog—and had come upon the dog in the trap, its right front leg a mass of foamy blood. The animal looked as if it had been trying to get loose for some time, maybe all night. Although it had been almost fifty years ago, Robinson had never forgotten the pained, haunted look of betrayal in the Lab's eyes.

He saw that look again this morning, in the face of Karen Elizabeth Hartley, a girl who called herself "Ellie."

He'd followed Reggie Stewart's ambulance from the coast inland up the Coast Range of mountains to Cassville, the old logging town where the logger who'd found Ellie had taken her. It was in a little flat stretch by a bend of the Altona River, and was surrounded by forest and mountains on all other sides.

The girl was inside the Jacobsen's General Store—the only establishment still operating in the collection of old buildings—warming by the wood stove, with a blanket wrapped around her. Deb Jacobsen, wife of Jake Jacobsen and half-owner of the store, hovered over her. Ollie Parker, the logger who found her, was standing with Jake by the counter.

Stewart gave Deb .a questioning look, and got a shrug in return.

"Sheriff. Reggie." Jake nodded his greeting to both men. Robinson had known Jake for thirty years, and considered him a friend. The store owner was a retired logger, a man of about seventy now, who had stayed on in Cassville when the mill closed. He and Deb ran the store mostly for fishermen and vacationers, and for something to do. Robinson approached the counter, and Reggie bent down by Ellie and Deb.

"Maybe Reggie'd better hear this too," Jake said quietly, looking at the girl. His voice had a funny sound to it, Robinson thought, like he'd just seen something he couldn't talk about, something dark and twisted.

Reginald Stewart, Reggie to his friends and most of Adams county, moved his frame to join Robinson at the counter, his black face wrinkled with concern for Ellie. He was a good medic, well-liked and respected.

"You all right, Jake?" Robinson asked.

"I dunno, John." Stewart joined them at the counter, and they stood for a moment looking at the woman. Deb was gently cleaning the younger woman's face with a washcloth.

Bad. She looks bad, Robinson thought.

Jake introduced the logger to the sheriff and Reggie. "What happened to her, Jake?" Robinson asked. "She looks bad, real bad."

Jake nodded at Ollie Parker, the logger. "He'd better do the tellin', Sheriff."

"It was down there on this side of the tunnel, Sheriff," Parker said. "I was on my way to get my loader, had some logs to get out today, and had just poured some coffee from the thermos, and then I saw her, right smack in the middle of the road. My old pickup slue into the ditch, and I burned my britches with coffee.

"Almost hit her," the logger said.

"What was she doing?"

"Just sittin' there, Sheriff, the damnedest thing you ever saw. She was just sittin' there. Damned near hit her. Her clothes was all tore, and she looked like someone had thumped on her face some.

"I said to myself—." Parker looked around to see that he had their attention. "I said that it was prolly some little pecker who wouldn't take no for an answer, brought her up here and had his way with her. Then I saw how cold and bad off she was, and brought her right here. Only thing was . . . she says she's from Phoenix, Arizona, and that somebody kidnapped her."

Reggie glanced at the sheriff, and walked back over to Ellie. She was rocking slightly, her lips moving. Deb stood behind her, holding the blanket closed.

Reggie squatted down in front of Ellie, between her and the stove, and placed his face directly in front of hers.

"Hey, little momma," he said softly. "You're gonna be all right. Reggie's gonna take you to a hospital and get you checked over, and Deb here, this pretty lady standin' behind you, is gonna go with us." He looked up at Deb and got her nod of agreement. "What's your name?" he asked, standing up, his legs beginning to cramp.

"Ellie Hartley," she said in a monotone, her voice barely audible.
"Where do you live?"
"Phoenix."
"What happened?" the big medic asked quietly as the sheriff watched. Robinson knew how people responded to this gentle giant, and he was content to let Stewart question the woman, to get the initial information so they could figure out just what the hell they had fallen into.

Ellie rocked slightly, and shook her head from side to side. She started to cry, and Deb put her arms around her and rocked with her.

The logger and Jake and the sheriff watched from the counter. Reggie held out his hands, palms up, and stood by his patient.

"Use your phone?" Robinson asked. "Can't get a cell signal from here." Jake produced one from behind the counter. The sheriff dialed directory assistance and got the number for the Phoenix Police Department. They answered immediately and transferred his call to the detective working the case. Strange to have a detective working on a Sunday, and this early, Robinson thought, but this is the big city

"This is Sheriff John Robinson, calling from . . ."

Reggie looked at the sheriff, and saw his friend's face grow old. Robinson's shoulders sagged more with each passing minute he spent listening on the phone. He had grabbed an order pad from the counter and was writing furiously. The medic walked over to Robinson and looked over his shoulder as he wrote. The sheriff had written six names, and circled the last one—Karen Elizabeth Hartley.

Sheriff Robinson told the Phoenix detective what he knew so far, which was nothing. He listened for a minute, then began writing again. He wrote and listened for fifteen minutes.

He circled "blood sample" on his notes and then underlined it several times. *Jesus-on-a-pogo-stick . . . why here? Why me? Who is this bastard?*

In Phoenix, Dennis Patterson promised Robinson that he'd send help, and hung up. His excitement had brought him wide-awake. He'd been about to leave the office when Robinson called. He had been working on Hartley and the other missing women all day Saturday and all night. His detectives and the uniformed officers called to assist had spent most of the day at the airport trying to find some jackass who had been thrown out of the Hartley woman's shop. Turned out to be a drunk who had just arrived from L.A. for a convention.

Finally we have a break, he thought. Whether she'd escaped or been released, the lady was very lucky to be alive.

Patterson had agreed to send a nationwide APB bulletin for Robinson. As soon as he'd called it in, he immediately picked up the phone again to talk to his captain. Maybe I can go another few hours before I need to sleep, he thought.

Stewart went out for another blanket for his patient, and when he came back in, Robinson looked around the room at each person.

"Folks, we got us one hell of a problem."

Deb stayed with Ellie as Reggie cleaned her hands and began to gently bind them. Ellie stared at them, saying nothing.

Robinson signaled for the medic to join them at the counter. Stewart patted Ellie, looked up at the older woman, and walked to where Robinson was clustered with the rest of the men.

Robinson grimly told them some of the information that he'd gotten from the Phoenix detective.

"You see any other women, any bodies?" Robinson asked the logger.

"Nope, just the girl there," Parker said, nodding at Ellie. "Can you show me where you found her?"

"Sure can, Sheriff, was right down there this side of the tunnel. I can take you right to it."

Robinson called his dispatcher and began to give instructions. The goddamn fiscal year was only two days old, and already they had a hell of an overtime problem, he thought bitterly. He would exhaust the annual overtime budget in a week, but what the hell, there was nothing else to do. Trying to explain the realities and costs of professional police work to the county commissioners was like trying to get a monkey to screw a football.

He rubbed his massive stomach, rolling the acid around, and told Stewart to stay with the girl until he could personally relieve him.

Stewart nodded grimly.

Robinson knew that it would take several very stupid or deranged persons to get by his large friend.

"Might as well show me where you found her now," he told the logger, and turned to the store owner. "Jake, I want you to come with us." Robinson walked outside into the grey morning. It was not even seven o'clock yet.

He thought of the days ahead with a weary resignation, and a tiredness came over him. He was too old for this shit. More than tired, he was sad, empty. He had seen a great deal of death in his thirty years as a cop in three different jurisdictions, and it never failed to affect him.

This'un could be a real cock-dragger, he thought, as he watched the rain from the porch. The little town was quiet; the only residents stirring were inside the store he'd just left.

He watched as Stewart came out first, followed by Deb holding a blanket around the girl. Deb got into the back of the ambulance with the patient. Might not be too acceptable of a practice in the big city, but that's how we do it here, he thought.

The city. Robinson wondered why he thought of that, and then he knew. This was city problems being dumped in his county.

The ambulance drove away and he went to collect Jake and the logger.

Denver International Airport
CHAPTER
17

Meredith leaned against the bench and closed his eyes, exhausted, his face feeling as if it had been blasted with hot sand. Blue flashes of light pulsed under his eyelids like a weak strobe. He let his shoulders slump. The noisy, busy airport crowded around him.

He had picked up his duffel bag from a carousel on the lower level, and wandered back up the escalator when his knee told him it was time to sit.

He turned on his cell phone and saw that he had several messages, all from a familiar number, with a Washington area code. Gardiner. Meredith dialed and watched the crowd in front of the United ticket counter.

"Gardiner here."

"This is Meredith," he said, trying to shake the fog from his head.

"You ready to write?"

"You sure sound cheerful this morning," Meredith said.

"Why shouldn't I be? I didn't spend all night traveling around the country and the morning in an airport."

Meredith pulled a notebook from his attaché case. "I'm ready to write—go ahead."

"You, Meredith old buddy, are going to Oregon, posthaste."

"Oregon?"

"Oregon."

"Then why have I been trying to get to Phoenix all this time?"

"Beats me. They've found one of the missing Phoenix women in Oregon. Ward wants you there as soon as possible."

"When's the autopsy?" Meredith asked.

"Autopsy? Did I say body? Hell, we ain't doing an autopsy--this one's alive."

Meredith woke up completely then, fatigue replaced by the excitement of the discovery.

"How did—?"

"I don't know the particulars," Gardiner cut in. "I just know directions to the hospital where she is. A little place on the coast."

Meredith wrote down the directions, scribbling furiously, wanting to be off the phone and at the ticket counter.

He found a flight leaving in an hour for Eugene, Oregon. He boarded the plane with a thousand questions that would have to wait.

Newharbor, Oregon
CHAPTER
18

Meredith dozed on the flight from Denver to Eugene, waking just as the plane touched down under grey skies. He rented a Pontiac sedan and drove to the coast, rolling the window down the last ten miles to stay awake.

He found Sheriff Robinson at the hospital, and did his best to set him at ease. The sheriff was wary, but seemed cooperative enough. Meredith didn't want to get into a pissing match with local law enforcement and would go a long way to avoid it.

Robinson showed him to the door of the victim's room. Meredith opened the door and slipped inside, leaving the sheriff standing in the hallway. The blinds were closed most of the way, the room dim with afternoon shadows. The victim lay on her back, sleeping, her breath coming in shallow puffs; against the stark white sheets and pillows, she seemed very frail, smaller somehow than she really was. He thought at first that he had the wrong room. The woman in the bed looked like a little girl, minus her teddy bear, who had been mistakenly placed in an adult ward. She looked bad, real bad, but she was alive.

Her face was a collage of bruises and scratches; a large bruise around her right eye was turning from black to yellow, there was a nasty-looking scratch on her forehead, her nose was swollen, and her lips were cracked.

He saw that her hands were completely bandaged up to her wrists, as if she were wearing large gauze mittens; an IV tube twisted upward from her right forearm. *Sheriff didn't tell me about the hands*, Meredith thought. He had a thousand and one questions now.

Motionless, just inside the door, he watched her, thinking that the real damage would not be visible. He pulled the door open a few inches, still watching her, and turned to see Robinson a few feet away in the hallway.

"I'm going to stay here for a while," Meredith said quietly.

Robinson nodded and Meredith closed the door, leaning back against it as he looked at the sleeping woman. He heard the sheriff say something to the deputy stationed outside the room and the creak of the leather gunbelt as the large man walked down the hall.

Robinson had told him that Ellie Hartley had not been interviewed since she had arrived. Meredith surveyed the room, which looked identical to every other hospital room he had been in, but more severe somehow. Then he realized that there were no flowers or cards here . . . this woman's family and friends were in Arizona.

He knew instinctively that this could work to his advantage, since he might be able to establish a bond with the woman in the absence of family, a bond that would allow her to open up to him, to tell them what they needed to know.

Meredith reached over Ellie's pillow and pushed the nurse's call button. Ellie moaned, her forehead twisted into frown lines, and mumbled, batting her bandaged hand against the IV.

Meredith bent down to listen to her muttering, which was barely audible.

"Hey . . . Hey . . . Ho . . ." she breathed, and was quiet.

Meredith walked to the door and put his finger to his lips when the nurse slowly pushed it open. In a low voice, he explained what he wanted and she nodded, returning in a few minutes with a small white basket of white and yellow mums. Flowers left by a discharged patient, she explained. Meredith removed the card and put it in his jacket pocket, then carefully placed the basket on the night stand.

Ellie stirred, and began blinking. Meredith kept this memory of her for years afterward—the pale, scratched and battered face that looked so painful, her nose and lips cracked and swollen, her blond hair clinging to her head, wet with sweat.

And with all of it he could see her beauty.

He leaned over and pushed the call button again for the nurse, and remained by Ellie's bed. He didn't want to scare her, and someone in an official hospital uniform would help assure her of his identity.

CHAPTER
19

Ellie let the sheets swaddle her as she floated on a mild sedative; she had known for some time that she was in a hospital bed with her head propped up slightly, higher up from the floor than she would have been in her double bed. She let herself drift, not wanting to come out of this comfort, this feeling of security. The faint hum of machinery and hospital efficiency, the quiet swish of a nurse's shoes on tile, the library whispers of visitors and patients, all served to give her a feeling of snugness.

She was vaguely aware of doctors and nurses coming and going in her room during the day, of being cared for. Her early morning admittance to the hospital and the initial examination by the doctor on duty was a distant memory. The doctor, a tall, gangly man of about thirty-five, who wore cowboy boots and jeans under his white coat, was kind and patient. He gave her a sedative while he was bandaging her hands, and she drifted away. An. IV bag hung on a stand by her head, the line winding its way down to her right arm. Sometime during the morning, a nurse had attached a new bag and left the room, leaving the bag swinging gently, throwing a fluttering shadow on her shoulder, a shadow that grew into darkness.

She came awake back in the van again, with the shadow of a grisly bird floating down to land on her shoulder, throwing a shadow even darker than the blackness of the van with its slick, foul, plastic abattoir.

Ellie shuddered and cried out.

The dead thing crawled and crabbed toward her. She whimpered and threw her hands up, struggling against the bandages, her eyes shut tight against the horror. She pushed against the arms that suddenly gripped her, held her; she heard someone yelling. . . .

"Doctor!"

The arms held her tighter and she pushed, her hands flapping with bandage trails and the IV line.

"Hey! Ho! . . . off to dig . . ." Ellie yelled through her cracked lips in a little girl's singsong voice.

"Doctor!" The arms above her yelled, and then said, quietly, "Hush, hon, I'm a nurse. It's okay. It's okay."

The arms rocked her and then whispered, "You're safe."

Ellie muttered in a little girl's voice and drifted, slowly letting the white sheets and the arms rocking her take her from the dark place, back into the hospital room.

Ellie had been hospitalized two times in her life—the first time as a six-year-old with tonsillitis, the most recent four years ago with the birth of her daughter. The last hospitalization had been a happy time, and even without a husband and father to help in the delivery, it was special. She had made her choice, and for the most part, she was comfortable with it. Her mom and dad had been there when she went into St. Luke's in Phoenix for Stacey's arrival. They had celebrated with champagne in her room, looking with wonder at the red, crying bundle at her breast.

She drifted, content to come awake slowly, to become familiar with her surroundings before she opened her eyes, She was in a hospital, that much she was sure of. This stay in the hospital was a stark contrast to that happy occasion that was her last one. Had she been in an accident? Ellie opened her eyes.

A petite young nurse with short dark hair was standing to Ellie's right, in front of someone sitting in a chair. The room was a private one, with a tray stand on wheels and the chair the only furniture.

The nurse came closer and bent over her. The tag on her starched uniform said "Judith Morely R.N."

"How are we feeling now?" Morely asked, with a smile that Ellie thought professional yet warm.

"I—I'm . . ." She tried to answer and it came out as a croak. Her mouth was dry and her lips hurt vaguely through the fuzz of the medication. She raised her right hand up to her mouth, bringing the IV line with it. She stopped her hand halfway up, confused by the bandages. Why were her hands wrapped? She had no memory of her frantic struggle to escape, her digging at the rocks with her bare hands.

She brought her left hand up from her lap and let it drop, struggling to sit up, pulling on the IV line as she flailed her hands.

"Easy, take it easy. Here, let me help," the nurse said, and put a firm but gentle hand on Ellie's shoulder, holding her down.

"I'll clip the control light here on the side of your pillow," Morely said, and punched the button to raise the head of the bed up to a half-sitting position. The nurse checked her patient, automatically looking for signs of a worsening condition. Morely had arrived for work after

Ellie was admitted, and the doctor hadn't said much about Ellie's injuries, but Morely knew that her patient had been through a terrible ordeal, a kidnapping, and she had listened to her patient's mutterings as she slept. It was a good thing that this one did not have serious physical injuries; even though they called themselves a hospital, they were little more than a clinic. With a dozen beds and a small emergency room staffed by local doctors, they were not equipped to handle serious trauma.

Ellie lifted her head and looked at the man in the chair behind the nurse. He gave Ellie a faint smile and sat there watching as Judy Morely brought a glass with a straw up to Ellie's lips, and Ellie took a few sips, the cool ice water taking away the dryness and clearing her head a little. She instinctively brought her hand up to grasp the glass, and found that she couldn't hold it. Frustrated, she dropped her hands down and let the nurse take the glass away. She was so tired. She closed her eyes.

"Nurse." It came out as a whisper.

Morely bent down close to Ellie's face. "Call me Judy," she said with calm assurance.

"Judy," Ellie said, opening her eyes and searching the young nurse's face. *She must be all of twenty-three*, Ellie thought.

"Judy . . . where am I?"

"You're in Newharbor . . . Newharbor, Oregon."

"But how did I . . . how did . . . I get here?"

Morely straightened and nodded at Meredith. "I'll let him explain that." She turned back to Ellie. "If you need anything at all, push this button." She lifted the control and laid it gently in Ellie's bandaged hand. "And I will be right here." Morely walked to the door, then paused.

"Oh, I forgot, this is Mr. Meredith," Morely said, nodding in his direction. She opened the door and stood to the side as Sheriff Robinson's massive bulk filled the doorway. The door closed and Ellie was left with the two lawmen. Judy Morely stuck her head back in, reluctant to leave.

"If you get tired and can't answer any more questions, call me. I'll kick them out—you're still my patient," she said, with an authority that challenged anyone to defy her. Ellie gave her a wan smile, and the door closed again.

Ellie nodded to Sheriff Robinson, remembering the big man in the tan uniform from the early morning meeting at the small store in the logging town. Robinson told her that Meredith was "from the federal government." She glanced at him, and turned her attention back to the sheriff, who remained standing by the door, as if he were uncertain about how to proceed.

"Is your name Karen Hartley?" Meredith asked softly, leaning forward in his chair. The question sounded foolish.

Ellie nodded. She looked at Meredith.

"We know some of what happened to you," he said gently. "We know that you are very tired and a long way from home, and I won't bother you with a lot of questions now. We'll try to make this as easy as possible."

She heard his voice—a nice voice, she thought—and listened to the voice and not the words, letting its quiet, almost hypnotic quality take her back to her job at the airport.

Ellie smiled, remembering . . .

Meredith, encouraged by the smile, continued.

"Do you remember who—?"

She remembered her job at her shop, her car. She thought of the white Camaro and frowned, the lines on her forehead bringing Meredith's questions to a halt. There was something . . . something about her trip home, a trip that seemed like a dream, like something that she had watched in a movie, something that happened to someone else a long time ago. She had been on her way home to swim with Stacey.

Stacey!

Fear for her daughter suddenly hit her, an all- encompassing, gut-wrenching fear, and she cried out her daughter's name.

"Staaaaceeee!"

Both men, now silent, looked on. Meredith shifted uncomfortably in his chair, wanting to help but unable to.

My baby, is my baby all right? Ellie thought madly, and the tears came, tears she might have held back had she been alone.

She sobbed and jabbed angrily at the call button with her bandaged hand, her mitten-like bandages making it awkward. She threw the control down on the bedspread and made a frustrated stab at it. She was still sobbing, sitting up and clutching the control when Judy Morely came rushing into the room. The petite nurse, taking brisk sliding steps, rushed by the startled Robinson, moving the large sheriff out of her way. Morely looked accusingly at Robinson, and then at Meredith as she checked her patient.

"I'm afraid that you gentlemen will have to leave for a little while. She needs to rest," Morely said without looking at the cops, putting her arms around Ellie as the sobbing continued.

"No!" Ellie said, her voice suddenly strong. She looked up, tears running down her discolored face. "Phone . . . I need . . . I need . . . to call my daughter."

"Your daughter's fine," Meredith said quietly, leaning forward in his chair.

"What the hell do you know about it?" Ellie screamed at him, splitting her cracked lips even more, the scream vibrating through her swollen nose. Meredith glanced quickly at the sheriff, who was motioning for them to leave.

Ellie's anger and the drugs and the sudden rush of blood to her head brought the water she had consumed up from her otherwise empty stomach. She choked back the nausea, and yelled, "And where the hell were you when someone . . . some bastard was trying to . . . to kill me?

"Where were you?" she screamed at them and threw her hands up to her face, sobbing into the bandages.

Morely glared at the two men and jerked her head toward the door, dismissing them summarily.

"I want my baby," Ellie sobbed, "my baby."

Morely gently drew her back down on the bed.

Enes Smith

The Mountain
CHAPTER
20

The rain had stopped, Meredith saw, but the grey pall of overcast suggested that this was going to be a short interlude.

He started the rental car and followed Robinson into the middle of Newharbor. He caught an occasional glimpse of the Pacific Ocean on his right through the afternoon mist. In the small coastal town of about forty-five hundred residents, the highway became Main Street, with the commercial part of the town strung out along the highway and beach. The residential areas were, for the most part, a part of town that the tourists never saw, a town built on the hillside that surrounded the bay.

Robinson passed the courthouse and turned off the highway, with Meredith following. Once away from 101, the land rose steeply on the north, east, and south sides of the harbor. They went up a steep wooded hillside into a residential area that overlooked the harbor, and Robinson pulled into the driveway of a two-story house whose weathered shingles gave it a cozy look. Meredith parked on the curb, got his bag from the back seat, and joined the sheriff on the front walk.

The low cloud cover and the mist prevented Meredith from seeing the beach and coastline. On clear days the view from here must be breathtaking, he thought. The shingled roofs of the houses below them poked up through the mist like so many steps to a giant stairway. Meredith noticed how quiet it was up here in the trees.

Robinson pulled a key ring from his pocket and opened the front door, leaving Meredith on the sidewalk. Meredith had a sense then of just how bad the killings were for Sheriff Robinson and those in Adams County who knew about the killings. Their tranquility had been disturbed. It was one thing to encounter this sort of madness in a large city, but in a town like Newharbor, a town isolated by its small size and geographical position, it was a drastic change from their usual way of life.

When the people of Adams County found out about what had been happening here, they would never feel safe again.

Robinson was opening drapes when Meredith came into the small living room. The house was comfortably furnished with a mix of modern and antique furniture. With the drapes open, Meredith saw that

94

the large window faced the ocean. There was an old oak desk in front of the window, a. desk littered with reports, books, a typewriter, jackets—a bachelor's desk.

"Just go on upstairs and put your bag in the bedroom," the sheriff told Meredith. "I know that you'll tell me that you have a gov'ment credit card for a motel, but you can stay up there." Robinson moved through a doorway out of sight toward the back of the house, still talking. "We ain't gonna have much time for sleeping in the next couple of days anyway," he said, louder, so Meredith could hear.

Meredith went upstairs and found a neat attic bedroom, with a single bed, and a window looking out over the harbor and the highway. The bedspread and curtains were made from the same material, a yellow and white cotton. It was a room that still showed the influence of Robinson's wife. Meredith changed out of his suit into jeans, a work shirt, and heavy leather boots. He got a light jacket from his suitcase, and joined the sheriff downstairs.

"You hungry?" Robinson asked.

"Yeah." Meredith, who hadn't thought about eating since his plane ride from Denver to Eugene, realized now that he probably needed food more than Di-gel.

"So am I," Robinson said. "I don't cook much—never did—and since my wife died a few years back, I let someone else do it."

They drove downtown in Robinson's car, stopped at the courthouse for some raincoats, then walked to a restaurant. Over lunch, Meredith told the sheriff about himself, and learned that Robinson had almost thirty years on the job—first as an officer for the Seattle Police Department, then as a deputy for Adams County, and then as Sheriff.

They left town in the sheriff's Blazer at three thirty in the afternoon, following the highway up the Altona River canyon. Except for an occasional log truck, traffic was light, and the sheriff was able to drive fast; he kept his concentration on the road and was quiet. About ten miles out of town, Meredith spoke up. "How far are we from the area where Ellie Hartley was found?" he asked.

"Cassville is about thirty-five miles from Newharbor, almost twenty miles directly east, as the crow flies, in the Coast Range of the Cascade Mountains. There's thick woods for the entire distance. Hell, last time I stayed up there I heard a cougar. The country is rugged and desolate, yet fairly close to some of the larger coastal towns. The girl was found about five miles this side of Cassville, on the road."

Robinson glanced at Meredith, and turned his attention back to the road. "I went up there after we took the girl back in the ambulance, and saw the remains." He paused, the lines on his face deeping.

"There were—." Robinson stopped and looked straight ahead, clearing his throat. "There is a skull there and at least one more body. And . . . I looked just long enough to decide that there wasn't anyone left alive, and posted a deputy up there to secure the crime scene. There should be plenty of people up there now, what with the state lab folks and our ambulance and other couple of deputies, and if any of them has told the press, my God, they'll wish to Christ they hadn't. I want as much time as I can get to find a handle on this thing before I have to deal with them."

Robinson stopped talking and they rode in silence. Meredith looked at the sheriff. He's scared, Meredith thought. The sheriff's scared shitless and he knows that he has to be the man in charge. He's at an age when life begins to blur, to soften around the edges, and what were once goals become distant dreams, an aching memory of what could have been. He's scared for the girl in the bed at the hospital, scared for the folks in his county, scared for himself . . . and so very scared of this unknown bastard who's killing people in horrible ways.

So am I, Sheriff, Meredith thought. *Baby . . . so am I.*

Had he known then just how bad it was going to get, he might have just chucked the whole thing and gone back up to Portland and hugged his son and planted a flower garden. Something with some color—maybe some zinnias, snapdragons, and dahlias. He could live on his medical pension and take some odd jobs to get them by . . . take Josh fishing on weekends.

He wished he could tell the sheriff; Look, take off and let someone younger do it. Grab your woman there, the one who works with you, take her to a cabin down the coast and walk on the beach in the morning and drink a few cans of Coors in the afternoon. Get the hell out.

I wish we both would, Meredith thought. I know we won't—can't, but, my man, I wish we could. Damn.

"Let's turn this thing around," he muttered.

Robinson had slowed the Blazer on the narrow, twisting highway. He was looking ahead, seemingly lost in thought, his mouth grim.

He blinked and looked at Meredith, and then turned back to the road.

"I'm sorry," he said, "I didn't hear. What was that you said?"

"Just muttering to myself."

Robinson pointed ahead. "There's the tunnel. The girl was found on the far side. Our people should be over there." He slowed as they approached the entrance to the tunnel, a crescent-shaped concrete slab that appeared to be holding the mountain up. There was a sign, Meredith saw, that said *TURN ON HEADLIGHTS*, and another, *BICYCLES IN TUNNEL WHEN LIGHTS FLASH*, on a pole with a mounted switch for cyclists to activate. And then they were in the tunnel. It wasn't a straight-ahead tunnel; it curved in the middle, a sweeping curve to the right and downhill. Some of the ceiling was smooth cement, but most of it was carved out of basalt rock. Water dripped from the rock onto the tunnel floor; in a couple of places, it was coming down from the roof in sheets. The Blazer punched through like a boat going under a falls.

Robinson slowed even more, and they were out of the tunnel. Brush grew on the sides of the road where the fir trees had once been clear cut for passage. For thirty feet on each side of the roadway, vine maple, wild rhododendron, and seedling firs grew up to twenty feet, the ground underneath littered with Boston and bracken ferns. Past the brushy area, the hillside rose up on their right, a hillside covered with tall fir trees, the boughs touching in a thick, unbroken chain up to a hundred feet or more. There was a break in the trees on the left side, where the north fork of the Altona River, indifferent to the event, made its way noisily past the group on the road.

Meredith saw several cars parked on both sides of the road, including three white cars with the Oregon State Police logo on the doors. There were a couple of brown-and-white units from the Adams County Sheriff's Department, a fire truck with a large aerial snorkel, several unmarked cars of obvious government issue, and a long, Class A motor home. A group of men were standing in the road beside the motor home, which was, Meredith guessed, a mobile crime lab from the Oregon State Police Lab in Eugene. The road was blocked further down, he saw, with a white Oregon State Police unit parked sideways. Yellow crime-scene tape stretched from each bumper into the brush. Robinson had indeed been busy.

Behind the mobile crime lab was a news van with a Portland TV station's call letters painted on the side. A cameraman, standing on a rack atop the van, appeared to be filming the Blazer's approach.

"Shit," Robinson said, and slapped the steering wheel with his hand. "I was hoping that we would have more time without having to deal with the media—at least until tomorrow."

Meredith glanced at the sheriff as he parked behind the news van and shut off the engine. The wipers stopped and rain began to cloud their view, shielding them from the camera and the others on the road.

"I've been a cop for thirty years, and I don't want to see again what I saw early this morning. And—." Robinson half turned and pulled two raincoats from the rear seat. He handed one to Meredith, peering intently at the younger man. He continued in a quiet voice that struck Meredith as somehow incongruous with his physical stature, "and I suppose I don't handle these things as well as I should. Hell, I've never seen anything like this before. If you see something that should be done, something that I've forgotten or overlooked or don't know about, please tell me. You won't be stepping on any toes."

"I'll do whatever I can," Meredith agreed. "The first thing we need to do is put someone in charge of this crime scene, and that someone can't be either one of us."

They got out and walked toward the group by the mobile lab, the sheriff lumbering in an oversized yellow slicker, the smaller man limping beside him. The grayness of the day mirrored their thoughts.

Eugene

CHAPTER 21

Sixty miles southeast of the crime-scene search, Thomas Brunson pulled his van into the parking lot of a small shopping center on the west end of the city of Eugene. The rain had followed him from the coast, making the shoppers hurry from their cars like so many barnyard chickens, running for the shelter of the mall.

No one paid any attention to the van.

His driving from the coast had been purposeful, determined. He'd slept for six hours in the van and awakened refreshed.

Brunson left the van, after making sure that it was locked, and walked to the mall, ignoring the rain. The flower shop was not far from the main entrance.

He entered quietly. He was the only customer in the shop. The clerk, a small woman with greying hair, was working on a display in the center of the store, facing away from the door.

She didn't hear anyone walk up behind her; she felt rather than heard his presence. She turned suddenly, to find him standing a few inches behind her.

"Oh!" She threw her hand up to her mouth and stepped back.

"I'd like some flowers," he said with a pleasant smile.

"I'm sorry. You startled me," the clerk said, moving back toward the counter. "Let me show you what we have."

Brunson walked behind her, watching her move toward the counter on trembling legs. He smiled, a cold, calculating smile, knowing that he could break her neck with a simple twist. He stayed close to her, sensing her fear. He knew that it would take the assembled lawmen a day or so before they could track the flowers, and maybe longer. They had enough to occupy them now, and, the more fear she felt, the less reliable her description of him would be.

The clerk stopped in front of the refrigerated display case that covered the back wall, her movements jerky, as if she were willing herself to turn around and wait on him, probably telling herself that the customer, a nice-appearing man wearing a white shirt, corduroy pants, and boots was harmless.

Yeah, there's something about me, Brunson thought. *It's becoming harder to hide.* He felt the power of what he was doing ripple through him, and he shuddered.

"We have some lovely . . . some lovely assorted arrangements for nine-ninety-five," she said, looking at the glassed-in shelves.

"I'd like some roses."

"Oh , well, we have some really nice miniature ones"— she risked a glance back at Brunson—"and white and red long-stemmed . . ."

"I'll take a dozen of the long-stemmed red ones," he said. "Can you send them to an address in Newharbor, over on the coast?"

"Well, yes, we could wire them and they will deliver this evening. Do you want them to put in a card?" She moved behind the counter, where her shaking was not quite so obvious. She crossed her arms, massaging her bare forearms, looking down. A nametag on her blouse read "Victoria Summers."

"Yes," he said. "But you'll have to write down the message for me. I can't write very well with this." He directed her glance to his right arm, which he was holding close to his body, as if injured.

"Oh," she said, "I didn't see—"

"That's okay," Brunson said, giving her his most charming smile, "this is what I want you to write."

Instead of calming the clerk, his smile seemed to alarm her even more. She began to write out the message, stopped, and then continued, her shakiness transferring itself to the pen she held in her hand. Brunson paid cash for the order, and left the shop, pleased with himself. He looked at the window display of a Barnes and Noble bookstore, and walked directly in front of two Eugene Police Officers. The one nearest him, a tall young woman with brown hair, was engaged in animated conversation with a stocky man whose sleeves bore sergeant's stripes. The woman moved around him without a glance, her web gear creaking lightly. They stopped ten feet past Brunson as he stood mirrored in the window, and the woman's voice trailed back to him.

"When I got there, this grandmother type with binoculars hanging from her neck, said to me, 'Officer, this young man, my next-door neighbor, is chasing these young girls around in his house all hours of the day, and he's *nude*! I didn't think police officers acted like that."

100

The sergeant's laughter boomed over to him, mingled with the woman's. They walked on, Brunson tracing their movement by the fading laughter.

They didn't see me.

I'm a shadow man.

He walked to his van and left the parking lot, turning on the wipers against the afternoon rain, feeling secure in his private, familiar space. He drove to Belt Line Road and took I-5 north. He had some shopping to do in Salem.

In the flower store, Victoria Summers slowly put the phone down. She reached for her sweater, the chill of the man's visit still with her. She knew that it was crazy, but he reeked of something . . . something dead? Something gone over. But that can't be, she thought. He's just a customer, and I've seen a lot of them in the past fifteen years.

But there was something about the note, which chilled her even more, although she supposed that it wasn't all that peculiar . . . some people had strange relationships. She wondered if the guy's girlfriend in the Newharbor Hospital was weird as he was.

She pulled her sweater more tightly around her, her eyes fixed on the front door, trying to push away the idea that he might come back.

CHAPTER 22

Meredith stood to the side of the mobile crime lab and looked on as the sheriff talked to the press. The rain falling lightly on his yellow raincoat worked its way down his neck. He pulled the hood up and waited, shivering with cold and thoughts of what he imagined he would see. Robinson, a savvy country sheriff, handled the press deftly. And why shouldn't he? Meredith thought. He's a politician as well as a lawman.

The questioners with their long narrow pads were standing in a group, facing Robinson. They bent over as one, shielding their notepads from the rain and observation, like a class of students working on a difficult quiz. Three camera operators were circling as they filmed, jockeying for the best angle, the woman among them adroitly fending off her male adversaries. A TV reporter wearing designer glasses and a large blue raincoat had the floor for the moment, holding a microphone in front of Robinson.

"Sheriff Robinson, can you tell us how many bodies,"—he suddenly swung his arm around in an arc and pointed to the OSP vehicle blocking the road, a gesture more theatrical than functional, aware of the cameras—"how many bodies are out there?"

The cameras panned around to frame the car with the evidence tape trailing from each bumper. The overhead red and blue strobe lights bouncing off the trees suddenly reminded Meredith of the surreal scenes from the movie *Resident Evil*. He shivered again.

"Well, we don't know for sure," Robinson answered. "I looked this morning, and there appears to be the remains of three . . . ah . . . bodies there, but until we begin the search in a systematic way, we really don't know."

"What about the girl you have in the hospital? Was she found on the road here?"

Christ, they know about her already, Meredith thought.

"Yes . . . ah . . . yes, she was," Robinson said, with a quick glance over at Meredith. "We don't know how she got here, for sure, and we don't know who might have done this."

"Do you know who she is?" a woman asked, her dark hair matted with rain.

"I believe that we do, but we will not release her name until we are sure that her family has been notified. We believe that she is one of the young women abducted from the Phoenix area in the past several months."

They all spoke at once. Robinson held up his hands, more like a benediction than asking for silence, and waited. It worked. The reporters obediently grew silent, pencils poised, antennae quivering.

"We all have a lot of work to do here today," he said. "I recognize that you have a job to do, but please bear with us as we do ours. I will attempt to keep you posted as I learn more, and I need your cooperation. This is a crime scene, and we don't know if we have it contained. Hell, we could be standing on evidence and don't know it. So please, stay behind the tape, and if you see anything that looks funny, like it doesn't belong here—and I mean anything—let us know. I will be back with you in an hour."

Hell, I'm beginning to like the old guy, Meredith thought, admiring the way Robinson had the sophisticated, jaded, urban reporters on his side in a matter of minutes. He was asking for their help, enlisting their aid. A Washington bureaucrat in charge of a large federal agency would never have been able to pull it off.

Robinson did. They trusted him. And so do I, thought Meredith.

"I will talk with you as soon as we have something," Robinson said, concluding the interview.

"Sheriff!"

"Sheriff, what about Phoenix?"

Robinson walked past the group of reporters, and entered the mobile lab, motioning for the other officers to follow. He might, by God, tell us that we're in charge, Meredith thought as he followed the sheriff, but he is very much in control here. Meredith began to understand why the voters in Adams County continued to return this man every four years and why no one would even run against him. His admiration for Robinson went up another notch. He entered, slipped up front, and sat on the engine cover, between the seats.

The motor home had seen extensive remodeling; the beds, cabinets, and stove had been replaced with work counters and drawers, computers and lab equipment, bags, ropes, saws and other tools that could be used for gathering evidence in the field, giving the inside a sterile look.

The officers crowded inside, probably a dozen in all, the motor home rocking under the shifting weight. The tile floor was slippery and muddy. Meredith recognized the state medical examiner, a first-rate forensic pathologist, and nodded to him.

Robinson yelled for quiet. He introduced himself and the others, as many as he knew—the state M.E., Dr. Vance; Lieutenant Shardz, commanding officer of the OSP Eugene crime lab and a fine investigator, as Meredith knew; his lab techs; Criminalists Ted Levy and Sarah McBain; two troopers assigned to crime scene security; deputies; the big medic, Reggie Stewart; and Jerry Snyder, Adams County District Attorney. Robinson pointed through the press of bodies to Meredith.

"Gentlemen, this is Mr. Patrick Meredith, from the Justice Department. He's a field coordinator for the Violent Crime Investigation Administration—used to work Portland Homicide, so he knows his way around a crime scene. Hopefully he can take what we find here and figure out who this bastard is."

Faces turned toward Meredith, curious, expectant. They waited for him to say something.

"You all know your jobs or you wouldn't be here," Meredith said quietly. "And, I don't know that I'm really needed. But too many times killers like these escape detection because they are extremely mobile. They kill in many police jurisdictions, and in the past we didn't have a central clearing house to compare information from one state to another. After the evidence is collected, maybe my agency can recognize something that has happened some other place."

Sarah McBain, the young criminalist working for Lieutenant Shardz spoke up, her slight figure hidden in the group.

"Anything you want us to look for specifically?"

"Your Lieutenant Shardz will be in charge of the crime scene, and this will be treated like any major crime-scene investigation. It is likely that this is a dumping site for the remains of the women abducted from Arizona. I should receive all investigative information from Arizona by tonight. You will have it as soon as I do. Keep in mind that the women were probably not killed here. Because of its proximity to the road, it is likely just a dumping site, and just because we have located two or three bodies, that doesn't mean that we have found every victim. There may be one more, or dozens more, and they may be close by or in other states."

"Why dump them all in the same place, anyway?" McBain asked.

"They may not all have been placed here at the same time," Meredith said, "but once a killer becomes familiar with an area and comfortable with it, he will tend to discard the bodies there. Again and again. That may even become part of his fantasy and desire. Keep in mind that if the bodies were not all dumped at the same time, we should find evidence of multiple trips into and out of the area that could indicate a time frame."

Meredith was sweating inside his raincoat. He stood up from his seat on the engine cover.

Lieutenant Shardz took over. "I want my group to stay in here for a few minutes while we go over assignments. The rest of you remember that we are all responsible for crime-scene integrity." He turned to a small man of about sixty standing next to the door. The man was, Meredith had learned from Robinson, Jerry Snyder, the Adams County District Attorney.

"Mr. Snyder, in your opinion, do we need a warrant for any of this property that we are about to search?"

"Nope," the D.A. said, matter-of-factly. "I haven't seen the exact area where the remains are, but if they are up there by that police car, just into the brush or woods, they are on land belonging to the U. S. Government—the Siuslaw National Forest. The killer has no property rights nor does he have a right to privacy on that land." Snyder opened the door to the motor home and stepped out, followed by the troopers and deputies who were not assigned to the preliminary survey.

Lieutenant Shardz extended his hand to Meredith. "Glad to hear that you're back in the state. We're going to begin the preliminary survey now, with aerial photos from the ladder truck, and sketches. You tell me what you want, and we'll do it."

"I'm just here as an observer, Meredith said. "I would like to go over the evidence with you as we get it, so we can decide what work your lab will do and what work the fed lab gets.

"Well, let's face it," Shardz said. "Some things we are not prepared to do. There won't be a problem there."

Sheriff Robinson spoke from the door. "Before you get started, Lieutenant, I need to know if you plan to go back to Eugene tonight. If not, I'll arrange for lodging for your men in town. Also, I can use some help with the overnight crime-scene security, since we won't begin to complete our work here today."

"We're staying, and I'll assign a couple of troopers to watch the scene when we leave."

Robinson went outside, with Meredith and the others following. They were about to find out what was in the brush.

The drizzle that had followed them from the coast was still coming down, forcing the members of the media into their cars and vans. Upon seeing Meredith and the state police lab team exit the motor home, the camera operators poked their heads out, not wanting to miss a shot.

Shardz stopped beside Meredith. "I'm going to set the aerial ladder up on the highway, as far away as I can get from the actual scene and still be lowered over it. I want you to come up with me."

The OSP car backed away and the big ladder truck moved slowly up into place, its diesel blasting out black smoke. Two firemen in turnouts got out and began to lower the hydraulic stabilizers. Meredith, Shardz, Robinson, and Stewart, the ambulance driver, waited. When the truck was ready, Shardz climbed up into the bucket, pulling his camera equipment with him, followed by Meredith.

Stewart lowered his large body into the bucket and placed his hands on the controls. In addition to running his ambulance business, Reggie Stewart was a volunteer fireman; he operated the aerial ladder because he was damn good at it. He was their pilot for the afternoon.

The aerial ladder truck, an American LeFrance Ladder Chief, could extend vertically to eighty-five feet—plenty high enough to scare the shit out of someone as unaccustomed to heights as Meredith was. He could operate at extreme heights if he had to, but just the same, he didn't like it.

Stewart stood in the bucket and gently squeezed the lever to lift the bucket away from its mooring. He faced outward from the rear of the truck, his oversize yellow raincoat dwarfing Meredith and Lieutenant Shardz. Near the ground, the boom that extended the bucket upwards was forgiving; at full extension, or eighty-five feet, a heavy hand on the controls could cause the truck to topple over, with death to the crew the probable result.

Stewart slowly moved them up off the fire truck, as the wind gusted rain into the bucket. The officers below stood in a group by the mobile lab, watching the ascent.

Sheriff Robinson stood with the group of reporters, his face turned up to the three men above him, his hand shielding his eyes. TV cameras, lenses shrouded against the rain, followed their progress.

From twenty feet they could see the jumble of cars surrounding the fire truck and motor home. To Meredith they looked like what they were . . . a collection of government cars . . . individual buyers do not drive such an ugly collection of rolling stock.

Stewart brought the bucket to a halt with a slight jerk, causing the bucket to bounce. Meredith grabbed the side railing.

"Hell of a place for a tailgate party," Stewart muttered. Meredith leaned forward, careful to keep his hands on the railing, water running off the top of his hood.

"What's that?" he asked, unable to see the medic's face.

"Uh, I said that those guys are partying down there," Stewart said, pointing to the group of reporters, "and I get to act as a chauffeur to a couple of overpaid government scouts." He laughed, shaking the bucket.

Meredith tightened his grip on the railing. Stewart turned to him and Shardz, replacing the laughter with a serious look. "Where to, gentlemen?"

Meredith pointed up. "Take it all the way up." He tried to breathe slowly, to relax, but he kept holding on as tight as possible.

The ground fell away to the sway and swing of the bucket, giving them a view of the surrounding forest. To Meredith's right, he caught a glimpse of the turbulent muddy waters of the Altona River, waters that looked to be at almost flood stage. The river was separated from the road by a screen of trees.

Straight ahead, to the rear of the truck, the tunnel entrance stood as a mute sentinel to the activity. Meredith glanced uneasily at its mouth. It seemed to him a sinister presence, a witness to unholy secrets.

To his left, the mountains rose up from the road. The land was steep; in places rock cliffs of basalt could be seen in the trees. A sudden swaying of the bucket gave him another queasy jolt. He had a sudden thought of the futility of it all. Here they were, a group of officers with their cars parked on a lonely road, trying to locate the remains of one or more unfortunate women—in an attempt to preserve some trace evidence. Evidence that might not exist, and if it did, it might not mean anything.

Stewart was bringing the bucket up to its maximum height by raising the scissor-like boom, then extending it, then raising it. Meredith kept his black thoughts to himself and gripped the lip of the swaying bucket with numb hands.

The medic stopped the bucket at eighty feet, the bucket swaying frighteningly, even with the gentle release of the lever. The truck far below bounced on its stabilizers.

Lieutenant Shardz began to take pictures of the surrounding area. Meredith followed his example, bracing his knees against the side of the bucket. Gardiner wanted pictures as soon as possible.

"Take us down to sixty feet," Meredith said.

The bucket dropped and swayed.

"There!" Shardz was pointing to the woods just off the road to their left, at the base of the mountain.

Stewart stopped the bucket. They all looked from sixty feet.

Meredith could just make out the form of a body lying in a slight depression, just visible through the boughs of a large fir tree at the base of the mountain.

Meredith and Shardz were both busy with their cameras now, taking pictures that would become evidence.

"Take us down . . . slowly," Meredith told Stewart, and the medic gave him an uneasy glance, his fun-loving personality subdued by what was below.

Meredith removed a small tape recorder from his shirt pocket and fumbled with the switches, his hands shaking He gave the date, time, place, and his name, as if he were speaking to Gardiner.

". . . adult female, nude, lying on her back in a slight depression." Stewart angled the bucket over the brush, until he was directly over the body, at a height of about twenty feet.

". . . her facial features covered with matted hair and dirt."

Stewart and Shardz listened quietly to him.

". . . and pine needles. . . ."

Shardz began to take pictures again, the shutter and auto wind a mechanical counterpoint to Meredith's soft voice.

"From a height of about . . . uh . . . twenty feet, there appears to be the remains of a second body . . . partial remains from here . . . unable to tell if male or female . . ."

A picture of Josh's mom forced its way into his mind, with a haunting vision of Josh, alone, asking accusingly, *why do you do this work?* He forced himself to become clinical, pushing emotions aside. He shook his head. The picture faded, and he was left thinking, *Josh is alone, and why the hell am I here?*

He spoke louder now, to Stewart, leaving the tape running.

"Take us down lower, into the branches if you have to, as directly over the bodies as you can."

Stewart nodded. He reached out for the controls and touched them tentatively, as if they were alive, squirming. The bucket brushed the branches, and Stewart lowered them to a height of about six feet. Yells from the road made the three of them look back, and Meredith saw that the truck was tilting dangerously, the bucket's extension to the side acting as a lopsided counterbalance. The bucket stopped, bouncing up and down above the grisly horror below.

Meredith shivered and the skin of his testicles tightened, sending painful shocks down his legs and up his torso, racing up his back and arms. The chill he felt wasn't from the weather.

"From here we can see the second victim more clearly. There is some hair left, maybe female due to the long length . . . with almost complete decomposition . . . the lower mandible is missing . . ."

Mother of God. Meredith was no longer aware of the swaying of the bucket, the rain, the cold, the group on the road. His companions, who shared this view of the horrific scene, no longer existed for him.

Lieutenant Shardz, standing shoulder to shoulder with Meredith, slowly lowered his camera.

Clinical, old boy, stay clinical. Meredith took a shuddering breath, and glanced at Stewart. The medic's dark skin was drawn tight, looked greyish, sickly.

To the left of the first body they could see a skull, old, mummified. A third victim.

Meredith had a sudden flash of raw terror for what it must have been like for Ellie Hartley to be dumped here in the dark by a killer, with the threat of a terrible death hanging over her for days . . . to be dumped here among these . . .

These reminders of her fate.

Shardz took some Polaroid shots, and nodded at Meredith.

"Take us back," Meredith said quietly.

Reggie Stewart gripped the sides of the bucket with his big hands, staring down at the bodies. He shook his head as if to clear it, the odor from below coming up strong for the first time.

"Man, I've seen bodies before," he said, hushed, his voice quavering, "but never nothing like this, not in my county, anyway. What kind of person would do something like this?" He brought his hands up, staring at his palms. "If I could get my hands on his neck, we wouldn't have any more of this shit."

Meredith thought that Reggie's big hands might just do that very thing. They certainly looked strong enough to crush the necks of pro wrestlers. Later, when Meredith thought back on the events of the summer, he realized that Reggie Stewart, the owner of the ambulance service, a gentle man dedicated to saving lives, did, in fact, get his chance to crush a neck.

But by then it was too late.

Too late to save lives.

And as it turned out, it was much too late for all of them.

Stewart gripped the controls and lifted away from the trees. Slowly, almost absentmindedly, he returned the bucket to the truck.

Meredith climbed down from the bucket, stiff-legged. He had locked his knees during the ride, and both legs were complaining. It took him a minute or so to get the blood back in them. Sheriff Robinson walked up and waited for Meredith to speak. Meredith held his hand up, signaling for Robinson to wait. He found Stewart sitting on the front bumper of the fire truck. The medic had his arms wrapped around his chest; his head was down, and the hood of the raincoat gave him the appearance of a turtle looking out from under its shell.

"You okay?" Meredith asked, putting his hand on Stewart's shoulder.

"I'm okay." He shook his head to show otherwise. "I'll help where I can, but, man, don't ask me to do that kind of shit again." He got up slowly, stretching to his full height, towering above Meredith, and gave him a slight smile.

"You're all right for a government man, Meredith." Stewart walked around the truck in the direction of his ambulance.

Meredith found Robinson in the motor home with Lieutenant Shardz. Shardz was seated at his desk, going over the Polaroids with his team. Sarah McBain had completed a preliminary sketch and had assigned numbers to the victims, number one was the first one they saw, number two the second, and number three was assigned to the skull.

Shardz was working up a narrative description of the scene. When he had his game plan complete his team would begin a detailed, systematic search of the crime scene, which would include the removal of the bodies and the collection, recording, and marking of evidence.

Shardz waved Meredith to a folding chair. "Sit down. Let's discuss this thing."

Meredith let the heat of the lab warm him. He pulled the raincoat off and stretched his game leg out.

"What's this guy telling us here?" Shardz asked.

Meredith had been thinking of little else since he saw the bodies. Although there were horrors to come that were much worse, for the next few days his mind continually went back to his first view of the bodies: the skull, the rotted flesh and body of what were once living, vibrant women.

And Ellie Hartley had been placed on the roadside with them. For Meredith the answer to the lieutenant's question was easy. He began talking, softly, not just to Shardz, but to everyone else in the motor home, and to himself.

"He's telling us that he's been at this for a long, long time. Maybe years. We've got a body there, the one we saw first, a woman who may have been killed within the last couple of days, certainly no more than ten days."

Shardz nodded.

"Then we've got number two, mostly decomposed, with skeletal remains mostly intact, who has been dead much longer, but where has the body been? It might not take long for a body to completely decompose in this warm rain, but where do you keep a body in the woods so it remains away from animals and stays intact? Our evidence may give us more questions than answers."

Meredith looked slowly around the motor home. The technicians had stopped writing and were listening intently. Shardz was looking at his Polaroids, waiting for Meredith to continue. Robinson stood by the doorway, uneasily shifting his weight from one leg to the other.

"And then we have the skull," Meredith said. "The skull that shows no evidence of any flesh, hair, or other body parts. Without the benefit of a lab, I would be guessing, but I would say that the skull has been out here for the better part of a year. Possibly longer.

"What he's telling us, gentlemen, is that he has been out here doing this for a long time, much longer than the current problem in

Phoenix. Although I have no doubt that at least one of the bodies out there is a woman missing from Arizona."

"Why put the skull there at all?" Sarah asked, "Why not just leave us guessing?"

"The bastard put the skull there to tell us just how had he is," Meredith said.

Shardz called his team together.

Meredith walked with the sheriff toward the Blazer, passing the media vans with their fogged windows. The door of a TV van opened, but the camera operator was too late. Robinson had the Blazer turned around, and they headed into the tunnel.

They made it back to Newharbor in just under an hour.

Newharbor
CHAPTER 23

Sheriff Robinson approached the driveway to his house, slowing as he passed Meredith's rental car. The car, a new Ford four-door, looked forlorn, out of place with the windblown pine needles and twigs littering its shiny exterior. The house was dark and matched their mood—neither of them had had much to say on the trip back.

They went inside, heads down against the gusting rain; it was stronger now, with another storm coming in from the Pacific. Robinson turned on all the lights on the first floor, as if he could turn back the darkness of the day.

Meredith stood in the living room, the fatigue of the travel and no sleep and the events of the day settling in. His knee was on fire, as if someone had carved on it again. Robinson opened a door off the kitchen and yelled. Excited barking and a loud whine came from the kitchen, and Meredith heard a mad clatter and slide of claws on the linoleum.

"Mac!" Robinson yelled.

A large black Labrador retriever hurtled through the open doorway of the kitchen and struck Meredith, pushing him back a step, the Lab's tail beating against the desk.

"Whoa, boy, wait a minute," Meredith said, trying to dodge the dog's tongue, holding him out by his paws like a reluctant dancer.

"Mac, get down!" Robinson yelled from the doorway. The Lab dropped away from Meredith, looking guilty, his tail still wagging staccato against every piece of furniture in reach.

"Sorry about that, but he just doesn't get much company and not much attention, I'm afraid, and . . ." Robinson shot the lab another look as the dog started for Meredith again, the look stopping Mac short.

Meredith called the dog to him, grabbed his head, and vigorously thumped his round side. The tail moved even faster, a puppy-like movement that belied the grey on the Lab's chin.

"I've never seen a Lab as big as you are. What the hell do you eat, boy? People food?"

He sat on a corner of Robinson's desk and rubbed the retriever's head. He looked out the window and could just make out the lights of the bridge.

Robinson came out of the kitchen, carrying an unopened half-gallon of Black Velvet and two glasses. He silently handed the glasses to Meredith and returned with an ice tray.

"Make us one, Meredith, and don't spare the whiskey." Robinson sat heavily in the chair by the desk, looking as tired as Meredith felt.

Meredith handed him a drink and took a swallow of his own. The Lab curled up by Robinson. The whiskey slid down Meredith's throat, warming him, carrying the fatigue away.

"Wonder how our patient at the hospital is doing?" he asked.

"Christ, I forgot to call and meant to when we hit town." Robinson set his empty glass down and reached for his desk phone.

"No need to," Meredith said, stopping the older man. "I'm going over there to check on her in a few minutes, that is if I can use your shower. The way I smell, they'll probably kick me out."

Robinson waved his glass at the hallway. "Shower's there."

Meredith went out to get his bag from the rental car, and limped back in, chilled and wet, his knee reminding him that he had been on it too long. He poured another generous shot into his glass and carried the whiskey to the bathroom.

The strangeness of the situation hit him then, as it almost always did when he was away from home. The routine, daily things that he did in a strange place, eating, taking a shower, sleeping—reminded him that he was away from home on a what? A case? A job? Something he needed to do? His ex-wife, Barbara—he actually thought of her as his "former" wife; to him the title of "ex" was harsh and somehow derogatory—used to tell him that he needed the job, that he needed the sight of blood and the thrill of the chase the way some men needed alcohol to get through the day, or the way some needed a love affair when the edges of their marriages began to blur.

When his long-ago marriage turned sour, he carried the guilt of what she said (*You need this, Patrick, this death . . . this horror . . . why can't you do something normal?*) with him on his appointed rounds, his homicide cases. It took him a long time to realize that he performed a useful, necessary function, and that he carried it out especially well.

But, sometimes he wondered, Do you "*need*" it, Patrick, old son, or is it just a job?

Maybe both.

Yeah. Maybe both job and need.

Meredith lathered and reached for the whiskey. He went over the current case in his mind, beginning with the missing women from Arizona. So many missing, and Ellie Hartley the only one found. He was certain that the bodies of the other women were out there, not far away. And the Arizona women were not the first victims of our killer. Not by half.

This guy had taken the six from Arizona as a part of a plan. He had placed the skeleton of a victim from possibly last year, or the year before, with the remains they found by the road to show them that he'd been at this for a long time.

The killer let Ellie go to up the stakes. He had been killing for so long without even coming close to being caught that he had to get the law involved.

The killer would come to know all of the investigators assigned to the case, if he didn't already. Meredith turned the water off, the bathroom was beginning to feel like a sauna, and toweled himself dry.

He thought some more about this killer. When he finally met the killers, the ones who killed a lot of women, they never did quite fit the picture he'd constructed during the investigation. They seemed smaller somehow.

What are you doing now, pal, right this minute? he wondered. And why the blood? Why did you go to the trouble of getting blood from a victim, and leave a vial of that blood at the crime scene of the next victim? Are you helping the police? Are you doing this to help us find you, or to confuse us? Meredith knew that one of the hardest tasks for an investigator was to figure out if the death of one victim was related to that of another. If victims, in this case young women, were murdered in different police jurisdictions at different times, it might be impossible to tie the deaths to one suspect.

That's my job, Meredith thought. *Only thing is, the son-of-a-bitch is doing it for me.*

He opened the door to let the steam out, and dressed in brown slacks and a white shirt. He grabbed a tan corduroy jacket from his bag, picked up his empty whiskey glass, and joined the sheriff.

Robinson was working on another glass of Black Velvet when Meredith returned to the living room. His head was nodding on his chest, the Lab sleeping at his feet. *He looks ten years older than when I first saw him this afternoon*, Meredith thought. He called to Robinson from the hallway.

"Better get some sleep, Sheriff. I have a feeling it's gonna be a long day again tomorrow."

"Huh?" Robinson jerked his head up.

"I'm going to the hospital now. It's nine o'clock. I might sleep there if it works out. As for you, get some sleep, yourself," Meredith said quietly, kindly. Robinson was a damned good man, and he liked him. Gonna need all the feelings of friendship that we can muster before we get through this thing, he thought.

Robinson grabbed his Blazer keys and tossed them to Meredith, and said, "take mine, it's got a radio."

The door closed softly and Robinson heard Meredith cross the porch. When he heard the Blazer's engine start, he said softly, "Just in case you need to call for help." He sat there for some time after the sounds of the engine faded, looking at his glass. He wasn't much of a drinking man, but a shot of Black Velvet was just the thing whenever he came home cold and wet. He'd already had much more than his usual one drink, but he didn't give a rat's ass about that now, he thought as he put ice in the eight-ounce glass and filled it with whiskey.

"Old fool," Robinson muttered to himself. "Fat old fool. You got some crazy sumbitch cuttin' people up for months, maybe even years, right under your nose. Hah!" The yell startled Mac, and the Lab raised his head and gave his master a curious look.

Robinson ignored his dog and continued his soliloquy.

"Some sheriff you are. Can't even figure out what's happening in your county. But I'll tell you what, you crazy sumbitch, get you if it takes *forever*." Robinson slammed his glass on the desk, spilling whiskey on his arm. His jowls and large belly were shaking with rage. He sat there, breathing heavily, and after a few minutes, filled his glass again.

He knocked back half of it in one toss.

He was mad.

And scared.

Salem
CHAPTER 24

While Meredith and Sheriff Robinson were arriving at the crime scene, where Meredith would review the grisly remains, Thomas Brunson was just south of Salem on Interstate 5, driving his van north against the wind and afternoon rain. His trip up the freeway to Salem had been quick and uneventful.

Thomas slowed the van when he came to the double bridges that crossed the Santiam River. He rolled across, glancing briefly at the turgid brown water below; the river was swollen way past the norm for this late in the year. He slowed down again, letting the speedometer slide down another twenty miles, and turned into the rest area on the river bank.

The lot was crowded with motor homes and camp trailers, the vacationers looking fairly pissed off at the late summer rain. He parked in front of the restrooms, between a station wagon and a Southwind U-Haul rental. Thomas rolled up the sleeves of his white western shirt as he walked around to the passenger side of his van. He unlatched the cargo door and slid it open. His inspection was perfunctory. The main cargo area had cabinets on both walls, from floor to ceiling. Thomas continued his ritual—he had stopped here in the past for just the same type of inspection. He stepped back and closed the door, unmindful of the rain, and walked to the rear doors. He opened them and looked at the small area behind the display section, an area he had constructed and covered with plastic. The floor, walls, and ceiling were coated with the plastic that made it possible for Thomas to remove evidence of his unwilling passengers in just minutes. He ran his fingers lightly over the slick surface, listening to the crackle of the plastic. He could sense the terror of Ellie Hartley and the others who had waited out the last hours of their lives in this slick cocoon of horror.

His fingers tingled.

He smiled.

Clean. As it should be.

He got back in the van.

He would be in Salem in a few minutes.

The plant nursery and garden store was one of Oregon's largest. Thomas drove through the lot, past rows of spruce and boxwood evergreen shrubs, azaleas, and rhododendrons.

He needed potting soil and steer manure for his garden. He stopped behind a line of cars; a teenage girl with a clipboard was taking orders. She came up to his window.

"What can I get for you today?" she asked.

"Some bags of steer manure and potting soil," Thomas said, looking at the steering wheel, seeing her as she would look in the back of his van, in his plastic-covered prison.

"Straight ahead, but it might be a little wait—everyone's gardening today." She walked to the truck in line behind Thomas.

The van's wipers clicked across the windshield. Thomas stared at the car in front of him. He wondered if the flowers he'd sent to the Hartley woman had arrived yet.

She would need them.

She was going to be his prize. His exhibit. His centerpiece. He knew she was the one who would attract those people who would join him. And scare the shit out of the rest of the country.

Thomas grinned.

The wipers pulled across the windshield under the low, overcast sky.

Thomas liked the rain. It cleaned things. He hated the dirty sand, the heat of Arizona.

Thomas Brunson never did know who his father was. As he grew older and bigger, he wasn't even sure that his mother had ever figured it out. It didn't matter to him. His father could have been any one of a hundred drifters, losers, drunks, and small-time crooks that floated up and down the coast highway, a human oil slick that slid from Seattle to San Diego.

His mother, Charlene Brunson, "Cherry" to her friends and customers, was married to a logger by the time she was sixteen. Her husband, Andy Brunson, was ten years her senior, and had been working in the woods since he'd turned fourteen. He worked for one of the small independent "Gyppo" outfits, and followed the company's timber-cutting contracts around the state.

Andy lived in a trailer, and it was here that he brought his bride to make their home. It was small, not really big enough to be called a mobile home. They would pull in to some old, broken-down trailer park, set down there, and Andy would go off to his new job and come back fourteen hours later.

Cherry soon found that the trailer parks were monotonously all alike, that this so-called traveling was so much bullshit. The parks were on an old state highway, one the highway department maintained pretty well in those days, but has forgotten since the interstate went in. The trailers, none of which was over eight-foot wide, were decrepit, and the inhabitants were either very old and stuck there in quiet desperation, or young, noisy, and transient.

Andy would drink beer on the way home from the job site every day. The company provided a "crummy," a large panel truck, to transport the loggers to and from the woods, and he could usually down a half-rack or so of Olympia, by the time he was dropped off at the trailer. After he got home, he would work on a quart of the cleanest whiskey his hard-earned money could buy, slap Cherry around a few times to get her tuned up, something everyone in the trailer park could hear. But what the hell, they thought, what happened in Andy's trailer was his business—and jump on her and perform what he called "just plain old humping," but what amounted to rape. He would then go immediately to sleep, ending the nightly ritual. Loggers had to go to sleep early.

When Cherry was seventeen, she'd had enough of this wonderful marriage, thank you very much, and left for the three days that it took Andy to find her. She couldn't leave the trailer for three weeks after that.

Andy failed to get off the crummy one spring day, when they were staying at a trailer park just outside of Coos Bay. A fellow-logger brought a sack to the trailer and told Cherry that a log had rolled on her husband. She was left with his boots, a knife, and an old wallet with $107 in it.

Cherry was in a period of mourning for a few seconds, and got a job the next day in the Jupiter Tavern, where she worked as a waitress and bartender, and learned to pick up an extra tip on occasion, after work. One of these "tips" became Thomas' father when Cherry was twenty-one.

Cherry moved on, working in little taverns up and down the coast. She never did quite make it to the status of "cocktail waitress," no matter how modest the title. She kept her baby, dragging him with her in the trailer to her next job.

By the time Cherry was twenty-eight, she was a bleached blonde and overweight by forty pounds. The booze, the constant greasy food, the long hours of work, all helped to erode her average-to-begin-with looks. It became harder for her to pick up that extra tip after work.

Harder, but not impossible. As Thomas grew older, he found that when it's closing time in a darkened bar, there are no old or ugly women, that when a man is down two six-packs and a shot of tequila from sober, everyone's a prom queen.

Some of the tavern owners would let Thomas sit in the kitchen while Cherry worked nights. When they didn't want him around, he would sit in the trailer and listen to the radio.

And listen to the rain.

The "dates" that his mom brought home were not always as considerate as the people Cherry worked for. She would bring her drunken dates over to the trailer after the bar closed, and take them to her little bedroom in the rear of the trailer, a bedroom that didn't have a door.

Thomas would listen from his bed on the couch in the front. One night one of her drunken dates stood swaying in the doorway, dripping from his dash for the trailer in the rain, and looked over at Thomas.

"Put him out, Cherry," the drunk said as if Thomas didn't exist, "I ain't gonna do you in fronta the kid."

Cherry turned to her son, her face puffed with booze, her speech slurred to the point of incoherence, and said, "Why doncha go out, Tommy, thass a good boy, just for a while."

He stood by the corner of the trailer and listened to another drunk slap up and down on his mom's varicose, lard-like thighs. He stared straight up at the raindrops, letting them hit his face. He put his hands in his crotch to warm them. The rain washed his face and he felt clean.

When he got to be a big boy of about seven, he would leave the trailer whenever his mom brought a date home without waiting to be asked. He didn' t like it inside then.

He would go stand outside in the rain and listen.

The rain hid you.

And it cleaned things.

When Cherry brought a local drunk home, Thomas would crawl back into his bed when the drunk staggered out. When the date was someone who was traveling through, Thomas would wait until the movement stopped, then he would enter the darkened trailer being quiet, careful, like a thief, feeling conspicuous, embarrassed.

When Thomas would stand outside too long, his mom would say, "Tommy, come in, don't stand in the rain," swaying boozily in the doorway, as if nothing had happened, as if he were a dipshit for standing in the rain. She'd pull him into her already sagging tits and smother his head in her crusty blue terry cloth robe.

"Whatcha doin' out there, you sweet little jerk? Here, let Mommy dry you off," she'd say.

When Thomas was eight, he was awakened in the darkened trailer by a burly man who smelled of stale booze, vomit, and cigarettes. The big mercury vapor light in the trailer park glittered through the window and backlit the man. He was naked, Thomas could see, and was muttering something. The man stood holding his erect cock in one hand, and yanked Thomas's blanket off the couch with the other.

Thomas curled up into a ball, trying to cover himself up, the fear hitting him all at once like a sudden plunge into an icy pond. The man was still muttering, slathering something onto his cock with his right hand, something that looked to Thomas like a stick of butter.

He whimpered, and tried to crawl off the couch past the drunk.

The man caught him, and ripped his underpants off with one swipe of his left hand. He flipped Thomas over on his stomach on the couch, and guided his cock into him.

The pain was excruciating. He twisted and screamed. Cherry, in her self-induced alcoholic coma, was no help, and Thomas couldn't get away.

After some time had passed, Thomas realized that he was alone. His eyes were shut tight, and his arms were pulled under him in fists. There was something on his leg, running down, warm . . shiny and glistening black.

He cried out.

He was bleeding.

He fumbled for his underpants and found them, torn, on the couch. With the blanket he got the bleeding stopped. He sat on the couch, too afraid to go to the kitchen for the knife that he wanted.

He didn't sleep.

In the morning Cherry wondered aloud why she came to have an extra five on her night stand when she woke up.

After that, Thomas began to wander around at night, returning to the trailer when he was sure that no one was with Cherry. He slept with a rusty butcher knife that he stole from the tavern.

During his journeys out into the dark, he would look into windows and watch families—kids, mothers, fathers—and he knew that he would never be like them, He would see kids with mothers who stayed home and fathers who worked down at the Boise-Cascade Mill, or Georgia-Pacific Corporation, or Weyerhaeuser. He would watch kids with fathers who took their sons camping and fishing and hunting and watched them play baseball.

Walking around at night, often in the rain, Thomas became adept at moving from one side of town to the other undetected by the kids in the houses, by their fathers and mothers. Most importantly, he remained undetected by the cops.

He came to know the cops in the larger coastal towns— Coos Bay, North Bend, Florence, Newport, Newharbor, Lincoln City, and Seaside. They in turn came to know him as "Cherry's kid."

He knew what they did and how they did it. He knew where they lived, where they ate, and where they drank. Thomas knew whether or not they were lazy, scared, kind, and who the assholes were. He knew which ones beat their wives, and which ones knew Cherry.

He especially knew the ones who knew his mother. They treated him the worst, with unspoken threats of what they would do to him if he ever disclosed their relationship with his mom.

Through his years of growing up on the coast and wandering the towns and nearby woods at night, Thomas Brunson knew that he could do anything during the hours of darkness, and he learned that he could do most things in the daytime, and no one would ever find out,

He learned how to become a shadow.

The car in front moved, causing Thomas to jerk his head up and look around, the dream of his mother and her dates fading as he opened his eyes. The wipers scraped on the windshield; the rain had stopped. How long had he been waiting in line? He glanced in the side mirror and saw that the girl with the clipboard was behind his van, waiting on customers. He watched as she touched her hair, smiling.

She didn't look at Thomas.

A high-school kid with football muscles helped Thomas load the bags of steer manure and potting soil into the back of the van. When they finished, Thomas closed and locked the doors. The kid was looking in the van from the side window, and Thomas suddenly thought of the glove box. (*A head—did you leave a lovely head in there?*) He walked forward to get rid of the kid. It wasn't getting caught that worried him—it was the unfinished work.

"I need one more thing," Thomas said as he approached the kid.

"Huh?" The football player looked up.

"Can you get me one of those large bags of mixed flower seeds, the six-pound one?"

"Sure." The kid pointed to the van. "You got DVDs of something in there?"

"Yeah, a few," Thomas said.

"Hey, you got any of Arnold Schwarzenegger's movies in there? Can you believe that governor dude, ripping people's heads off and shit like that?"

"No," Thomas said, smiling, up close to the kid now, thinking about the glove box and its contents. "How about the seeds?"

The kid shrugged and walked into the building, flexing his muscles as he went. He brought a bag of seeds to Thomas, and walked to the next car in line.

The printing on the plastic bag declared. that the seeds would grow marigolds, impatiens, and petunias. A profusion of color—yellow, purple, pink, red, white.

Flowers for his lovelies.

He wanted his garden to look especially nice for Ms. Hartley's next visit.

CHAPTER 25

It was 9:30 P.M. by the time Meredith made it to the hospital. He walked down the wide, bright hallway, grateful for the empty nurses' station, his limp pronounced, showing his fatigue. There was moaning coming from an open doorway to his right, a private room. He caught a glimpse of a white-clad nurse inside.

"Fraaaannk." The moaning changed to a yell as Meredith passed the room. He could hear the nurse's quiet, controlled tones behind the yell.

"Frank? Izzzatt you, Fraaaank!" The voice was cracked with age, sounded female, and was calling to an empty hallway.

A deputy was at the door to Ellie's room, sitting in a classroom chair, the kind with the desk attached, reading a paperback. He looked to be about fifty and feigned interest when Meredith showed him his ID card from the Justice Department.

Ellie Hartley was engaged in animated conversation with a nurse when he walked in, her bandaged hands moving, gesticulating. They looked at him when the door opened, Ellie's hands stopping in mid-sentence. The nurse placed a pitcher of water and glass on the hospital tray suspended across Ellie's lap. A small lamp was on in the corner, lighting up a beautiful bouquet of red, long-stemmed roses.

Were they from a relative perhaps? He reminded himself to ask the nurse about the flowers when he left the room.

"Sorry to barge in like this," Meredith said. "I can come back "

"No, hey, come in," Ellie said brightly, waving one of her bandaged hands. She had that fresh scrubbed look, her cheeks clean and shiny, her blond hair billowing as she moved. She's put it behind her, Meredith thought, buried her ordeal somewhere far away.

"Call me, Ellie, if you need anything," the nurse said and walked quickly from the room.

"Please, come and sit down here," Ellie said to Meredith, motioning to the chair that he had used earlier. "I'm sorry, but I forgot your name and all. I'm afraid I wasn't doing too well this afternoon."

"Meredith. Patrick Meredith. I go by either one. I'm afraid if I sit, I'll be asleep in a few seconds. It's been a long day, and . . . no need to apologize." He stood at the foot of the bed, struck by her beauty and impressed by the way she was taking charge of what was to be his interview.

"Can you tell me what you do, I mean, are you a detective?"

"I, uh, work for the Federal Government, the Justice Department, to be exact, and I assist with the investigation of . . . of homicides."

Ellie shifted in the bed, and struggled to reached a sitting position, the back of her hospital gown falling open. She tried to pick up the glass in front of her, but it slipped through her bandaged hands and fell back to the tray. They both watched it wobble, staring like kids as gravity pulled the glass motionless. She grabbed it again with both hands, visibly exasperated, and Meredith moved quickly to help. He filled the glass and held the straw up for her. She drank and nodded her thanks.

"They gave me a sedative earlier, and 1 think that it dehydrated me, I've been drinking water nonstop for the last couple of hours."

"You certainly look as if you feel better," Meredith said, unable to come up with anything that made more sense. Fatigue was constantly with him now, and he felt tired, foolish.

"I know that you need to talk to me about what happened," she said in a low voice, and plopped backward on the inclined bed. "That's all right with me. In fact it's probably good for me to do it."

She looked up at Meredith then, holding his eyes. "I'm a businesswoman, Mr. Meredith, and I have a daughter to raise. I won't fall apart. I talked with my Stacey today. She's being well-cared for and I will see her tomorrow."

Meredith was surprised by her strength and apparent recovery, the change from the disheveled, fearful woman he'd seen earlier in the afternoon. He admired her gutsy response to what had happened, particularly in light of what he had witnessed on the mountain. Had their roles been reversed, he didn't know if he could be so calm. He shut out the scene of the bodies, the remembered odor of death. He answered Ellie.

"I, or I should say, 'we' need to talk with you at length about what happened," he said, trying to keep the fatigue from his voice. "The sheriff here, Sheriff Robinson, will want to talk with you, and so will the FBI and more and more of us eventually."

"I realize that. I think that I can do it," she said, emotion creeping into her voice.

"I wish that I could tell you that the bogeyman didn't hide under your bed, that the world is a safe place, that horrible things don't happen to nice people," Meredith said, thinking as soon as he said it that it was a dumb thing to say.

"But I can't tell you that," he finished.

Ellie held her right hand up to Meredith, the bandage making it look like a wounded wing. He took it lightly.

"I know you can't," she said softly, "but thank you for the thought.

He held her hand, not wanting to put it down just yet, leaning awkwardly over her bed. She took her hand back and placed it in her lap, looking at the bandages.

"Do you know who kidnapped me?" Ellie asked, her voice low.

"No, but with your help, maybe we can figure it out." Meredith looked behind him and sat in the chair.

"How many women did you find up by the road where I was found? Are they all right? Did you find some bodies up there?"

He paused, thinking that the truth was ultimately better for her, even though he would rather not disclose it. Not just yet. He waited, watching her. Her mouth pulled down as she sensed the truth or possibly remembered the last part of her ordeal. At last he spoke.

"Three," he said. He didn't have to say more. Her lower lip quivered. She shook her head, her blond hair following, flowing. And he knew then that she didn't know, possibly never knew, just how pretty she was.

"From Arizona?"

He nodded.

"Are they all from Arizona, the ones who were missing before he kidnapped me?" Ellie's voice was steady.

"No, at least we don't think so. At least one is from an earlier time."

"Oh, those poor, poor women," Ellie said, carefully enunciating each word, as if she were giving them a benediction. And who better to do it? Meredith thought, his bitterness and hatred for those who could so easily destroy lives coming up in him. She started to shake, and Meredith got up, moving toward her, Ellie waved him hack.

"No. I'm—I'm all right. I'm alive, and those poor women—"

"Miss Hartley, do you want me to come back later?" Meredith asked softly.

"Ellie. Call me Ellie." She gave him a brief smile. "O.K., Ellie, do you—"

"No. I want you to stay. Ask anything you want. I just don't want to be alone right now. Okay?" She lay back and closed her eyes.

"Okay."

She talked for an hour, with her head back on the pillow, her eyes shut. She leaned forward once for more water, and Meredith held the glass again.

She started with her drive home from work, and told the story, interspersed with information about Stacey, her job, and the terror. Meredith had gotten Ellie's permission to record their talk; a pocket recorder sat on the tray in front of her. Other than making an occasional entry in a small notebook, and asking a few questions, Meredith didn't move. Ellie finished with her trip to the hospital.

There were gaps in her story, of that he was sure. She didn't remember anything from the time she reached Oregon until she was found by the logger. There must be more; there had to be.

"Can you describe your kidnapper, enough for someone to draw him?" Meredith asked.

"I think so, but it may not be very good, it's kinda fuzzy."

"Will you try?"

"Yes, when?"

"Tomorrow, the sooner the better," Meredith said.

"I'm going home tomorrow." Her voice was stronger now.

"All right, if the doctor will release you."

"He will," Ellie said, matter-of-factly. "I'm going home to see my baby, and to go to work, and to put all this madness behind me."

"Yes," Meredith said.

"So, how can you do the drawing, or whatever—"

"Easy, we'll do it in Phoenix."

"We?" She opened her eyes and sat up, waving her bandaged hands in the air for balance.

"Yeah, didn't I tell you? I'm in charge of this investigation, and I'm going with you. To Phoenix." He smiled at her.

She lay back down, tiredness showing in her face. Meredith stood up and retrieved the recorder. Ellie opened her eyes partway and blinked.

"You leaving?"

"Just for a minute. I have some phone calls to make."

127

"Comin' back?" she asked in a slightly slurred voice.

"Yeah, I'll be back. I might even be able to doze in that chair," he said, walking to the end of the bed. He left his jacket on the chair.

"Okay, hurry back," she whispered, more to herself than to Meredith. She was almost asleep.

Meredith opened the door, the bright lights of the hallway making him wince.

Ellie drifted off, feeling secure for the first time in days. There was something sincere about this Patrick Meredith, this government man, and she felt better with him in her room, even though she knew there was a deputy just outside the door.

She slept.

The bird of death didn't return.

Yet.

This time, she didn't dream.

Meredith moved as quickly as his stiff leg would allow, and found the nurse sitting at a desk at the station down the hall. She looked up from her paperback, an early Stephen King novel, 'Salem's Lot.

"How can you read that at night, alone in a hospital?" Meredith asked with a grin. She was about thirty-five, short and plump, with a cute face framed by a short, efficient haircut. She smiled, showing dimples and lines suggesting that she laughed often.

"Easy," she said, "I have a deputy down the hallway, although it looks as if the cops in the book couldn't help themselves against vampires." She put the book down and introduced herself as Sharon MacDonald. "Come around here and sit. Say, you want some coffee or something?"

"Coffee would be great." Meredith limped around the desk and found a chair.

"You ain't a patient—the coffee's through that door," Sharon said with a laugh.

The coffee, which he took black in a styrofoam cup, smelled old. He returned to the chair, and sat tiredly, sipping the coffee. His nose was right, he decided. It was bitter. He asked about the roses.

"They came in about six, delivered by a local florist."

"Card with them?" Meredith took another sip and winced.

"Yeah, said something about 'lovely.' No signature though, and yeah, I read it," she told Meredith, and watched as his eyebrows jerked up.

"Did Ellie Hartley read the card?" Meredith asked with a hard edge in his voice, the conversational tone gone. "Yeah . . . well, no, I don't know. I mean, she was sleeping so I put it under the flowers."
"Shit!"

Meredith lurched out of the chair and stopped, swaying in front of the counter like a drunk. "You have some tweezers? Get them, and a plastic baggie," he commanded. She produced the tweezers from a drawer, and found him a garbage bag. Moving swiftly despite his limp, he went back down the hall to Ellie's door. The deputy raised his eyebrows and said nothing.

He stopped just inside the room, letting the door close softly behind him, waiting for his eyes to adjust to the dim light.

The small lamp was still on, its soft light showing Ellie on her side with one arm thrown over her head. He walked quietly around the bed to the table and lifted the roses. There it was. Maybe she had seen it and put it back there to hide it. That in itself would not be too unusual. He had known rape victims who hid evidence and refused to reveal certain parts of their assault. It was too personal. Too embarrassing. Too terrible. He carefully set the vase to one side. He picked the card up with the tweezers and placed it in the bag. He looked at Ellie again, and made his way to the door.

The deputy looked up and nodded.

He walked back to the nurses' station and spread the bag out.

"You'll have to be printed, of course," he said to the nurse. "Chances are that the order for the flowers came from a wire or phone order made in another town, and the card won't have the suspect's prints on it."

He would try, anyway. He carefully pulled the top of the bag open and gripped the card with the borrowed tweezers. The nurse was looking cautiously and somewhat tentatively over his shoulder, ready to run if something bad happened. It was a look you see in biology class when the instructor is about to dissect the first worm of the year. Meredith put the tweezers down and asked for some surgical gloves. He felt absurd, an imposter, posing as a doctor and asking a nurse for medical supplies to perform delicate surgery on a greeting card. He pulled the card out and carefully opened it by the edges.

It was a small plain white card, the kind that comes free with an order of flowers. The inscription was written in cursive, the small, looped, exact writing of—a clerk? A shop owner?

The inscription itself was chilling. He knew then for a certainty that Ellie had not read it.

MY LOVELY MS. HARTLEY
I HOPE TO SEE YOU AGAIN *SOON*
TELL THEM ABOUT ME

Meredith was suddenly cold. He gave a quick glance down the hallway to the deputy. With everything that had happened so far, he had no doubt that the killer meant what he said, that he was going to come after her again. He was taunting them.

With Ellie's life.

The message said "soon."

Meredith made four phone calls in quick succession. He called the lab in Washington, D.C., and left a message on Gardiner's answering machine, realizing that it was after one in the morning on the east coast.

He called Ward, his boss and the Director of the Violent Crime Investigation Administration. Ward wasn't too happy about the call, but he never was. He listened, and gruffly granted Meredith's request. The gruffness, Meredith knew, had nothing to do with the cost.

He called the Phoenix PD and left a message for Detective Patterson, telling him to expect Ellie Hartley sometime tomorrow, and that he would call back with the flight time.

He called his mother and Josh last. "When you coming home, Dad?" The loneliness in Josh's voice gave Meredith a painful stab of guilt. He should be home with his son (*You need this Patrick? Why can't you do something normal?*) and not chasing around the country dealing with some freaky mother.

"Well, Josh, I'll see you for a little bit sometime tomorrow, but only at the airport. I have to fly to Phoenix for a couple of days, and then I—" Meredith stopped. Josh was silent, his disappointment hanging between them.

"See you tomorrow, son," Meredith said gently "Put Grandma on, okay?" He could hear Josh handing the phone to his grandmother, not telling Meredith goodbye.

Meredith's mother came on the line and he listened to her tell him about Josh and that they were doing all right.

The boy was okay, listless, lonely, she said. *Yeah, Mom, I know.* He told his mother to bring some specific items to the airport with her the next day.

"I'll bring them," she finally said, "but I won't tell the boy." The worry in her voice added to his feelings of guilt. She told him goodbye, and Meredith held the phone, staring dumbly at it until the abrasive voice of the recording came on and told him to hang up, dumbshit.

Sharon MacDonald was down the hall looking in on the woman who had been calling for Frank. She had started yelling for him again.

He got a pillow from the nurse when she came back to her desk, and took it to his chair in Ellie's room.

He fell asleep, absurdly weary, thinking that he couldn't do many more days like this.

Before he drifted off, he thought there was something about blood . . . a vial of blood, and he almost knew what it was all about.

<u>MONDAY</u>
JULY
3

Newharbor
CHAPTER 26

Ellie Hartley waited impatiently for daylight, wanting the day to get going so she could be on her way home. Newharbor Hospital was small; she heard it come awake. At five she started hearing occasional kitchen sounds—the clanging of a pot, a dropped spoon. There was an increase of activity in the hallway as well, with the cleaning staff moving beds and a shift change in progress for the nurses.

The woman across the hall and down a couple of doors had stopped yelling for Frank about 3 a.m.

There was some light in her room, enough to see that Meredith was still sleeping in the large overstuffed chair in her room. He had taken off his jacket and had located a pillow somewhere. His mouth was open, his face lined with tiredness, his legs hanging over the side of the chair.

She didn't know him, but she knew since last night that she felt better having him with her in the room. And besides, she told herself, he didn't have to stay here, did he? She was sure that he didn't. She had a small business owner's disdain for government, and was amazed at the dedication of this man.

Her door opened, and Judy Morely stuck her head in.

"Good morning," she said brightly, and stopped short when she saw Ellie's finger go to her lips, motioning for quiet, pointing at the sleeping Meredith.

"Oh," the nurse whispered, and grinned, letting herself the rest of the way into the room. She approached Ellie and took her patient's bandaged right hand with both of hers.

"How are we feeling this morning?" she asked softly.

"Fine. I'm going home. But I need some things. "

"Name it, kiddo," Morely said.

"Well, first of all," Ellie replied, "I need to go the bathroom. Then breakfast. A lot of it." She was starved. Judy helped her off the bed, and they carefully walked to the bathroom. Ellie was weak, but able to move. She winced when she saw the discolored and swollen face in the mirror, but she couldn't help smiling. She felt so damned glad to be alive, to be going home!

Judy was waiting with a bathrobe for her, a blue terrycloth one. Together, they got her into it. They hugged, and Ellie drew back and looked at the friendly nurse. They both smiled.

She felt human again, for the first time since she'd left Arizona.

Judy helped her into bed. "I'll be right back," the nurse told her. "I have something for you." She left and came back seconds later with a large paper sack, which she placed in Ellie's lap.

Ellie pulled out a pair of blue jeans, a red cotton sweater, new underwear and athletic socks, and a new pair of white Reeboks still in the box. "What is this?" She dropped the clothes on her lap, her lip quivering, ready to cry. She felt like such a baby. It was as if she were pregnant again, with her emotions close to the surface, as if she were going through the accompanying hormonal change when she'd cried at everything and for no reason at all.

"Some things for you," Judy said. "You can't very well travel back to Phoenix in a hospital gown, can you?"

"Will if I have to," Ellie said defiantly, and they both laughed. Ellie glanced over at the sleeping Meredith, not wanting him to wake up just yet. "Where did you get—?"

"The jeans and the sweater are some things I had. They might be a little big but I doubt it. We're both dinks in the size department. The shoes and bra and panties I bought for you last night on my way home from work."

"You don't know how . . . I . . . how can . . ." Ellie stopped, and finished with a quiet "thank you."

"Glad to," Judy Morely said, grinning. "Let's try'm." Once again, she helped Ellie from her bed and into the adjoining bathroom. They laughed over a sponge bath. Judy carefully washed her patient's hair, and artfully applied makeup, hiding much of the bruised face.

The clothes fit, and Ellie found that she could almost dress herself, although she'd tried to hook her bra with bandaged hands and gave up, feeling like a clumsy teenager. She walked slowly back to her bed unaided, skirting Meredith's chair. She slumped back on the bed, weak and hungry, but feeling good, and she knew that everything would be all right now. She just needed to get home.

"I gotta go. Your breakfast will be up any minute," Judy said. She looked at Meredith. "Let me see if I can get a tray for him." She gave Ellie a wink and left the room. Meredith stirred.

Ellie watched him as he stretched. He looked over at her and sat up suddenly, his curly hair matted on one side and sticking up on the other, with streaks of grey showing through. Even his neatly-trimmed moustache looked crooked. She grinned at him.

"Look that bad, huh?" he rasped.

"You look like you just woke up, I think," Ellie said tactfully, her grin telling the truth. "And besides, I think I owe you that, you've been watching me sleep. Fair's fair." She thought that he looked rumpled, but with a strong, pleasant-looking face, his disheveled hair giving him a vulnerability that she hadn't seen before. He looked a little like someone who did commercials on television, or maybe the actor Mark Harmon, but it was probably just the curly hair that made her think that. You're being silly kid, she told herself. You just want to go home.

Nurse Morely brought in breakfast trays, and Meredith watched as Ellie devoured scrambled eggs, hashbrowns, toast, coffee, and was eyeing his toast before he had a chance to really get started.

He gave Ellie most of his breakfast without too much complaint from her.

On the mountain, Lieutenant Shardz and his crew started their second day at the crime scene. They were in the mobile crime lab, waiting for the first morning light, generally bitching about the short night, the rain, and why the hell the good ol' Superintendent of the Oregon State Police didn't ever get up this early and come to these things.

Shardz sat in front of his computer console and sipped his coffee, letting the complaints run without response. They were talking, Shardz knew, to keep the thoughts of today's work away from the motor home. Today they would take from the mountain the most crucial evidence in the case.

The bodies.

"Morning, Sheriff," Meredith said. Robinson was seated at a small dinette in his kitchen, dressed in a starched and pressed khaki uniform, eating toast. His Lab, Mac, was sitting with his large head at the sheriff's elbow, watching every move, his tail thumping expectantly on the refrigerator door. Robinson grunted a reply.

"You look pretty good," Meredith said, grinning. "Amazing I'd say, judging from the level of that Black Velvet bottle on your desk out there."

"Just because you think you're an investigator, it don't mean nothing in this house," Robinson growled. "How's the girl?"

"Rarin' to go home. She'll be released this morning." Meredith told him about the flowers.

Robinson's face grew red, his jowls turning a shade of purple. He jumped up and moved so fast that it startled Meredith, who thought such speed impossible for the big man.

"Does the girl know?" He growled the question from the door.

"No. Your deputy does."

"See you at the hospital. And Meredith," he said, his tone softening somewhat, "put Mac in the garage for me, will you? He gets four cups of the dry food."

Meredith took the big dog out and fed him. He took a quick shower, shaved, grabbed his suitcase, and was ready to go in no more than fifteen minutes after the sheriff left.

He stood just inside the door of the sheriff's neat cottage, looking at the desk, the half-full bottle of BV, the home of a good man with an overweight, aging Labrador retriever. He thought of the sheriff and the way he looked when he left, his face flushed with anger, his eyes glaring.

He closed the door softly and walked to his rental car in the morning mist. The house stood empty, reproachful, it seemed to Meredith, at being left alone. Almost prescient, he thought later.

Sheriff Robinson never saw his house again.

CHAPTER 27

Robinson had insisted on driving Ellie and Meredith to the airport. As they drove up a mountainside into a thick forest, inland from the Pacific a mile or so, Meredith wondered how an airport of any size could be in the trees. He sat in the back seat of the sheriff's Chevy Blazer, with Ellie settled quietly in the front passenger seat. He had stood with Robinson and watched as the hospital staff said their goodbyes to Ellie. Nurse Judy Morely had made a big deal about helping Ellie into the Blazer, giving Meredith and Robinson a look that warned them to take care of her patient or else. Now, Meredith was about to ask the sheriff if he understood that they wanted an airport, with planes and all, when they came to a break in the trees and were suddenly on the runway.

The runway, which to Meredith looked more like a road, was paved and level, and ran parallel to the coastline, pretty much north and south, with the forest closing in on both sides. Like a mountain road, he thought, and he tried to suppress the picture of what it must be like to land a plane in the mist on that small runway.

Robinson drove toward a small office, which was flanked by some weathered hangars. There was a blue and white plane on the apron in front of the office, a twin-engine Cessna Three Ten. His boss had come through. The pilot walked out and helped with the loading. He was a small, trim man, with a fringe of grey hair, wearing aviator glasses.

He introduced himself as Glenn Williams. He looked at Ellie's bandages and helped her into the front passenger seat without comment. Meredith walked back to where the sheriff was standing by his Blazer.

"Take care of yourself."

"I will," Robinson said, extending his hand, "and you have a good flight."

"No such thing," Meredith said grimly. "Call the Phoenix P.D. if you need us for anything. Where are you going to be?"

"Area around Cassville. As soon as you leave, I'm going to drive up there and spend the next few days organizing a search for whatever else the killer left up on the mountain. Plan to stay at Jake and Deb's store. Get hold of me there or call my office, and take care of that girl."

Robinson handed Meredith three packets of photographs. "Your crime-scene photos, developed this morning."

Meredith waved, and walked to the plane, wondering why he needed to fly. He strapped himself into the back seat, and sat waiting for the flight to be over.

The pilot chatted with Ellie as he taxied to the end of the runway. "Tight-assed little airport you got here. I almost overshot the little sumbitch when I came down out of the soup." He ran the throttles all the way up and the plane vibrated. Meredith was about to ask for a car, when the pilot released the brakes and they rolled forward, quickly picking up speed.

"Why'd you plant all these trees so close to the friggin' runway, anyway?" Williams said, as the trees flashed past. *Must be nearing the end of the runway now,* Meredith thought, and then swallowed air as the pilot pulled them smoothly up, neatly clearing the trees by what seemed to Meredith an uncomfortably close margin. Williams and Ellie kept up their conversation, Ellie excited and pointing first to the trees, and then to the ocean on their left. The mist and clouds began to close in around them and Meredith relaxed a little.

"Looks like indoor-outdoor carpet with spikes from up here," Ellie said, pressing her face to the side window like a little girl.

"When you can see," Meredith added dryly, speaking for the first time. Ellie and the pilot laughed.

They made it to Portland International Airport in less than an hour. Ellie walked with Meredith through the airport, at home in the busy concourses and crowds, aglow with the feeling that her life would be all right when she arrived back in Phoenix, away from the madman and his killing. She would be with Stacey again, in her own home, and back at her business.

She glanced up at Meredith, glad he was accompanying her, realizing that his presence made her feel more secure.

"Dad!"

The voice came from in front of them, and Ellie saw a blur of movement through the crowd. A young boy wearing a blue Seattle Seahawks jersey and tennis shoes was racing toward Meredith, who just had time to drop his bags before the youngster leaped at him and wrapped his arms around the agent's neck.

Meredith hugged Josh as Ellie looked on, smiling at how father and son were oblivious to everything but each other. An elderly woman wearing a dark blue rain slicker waited patiently a few feet away. Her face was very wrinkled, making it difficult for Ellie to guess her age. Maybe seventy or so, she thought. A little taller than me, which makes her a gigantic five foot three or so.

Meredith reached around his son and touched the woman on the arm.

He has his son here, Ellie thought. And this is most likely his mother. Only thing missing is the wife.

A family.

Suddenly she wanted to be out of here, on her way home to her baby, her house, her friends, her business. She waited, impatient now to finish her journey, becoming annoyed at the useless trip to Portland, when they could have just as easily flown to San Francisco from Newharbor and then on to Phoenix. What right did he have to take her to Portland just so he could visit with his family. And on Government time at that? A wave of bitterness suddenly hit her, rising up to strangle her. The unfairness of it all, her kidnapping . . . her terror!

Aren't you really annoyed 'cause he's married? Nonsense. Doesn't matter to me.

But it did matter to her a little bit.

All she wanted now was to go *home*. Meredith glanced back at Ellie, and set his son down on the floor.

"Mom, Josh," he said, with one arm around his son's shoulder, "This is Ellie Hartley. I'm taking her back to her home in Phoenix."

Ellie held her hand out to Meredith' s mother, then, looking at the bandages, dropped it to her side, feeling awkward. She nodded to Mrs. Meredith.

"Hi, Josh," she said evenly, wanting desperately for this to be over, not feeling very charitable.

"Hi."

Meredith picked up his one of his bags and Josh struggled with the other, and they walked down the concourse, Meredith flanked by his family and Ellie following.

Meredith's mother gave him an attaché case. He checked his other two bags at the United counter, locked his attaché, and handed it to the clerk. "I need to check this also," he said.

I might not need the attache or what's inside—but I'm sure as hell not going into this thing without it.

They had coffee in a small concourse restaurant. Meredith's mother sat next to Ellie in a booth and said little. Ellie learned that her name was Lillian. Josh called her Grandma and Meredith called her Lil. Both Josh and Lillian looked at her bandaged hands but didn't comment or ask any questions.

When their flight was called, Ellie was the first one up, waiting while Meredith paid the bill. Josh stood beside her and looked at the bandages.

"Uh, where's your mom? She working?" Ellie asked.

"Dead," he said matter-of-factly.

"Oh." It was all she could think of to say.

Meredith got his change and they walked to the security area. Ellie went through the metal detection gates and waited on the other side while the agent said goodbye to his family.

Meredith, bending down in front of his son, with his hands on his shoulders, was listening intently to the child. Ellie saw him shake his head and then say something to Josh. They both looked at Ellie and Josh gave her a small wave.

Ellie waved back.

They boarded the plane a few minutes later.

CHAPTER 28

Ellie let the takeoff push her back into the seat. She was next to the window, with Meredith alongside her. The aisle seat was empty; the privacy suited her. She was able to relax with this man, and although she didn't know much about him, she trusted him.

She crossed her bandaged hands on her lap and leaned her forehead against the window. He wasn't married. What does that matter? she thought, and tried to tell herself it didn't. But it did.

I'm being silly. He's just doing his job. I've almost been killed by a madman and I just want the security. Why didn't he kill me? I should be dead.

She pressed her head further into the window and stared at the grayness. The tears started and she sobbed against the window, closing her eyes against the sudden sunlight as they broke above the clouds. She turned to Meredith, shaking and crying, her eyes still shut, holding her bandaged hands out to him.

"H-hold me."

Meredith unbuckled his seat belt, pushed the armrest up that divided their seats, and took her into his arms.

"Wh . . . why didn't he kill me?" she sobbed, with her arms tightly around his neck, her face pressed against his chest.

He held her, rocking ever so slightly. He didn't answer her right away, thinking that this was probably the best way for Ellie to work out her fears, to deal with the horror of what she'd seen. They held onto each other long after the crying stopped. Ellie lifted her face up from his chest, still holding onto his neck, and smiled.

"Thanks," she whispered. She made no move to take her arms from his neck. Meredith kept his arms around her waist. She pulled her face back a little more, looking at his chest.

"I got your shirt wet."

"I know."

"Sorry."

"That's okay. I brought another one."

She gave him a fierce hug and sat up and looked for something to wipe her eyes with.

What the hell am I going to do now? Meredith thought. *Better be careful pal, this is your job.* He still felt the weight of her body on his chest and the closeness of the hug. This was stupid. She would need to be close to any person who accompanied her. Ellie may like you, he told himself, but she is very vulnerable right now, and it will be hard for her to separate her emotions. He sat up straight in his chair.

"Why didn't he kill me?" Ellie asked again, quietly.

"He's telling us something. He wants to be challenged . . . he wants to be known."

Ellie hugged herself and looked out the window. She would not give in to the fear. She was going home.

They had a lunch of baked chicken breast and white wine. When Ellie was finished with her meal, Meredith ordered another one for her. Her appetite had returned with a vengeance.

She belched and laughed. "I'm going to gain fifty pounds if I don't stop eating." She excused herself and slid past Meredith to go the restroom, and he watched as she walked down the aisle, the sun catching her blond hair as it brushed her shoulders. His stomach was suddenly queasy as she went out of sight around the forward bulkhead. The killer's threats frightened him, and he had to admit, job or not, he cared for her. When she came back, they talked.

She asked him about Josh, his family.

He told her about Josh's mother and his newness as a father.

His voice changes as he talks about his son, Ellie thought. *God, I need my Stacey.* She placed a bandaged hand on Meredith's arm.

"Thank you for the roses."

"Roses?" he asked, stalling for time.

"The dozen red ones in my room. I thought you sent them—"

Meredith shook his head, avoiding her eyes as she turned to face him.

"But if you didn't send them, who—?" And suddenly she knew. Shaking her head, she whispered "Oh my God," then screamed, "that son of a bitch!" The passengers around them looked, but Ellie, not caring, was crying, shaking with an anger that she had never known. She glared at Meredith. "How did you know who sent them? Did he just *walk in* and put them on my table?"

"No . . . he wired the flowers with a note."

Ellie turned angrily away and put her bandaged hands to her face. The anger kept the fear down, but it was there, boy oh boy was it there. And I've got to put a smile on for my baby, she thought.

The dead thing with black wings brushed across her face (*Hey! Ho! It's off to dig we go*) as the captain announced that they would soon be landing in Phoenix.

Even with her fear, Ellie's excitement grew as she saw the familiar landmarks of her airport. With the landing, she felt safer . . . home.

Meredith hoped they would be able to get through the airport without causing a great deal of commotion. As they left the plane and entered the concourse, Ellie began to nod and say hello to several airport workers. Of course! What an idiot I am, he thought. He should have realized that she couldn't sneak into her own airport, where she had her business and was well known.

Camera crews were waiting on the other side of the security gate, along with many of Ellie's co-workers and friends. Meredith was about to ask her if she wanted to go another way, when she screamed and ran through the crowd. He lost sight of her when she ran past the security gate, her movements jerky, her blond hair flying out behind her.

He found her on her knees, hugging a miniature likeness of herself, clutching the child with her bandaged hands. Stacey sucked her thumb and looked over her mother's shoulder at Meredith as he approached. A small woman with black hair stood nearby, crying. Must be the housekeeper, Maria, Meredith thought.

"Mr. Patrick Meredith?" The voice was at his elbow. He turned and looked at the speaker, who was pushed up against him in the press of bodies. The man was short, had receding white hair, and a belly. Cop, he thought.

"I'm Sergeant Patterson, Phoenix Police." He stuck out his hand. Meredith took it and nodded at Ellie. "Karen Hartley," Meredith said, raising his voice almost to a shout to be heard over the noise of the crowd.

He watched Ellie clutching her child, and suddenly wanted to get them out of there. Patterson nodded to a uniformed officer, and four more uniformed men appeared and effectively surrounded Ellie, cutting her off from the press. Ellie picked up Stacey, and she and Maria walked with the officers. Meredith and Patterson followed, trailed by the camera crews.

They stopped at Ellie's store, where she was greeted by her staff and Herbie.

"The small man's the former owner and family friend," Patterson explained to Meredith, as they watched from the concourse entrance to the store. Meredith looked at a display of original pottery, a beautiful set in reddish- brown with a bluebird design. "Eight hundred dollars for a dinner set!" he said in amazement.

"Yes, she does well with the shop," Patterson replied.

"My detectives tell me that Miss Hartley has a keen business sense and is becoming a fairly wealthy woman."

Meredith watched Ellie chattering excitedly with her friends and employees, thinking she looked younger than her clerk; her face flushed with excitement, her blond hair on her borrowed red sweater, her petite figure in jeans.

She saw him watching her, and walked over to the entrance, still carrying her daughter. Her tears had washed away some of her makeup, Meredith saw. She was smiling, beaming was more like it, clutching and hugging Stacey, unconcerned about her bruised, tear-stained face.

"Stacey, honey, this is Mr. Meredith," Ellie said, looking down at her daughter's face. "He's been helping Mommy."

"Hi, Stacey," Meredith said and gave her a grin. She pulled her thumb from her mouth, said hi, and immediately plopped it back in.

Meredith introduced Patterson, and they escorted Ellie, Stacey, and Maria from the store. The detective led them quickly through the Phoenix Police airport office to a secure parking area, where he had a car waiting. He gave Meredith's baggage checks to a uniformed officer with instructions to bring the bags to them later.

They left for the Hartley residence, with Patterson driving the lead car and Meredith with him in the front seat. Ellie and Maria sat in back with Stacey between them.

A second car with two officers followed. The threats to Ellie's life were being taken seriously.

Stacey had her right hand in her mother's hair as they left the airport; her left thumb was stuck securely in her mouth. She twisted a strand of Ellie's hair, pulling it down and trying to wind it around the thumb in her mouth. Her cheek was nestled in Ellie's neck.

She was humming the tune, "*Twinkle Twinkle Little Star*" very softly, over and over again

She had cried when her mommy didn't come home. She had heard Maria talking on the phone, and heard her say that a bad man had taken her mommy for a while. She didn't want her mommy to leave ever again. She was afraid. Even with her mommy here, she was afraid that maybe she might go away again.

Mommy's face and hands were hurt.

Stacey thought that she might have to cry.

She hummed again instead.

Twinkle Twinkle Little.

Ellie closed her eyes as they left the airport, content to hold her daughter. She reached over and touched Maria, the sister that she never had, and a dear friend. Her friend was, in fact, another parent to Stacey, and Ellie knew that Maria loved Stacey as much as she would a child of her own. Maria took her hand and gently held it.

The trip from the airport seemed to take just seconds. When Ellie saw her house, it seemed as if she had been away for months rather than just four days.

Meredith opened the door for her, and she got out still holding her daughter. She walked up the driveway and didn't look back. Maria was right behind her, talking excitedly.

Meredith started to follow, giving Sergeant Patterson a concerned glance.

"It's clean," Patterson said, waiting by the car. Meredith stopped. Two uniformed officers entered the driveway from the pool area.

The heat from the driveway was making him nauseous. He walked to the open front door of the house and entered the cool interior. Ellie was on the far side of the living room, holding Stacey with one arm, her other arm around Maria. Meredith held up a hand and said, "I'll see you later." Ellie nodded and leaned her head against Stacey.

He walked outside and got into the car with the homicide detective and they drove toward downtown Phoenix. Meredith liked the dry heat of the Southwest, but the lack of sleep was taking its toll. He fought to keep his eyes open in the brightness of the afternoon. Patterson woke his passenger as he pulled up in front of the Sheraton.

"We need to talk," Meredith said, struggling to get out of the car.

"Later. Get some rest. pick you up at seven in the morning. You can buy me breakfast."

Meredith forced himself to take a shower, and fell into bed. When he woke up at 4 A.M., his knee was stiff and painful, and his bladder was screaming. He had slept almost thirteen hours.

Hell of a way to start the Fourth of July.

And the terror was just beginning.

<u>TUESDAY</u>
JULY
4

Oregon
CHAPTER
29

Sheriff Robinson began his second day in Cassville by sending teams of searchers into the mountains to look for bodies. He stood on the porch of the Jacobsen's General Store, holding a mug of steaming coffee, watching a van of explorer scouts prepare to leave with one of his deputies. You could hide the city of Los Angeles up there in that brush and not find a body, he thought bitterly. in fact, so far, they had found nothing but trees, brush, and rocks.

The slow-moving warm front coming off the Pacific Ocean meant that the rain would continue for several days. This was unusual for early summer, but not unheard of. The already saturated ground could hold no more water. The runoff filled streams to capacity and beyond, and low areas began to flood.

Large sections of earth shifted, mostly where man had cut roads or too many trees.

While this warm front would bring a lot of rain for an extended time, it was not like the intrusion of warm equatorial water into the Oregon coastal waters, such as the frequent El Nino weather patterns in the Pacific Ocean. Some might argue that El Nino was back, with this being the wettest spring on the Pacific Coast since those seasons.

It would be 101 degrees in Phoenix at noon today.

The rain fell out of the nimbostratus clouds on most of the Pacific Northwest. The clouds gave a low ceiling to those areas, giving the inhabitants another grey day.

For those on the mountain, left to lie and gaze unblinking at the rain in a circle of decay, the clouds and desolation hid their silent screams.

The rain worked its way perniciously into bridges, roads, reservoirs, tunnels. The most serious damage was sustained in those places where man's grip was tenuous at best, mountain roads that clung to steep hillsides.

The mountain roads near the old logging town of Cassville looked down upon buried dreams.

Nevada

CHAPTER 30

The dawn grew over the Nevada desert, cold and striking.

Thomas Brunson sat up on his sleeping bag and slowly looked around the dim interior of his van. He had unrolled his bag on the floor behind the front seats, crowded among the boxes of video cassette tapes. He worked his legs into denim pants and laced up his hiking boots, thinking with almost a kind of joy that this trip would be the last one he would have to make to Phoenix.

He crawled to the door, opened it, and slowly looked around.

Nothing.

He was alone in the desert.

He stepped out and stood by the van, shivering in the cold morning air. He stretched, working the stiffness from his cramped muscles, and walked a few feet away to empty his bladder. The sun lit up the rocks of the low hills that surrounded him. He gave an involuntary shiver and zipped up his pants. He walked back to the van, grinning, thinking about what he would do on this trip to Phoenix. He would be in Phoenix by late afternoon, and he had plans for Karen Elizabeth "Ellie" Hartley.

Oh, yes.

She could not forget him so soon.

It would be like a date.

He had never had a normal relationship with a girl, sexual or platonic, and he knew at this time in his life, he never would. It didn't matter. He did more with his lovelies than he ever could on a date.

He would make a date with Ellie, all right. Maybe they could even bring her daughter along.

He turned the key in the ignition and waited for the engine to warm up before he drove back to the highway. Only a few hundred more miles and the van would have to be destroyed. He caressed the steering wheel with a tenderness that was as close as Brunson ever got to caring for something, or someone.

This van had been with him for the past two and a half years.

If only it could talk.

It had served his business and his desires well.

149

His business allowed him to travel constantly, without schedules. He could pick and choose his routes, his times. He kept no appointments. His business was making money, actually quite a lot of it, but it served only as a support function to his life in shadows, his lovelies.

His gardens.

Brunson was a modern-day drummer, a traveling salesman who called on small businesses, restaurants, service stations, and convenience stores, some of which were community centers for their small portion of the outback of the American West.

He'd bought the business almost ten years ago from old man Henry Johnson. Brunson soon found that Johnson had been selling a conglomeration of junk that made the business unprofitable. During the first year of operation, Brunson had streamlined the business and changed the name to "Counter Products, Inc." He'd marketed shrewdly, and sold only those items that could be placed on a countertop near a cash register, items that people would buy while they were shooting the shit with the store owner. The cardboard displays were filled with things that customers could use, those items that they frequently lost or misplaced: fingernail clippers, disposable cigarette lighters, and eye-glass cleaner.

During the last year, Brunson had begun selling pirated DVDs. His net income had quadrupled.

He'd also given rides to many lovelies during the last year.

Brunson slowly drove down through the sagebrush and sand back to the highway. When he reached Interstate 95, he turned south. The two lanes of the blacktop stretched out before him as far as he could see, surrounded by desolation and jack pine, juniper, and cactus.

He drove for twenty minutes. In the distant haze a group of buildings began to take shape. About three miles away, he thought. A combination service station and convenience store was on the left side of the road, and the motel, if you could call it that, was on the right. He pulled in at the service station and parked the van by the pumps. A faded Texaco sign swayed above the building in what was left of the morning breeze. The front of the store was a sand-blasted whitewash, with a poster announcing a revival meeting taped to the window.

Frank Jervis had been running the store for as long as anyone could remember. He was in his sixties, a small man with a face turned to leather by desert sun and wind.

"The last little bunch of doo-dahs that you sold me," Jervis told Brunson as he came in, "looked good enough to diddle." Jervis reached under the counter and brought out an empty display, one that had contained twenty air fresheners in the shape of a naked female body. The picture on the display showed a lot of skin and large, oversized breasts.

"Got any more of these?" Jervis asked. "Went so fast I didn't have time to lay one back for myself." He squinted up at Thomas. "Back kinda soon, ain'tcha?"

Brunson shrugged. He placed his latest DVD on the counter and watched the old man's eyes light up.

He had Jervis fill the van, even though he had plenty of gas to make it to Las Vegas. He walked around the vehicle, checking, while Jervis followed, keeping up a chatter.

"Say, that's a hell of a bumper that you got on your van. Hell, you hit something with that, with the bumper clean up past your headlights, why, you wouldn't even scratch it—and whoever you hit would be thinking that they should have cut their vacation short. Looks good painted black, though."

Brunson opened the sliding door on the passenger side and got some more DVDs for Jervis.

"How far south you say you're going in this thing? You don't want to get down there to Nogales," Jervis cackled, "or those Mexicans'll strip this so fast you won't have time to say 'cockroach.' "

He counted out the money for the DVDs.

"Just to Las Vegas."

Jervis packed a wad of Red Man leaf tobacco in his cheek, and spat out a brown stream on the gravel lot, watching a tractor trailer rig slow and stop across the highway by the motel. He turned back to Brunson.

"You got family there?"

"You might say that," Brunson said as he started his van, looking down on the store owner. "I've got a . . . lovely . . . woman, and . . .she has a baby daughter."

Brunson looked straight ahead, and pulled back onto the highway.

CHAPTER
31

Meredith stood on the sidewalk outside the front entrance: of the Sheraton and waited for Detective Patterson to pick him. up. He held his briefcase tightly, as if the pictures inside were visible to each passer-by, it was already warm and not yet seven a.m. Hell, he was early. He had slept for over twelve hours and had been up for three. He had dressed carefully, slowly, fighting impatience now that he was rested, putting on his knee brace, jeans, tennis shoes, and a blue polo shirt.

He left the shirt untucked to cover the .45 auto that he'd placed under his belt in the small of his back. The package that he had his mother bring to the airport contained a Sig Sauer .45 caliber automatic pistol, a weapon as unlike the original Colt .45 as a jet airplane was from a biplane. This .45 was made in Germany, and was state-of-the-art in handgun weaponry.

It was a true combat weapon—it didn't have a safety to worry about when people were trying to kill you.

The pistol felt hard, conspicuous. He had resolved to carry it. He knew from past mistakes that he was better off with the gun than without it. His knee told him that.

He had a sudden, frightening vision of the bodies on the mountain, the odd way they were placed together, the stench. He was standing once again in the swaying, swinging bucket of the aerial ladder truck, silent with Lieutenant Shardz and Stewart. He had a sudden impulse to give the gun to the hotel doorman, but he knew he wouldn't. Meredith paced to the corner and stopped. He stood on the sidewalk, trying to get his mind back in focus on what he had to do today. An old farm truck rattled by, a little girl in back with a box of sparklers. My God, he thought, it's the Fourth of July. Independence Day. Wonder what the founding fathers would think of this madness? The strangeness of what he was doing hit him, and the pain of loneliness, and the thought of his son spending another day without him. He and Josh should be fishing this morning, in some high mountain stream on the other side of Mount Hood, and returning in the evening to watch fireworks together. Father and son.

The Fourth of July. Thomas Jefferson must be weeping just a little at this sorry asshole who kills women and—

"Meredith."

He jerked his head around.

"Hey, Meredith!" Patterson was at the curb in front of the Sheraton. Meredith walked back and got in the ear with the chubby detective, the thoughts of Josh and fishing lingering.

"You certainly look better," Patterson commented as he drove. "You had breakfast?"

"Just coffee," Meredith said.

"Good. I happen to know a few places—"

The Phoenix detective was dressed in a white shirt and tie. A sport coat was folded over the seat.

"You wear that in this heat?" Meredith asked, pointing to the jacket.

"What heat?" Patterson said grinning. "Besides, it's my town, and I have certain responsibilities, not like some Fed who always works out of town. I bet you don't wear jeans and tennis shoes in D.C."

Meredith laughed. "No, I don't. But I do in Portland."

They talked about the case over breakfast. When they went back outside it was twenty degrees hotter than when they went in to eat. Sweat crawled down Meredith's back while he waited for the air conditioner in Patterson's car to kick in They reached the detective's office in minutes.

Patterson's squad room looked like most of the others that Meredith had been in—a jumble of desks, with case files and pictures and personal trivia scattered on each one.

Meredith spread the crime-scene pictures out on Patterson's desk, starting with the ones taken from the highest distance. He got an Oregon map from his briefcase and put it on the desk, too. Then he stood back, letting Patterson and his detectives gather around to look at the pictures. Meredith had an indelible picture of the mountainside where Ellie had been taken. He didn't need the photos.

Patterson finally looked up. His eyes seem older, Meredith thought.

"Rest of you guys, get back to work," Patterson told the others. Meredith joined him at his desk.

"Where's this guy live?" Patterson asked.

"Oregon," Meredith replied without hesitation. "Why?"

"Because he's shopping in Arizona, and probably other places. But he's dumping in an area that he knows quite well. And, from what we see at the crime scene, he has moved bodies. Bodies that were dumped in the area, according to Lieutenant Shardz of OSP. The preliminary reports indicate that the plant growth and bacteria and insect larvae are all indigenous to the western slope of the Coast Range of the Cascade Mountains. Some of the remains have been on the ground for a long time."

Meredith picked up a close-up of the skull.

"He's moving bodies."

He looked at the Phoenix detective.

"For our benefit," he added.

Patterson sat down heavily, looking at the pictures as if they would give him a name. Something to go on. He put the pictures back into the folders, and gave them to Meredith. "This guy, this killer," Patterson said, "is abducting women from Arizona, and God knows where else, taking them to Oregon, and God knows where else, and then he is, 'for our benefit,' as you say, giving us some clues as to what he is doing?"

Meredith nodded.

"That's bullshit," Patterson muttered.

"He's not giving us clues as much as he is communicating with us," Meredith explained. "He wants us to know that he's in charge. And he's right, he is."

They talked into the lunch hour, Patterson at times angry and visibly upset, at times calm and technical. They planned for the meeting scheduled for the next morning, the meeting in Phoenix with representatives from all involved agencies: Meredith's own agency, The Violent Crime Investigation Administration; the FBI and their forensic specialists; the Arizona Department of Public Safety; Maricopa County Sheriff's Department; the Phoenix Police Department; and the Oregon State Police.

Patterson abruptly jumped up, startling Meredith, and grabbed his coat.

"Let's go!" he yelled, and moved quickly to the door.

He moves too fast for the size of his gut, Meredith thought, and hurried after the Phoenix detective, limping slightly, even with the knee brace on. The sudden rush to his feet gave him a sharp pain in the back of his head. He caught up with Patterson in the hallway.

"What's up?"

"Don't you guys from the Northwest have any culture?" Patterson asked indignantly. He pointed to his watch.

"Lunch time," he said solemnly, as if explaining it to a child.

Over a buffet lunch of Mexican food, the two lawmen went over the evidence so far: The kidnappings, the bodies that were moved, Ellie's story, the physical evidence of the damage to her car, the blood, the kidnapping of the others in Arizona.

"Who found Ellie's car?" Meredith asked.

"One of our uniformed officers found the car and had our dispatch center check with the Hartley residence. The hell of it is, we normally wouldn't even stop at a car alongside the road if the driver was no longer there. But with the disappearances of the women, and the fact that they were all in car wrecks, and that like the others the wreck was a rear-ender—anyway, the officer stopped."

"Anyone else see it?"

"There was a person at the car when the officer arrived, a biker on a motorcycle who was just leaving the scene. The officer stopped him and he checked out okay. At least he claimed that he didn't see anyone, and he certainly didn't have the Hartley woman with him at the time. I haven't found him again to interview him."

"We got anything else to do today?" Meredith asked.

"No. We're pretty much on hold until after the meeting tomorrow."

Meredith suggested they use the afternoon to look for the biker. He paid the bill and joined Patterson outside. Looking at the detective's crisp white dress shirt, Meredith wondered how the man managed to look so put together. Meredith had already sweated through his polo shirt.

It was twelve-thirty, and just over 100 degrees. Patterson drove, and Meredith tried to breathe, waiting for the air conditioner to catch up.

"When can I see Ellie's car?"

"It's in the Police Impound Lot," Patterson said. "I can take you there any time. There really isn't much to see on the car. We photographed every print and partial, vacuumed it several times, and methodically took it apart on the chance that the killer was in it for a period of time. Most of the hairs appear to have come from the victim or her daughter, but we do have a few unidentified ones that we may be able to use for comparison when and if we ever catch the son-of-a-bitch.

"The car doesn't have much damage, just some to the left quarter panel, as if someone had possibly backed into her or rear-ended her at low speed—not the kind of thing you get excited about."

"Do we know for sure when the damage occurred?" Meredith asked.

"Everyone we talked to was asked about the damage, and no one remembers any damage to her car. The car was only a few months old," He glanced at Meredith. "You say that she doesn't have any memory of the wreck?"

"She doesn't remember," he told Patterson. "The doctor said that the memory loss is probably temporary, brought on by the trauma, and that eventually she will remember most of the events that took place. But if there were things—and I believe that there were—so gruesome, so horrible, things that either happened to her or that she witnessed . . . she may not ever remember those things. But she seems to be a competent lady, with her head square on her shoulders, and she has a good life here in Phoenix. If she doesn't fight it, we can hope that she will eventually remember everything."

"Especially the guy who abducted her," Patterson added grimly.

Meredith watched the small adobe houses drift past as they drove down Buckeye Road, houses with four or five broken, junked cars in the front yard. Adobe houses, bars, and old warehouses.

"The vehicle she was transported in to Oregon . . . did you get anything on it in Phoenix?" Meredith asked.

"The lab suggested a truck, due to the height of the damage to the Hartley car. In fact, the van or truck was probably used in all of the abductions. Everything matches so far—black paint twenty-eight to thirty-six inches from the ground—although the lab people tell me that the height and configuration are a little strange, as if the vehicle has a homemade bumper on front. And, by the way," Patterson added, "the lab also says that the spectrograph analysis of the paint transfer shows that the paint is from a kind commonly sold in a spray can. He's been repainting the bumper."

"We might be able to match some samples," Meredith suggested.

"If we ever find the van. Anyway, we have arrived." Patterson, slowing down, nodded to a flat-roofed, run-down adobe building.

A faded sign over the door said "Mary's Tavern," but Meredith doubted if anyone named Mary had been in the place for years. There were vacant lots on each side and in the rear. There was a warehouse across the street. Most of the buildings in the area were surrounded by chain-link fences topped with concertina wire. Must be the trustworthy clients of Mary's Place, Meredith figured.

Several motorcycles were heeled over on their kickstands, baking in the sun in front of the tavern. Patterson parked his unmarked Plymouth behind the row of motorcycles and left the engine running, the air conditioner still coughing out semi-cold air.

"Who we looking for?" Meredith asked.

"Oh, you'll really like this guy. He belongs to the Black Satan motorcycle gang, name of Gerald Christianson. Goes by 'Sonny.' He's got the usual biker record. Assaults, drunk driving on his scooter, menacing with a gun, and various dope charges and other minor bullshit that goes with guys who've been brain dead as long as these hairbags have."

Meredith laughed. "Everybody's gotta be somewhere. I take it you don't like them either."

"Whatever gave you that idea?"

Meredith could tell that it was going to be a fine tavern when he could smell the urinal as he got out of the car, and they were still a good thirty feet from the front door. The motorcycles, mostly black-and-chrome Harleys, were in various states of disrepair. A few were dripping oil, looking unsafe just sitting there on the oilstained cement. Where the hell was Ralph Nader when you needed him? Meredith thought. If he could take on General Motors, maybe he would have the balls to look at these pieces of shit the outlaw motorcycle gangs were riding.

Meredith saw two new Harleys among the wired-together ones. He knew that a biker with a new machine was a God to other members.

As Meredith and Patterson approached, four bikers filed out to the front of the tavern and leaned against the wall. They all wore the same uniform: a greasy T-shirt and a ragged vest with a skull and other garbage on it proclaiming their identity.

"Looks like we got a crew to greet us," Patterson commented.

Meredith, acting as if he didn't hear, went to the nearest new Harley, and kneeled down by the engine. At once, the owner hurried out of the tavern and strode over to the line of motorcycles.

"What the fuck you doin' with my bike?" he growled. He was at least two inches taller than Meredith, almost a foot taller than Patterson, and outweighed Meredith by a hundred pounds. He had a full beard, the ubiquitous beer gut, and tattoos.

"Uh, Meredith, this is Lloyd," Patterson said as an introduction, and followed it with a whispered caution. "You know that he's got to do something for all the brothers inside, don't you Meredith?"

"Yeah, Lloyd's got to be tough in front of his friends." Meredith appeared to scrutinize the transmission case of the hike, and then stood up in front of Lloyd.

"Lloyd, I'm a federal cop."

The biker's eyebrows came up a little.

"Well, no shit," Lloyd said loudly. "I knew you was some kinda cop. Nobody in their right mind would drive one of them plain turd-brown Chevys that they make you guys drive." The watchers against the wall laughed. Lloyd played to them, laughing, taking a swig of beer, spilling some on his beard, his massive gut rising.

"Time to squeeze his balls, huh?" Meredith said to Patterson.

"We call them caj*ones* here," he muttered, stepping up beside Meredith. "Sometimes we call them *huevos*," he added.

"Now, Lloyd," Meredith said. "What I'm going to do here is, I'm going to grab you by the balls and squeeze just a little bit, but I'm not going to touch you." Meredith said this quietly, keeping his eyes on Lloyd's face, and slowly put his palms out and up to keep the biker from advancing, trying not to spook the Neanderthal into rash action.

Lloyd stopped drinking his beer, and this time his bushy eyebrows went up more than a fraction of an inch.

"Lloyd, if someone took your scoot away," Meredith continued quickly, "it would be just like someone hit you in the balls, wouldn't it?"

Lloyd flipped the bottle to one of the loungers and snarled at Meredith. Patterson stiffened.

"If I'd known you were going to stir up these assholes," he muttered, "1 would have brought some more of our boys and girls with us." Meredith glanced over and saw Patterson move his hand under his jacket toward his gun.

Meredith spoke fast, trying to slow down the impending explosion from the biker.

"Lloyd—Lloyd!" Meredith moved his palms downward in what he hoped was a soothing manner. "Lloyd, look at it this way. I'm not going to take your bike."

"Damned right, you ain't," Lloyd growled.

"I need a favor, Lloyd," Meredith said in a rush, still holding his hands up. "I need to know where Sonny is, that's all. We're not asking you to give him up or anything, he's not in trouble, but we need to talk to him. However, you know as well as I do, that we can walk away and call in a whole bunch more of our friends with uniforms on, and really—" Meredith paused for effect, at least Lloyd hadn't hit him yet, "really scrutinize the numbers on your scooter here. Maybe even impound it. And maybe, just maybe, Lloyd, you have a stolen part or two on it, *not* that you would know about it, right, Lloyd? I'm sure that a good citizen like you wouldn't . . . but . . ."

"I get your drift, man," Lloyd said, somewhat subdued.

Meredith nodded. Taking a man's scooter was taking his identity, taking away his membership in the group.

"You say you aren't gonna arrest him?" Lloyd asked.

"No. No way, He may have witnessed the kidnapping of a young woman. That's all. We just need to talk." Meredith felt sweat roll off his face and vaguely saw it hit the cement as he waited for Lloyd to answer.

Lloyd jerked his head toward the door. "He's inside." He turned and walked to the front of the tavern. Meredith and Patterson followed. The Phoenix detective put his hand on Meredith's shoulder as they entered the door.

"Know what, buddy? I didn't even check us out here with the dispatcher. No one knows where we are. Good thing you didn't start a war with the reptile there."

"You only live once, Sergeant."

Meredith entered the darkened bar and stood just inside and to the right of the doorway, letting his eyes adjust to the darkness. Place not only smells like a urinal, he thought, it is a urinal. As he gradually became aware of shapes, he saw that there were only five or six other bikers in the bar; two of them were playing pool at the far end of the room.

A blonde waitress came up to them and waited. She was wearing jeans, tennis shoes, and a very skimpy laced tank top with her nipples on bright. She wore the t-top like a camisole, almost elegant, with a hint of sensuousness, like she was unaware of it. She was probably in her early twenties, but the hardness in her face said different.

Needle-user, Meredith thought, noting the yellowish skin of jaundice. Hepatitis.

"My," she said, eyeing Patterson's suit. "Help you Gentlemen?"

"Ain't no gentlemen—they's cops," Lloyd offered.

"Lloyd here is helping us," Meredith said. "I'll have two bottles of whatever Lloyd's drinking, and one for him of course."

They stayed just inside the door, and watched as Lloyd walked over to the pool table and spoke to a burly man of about thirty-five with reddish hair and beard, the muscles of a bricklayer, and the gut of a beer drinker. They looked at the cops. Sonny handed his pool cue to his partner, and walked over to the only booth in the tavern. The two beer drinkers in the booth scrambled out, and Meredith walked over and slid in across the table from Sonny.

Patterson sat down gingerly beside Meredith, looking ready to run. The bikers who had been outside, drifted in, blocking the door.

The blonde brought them three long-neck Budweisers, and Meredith took a sip. He brought the bottle down and held his hand out to Patterson. The detective gave Meredith the photo packets, and Meredith slid them across the table to Sonny.

"Go ahead, take a look."

"What is this shit?"

"Pictures, not exactly a family portrait."

Sonny stared at the envelopes, and then slid the pictures out and began to go through them.

Meredith watched as the biker's eyes narrowed and his face noticeably paled. Patterson shot a quizzical glance at Meredith, but said nothing.

Sonny's hands were trembling as he shoved the pictures back to Meredith.

"This is bullshit, man. I didn't have any—."

"Like hell, you didn't," Meredith whispered fiercely. "You found the car."

"Yeah, but man, I didn't—"

"Kill them? Maybe not, Sonny, maybe not. But you sure as hell took some material evidence in a murder case and I'm gonna step on your bails if you don't give it up." Meredith's voice was hard, unrelenting.

"Fuck you!" Sonny suddenly yelled, causing Patterson to jump. "You don't have anything on me." The biker's face was as red as his beard, and he was halfway up from his seat. Meredith could sense the others in the bar crowding closer.

Lloyd walked up to the table. "Hey, man, lighten up, we're just like Robin Hood—take from the rich and give to the poor, namely us." He grinned at Meredith.

"Robin Hood!" Meredith shouted. He leaned across the table, his face inches from Sonny's. "Robin Hood, my ass! He was a hairball, like you, Sonny, and like Lloyd here."

Patterson saw Meredith's eyes bulge like a madman's and the short detective looked around the tavern nervously.

"Robin Hood ran around with a gang of scuzzy psychopaths, like *you*, Sonny," Meredith said, and. slammed his hand on the table, causing Patterson to jump.

"Robin Hood raped and robbed and murdered good citizens, like *you*, Sonny, you douche bag!" Meredith ended up out of breath. Patterson had his gun halfway out of its holster. The room was very quiet.

"You think that we came here without backup? Do you want to bring heat down on all your friends here?" Meredith swept his arm toward the bar. He held his hands up again. "Hear me out, then you can do whatever you want. And Sonny"—Meredith leaned forward— "we had the graveyard shift stay over after work to help us here. I'm sure that you're acquainted with some of those folks."

Patterson groaned. Meredith almost had him believing this. Yeah, Sonny knew graveyard cops.

"Sonny," Meredith prompted, "I'm waiting for your answer,"

"Huh?"

"Look, Sonny, I know that you took something from the car that day." Meredith's voice softened to almost a whisper. "Why don't you save yourself a lot of trouble and tell us about it."

"Uh, yeah . . . I might've . . ."

"We want you on our side on this one, Sonny," Meredith urged. He picked up the packets of pictures on the table and held them up. "You don't like to see this kind of thing, do you?"

Sonny shook his head.

"What'd you take?"

"Okay." Sonny looked at Meredith, then at Patterson. "Okay, no arrest if I did?"

"No arrest."

"Okay, I took some stuff, but just a couple of DVDs."

"What kind of DVDs?" Meredith demanded.

"Just some tunes, man, some DVDs from the car, and another from the ground. But I didn't know that the girl was . . ."

"I don't care about that," Meredith said harshly. "Tell me about the DVD on the ground."

"It was some kind of movie."

"Let's go, Sonny."

"Where?"

"To get the DVDs."

CHAPTER
32

Ellie quietly opened the door and looked at Stacey sleeping, her arm flung over her head, her favorite blanket, no more than a rag now, twisted between her fingers. The room was dark and cool; stuffed animals and toys were crowded in the corners—a four-year-old's room. Ellie listened carefully. She could hear Stacey's faint breathing over the hum of the air conditioner.

Maria walked up softly behind Ellie, and they both stood there, watching.

Since arriving home on the previous afternoon, Ellie had been holding Stacey, touching Stacey, hugging Maria. Stacey wouldn't let her mother out of her sight, insisting on accompanying her even on trips to the bathroom. As tired and exhausted as Ellie was, they had stayed up late, and she let Stacey sleep with her. For one night, she told herself. In some ways, she thought, Stacey must have been as terrified as Ellie herself had been during her abduction, having her only parent missing and her whereabouts unknown.

Ellie closed the door and walked with Maria back into the living room. Maria touched Ellie's bandaged hand, and Ellie could see tears in her friend's eyes. Maria had cried when she changed the bandages that morning. Ellie put an arm around Maria and they held each other. "It's all right, Maria," she said softly. "We'll be fine."

The two police officers assigned to guard them were in the kitchen, talking quietly. She had insisted that they come inside when they arrived to relieve the night-shift officers, it was too hot for them to stand around outside. She suddenly felt bad, worse than when she had been crying. She was through crying, if for no other reason than it would terrify Stacey to see her mother sobbing.

The feelings of helplessness were intensified at home, not diminished as she'd expected. Nothing was resolved. She couldn't pick up where she had left off, not yet anyway. Herbie was being a dear, running her business in a caring, capable way. "For as long as you need, Ellie dear," he had said, so she didn't need to worry about that. She sat down on the couch with Maria, facing the patio and pool.

"Ellie," Maria said quietly.

She looked at her friend.

Enes Smith

"Ellie, you need to call your parents. They're coming in two days."
"I will."
She knew that they would have been here sooner if she hadn't put them off, but she'd insisted on having some time alone with Stacey, and she didn't want them to see her until she was more in control. She had minimized the ordeal when she called them and hoped that they hadn't read too much about it in the papers.

She picked up the phone and tried to dial, but the bandages on her hands made it awkward. She dropped the phone and walked into the kitchen. Both officers started to get up from their chairs when she entered. She waved for them to stay seated.

"Can you contact the detective for me, the one who brought me home?"

"Uh, yeah, we can," the younger of the two officers said.

"I want to get a message to him, to have Mr. Meredith call me as soon as possible. Will you do that?"

"Sure, right away." The officer began speaking into a small portable radio. He waited for a reply. "Message delivered."

"Thanks."

She left the kitchen, and got appreciative glances as she walked back to the living room in her form-fitting white shorts and bright blue T-shirt.

When the phone rang, Ellie snatched it up on the first ring.
"Hello."
"Ellie? This is Pat Meredith."
"Can you come over right away?"
"1 can be there within a few minutes. Is something—"
"I just want you here," she said quietly, almost in a whisper. "You can guard my family as well as these other guys can and I want to see you."

"All right."

She realized that she didn't even know where he was staying, she had been in such a hurry yesterday. "Can you get your suitcase and bring it here? I have a guest room and I want you to stay here. I . . ." She stopped, feeling awkward, foolish, but dammit! She was relaxed with Meredith. She didn't care how it looked; she wanted him to stay in her house while he was here.

"All right," Meredith said again, quietly. "Be there in an hour."

"Bye," Ellie said.

164

"Bye."

Ellie carefully placed the phone down on the cradle. Her heart was hammering, pounding in her chest and ears. She realized then how much she wanted to see Meredith again, if only to just talk with him. She knew that he would be going back to Oregon soon, and that she would have little contact with him, even if the case continued for years. But she didn't care. She wanted some feeling of security, some normalcy. (*Don't kid yourself Ellie old girl, you want an escape from this madness*) some . . . *love.*

She turned excitedly to Maria, who had been sitting on the couch with Ellie while she had been on the phone.

"Maria, do we have what we need for you to make one of your special dinners?"

"I think so," Maria said with a smile. It had been a long time since she had seen Ellie this animated, this excited. It had been long before the kidnapping, she realized. "We may need some fresh tortillas."

"Let's make a list and you can take my car, if you don't mind, and run to the store. Wonder what he drinks?" She stopped, seeing the look the other woman gave her.

"Maria, what is it?"

Maria said, gently taking her friend's bandaged hands, "You don't have a car."

"Oh." She jumped up and turned to Maria. "Damn. Well, call Herbie at the airport and see if he can rent one for us and have someone bring it out."

Ellie walked quickly to her room, calling to Maria as she went, talking about what she would wear.

"Mommy."

Stacey ran into Ellie's bedroom, trailing her blanket, her face flushed, creased from sleep. Ellie scooped he up, hugging and kissing her.

"Help Mommy get dressed, honey, and then we'll find something special for you to wear. We have a friend coming for dinner."

The rental car arrived just before Meredith did.

CHAPTER 33

As Meredith arrived at Ellie's house, Brunson located the motel he wanted just off Van Buren street, not far from Phoenix Sky Harbor Airport. In fact, the motel wasn't far from the biker bar that Meredith and Patterson had been at just two hours before.

The room was white adobe, with a rusty stain sliding down the outside wall beneath the air conditioner unit. The sign outside advertised X-RATED CABLE and WEEKLY RATES.

He took a cool shower and lay back on the bed, nude, his arms crossed behind his head, waiting for his heart to slow as he got used to his surroundings.

His throat was dry from the air conditioner.

And anticipation.

He looked slowly around the darkened room. He had his bag, his clothes, his two knives, and a Beretta 9mm pistol laid out on top of the dresser.

It was too early for him to go to work.

She's close!

He could feel her, here in Phoenix. She'd been here for years, spreading her filth and her legs the way she had done in Oregon.

Cherry.

He would take another one first . . . a lovely who could show them just how invisible he had become, one who could show them all of his lovelies, his *work*, his power.

Cherry would know that it was him. He was preparing a monument for her.

The last one, Ellie Hartley, would know as well. She still had important work to do for him before she could join the others again. He had her address on her driver's license in his bag. He wanted to visit her when her daughter was home.

And finally, the cops would know. He would tell them, and what better time to do so than when they were all together tomorrow. The *Phoenix Sun Times* had dutifully printed a press release that told of the meeting scheduled for the fifth, a meeting of all the law enforcement experts who had no idea that he was invisible, that he could do what he wanted, even when he left clues for them.

Clues that they were too stupid to see.

He felt the laughter rise up in him then, and he shook his head in irritation, trying to get rid of it before it took him away. His view of the room, of the darkened TV and the bag on the dresser, dimmed.

His head began throbbing.

Hey!

The laughter shouted.

Hey . . . Know what spreads easier than peanut butter?

The laughter shrieked.

Brunson squirmed on the bed, sweat standing out on his taut muscles despite the air conditioning.

What?

Yeah, what?

Cherry Brunson's legs, that's what!!

They would all join in then, laughing, and Thomas would run, too alone to fight all of them . . . he wasn't invisible then.

When Thomas was fourteen, he found that he didn't have to run anymore. He was working at the Sea Thrift food processing plant on the bay in Florence. He told the supervisor he was eighteen, got the job with a forged work permit, and dropped out of school.

He took off work early one afternoon; most of the fishing fleet was in the harbor to wait out a Pacific storm. First he walked downtown to buy a hamburger, fries, and a shake at the Wheel-Inn Drive-In, and then strolled back down to the park above the jetty. He sat on a small slide in the play area, and set his food down at his feet. He started on the milkshake. The breeze was brisk on his face, the air heavy from the impending storm. He was conscious of the fishing boats behind him in the bay, pulling at their moorings, and the waves thundering over the jetty in front of him.

"Well, lookee here, we got us a preevert, sitting on the kiddee slide!"

The voice caught Thomas from behind, and he jumped off the slide and turned to face the speaker. Bobby Roston came up to him, leering, followed by another senior, his younger brother, and two girls. Thomas held his shake and stared at them.

"Hey, he smells like fish, don't he?" Roston said, wrinkling his nose and turning to the others with a laugh.

"Yeah," Bobby's brother Gary said, stepping up beside Bobby. "It must be from sleeping with Cherry. Now, that must smell like a day-old tuna can."

Jane Poskell laughed a high shrill laugh.

Anger flared through Thomas, hot and unchecked. He didn't give a shit what they said about Cherry, but it was time for them to leave him damn well alone. He reached down and placed the milkshake carefully on the bottom of the slide, and pulled the plastic straw out with his teeth.

Gary and Bobby were still laughing.

He suddenly threw the milkshake at Gary and launched himself at Bobby, legs driving like a halfback.

"What the hell!" Gary yelled, as the container broke open on his shoulder, the vanilla shake spreading down his jacket.

Thomas grabbed Bobby's hair and twisted his fist through it, jerking back as he did. He whisked the plastic straw from his mouth and planted it like a stake in Bobby Roston's left eye. He grinned as the straw sliced through eye tissue and fluid gushed up on his hand. Bobby screamed, a high, keening sound, and went over on his back.

"My eye, my eye, my eye. *Oooohh God my eye!*"

Jane Poskell began screaming, too, her voice blending with Bobby's in an eerie duet.

Thomas jammed the straw in, driving it deeper as Gary came to his brother's aid, kicking and pulling on Brunson.

Bobby Roston mercifully passed out. They said later that he was lucky that all he lost was his eye. He could have died.

Thomas shook Gary off and rose to meet him, with Gary backing away, hands up to ward him off.

"Now, this ain't over yet, you jerk-off faggot," Gary yelled, as Thomas calmly picked up his fries and hamburger and walked off, knowing that it was time for him to get out of town.

Before the cops came looking for him that night, he caught Jane Poskell's poodle and cut off its head and tail and one of its rear legs. He put the parts in a green garbage bag and threw it through Jane's bedroom window. The plastic was slick on the inside with blood and fluid. The outside was clean. Slick.

Very slick.

The voices faded.

The laughter stopped.

He knew now, as he had learned at fourteen, that he could stop laughter. The air conditioner blew its stale, cool air on Thomas, drying his sweat, and he shivered.

He opened his eyes.

He had a throbbing erection.

Everything in the room was as it was before the laughter: The bag and clothes and knives and gun were on the dresser, the door and the curtains were closed, and the van was parked outside the room in front of the door.

Tomorrow he would find someone to help him spread the word.

His fingers closed on his erection and he thought of his lovelies on the mountain.

CHAPTER
34

The DVD seized by Meredith and Patterson from the biker's apartment was the first and only piece of evidence they had so far that had probably belonged to Ellie's abductor. They didn't think it belonged to Ellie; it was a skin flick—hard porn.

As Meredith was pulling into Ellie's driveway, the DVD was on its way to the FBI's forensic lab in Washington, D. C.

Ellie stood in the doorway, smiling at him, her arm on her daughter's shoulder. She was, Meredith thought, wonderfully and absolutely gorgeous, with her blond hair falling to her shoulders over a white, sleeveless tennis dress. The dress had thin shoulder straps, and Ellie wore it with a tan belt and matching sandals. The white bandages added to the effect, looking like formal gloves.

Stacey was barefoot, and was wearing a red and white striped sleeveless shift. At Meredith's approach, she opened her mouth and started bringing her thumb up, ready to pop it in her mouth. The thumb stopped halfway and she gave her mother a quick glance, slowly lowered the thumb, holding it behind her back as if it had a mind of its own.

When he thought about it later, he remembered them this way—mother smiling and daughter unsure, Ellie so beautiful, hair shimmering in the sun, so . . . so lovely.

Ellie reached out and grasped his hand, looking up at Meredith, still smiling.

"Come in."

"Hi," he said, taking her bandaged hands in his. She stepped back and pulled him into the entryway. Stacey came up to his side and put her thumb in her mouth, her index finger curled over her nose. She looked up at him and spoke without removing the thumb.

"Hi." It came out as a gurgle.

"Hi," Meredith replied, kneeling down beside her. She peered closely at him; an inspection, he thought. When she seemed satisfied, she ran off, with her thumb still plugged in, her blond pigtails bouncing. Ellie tugged on his hand, pulling him further into the hallway.

"Come on," she said, "Let me show you my house."

She kept his hand and led him into the living room. It was large and airy, with a tile floor in desert-rust-and-sand. The floor and adobe walls were covered with colorful Navajo rugs. One wall of the room was taken up by large sliding glass doors that opened onto a wide veranda and overlooked a swimming pool. Stacey was talking excitedly in another room.

They passed a piano in the far corner of the living room, and Ellie removed her hand from Meredith's and brushed the keys with bandaged fingers. They entered what Meredith took to be the master bedroom, a large room with a glass door that opened onto the pool area. There was an office area on one side, with an old scarred oak desk cluttered with papers. He could see a bathroom through an open doorway off the bedroom. The bedroom was filled with things from her past: a worn baseball glove, an ASU football team poster, an old steamer chest with a small TV on it, a picture of Ellie—a much younger Ellie—and a grey-haired man with glasses--her father? Meredith wondered— standing on the deck of a fishing boat, holding fishing rods and cans of beer, sporting silly grins. Meredith could see the stunning girlish beauty that would become the woman.

"Me and Dad, sneaking beers," Ellie said, watching Meredith.

She's not looking for my approval, she's showing me where she's most comfortable.

"I was all of sixteen, and Daddy and me, well . . . we used to sneak beers when we went to the beach, or fishing, and laugh at Mom's raised eyebrows when we got home. She didn't like it, but she respected our time together . . . and our . . . our love."

Ellie touched the picture frame and bent down to peer at the figures. The corners of her mouth suddenly turned down. She abruptly straightened and threw her arms around Meredith, her bandaged hands clutching his neck.

Meredith put his arms around her. His heart hammered at his shirt. He looked over Ellie's shoulder at her room, at the baseball glove, the posters, the pictures. A place where she's saved the past, he thought. That's what it is . . . that's why she's showing me her room. She won't accept what the present is dealing her. He felt her body pressing against his; her breath was warm in his neck. He struggled with the pang of guilt that intruded on the wonderful feeling of holding her.

Kinda taking advantage of the situation, aren't you, Meredith, old boy? And don't mention the fact that you are getting paid for all of this, yes indeed, thank you ma'am.

Bullshit. He did care. And he knew she did, too, even if she was vulnerable.

They broke, suddenly chased by demons not yet buried. Maria announced that dinner was ready

It was 6 P.M., July 4.

At eleven, Ellie tiptoed through the darkened living room to Stacey's door as Meredith watched from the couch. She opened the door quietly, performing the age-old parent's ritual of watching her child sleep, listening for her breathing, touching her not to wake up but to love. The twinge of anxiety that had always come to her during this nightly check was now a screaming, mind-numbing fear, a fear that ran through her like an ice storm, leaving her cold and weak. Since she had been abducted and left with the remains of the dead, she had a sense not so much of her own mortality but of her daughter's.

Her baby.

Meredith stood at the door, watching.

She motioned for him to join her at the bed. He walked into the room and stood behind her, looking at the sleeping child.

A family. We look like a family, she thought. Parents.

She knew now what parenthood was—she could define it for all of the pediatricians and child-care specialists and child psychologists and magazine writers and experts: Parenthood was fear. Heart-stopping fear.

Fear when you bring your newborn home and you think she might stop breathing. Fear when your eighteen-month-old has a cough that gets worse and worse and the doctor says if it doesn't get better he'll have to put her in the hospital. Fear when your toddler runs to the end of the driveway and you're too far away to stop her from going into the street.

And then some crazy comes along and raises the fear quotient right off the chart.

She smoothed Stacey's covers, and touched her daughter's hand, a caress. She left then, leading Meredith out by the hand and quietly closing the door.

She walked to the patio and slipped outside, feeling the heat from the tile on her bare feet. They stood at the edge of the pool listening to night sounds.

"There," Ellie whispered excitedly, pointing south toward the horizon. A multicolored glow lit the skyline. "Fireworks at Sun Devil Stadium," she explained.

"Oh."

She watched Meredith as he stood beside her, and she realized that she hadn't even asked him if he had any plans tonight. She had wanted to see him and talk with him, but maybe she should have let him stay at his hotel.

"Swim?" she asked.

"Didn't bring a suit."

"There's one in the guest room."

"Are you swimming with bandaged hands?"

Ellie laughed. "You can help me keep them out of the water."

They met back at the pool in five minutes, Ellie arriving first and watched as Meredith came out. She giggled as he opened the door. He was wearing navy blue trunks that were several sizes too large, the leg holes billowing and the drawstring pulled tight to keep them up.

She put her hands up to her mouth and laughed, watching as he walked toward her, taking in his muscular chest and arms, his open, caring face etched with the passage of time, the quick and friendly eyes, the brown—graying—curly hair that was starting to recede, the long, white, and very noticeable, ugly and twisted scars on his left knee.

She knew then that she could love this man.

As he walked out on the warm tiles, Meredith felt silly in the over-sized suit, and wondered who the boyfriend was who belonged in the damn thing. He stopped short when he saw Ellie, aware of her laughter.

She stood at the edge of the pool, shaking now with her giggles, her slender body accentuated by a white one-piece suit. The patio lights were turned off, with the pool lights casting a soft blue glow over the surrounding tiles.

She's unaware of her beauty, Meredith thought.

"Nice suit," Ellie said, still laughing, and held her hand out for him. Meredith grabbed the sided of his trunks and executed a somewhat inelegant pirouette.

"Thanks," he said. "It belonged to a stout acquaintance of yours, no doubt, a man of considerable girth." He stood next to Ellie and put his hands on her shoulders, aware of their closeness.

"An acquaintance, but not a lover . . . I don't have one of those," she said, looking at his chest from a few inches away.

"Never?"

"Nope."

"But," she quickly added, "I hope to have one some day."

"Just one?"

"No, dozens," Ellie said. She reached up and removed Meredith's hands from her shoulders, and suddenly threw her hip into him, playfully dancing out of his reach, laughing. Meredith waved his arms in a good windmill imitation, trying to regain his mental and physical balance; the sudden attack had taken him by surprise. He was sure he was going to tumble into the pool, but he recovered his balance with his toes hanging over the edge..

"Bandages or not, you're gonna get wet," Meredith said, turning toward her. She hit him with her shoulder before he could complete the turn. This time he didn't have time to pinwheel—he fell straight in, flat, the classic belly flop. The water was warm, almost hot.

He came up to Ellie's shrieks of laughter. She was doubled over, holding her hands up in front of her, shaking, trying to talk.

"You . . . you looked so funny when you"—she gave in to laughter again, watching Meredith warily as he swam toward her, "hit the water."

Meredith laughed with her, thinking that he must have indeed looked funny hitting the water in the over-sized, billowing swimsuit. This was the first time he had seen Ellie playful, laughing, enjoying herself.

He didn't want it to end.

"Okay, I won't pull you in," he said, and leaned his arms on the tile, looking up at her.

"Bandages," Ellie said solemnly, pointing with her right mitten bandage at the left hand. "Can't get them wet." She sat down on the tile next to Meredith and dropped her legs in the pool.

Meredith reached up, gently put his hands on her waist, and slowly lowered Ellie into the pool, holding her against his body.

She put her bandaged hands around his neck, and brought her legs up, circling his waist with her thighs. He walked backward until the

174

water level came up to his chest. She put her face down into his neck, nuzzling.

Ellie's legs tightened around Meredith, and her round, firm breasts pressed against his chest. He suddenly felt like a twenty-year-old, not at all like a forty-two-year-old ex-cop with a broken body, a body that he'd begun to regard as over-the-hill.

She's not doing this for you, buddy boy, she's vulnerable and scared, that's all.

"Ellie, I . . ."

"Shush," she murmured in his ear.

". . . don't think we should be doing this."

"Quiet. Don't you want to hold me?"

"Yes, very much," he admitted, "but . . ."

Ellie pulled her face away from his neck.

"Then be quiet," she commanded gently. She spoke softly and slowly. "I want to hold you and be held by you. I don't care what anyone thinks, and I don't care that this is a terrible time for me and maybe that's what all this is about, that I need someone right now, but I don't . . . I haven't felt like this in a long time, have you?" She grew silent then and put her head down on his shoulder.

He tightened his arms around her in response.

They stayed like that in the pool for some time. Minutes? An hour? Ellie couldn't be sure. Finally, Meredith carried her to the side and lifted her onto the apron, where she carefully untangled her arms and legs and lay back on the still-warm red tile. Meredith sat down next to her. She suddenly wanted to know everything there was to know about him.

"What did you do after you left here yesterday?" Ellie asked, closing her eyes, relaxing with the warmth of the tile and his closeness.

"Got a room at the downtown Sheraton and slept for what must have been twelve hours."

"Then what?"

"Had breakfast with Detective Patterson and looked at some evidence—"

Ellie opened her eyes. "What kind of evidence?"

"I don't suppose you would want to talk about it tomorrow?" Meredith asked.

"No." Ellie sat up next to Meredith and touched his arm. "If you have something new, I want to know about it."

Meredith sat facing the pool.

"Please tell me," Ellie insisted quietly.

"Sure this can't wail until tomorrow? We can't do anything tonight and we have a meeting tomorrow with all agencies involved. We might be able to make more sense out of it then." He turned to Ellie and put his arms around her.

"Tell me," she said.

"We looked at your car, and then we talked to a man who stopped to look at your car at the scene of the accident. He found some DVDs. One was Springsteen."

"His 'U.S.A.' songs," Ellie said, "I had that in the console in my Camaro."

"The other DVD was Alicia Keys."

"Songs in a Minor!" She was excited now. "That in the console, too, but how did he—?"

"We think that this man looked through your car and decided to steal whatever he could. He's not exactly in the running for the Citizen of the Year award."

"I can't remember what other songs I had in the Camaro," Ellie said. And suddenly she was driving her car on that day, on her way home from work, stopping at the store to buy popsicles for Stacey's swimming party.

She drove to the intersection of Castle Rock and Cottonwood, as she had done hundreds of times since they had moved into their new house over a year ago. She started through, and the van slammed into the rear of her car.

Ellie moaned, and stared unseeing at the pool, unaware that Meredith's arms had tightened around her.

And she got out into the heat of the day, her Coke spilled on her blouse and linen suit, furious at the driver of the van for wrecking her new Camaro and ruining her outfit.

She watched as if she were a silent witness. She watched herself as she walked to the van and the driver got out holding his right arm across his chest.

Watchout! She screamed silently at the figure of herself, walking toward the van.

Watchout! Don't go in the van. Don't go don't go don't' go!

But the Ellie figure walked to the van and leaned in to get the man's registration, and suddenly he was in the open door between her and freedom and the Ellie figure opened the glove box and the horrible, filthy face inside, screamed out and the foul-smelling rag came over her face and she kicked—

Ellie watched from a distance and cried, a shaky cry full of anger and—and guilt—and fear and nauseous anticipation of what she knew the Ellie figure would go through, the filth, the terror.

She watched as the Ellie figure struggled with the man and kicked something on the floor of the van and it clattered to the pavement, a—

"A DVD!" Ellie cried suddenly. "A DVD!" Meredith sat next to her on the tile, holding her tightly, waiting.

The sound of her voice broke up the images Ellie had from the past; the silent view of her abduction was fading. She looked at the tape one last time, trying to see the label, but she could not. She became aware of Meredith's arms around her, the warm tile, the lights glowing in the pool, the darkened windows of her house. She put her head on Meredith's shoulder.

"It was a DVD," she said quietly. "I don't know what was on it . . . but I kicked it out of the van. The DVD belongs to the killer."

Meredith continued to hold her. They both realized that there was nothing for him to say. Ellie hooked her hands around his arm, wanting to banish the images that lingered, wanting to give herself to this man, if only to chase the ghosts away, but she couldn't. She didn't want this night with him to end with thoughts of murder and kidnapping. She wanted to have a normal relationship; she wanted to be held, to be loved, to make love.

She got up and they walked into the darkened house.

From the guest room Meredith could hear the shower running in Ellie's room.

177

<u>WEDNESDAY</u>
JULY
5

CHAPTER 35

"Well, I see that the gang from D.C. is all here," Meredith said in greeting. He didn't expect an answer from Ward and didn't get one.

Ward and Gardiner were eating breakfast in the crowded basement cafeteria of the Phoenix Police Department. Ward grunted, and Gardiner nodded with his usual grin. Meredith took a chair and set his cup of coffee down.

"The DVD we got from the biker is on its way to Washington," Meredith said. "The lab technicians here took a look at it yesterday, and thought that the lab in D.C. would have a better chance at prints and origin. Detective Sergeant Patterson had the biker printed after we got the DVD."

"You sure this DVD belongs to our man?" Ward asked.

"Ellie says it does," Meredith answered.

"Ellie." Gardiner was grinning at Meredith.

"Yeah. Karen Elizabeth Hartley."

"Let's go up to the auditorium," Ward said. "I want to talk with Chief Maxwell before the meeting starts."

The meeting in the Phoenix Police Department on the morning of July 5th was something to behold, even to veteran lawmen like Meredith and Patterson. The auditorium was almost half-full when they arrived. Representatives were present from the Phoenix Police Department; the Maricopa County Sheriff's Department; the Arizona Department of Public Safety; the Scottsdale and Tempe Police Departments; the Oregon State Police; the FBI; the California Department of Justice; and the Nevada Attorney General's Office. Also present were various forensic specialists from the agencies, and Meredith's own employer, the Violent Crime Investigation Administration.

Gardiner immediately split off from Meredith and Ward and was soon engaged in conversation with other forensic specialists.

Ward and Meredith took a seat near the back.

Thomas Brunson walked through the concourse of Phoenix Sky Harbor Airport, empty at 8 a.m., holding his blue and red ticket folder in his hand, the seat assignment glaring in green ink across the bottom. He located his van and drove through the palm trees from the airport back to his motel. He didn't like leaving his van, but he would have to leave it soon. The thought of flying back north today brightened his mood . . . he had a garden to look after and the zinnias would be blooming for his lovelies.

But he had things to tend to in Phoenix first.

It was time to start the hunt.

Meredith stretched out his stiffened knee, half listening to the overview of the case given by Maxwell, thinking about the killer, wondering.

Where was he now?

It was almost 9 a.m.

The morning traffic was starting to thin out, with plenty of stragglers going to work late.

Brunson drove the van in the slow lane, with a measured, unhurried pace. He drove to the shopping center in the northwest.

Close to Ellie's house.

He would find someone to help him spread the word. It was unbelievably easy.

* * *

Chief of Police Jerry Maxwell of the Phoenix Police Department spoke first. He looks tired, Meredith thought, and why shouldn't he be worn out. If they didn't catch the killer soon, a lot of officers were going to be working without sleep. Meredith's boss, Jonathan Ward, was introduced, and as he began to speak to the assembled lawmen, Meredith thought of his swim with Ellie.

Is this real, this attraction between us? Or, do we both have a need? He pushed the thoughts away and listened to Ward's comments.

". . . and the blood that the killer left with the woman in Phoenix. We believe that this was his first attempt to communicate directly with us," Ward said. Meredith knew that he was forgetting something, or more correctly, not getting something. There was something about the blood that he knew, or should know.

Why leave the blood? What was he doing with it?

Meredith looked around the room. Most of those present were administrative staff from the involved police departments—Chiefs, Deputy Chiefs, Superintendents of Police—administrators who in some cases didn't even know the names of their primary homicide investigators, or their way around a crime scene.

They would all be invited to a press conference after the meeting.

The real work, the planning, the solutions—if any— would start with the officers from the various agencies sharing a few or a lot of— beers after the formal meeting was over.

". . . and at one o'clock, we will have a meeting with all primary investigators and forensic specialists, here in this room, while all of us administrative types talk to the press and get a chance to be somebody and stay out of the real cops' way."

There was a smattering of laughter in the room. Meredith smiled. The old man still knew about police work.

Gardiner set down next to Meredith and began to whisper excitedly.

Patricia Cochran got out of her Toyota Celica.

He saw her.

He sat in the van and swallowed, his mouth suddenly going from dry to wet with saliva. His hands were slippery on the steering wheel.

Lovely.

She was lovely.

He started the van, letting the air conditioner cool the interior, and watched her walk toward the mall. She had parked two rows up from him. Red shorts. White halter top. Maybe eighteen or twenty. Lovely.

Patricia came out fifteen minutes later carrying a small sack, her long brown hair swinging across her back. She had purchased an anniversary card for her parents at the Hallmark shop.

There was a blue van parked next to her car.

Patricia was looking, through her purse for her keys when the crutch fell into the side of her car. She hadn't noticed the van parked next to her when she walked out of the mall. She found her keys and opened the door to her Celica, impatient at having to pick up a crutch when she was in a hurry to go see her morn and dad.

And then she felt guilty and a little ashamed at her thoughts. She would take a few seconds and help the poor soul who lost the crutch. She walked between her car and the van.

"I don't think I'll ever get the hang of these things," a man's voice said.

She thought he looked awkward, embarrassed. He was wearing a long-sleeved white shirt and jeans, and came around the back of the van. He took a hop with his remaining crutch.

"Here it is," Patricia said. She held the crutch up so he could grab it.

"Thanks," Brunson said, putting the crutch under his arm. "I don't make a very good cripple . . . not yet anyway." He walked to the rear of his van in the unsure way of someone new to crutches, and bent over to lift a box into the van through the rear door.

The crutch fell over again as Patricia reached the door of her Celica.

Brunson remained bent over, watching the short red shorts come toward him.

"Here, let me do it," she said, and put a box inside.

"Well, it is a little embarrassing to be so clumsy, but . . ." He gestured at the boxes of tapes that remained on the ground.

"How'd you do it?" Patricia asked, leaning in the open door of the van, with Brunson behind her.

"Motorcycle."

She turned and grinned up at him. "We've got something in common, anyway. I spent a whole summer in a cast because of a damned motorcycle accident. A dirt bike that belonged to my brother."

Brunson rapped his leg. "Streetbike."

". . . and the hard evidence in the case," Ward said, "other than the forensic evidence associated with the remains of the bodies, has all come from the suspect." He looked out at the auditorium filled with lawmen.

"Who is he?" Ward asked.

And when no one answered, he asked:

"Where is he?"

"Oregon," a man in the audience answered.

"Why?" Ward pointed to the speaker, a criminal investigator from the state of California.

"Because you've had a kidnapping roughly every three weeks to a month this spring and early summer. He's not due back for another two weeks, minimum."

There were four more boxes on the hot pavement, DVDs the label said. Patricia started to put one in the van. The interior smelled funny, like disinfectant. The smell irritated her nose. She set the box down and scratched. "How come you have all the plastic covering?" she asked, swinging another box in, with Brunson standing to one side.

"Oh, I put potting, soil and junk in there, and then hose it out when I'm done."

Patricia wiped her hands together after placing the last box inside. "Well that's done—"

She was suddenly shoved forward into the rear of the van, and for a moment she thought that he was indeed clumsy and that he had fallen forward off his crutches. And then a powerful hand clamped around her throat and she took a sharp breath (disinfectant?) and went limp.

Brunson pulled on rubber gloves, picked up an envelope from the front seat of the van, and placed it in the front seat of the Celica. He got back in the van and wrote down the license number, color, make, and location of the car.

It wouldn't do for the cops to miss the note. He would give them good directions when the time came. He didn't think that they would find the car on their own. Hell, they wouldn't even take a missing persons report for days, and if the missing person was a college student, they might not take one for a lot longer.

But they would take a report this afternoon.

He would almost guarantee it.

"Mommy, watch!" Stacey yelled. She pushed away from the side of the pool, dog-paddled across the short end, and lunged for the other side. Ellie stood with Maria under the veranda, applauding Stacey as she reached the side of the pool. It was hot, almost noon, and not a time that Ellie would choose to swim, but Stacey had been begging all morning.

Ellie had finally slept last night, and then didn't awaken until after Meredith had quietly left the house. His note said that he would be back for dinner. She had gone through the morning humming, playing with Stacey, helping Maria with the housework. The world seemed brighter, safer, in the daylight.

More sane.

And she knew that she couldn't wait for Mr. Patrick Meredith to show up for dinner.

"Okay, hon . . . it's time to get out of the pool."

"One more time, Mommy, *please!*" Stacey pushed off from the side without waiting for an answer.

Ellie stomped in exaggerated steps to the poolside to meet Stacey, her hands on her hips in mock anger. Maria followed, giggling. Not only was it hot out here, Ellie wanted to do some special shopping for their dinner tonight, even if she had to take along the officers assigned to guard her.

She couldn't know it then, but she and Stacey were going to leave Phoenix well before dinner.

Meredith had once thought that he actually preferred to live the life of a bachelor, and he did, in fact, have a pretty good life. Even before Josh. With Josh, he had the love of a son and someone to care for, to do things for.

When he met Ellie, he realized that he was missing a great part of life . . . falling in love . . . being loved by a woman. And he was tired of the arguments that he kept raising, about her being vulnerable, and possible professional conflicts. He wanted to be with her.

He wanted this case to be over. He wanted to put to rest the haunting verbal jabs that his former wife used to give him (*You need this job, buster, you need to deal with all of this sick shit*).

He straightened his leg out slowly, working the aches out of the knee, half listening to Ward's presentation.

". . . that the FBI is working with the Phoenix PD to profile the victims, beginning with our live wit— " Ward stopped and watched as a Phoenix PD sergeant ran past him and stopped in front of Chief Maxwell, speaking urgently to his boss.

Meredith stood and stretched his knee. He moved to the end of his aisle and leaned on the wall next to an exit, watching as Chief Maxwell stepped in front of the microphone.

"I want everyone from my agency to remain here for assignment," the Chief said gravely, his face sad and stern at the same time. The low level of talk among investigators, which had been present during Ward's talk, was gone.

"We have had another kidnapping," the Chief continued, "at the Metro Center this morning, and our suspect left a message for us.

The room was buzzing.

Ward looked out over the auditorium, trying to get Meredith's attention.

Meredith was gone.

CHAPTER 36

Meredith ran for his car, limping badly, unprepared for the heat and brightness as he ran from the auditorium. He pulled out the keys to the loaner from Patterson and launched himself behind the wheel, the sweat breaking out instantly in the oven-like heat of the car.

Ellie!

The Metro Center was less than a mile from her place!

The note with the flowers said, "I hope to see you again." Was the killer on his way to Ellie's house?

He jerked the car into gear and backed out, the rear tires squealing his urgency. Patterson ran up and banged on the door, yelling. Meredith stopped and the pudgy detective jumped in. "Do you know how the hell to get there?" he asked, puffing, out of breath, holding onto the side of the door.

"Not exactly, but find it, "Meredith said grimly. He slammed the gearshift into low and shot forward through the parking lot, cutting off a police cruiser at the entrance to the street, the officer yelling at them as they left.

Patterson was talking urgently on the police radio, trying to make contact with the officers stationed at the Hartley residence. They slid around a corner, Meredith slammed his foot down, and they rocked forward, the entrance to Interstate 17 coming up fast.

"Slow down," Patterson croaked, grabbing Meredith's arm. "The officers at her house say she's okay."

If anything, Meredith drove faster, and Patterson wished that he had shut his mouth.

When they arrived, Meredith found that Ellie was anything but okay. She met them at the front door.

"You might as well come in," she said through clenched teeth, "I'm not going to be here much longer." With that she whirled around and ran back through the entryway and into the living room. Patterson and Meredith exchanged glances and Meredith shrugged. Meredith took a step forward as Ellie was coming back toward them, struggling with a suitcase. She dropped it in front of Meredith and ran back across the living room, giving the young officer on the couch a withering glare as she passed him.

She slammed her bedroom door.

The officer saw Patterson, and made his escape to the entryway.

"What's up?" Patterson asked.

"She's been like this for the past ten minutes," he whispered. In any other setting, Meredith would have been amused by the clear intimidation that the diminutive Ellie had established over the officer.

"What happened?"

"She heard on the news about some woman being kidnapped."

Meredith walked through to Ellie's bedroom door, and knocked softly. No answer. He turned the knob and went in. Stacey was sitting on Ellie's bed with a pile of clothes, helping Maria put them in a suitcase. Ellie was on the phone at her desk, opening drawers and selecting items and hurriedly shoving them into her purse. She was dressed for travel, wearing a soft-beige blouse and brown slacks.

"What are you doing?" Meredith asked, knowing that it sounded stupid, but he didn't know what else to say. It is obvious, you dumbshit, he told himself, what the lady is doing. She is packing for a trip. And she's in a hurry, you moron.

"Leaving." She brushed quickly by Meredith and put her arms around Maria, who was blinking back tears. "Maria, will you help Stacey take her suitcase to the car?" Maria held her arms out for Stacey and walked out of the room, talking softly in Spanish.

Ellie turned to face Meredith. "Look," she yelled, trying to keep her voice down and not succeeding. "That killer's here, and close, and we're leaving."

"We can protect you," Meredith said quietly and somewhat lamely. Ellie snorted, and lowered her voice.

"Yeah, for how long? A day? A week? A month? I really doubt it."

"Where are you going?"

"Oregon."

"What?"

"Stacey and I are going to be on a flight that leaves for Oregon in exactly . . ." Ellie glanced at her watch. "in exactly one hour."

"Ellie that's—"

"Stupid?" she shrieked.

Meredith reached out and put his hands on her shoulders. "Not necessary," he said. Ellie twisted away from him and snatched her purse from her desk. For the first time Meredith noticed that the pads of her fingers were bleeding through her bandages. "I'm going there and you'll have to throw me in jail to stop me."

"But what do you hope to accomplish there that we couldn't do . . . that we can't do now?" Meredith pleaded. "We can put hundreds of officers throughout the west on this case, on the killer—"

Ellie raised her hand, cutting him off. "I'm the only one who has been to his graveyard . . . his hilltop . . . and I think I can find it. Don't you see? It's our only chance to save that . . . that girl. We can beat him there." With that, she began to cry, and angrily jerked her purse open and pawed around for a tissue.

"What about Stacey?" Meredith asked quietly.

"I'm not leaving her anywhere, not ever. She goes with me." She walked from the room, still looking in her purse.

Guess I have to agree with her on that one, Meredith thought. Ellie was the only one who could lead them to the killer's dumping ground. If she could find it, and if he followed his past practice on this one, they could end this madness in two days. He walked to the guest room and got his suitcase. Ellie and her daughter might be going to Oregon, but they weren't going alone.

CHAPTER 37

Meredith called Patterson's desk as the loudspeakers announced their flight to Oregon. A detective told him that Patterson was in a meeting. While Meredith waited, he watched Ellie holding Stacey on her lap, looking tiredly at the people walk by on the concourse.

"Meredith, boy you sure as shit stirred up a nest here. The chiefs and such want to string you up by your balls and really show you how mad they are."

"I don't have a lot of time, and I need some answers."

"Shoot."

"Was it him?"

"Looks like it. He left a note."

"What'd it say?"

"I don't have a copy in front of me," Patterson said, "but the gist of it was that he would be back for the Hartley woman and her daughter, and something about 'catch me if you can.' "

"How'd he notify us?"

"Called a rock station in Phoenix. They called an affiliated TV station, and we got a call about the victim's car . . . a Patricia Cochran, ASU student. When the first uniforms arrived on the scene the place was crawling with media. We don't know how much evidence was destroyed by those assholes, but the public's gotta have something to digest each night."

"Where's Ward?"

Patterson lowered his voice. "He's right here, waiting to talk to you, and 'pissed' doesn't halfway describe what he is. Gotta go."

"Oh, shit," Meredith muttered.

"For chrissakes!" Ward exploded as he came on the line. "She's our only living witness! And what about the daughter?"

"I know," Meredith said calmly.

"We'll catch him if he tries to get back north," Ward said, the strain in his voice coming through to Meredith now, The loudness was gone. "We are putting every, I mean every, available cop on the road from here to L.A., the state of Arizona is pulling out all stops . . . hell, the Governor has even offered the National Guard for use in roadblocks, and we might take him up on using some copters to spot the van. Nevada, Northern California, and Oregon . . . everyone's on the road . . . hell, the bastard won't make it to the damned Oregon border. We'll cut him off at the pass, literally. And," Ward added, "I absolutely forbid you to go. Bring her back."

"Would if I could," Meredith said. "I told her the same things. She'll go without us. And she doesn't buy the bullshit about us being able to find him on thirteen hundred miles of highway . . . and quite frankly, Boss, I don't know that we will catch him that way either." Meredith watched as Ellie picked up Stacey and gave him a questioning look. They were announcing the last call for the flight.

"We'll catch him," Ward repeated.

"I doubt it . . . and so do you. She has an idea that she can locate his dumping ground, his killing ground, and then we can get some troops and wait for him to come to us. It's not a bad idea, Ward. We should have two days or so to find it, and after that . . . well, we'll see. I have to go. Call you from Oregon." Meredith hung up, hearing Ward's angry yell before he could put the phone back in its cradle.

"Let me take her," Meredith said, holding his arms out. After a moment's hesitation, Stacey put one arm around his neck, clutching a ragged, stuffed dog with the other. She'd had a tight grip on the dog since Phoenix. As he lifted her he was struck again by her likeness to her mother, a beautiful, miniature copy of her mother. He was filled with a sudden sense of foreboding . . . of fear . . . that he was doing the worst possible thing, that he should listen to Ward and stop them here.

He should be protecting them.

Instead, he felt as if they were being led into certain horror by a madman.

They ran down the ramp to the plane.

Fatal Flowers

Highway 32, near Cassville

CHAPTER
38

The rain continued, heavy at times, into the afternoon, and a flood warning was issued by the National Weather Service in Eugene, a warning for the valley floor and coastal and low-lying areas. Sheriff Robinson stood by his Blazer, the rain glistening on his yellow slicker, and watched the last vehicle of the search team drive back toward the tunnel. He glanced at his watch, surprised that it was only five in the afternoon; the overcast made it a dark, dreary day, and except for the heat, it seemed like a winter evening.

He had heard on the radio that the Willamette River was two feet above flood stage at the Harrisburg Station, and still rising. In July!

Folks near the river had moved their livestock to higher—certainly not dryer—ground, and those who had been flooded before got ready to leave their homes. The rain didn't look as if it was going to quit for a while. The Altona River was now filled with muddy, churning black water, and like most coastal rivers, it was a wild one, with no flood control like the valley tributaries. Robinson could hear its roar from where he stood.

They had been concentrating their search on the six-mile stretch of road from Cassville to the tunnel. In the three days that Meredith and Ellie had been gone, he had stayed at Cassville, using the Jacobsens' store as a base of operations. He had organized the Explorer Scouts and other search and rescue groups into search parties.

It was a futile effort, and they all knew it. All they'd been able to do, without any kind of location for additional bodies, was to search the sides of the road to the river on one side, and the mountain on the other. And even at that, Robinson thought, it was a real cock-dragger. They had a kid break his leg today, and Stewart was, at this moment, giving the kid an ambulance ride to the hospital. The medic had spent much of his time with them on the search, assisting Robinson in directing the teams.

Robinson looked at the trees beside the road. The firs seemed to close in, making the road a dark tunnel. He shivered. He opened the Blazer's door and heard a burst of static and chatter on the radio.

"Seven zero one!" Stewart was trying to call him.

191

Robinson picked up his mike. "This is seven-oh-one. Go ahead." He absently brushed water from his slicker and waited for the reply.

"Yeah, this is Stewart. I got the kid in and he's going to be okay, and a couple of other things . . ." Stewart faded out as static took over. Radio reception was poor under the best conditions this far from the courthouse.

". . . tunnel is bad, and it looks . . ."

Robinson waited for Stewart to stop.

"Stu, if you can hear me, you'll have to repeat. Reception is bad."

The medic repeated his message until Robinson got all of it. Another kidnapping in Arizona. The killer was probably on his way with another victim. Meredith and the Hartley woman were going to arrive tonight to try and find the location of the others before the killer could get here. Robinson's heart hammered under his raincoat. Christ in a sidecar, he thought bitterly. Don't we have enough problems already? Stewart had signed off after telling him another tidbit of wonderful news. The tunnel—the lifeline to Cassville—appeared to be deteriorating in the rain. A chunk of roof had fallen, narrowly missing the ambulance.

Robinson slowly replaced the microphone, got behind the wheel, and started toward Cassville. He would get Jake and take a look at the tunnel. The damned thing had to remain intact so the killer could get in. How else, he thought, will the bastard get here so we can find him?

They found out later that it would have been better, much, much better, to keep him out.

The small trickles of water left unchecked in the roof of the Cassville tunnel became small rivers, taking bits of concrete and rock and mountainside to the roadbed in the tunnel. Robinson and Jake stood at the mouth, looking at the debris on the road.

"Think it'll hold?" Robinson asked the store owner.

"Dunno," Jake said, looking at the darkened maw in front of them. Water ran down the sides, glistening in the headlights of the Blazer; the lights of the tunnel had long since burned out or broken. "Just dunno," added. "'The dang thing was built in the thirties, by some WPA workers, and it's gettin' tired. Worn out like the rest of us."

They drove back to Cassville, to Jake's store, twice stopping on the road to remove debris that had washed down from the mountain. The rain continued.

Fatal Flowers

In other parts of the Coast Range, whole hillsides became heavy with water, and liquid patches of earth and vegetation gave in to the force of gravity and slid lower, filling small valleys. Areas where fires and recent logging operations had removed trees and brush were the first to move. The months of rain made the mountains a shifting, churning place.

On the plateau in the forest high above Cassville the circle of death watched as the mountain trembled and slid by the opening in the rock, taking small firs and rhododendrons with the mud slide, exposing the basalt rock in some places, burying it in others.

After all, the rain did its work, cleaning.

<u>Eugene</u>

CHAPTER 39

Meredith's customary fear of flying competed with his increasing uneasiness over flying into unknown danger. Ellie's decision to go to Oregon truly scared him. It was naive to believe that they could catch this savage killer. The madman had managed to stay so far ahead of them for so long, to play with them . . . to taunt them. He had to know that they would be looking for him and his van—his cargo, on the entire route from Arizona to Oregon.

They would be waiting for the killer.

Logical arguments did nothing to ease Meredith's fear. He was missing something, that he was sure of. What? And what about the blood? They never did come up with a good answer to that one . . . but Meredith couldn't forget it.

He looked at Stacey and Ellie, sleeping next to him. Stacey was clutching her ragged stuffed dog, her head on her mother's chest.

Ellie opened her eyes and gave him a tired smile as they landed.

He rose as the whine of the engines began to fade, and stepped aside so that Ellie could move into the aisle. She pulled a bag from the overhead rack, grabbing it with her bandaged hands before he could react. Meredith bent over the sleeping Stacey and tried to pick her up without waking her. As he picked her up and cradled her in his right arm, she moaned and ground her teeth and opened one sleepy eye. Meredith gave her a hug. A white-haired woman in front of Meredith gave them a warm smile.

"Oh, ain't she a one," she said, and touched Stacey's hand, which was dangling down Meredith's back. She spied the dog that Stacey had left on the seat, and leaned in to pick it up.

"Your daughter would be very upset if you forgot this very important person," the grandmotherly woman said, and tucked the dog in between Stacey and Meredith.

"She's . . ." He started to tell her that Stacey was not his, that she was "just a job," but he knew in his heart that she was more than that—like Josh had been more than just a job from the moment he walked into Angie's apartment and saw him. He nodded his thanks. As they filed out of the plane and walked to the baggage claim area, Meredith was conscious of the picture that they made, and he was sure that Ellie was also, a picture of a family returning from a vacation, with the husband carrying their sleepy daughter through the airport. They found the right carousel and waited for the luggage to appear.

"You hungry?" he asked.

"Famished, and here, let me take her," Ellie said, reaching for her daughter.

"She's okay, and I don't think that she minds."

"All right," Ellie said, sounding pleased. "Let's get some food on the way out of town."

Meredith signed for the car at the Hertz counter, shifting Stacey into his left arm. She was awake, watching him with her thumb plugged in, looking at him intently with her sleepy eyes.

He called the Adams County Sheriff's Office, and learned that Sheriff Robinson was expecting them at Cassville. They were to stay at the store while they were searching.

Ellie decided she was too hungry to wait. They ate at the airport restaurant, then bundled Stacey into the back seat of the Ford Crown Vic rental and started for the coast.

It was dark when they left the airport.

Cassville Tunnel
CHAPTER 40

Thomas Brunson waited in the trees, well back from the tunnel, knowing that he couldn't be seen from the road. He had read about others who had done this . . . this work. He dreamed about them. And now people would read about him. Dream his dreams of horror and brightness. He knew the power of the shadows, and he knew that there would be others. There were those like him who toiled alone. He would find them and show them how to tend his gardens.

Brunson had been listening to the rocks fall in the tunnel for the past two hours. He looked through the trees to the tunnel's dark maw. A loud crash and thud shook the ground, and he knew that a large piece of the ceiling had fallen in.

The laughter had not returned. He no longer heard the voices of his tormented youth.

Cherry was here at last.

Brunson walked down to the road, feeling the power in his legs. He had a car hidden off the road, in the trees. The cops hadn't searched this area today. It was safe.

He drove toward Cassville.

As he drove, he thought of each lovely, individually, like a parent with loving thoughts of his children. When he found the trail, he drove past and pulled off the road behind a pile of brush. He walked up the shifting, slippery slope to the plateau. A car flashed by on the road below.

He started a fire in a large, wet brush pile, a fire that started with a small explosion as he threw the match. The gasoline and diesel mixture worked well.

As the fire grew, hissing and popping in the rain, Brunson visited his lovelies, walking in his shrine of madness.

CHAPTER 41

Meredith drove west toward the coast, with Ellie sitting beside him in the front seat. Stacey was in the back, happily munching on a snack. She had been too excited to eat at the airport.

Ellie had her hair done up in a ponytail. He glanced at her, more than aware of the looks that she had received from the men in the restaurant.

"Frankberry!" Stacey yelled suddenly, waving her free hand in the air to punctuate the new word. The other hand held a crumbled mass of small berry-colored puffs, which she was happily munching from the cereal box beside her on the seat. Booty from Meredith's quick trip to 7-Eleven.

"Frankenberry," Ellie corrected, and turned in the seat to look at her daughter.

Meredith looked in the rearview mirror and grinned. Hertz was going to have Frankenberrys in the back seat of this Pontiac until they retired the car from service. He looked at Ellie.

"Did I do good?"

"Yes, for a new papa, you did fine." She gave his arm a squeeze. She left her hand there, holding on to him.

"I thought maybe she would like them."

Yes, Ellie thought, and we both like you. It seemed that Stacey was already competing with Mom for Mr. Meredith's affections.

"Mommy," Stacey whispered loudly between bites of her cereal. "C' mere."

Ellie released Meredith's arm and leaned over the back seat.

"Do you like Mer'dith? I do."

Ellie glanced at Meredith, who was looking straight ahead at the twisting road, grinning. "Yes I do, honey, very much," she said in a stage whisper. She giggled. Stacey and Meredith laughed, and suddenly Ellie felt fine, better than she had for days. Here in the coziness of the car, with her . . . her family.

The road became steeper; Meredith was driving smoothly, the headlights picking up the green forest as it swept by. Ellie liked the cooler weather, the lush green in contrast to Arizona, but she glanced at the woods with increasing apprehension. She pushed the fearful thoughts from her mind, and willed herself to think of the evening before, of their passion; their caring in the pool. He hadn't said anything about it since, but she was sure of her feelings for him, and it was all she could do to keep from grabbing him and hugging him and giving herself to him.

He caught her looking at him.

"What?"

"Just looking at you, Mr. Meredith. Wondering if you'll go back to Washington and write to us when this is all over." That was safely said. What was it about him? She'd never felt like she had to mince words before.

"So who says I'm going back to Washington? I live here."

"Washington is where you work. You have to go back . . ."

"Write to you?"

"Right, or tell them that you're coming back to live out here . . . and move."

"When you say 'out here,' do you mean Arizona?" "I mean . . . anywhere you want to live," Ellie said. "Maybe Arizona. It gets hot there."

"Yeah, I found out. What if my boss says no?"

"Quit."

"Oh, quit, she says." He laughed. Ellie snuggled on his shoulder and laughed with him.

"Okay, so I quit. What then?"

"Do whatever you want."

"What if I wanted to be a beekeeper?"

"Would you be happy?"

"That wouldn't bother . . . that wouldn't bother . . ."

Meredith stopped and started again. "Would it bother you if we dated, if I were a beekeeper? I guess I should say, would you date me if I were a beekeeper?"

"I would date you if you were unemployed or were retired and not even looking for work."

"What I mean," Meredith said, nudging the steering wheel to negotiate a curve, "is wouldn't it bother you that I'm not president of the local beekeeping company?"

"No."

"No?"

"Presidents of companies have no time for dates, or . . ." Ellie glanced at Meredith and then back at Stacey, "or for families . . . or other stuff," she finished.

They did look so much like a family, he thought, and fit so well together. When he'd carried Stacey into the restaurant, she'd had her arm casually around his neck, chattering about the trip and what she wanted to eat, and Ellie had come up behind him and given him a hug.

Like a family.

Only thing we need to be complete is Josh.

"What do you mean . . . other stuff"? Meredith took his attention from the road for a second to watch Ellie. "What other stuff?"

"Wouldn't you like to know," Ellie whispered, and after risking a quick glance back at Stacey, who seemed engrossed in looking out the window, she touched his ear with her lips. Meredith suddenly realized how much he wanted her. His hands tightened on the wheel, gripping it harder until they turned white, trying to keep the car straight. Ellie moved her lips and pressed her cheek into his shoulder, with one bandaged hand lying on his neck. He allowed himself to think of them as a family: Ellie, Stacey, Josh. Yeah, he wanted Ellie, and he wanted the family part as well. His thoughts twisted back to the reason for this trip, something he could never allow himself to forget.

Someone else wanted them, too.

That's why we're here, Meredith thought bitterly.

"How far are we from Cassville?" Ellie asked. They had been driving for almost an hour. The road, a two-lane blacktop, rain-slick and narrow, twisted its way up the western slope of the coastal mountains. Meredith turned the wipers to slow.

"I think we have seven or eight miles to go. We turned onto the road to Cassville about ten minutes ago."

"Hope they have a good place for us to stay . . . like one big room," Ellie said huskily, a little shyly, searching Meredith's face.

"Well, there may be only one room for all of us."

"I wouldn't want it any other way," Ellie said, and she could feel her cheeks begin to burn. But she didn't care, dammit.

Meredith suddenly hit the brakes, swerved, and came to a stop in front of a mud slide. The road was almost blocked. He drove over on the left lane, and carefully guided the car around the rocks and mud, branches and small fir trees from the mountainside that had slid down upon the road. As it was, their tires crunched over the smaller pebbles, and then they were past it, picking up speed in the right lane.

"What if that were all the way across the highway?" Ellie asked.

"Well," Meredith said, "I guess that we would turn around and go to the coast. As far as I know, this is the only road into Cassville in the spring. Sheriff Robinson told me that there are some old logging roads that go up over the crest of the Coast Range mountains, but that they are impassable this time of year until late summer, and are not maintained."

"So if this road was closed, the sheriff and those people in Cassville would be stuck there?"

"It looks that way," Meredith said. "They would be stuck there at least until the road opened."

Ellie shivered. She suddenly felt cold, and drew her sweater tightly around her. She should get her jacket from the back seat.

"I was there once with Sheriff Robinson," Meredith said.

Ellie shook her head and turned to him. "What?"

"We have a couple of miles to a tunnel, and then about five or six miles on the other side of the tunnel to Cassville. Robinson says that the general store is in the center of town, and that this older couple, Deb and Jake Jacobsen, run the place. I guess Cassville used to be a booming lumber company town, but since the mill closed, the old store is operated primarily for the few people who still live there, and some fishermen and hunters who drop in. Even at this speed, we should be there in about twenty minutes."

Meredith stopped talking as they came around a long, sweeping curve to their left, and saw the mouth of the tunnel. They passed a sign that said TURN ON HEADLIGHTS, and came to another one that said BICYCLES IN TUNNEL WHEN LIGHTS FLASH. The tunnel swept downhill and made a gentle curve to the right so that you couldn't see the other end when you entered. It was almost a quarter of a mile long.

Ellie was somber, looking out at the gray cement sides of the tunnel. Even Stacey sensed the change in their surroundings as they entered, and stopped her singing. The headlights picked out the water running down the tunnel walls.

Meredith thought something was different. As they went into the curve a little further, he realized what it was.

The lights in the tunnel were out.

The last time that Meredith had been through, the tunnel had been lit up, so headlights weren't even necessary.

When they had cleared the last small slide, a mile or so back, it seemed to Meredith that the rain was slackening, and he'd boosted their speed to fifty. As he'd entered the tunnel, he had slowed to forty-five. It was a pretty good road at this point. Ellie was sitting leaning forward, gripping the dash with her right hand, and Meredith shot a glance at her.

"Meredith, there's something in the—!" she screamed.

He saw the blocked passage much too late. He jerked his foot off the gas as the car swept through the tunnel and through the curve to the right. The headlights glanced off the walls, sending up shadowy figures dancing past. The lights picked out things that shouldn't be there, rocks, boulders, large jagged pieces of cement.

They were still going forty when they hit the first of the rocks.

Meredith jerked the wheel savagely to the left to avoid a large chunk of cement that had fallen from the ceiling. The damned thing was as big as a compact car! The car went into a skid to the right, and Meredith heard Ellie scream and Stacey crying as he fought the wheel, the squealing tires and the gunshot sounds of the rocks hitting the car adding to the cacophony.

The car slid to the right, the front end heading for the left side of the tunnel. Meredith thought they had made it by the rock and was counter-steering to bring the front end back around when the back end hit with a sickening slam. It threw them all to the right, and Ellie's head struck the side window. The window shattered and showered her with glass.

"Hang on!" Meredith yelled.

The front end of the car twisted around again, Meredith fighting with the wheel, spinning it, trying for control, but unable to get traction on the mud and gravel. He stabbed the brakes. The headlights flashed across the tunnel in a wild shower of light, showing more boulders and a massive slide up ahead.

Blocked!

The goddamned thing was blocked, and they were still moving, fast, and Meredith thought of how ridiculous it was that they were now doing about twenty miles an hour, and that twenty usually seems so slow. They bounced off another good-sized rock that he didn't even see, and he jammed on the brakes. They slid forward, this time going in a looping skid to the left.

The car turned completely around, the bending metal screaming as it bounced over the narrow walkway, and the side of the car hit the wall, with Ellie's head inches from the cement wall flashing past the broken window.

The car came to a lurching stop, facing back toward the tunnel entrance. Both headlights were out, broken, Meredith guessed, and the engine was dead, hissing and ticking where water hit the manifold and exhaust and turned to steam.

Ellie!

She was slumped over facing forward. A trickle of blood was on her head. Meredith removed his shoulder harness, bent over Ellie, and gently took her head in his hands. She moaned and stirred, then opened her eyes to look at him, bewildered.

"Stacey!"

Ellie screamed and tried to twist around to see her daughter. Meredith's fear came to the surface, dark and powerful. He felt weak.

He looked behind them.

"She's all right. Put your head down for a minute." He could hear the water running somewhere, and thought that they might not have much time before the tunnel became a tomb.

Stacey was sobbing in the back seat. Rivulets of tears streamed down her face, and she looked first at her mother and then at Meredith. Meredith reached for her. She held her arms up and he pulled her into the front seat. She threw her arms around his neck before he could pull her all the way into his lap, her tears wet against his cheek. She tried to go to her mother, and he held her back.

He reached for Ellie, brushing her hair from her face with his hand.

"It's all right, it's all right," Meredith whispered to the child over and over again, watching Ellie. She was the one he was worried about. Ellie's eyes were open.

"Stacey!"

"Right here, she's fine," Meredith said calmly, although he felt anything but calm at this point. He struggled to get a grip on himself.

Stacey climbed into her mother's arms.

Meredith looked at the windshield, unable to see out into the dark, seeing himself in the mirror effect set up by the weak interior light.

They all flinched as more debris from the roof suddenly crashed to the pavement close to the car. Gravel and water hit the roof, and Meredith put his arms around Ellie and Stacey.

"We must be the first car through here. I mean, it must have happened a short time ago. I don't see any other cars . . . at least from this side."

"What are we going to do?" Ellie asked. Meredith heard the fear in her voice.

"Well, it's sure that we can't stay here; the damn roof may go at any time." And with his words, a large chunk let go, a chunk of cement as big as a truck tractor, Meredith thought. It sounded as if it were somewhere down the tunnel, toward the entrance. The tunnel shook, and pebbles and smaller chunks fell. It was as if a monster were stomping toward them, saying, "I'm coming and yoouuu messed up."

"Let's get out of here, now!" Ellie's voice shook. Meredith tried the ignition key again, in a last, futile effort.

Nothing.

The interior lights winked once, and went out.

"Mommy!" Stacey clutched her mother and screamed.

Meredith found his duffel and pulled it into the front seat. He felt the round smoothness of a flashlight, and turned it on, showing shadows and scared faces. His own frightened image stared back at him from the rearview mirror. At least something worked, he thought, as he left it on and sat it on the dash.

He began gathering their belongings. He pushed the door open and crawled around to the back of the car, crawling in water and grit, fighting off feelings of terror and claustrophobia. At the trunk, he moved rock and cement until he could get it open and get at their suitcases. He placed them in the road amid the debris from the ceiling, feeling his way with the light coming from the flashlight on the dash. Ellie's door was too close to the wall of the tunnel to open. Meredith felt his way around the front of the car and got back in.

Pieces of roof continued to fall. Stacey had stopped crying and was looking at Meredith with large eyes, when a large part of the ceiling fell close by, rocking the car. A flood of gravel fell on the roof. Meredith reached up and brushed Ellie's hair back from her face where the blood was beginning to coagulate. She winced as he touched her.

"You've got a hell of a goose egg here," he said softly. "You all right?" Their noses were almost touching, Stacey quiet between them.

"Yeah, it's just a bump." She cocked her head, listening. The tunnel continued to rumble. "But unless we get out of here pretty fast, the bump on my head won't matter at all."

Meredith agreed. He removed the flashlight from the dash, and they all got out the driver's side and stood beside the car. The gravel and mud on the pavement made the footing treacherous. Meredith moved the beam of the flashlight slowly around the walls and roof of the tunnel, the shadows and bouncing light a counterpoint to the ominous rumbling, which sounded much louder now, outside the car. Handing the flashlight to Ellie, he quickly removed Stacey's clothes from her small suitcase and added them to his own bag, the falling chunks of ceiling a constant reminder of the need to hurry.

Stacey was trembling and clinging to her mother's side. "Can you manage with her?" he asked Ellie.

She nodded, and they stood on a foot of mud and gravel while Ellie held the light on the muddy cement that blocked their way. Meredith started to climb over the debris, dragging his duffel and Ellie's suitcase behind him. The blockage was almost to the ceiling on the west side, but on the east side of the tunnel it looked as if they had only about eight or ten feet to climb over.

He started there. Water poured from the cracks in the ceiling. He motioned for Ellie, and she came up close behind, holding the flashlight and Stacey, the moving light casting leaping shadows on their tomb. A portion of the tunnel behind them suddenly collapsed, sending a shower of water and gravel down on them. Meredith threw the duffel and suitcase over the debris, pulling Ellie and Stacey next to him.

"Hold on to the light," he yelled, and lunged upward, until he realized that they were sliding down, looking at the fading light at the end of the tunnel. The tunnel rumbled again, the bowel of a monster grumbling for food. Meredith gathered Ellie and Stacey into his arms and they continued to slide down to the pavement, Meredith gritting his teeth against the stabbing pain in his knee.

Wincing, he stood on one leg, took the flashlight from Ellie and looked at the end of the tunnel. To his left, part of the wall had caved in, and as he flicked the light past, he saw a red fender and part of a bumper. There was a car buried in here!

A large part of the tunnel caved in somewhere behind them, making the pavement jump and the tunnel shudder. Monsters walking, Meredith thought wryly.

Gravel from above fell on them, making a crackling sound as it hit the pavement.

Ellie clutched at his arm, and said in a wavering voice, "Let's get out of here."

Meredith grabbed her arm and they ran for the end of the tunnel, Meredith limping badly and carrying Stacey. Ellie looked back and saw their bags at the bottom of the debris pile, and then they were out in the open air, the rain feeling cold and surprisingly good on their faces.

Meredith set Stacey down, and she put her left arm around her mother's leg, her right thumb in her mouth. They walked out until they were well clear, fifty yards or more, and then all three turned to look back.

They stood in the drizzle, and watched the mouth of the tunnel, as if they expected the monster inside to emerge and give chase. Meredith started limping back toward the exit.

"I'll be right back," he told them.

"The red car!"

"I'll check it, be right back." He turned to look at Ellie and Stacey, both shivering on the road. Have to get them inside soon, he thought. He didn't want to go back into the tunnel. But someone might just be alive in that car. And he felt now more than ever that he would need what he carried in his duffel bag, if they were to survive.

He turned back to look at them and walked into the maw of the rumbling, growling tunnel.

Meredith was filled with apprehension; the back of his neck hurt from the tension. He passed the red car and went directly to their bags and pulled them up. He came back to the car and saw that a large piece of tunnel had collapsed directly on it, smashing it like a sledgehammer on a toy.

He flashed the light in the opening where the driver's window had been, now distorted, the glass broken. A face grimaced at him, ugly in death, a bloody frozen rictus of fear, a sudden reminder of Meredith's own mortality as the tunnel continued to shake.

He moved on, toward the exit, thinking that it was important, this finding of the body, but he was too tired to figure it out. He hobbled quickly into the open, and looked back over his shoulder as if he were being chased.

Ellie's heart jumped and she realized how scared she was, for Meredith, for Stacey, and for herself, too. She had been pushing away the thought that she and Stacey might have to spend a night alone in the woods, the woods that she had already . . . the woods where she'd lain with death (*hey, ho, it's off to dig we go*), and the woods that she was looking at now—dark, threatening, close to the sides of the road.

Meredith limped up, the flashlight bouncing crazily as he lurched along. They both clutched him as he came to them, and they stood there, swaying.

He pulled back and picked up Stacey. He looked at Ellie from over the little girl's shoulder and shook his head from side to side.

No one alive.

"Meredith . . do we have to walk a long ways?" Stacey murmured.

"No, I don't think so, Honey," he told her gently, still looking at Ellie. "Last time I was here, I saw some cabins just around the corner."

"But what if there's nobody home?"

"Well, we'll just borrow the cabin, and leave some money, like a motel." He brushed the hood back from Stacey's face and pulled back to look at her with a smile and a big wink. "And I'll fix dinner, and your mommy can build a big fire, and we'll be toasty warm."

"How do you know if I can build a fire?" Ellie asked, joining in. "I'm from Arizona, you know. Most of the time we don't need fires."

"You were a girl scout, and they—"

"Sell cookies," she finished for him.

"Cookies!" Stacey yelled.

"See what you've done," Meredith said with a laugh. "Now one of us has to bake cookies tonight."

"Yay!" Stacey clapped her hands.

"How did you know I was a girl scout?"

"I could tell by the way you walk," he said. "Short legs from carrying all those cookies around."

"Thanks a lot!"

They stood in the rain.

Meredith set Stacey down, and removed two large ponchos from his duffel bag. He helped Ellie with one, and put one on himself. Then he picked up the duffel bag and suitcase.

"Come on, Stacey. Let's walk to the cabin." He leaned down so she could put her arms around his neck, and then straightened, willing his leg to move.

They set off, Ellie protesting about having nothing to carry, but not too hard. Three tired, hungry, cold—and scared—travelers, Ellie thought. In less than a quarter-mile, they saw a driveway that led to a cabin, a dark shape that was set off from the road by a stand of small fir trees, right there with the Altona river to its back, and the road in the front. The driveway was almost in sight of the area where Ellie was found by the logger, where she had slept with death.

And now she would spend another night in the woods.

CHAPTER 42

Ellie could tell by the way Meredith's shoulders sagged that he was weary. Who wouldn't be, with two others to care for, with the drive, the crash, the car he found in the tunnel, the rain, the cold, and all their gear? It would be easy to forget the real reason for being here; at this moment she just wanted some warm clothes and some food and a place to sleep. She didn't think that a person could get this tired and still move.

The driveway leading to the cabin was covered with fir cones, needles, and wind-blown branches. It looked deserted, as if no one had been here for a long time, possibly not all winter. The driveway—more like a path—curved down to the left, lined with thick stands of fir trees on each side.

Dark.

Wet.

Forbidding.

The face.

Ellie screamed, but the sound wouldn't come out. Meredith was walking up ahead, carrying Stacey, not looking back. The face was just inches now from hers in the trees on the right side of the driveway.

She froze.

Her heart stopped and then burst in her chest, beating madly. The bird with the rotted face settled on her shoulder, a dark shadow of death.

(*Hey!*)

(*Ho!*)

(*It's off to dig we go!*)

The darkness came up and washed over her as Meredith and the flashlight beam got farther and farther away, now twenty feet away, now thirty, the light wavering toward the cabin.

She had to scream, to warn them about the face.

She turned back to look at the face, not wanting to, the muscles creaking in her neck.

The killer.

And suddenly it was gone.

In its place, a bushy vine maple grew between the firs; the shadows within its leaves and branches looked like faces. The intended scream ended up as a whimper.

Meredith was a shadow himself in front of her now. At last he turned and looked, and saw Ellie frozen on the path, hunched over, her arms wrapped around her chest, trembling. He dropped the bags and hurried back, gripping Stacey to his chest, looking at Ellie's stricken face as they got to her.

"What is it, why did you . . . ?" he trailed off as he saw the look that she gave the woods, a look of terror.

"I just thought that I saw . . . a . . . a face in the woods. The face of the man who took me." A shiver passed through her.

Meredith looked into the darkness, shifting Stacey around so he could put his hand on the .45 under his coat. Nothing.

"I don't think that I really did see a person," she added weakly.

"Whether you did or not doesn't mean that the killer is not here somehow."

It came to him then—what had been bothering him since they left Arizona. Was the killer still running them, still ahead of them, still controlling them? He pushed the thought aside, trying to resist the fear that Ellie was feeling. *And why shouldn't she be scared? You certainly are, Meredith, old kid. She is very close to where she was taken by the killer.* He helped her to straighten up, still holding on to Stacey. "Let's go," he said gently. "If there was someone there, he's gone, and we can't stay here all night."

They were at the house before she saw it. It was a log cabin, with a long porch facing back down the driveway. Ellie could hear the river somewhere close, the muffled roar coming from behind the cabin.

Black water, she thought for no reason at all, black water, murmuring as it rushed past the bushes on the bank, black water (*stop it*) with hideous dead things (*stop it*) in it.

She shook her head as if to rid it of the thoughts and bumped into Meredith's back as he stopped.

They both listened. The rain continued, muted here in the trees, with drops hitting needles, old leaves, making a constant rustle that combined with the roar of the river to mask other sounds.

Meredith dropped the bags he was carrying, and the pain between his shoulders eased somewhat. Stacey stirred beneath his poncho. She didn't weigh much, but he had been holding her in the same position for the last fifteen minutes or so, and his arm had been a lump of pain for the past fourteen minutes. He had often seen parents carrying their children for long periods, kids that got tired at the zoo, kids that got tired of standing in line for tickets, kids that got tired shopping, and he never before realized that there was pain associated with the love that told a parent to carry this child.

I mean, just to see someone carry a kid, big deal, he thought. His arm said that it was.

Meredith went up the steps, and Ellie followed, zombie-like. He set the duffel down and shrugged out of his poncho while juggling Stacey.

The porch was dry. He handed Stacey to Ellie, and turned to try the door without ceremony.

No sense knocking; there were no lights on and no cars in the driveway. The door was solid, and looked like oak. There must be some type of bar inside, he thought. He removed his .45 from under his coat and walked to the window to the left of the door. He smashed the glass with the butt of the gun and reached inside and unlocked the window. He slid the sash up, feeling self-conscious, guilty. A thief. He crawled inside without hesitation and found the door locks, letting Ellie and Stacey in. Both were shaking with the cold.

Meredith directed his light around the cabin. There was one large room on the ground floor, and a sleeping loft above that ran the length of the cabin.

They stood just inside the door and watched as he moved the light around, Ellie ready to run if something bad happened, her heart beating fast. Run where? she thought.

Off to the right was an open kitchen, with a sink and hand pump, and a steel, airtight wood stove. Next to the kitchen there was a long picnic table, made from split logs, with matching benches. To their left was a couch and two easy chairs. The large, square room seemed to Meredith rather nice for a fishing cabin—as livable as a conventional house. And a fishing cabin was what he was sure it was, with the closeness to the river and the fishing tackle hanging from each wall. The light flashed over poles on hooks, an old wicker creel.

As the light moved, it left dark areas behind. Meredith brought the beam back to Ellie and Stacey. He walked to the picnic table, set the flashlight down, and picked up the largest of two lamps on the table. It was an Aladdin, a kerosene lamp with a round wick, capable of putting out as much light as a 60-watt bulb. There were matches next to it.

Meredith saw that the lamp was full of kerosene. He lifted the mantle, struck a match on the table surface, and lit the wick. The light instantly pushed back the shadows, and started to put out a surprising amount of heat. Ellie and Stacey, who had been watching from the doorway, walked across the room and stood behind Meredith. He moved to the wood stove, opened the door, and grunted with satisfaction when he saw that a fire had already been laid, with kindling stacked over an old copy of The Oregonian. Ellie and Stacey moved with him as he lit the fire. Ellie dropped to her knees beside him, and Stacey moved to the opposite side, watching the fire grow with her thumb in her mouth.

Meredith put his arms around them and drew them close. Within minutes, the fire began to warm the small cabin.

Ellie brightened visibly as the room warmed. Stacey ventured a few steps away and sat on a bench, watching the Aladdin lamp. Ellie stayed with Meredith, leaning against him. "Were you ever a boy scout?" she asked, content to be close and to watch the flames.

"As a matter of fact, I was."

"Well, you're a good scout to find this place," she said, and she slipped her arms around his neck.

"If you don't leave the good scout alone, he'll never get to do any good deeds, like . . ."

"Like helping ladies to keep warm."

"Like that, and drying them off."

"So what happens, good scout, if the lady gives you a kiss, like this?" Ellie said as she brushed her lips across Meredith's. Then she grabbed his head and kissed him hard, her tongue slipping suddenly into his mouth, surprising them both. Meredith twisted slightly to look at Stacey. She was watching the lamp, humming. They broke away, hugging.

"Can you work with this kind of help?" Ellie asked.

"Only . . . only," he said, his throat suddenly dry, "only if you don't stop."

"Oh," Ellie said sweetly, and they kissed again, and she hugged him tightly, her hands finding their way inside his shirt, touching his chest, sliding down to his stomach. She heard him gasp. She so wanted this man, to please him, to have him make love to her, to have him . . .

"Stacey," Meredith croaked.

Ellie stopped moving her hand. She whispered his name, the whisper sounding like a moan. Still holding on to him, she looked at her daughter, then pulled Meredith's head down and whispered into his ear. "I want you."

Meredith squeezed her and nodded.

She had said it matter-of-factly, and she did want him. She felt—no, she knew, dammit—that he wanted her. Meredith was letting his silly pride, his thoughts of her kidnapping, his job, get in the way.

They had almost been killed . . . all of them. And they still might be.

Soon.

They were surrounded by fear and death. Ellie knew now that love drives fear away. Love drives death away.

The lamp and the stove soon changed the cabin from a cold, alien place, to a warm, dry, cozy, and yes, even homey place.

Ellie went into the kitchen and began to open cupboards. Meredith picked up Stacey in his arms, and they inspected the cabin. "Let's go up there, Mer'dith," the little girl said. She pointed to the loft. Meredith pushed her up the ladder ahead of him.

"I wonder where they live," Ellie said as she continued to poke into the cupboards.

"Huh?" He looked down at Ellie.

"The people who own this," she continued. "I wonder where they live."

"Well, if you keep looking in the cupboards, I'm sure that you'll find out."

"I'm not looking for his address, dummy," Ellie said, grinning. Meredith returned the grin

"Which bed is mine?" Stacey asked. There was a twin bed on each side of the loft.

"Which one do you want?"

She pointed.

"Well, that's your bed." Meredith grabbed her and threw her down on the bed she'd chosen, tickling her as she bounced. She screamed with delight.

Ellie looked up at the loft from below, humming. She felt as if they could stay here forever. It was the first place that she'd really been happy in a long time.

Meredith and Stacey came back down the ladder. Stacey went to help her mom in the kitchen.

Meredith walked to the front door and locked it. He located a dustpan and a broom and swept up the glass on the floor, and then fastened the shutter as best as he could. It would keep the cold out, and the light would not show outside. The room was almost too warm now. Ellie was pulling out pans and had opened some cans of stew she had found in the cupboards. Meredith walked to the kitchen area and stood behind her. Her movements slowed as he reached for her, and she placed the cast iron pan she had been holding down on the counter.

She turned quickly and threw her arms around Meredith, feeling his arms come around her. She pressed herself to him, her face against his cheek, feeling his rough beard, feeling his body, his sudden hardness.

She'd always been in control of her life, even when she had been a single pregnant mother. But this was right, dammit, right for her, right for now. Meredith kissed her warm, wet lips. She slid her tongue into his mouth again to touch his, and that was almost their undoing, and it would have been if Stacey had been in bed.

They stayed like that for what seemed minutes, Ellie pressing her groin to his, her eyes tightly closed.

Meredith finally broke off, panting harshly.

"Wow!" he breathed.

"Double wow," Ellie said. She slid her hands down his back, and cupped his buttocks, feeling the muscles stiffen. Stacey was pulling cans out from a cupboard behind Ellie.

"You hungry?" Ellie asked him.

"Yeah."

"Food?"

"That, too," Meredith said, not trusting his voice.

"Why don't we fix some food," she said in a conspiratorial whisper, "and lock this place up tight, find Stacey a warm bed, and . . ”

“And then find us a warm bed."

213

"You may get a merit badge yet, Buster."

Cassville
CHAPTER
43

"I'm telling you, Sheriff, all we can do is wait for morning," Jake said. "They had to turn back like you were thinking. Road's probably out." The owner of the Jacobsen's General Store, tavern, post office, and service station was holding forth behind his tiny bar. He polished a glass and held it up to the ceiling light to check his progress.

"Bullshit," Robinson growled. "That girl is bringing her daughter up here with Meredith, the federal agent, the one I told you about. They shoulda been here hours ago." Robinson was leaning forward on the bar, his large stomach pushing into it. He had taken himself off duty hours ago. He took a sip of Black Velvet and peered at his watch.

"It's almost ten thirty, been dark for over thirty minutes, if you can call what we had today daylight, and I'm telling you that they should have called or got word to us somehow. I don't give a shit if your power is off—your generator's working, ain't it?" Robinson could hear its roar, muted to a muffled drone through the wind and rain, but the generator out back of Jake's place was on, all the same.

"I'm gonna go back down the road a ways, and see if I can get my radio to get through to the coast. Maybe I can raise the dispatcher or one of my deputies." Robinson tipped the glass up, drained it, and stepped away front the bar, half expecting to hear Jake argue with him, when the front door to the store opened. They heard Jake's wife, Deb, call to someone in the grocery part of the store, a room in front of the small bar. Since the bodies had been found, Jake and Deb had experienced a rush of media people, the just plain curious, and some others they classified as mentals. Cassville was the closest thing to civilization in the mountains, and it numbered only eleven full-time residents.

Robinson looked back at Jake as the voices reached them.
Charlie Heffner, one of the permanent residents, came in with Deb. He was weaving slightly, his face flushed with excitement and almost sixty years of the best booze he could buy.

"Road's closed," he croaked, and sat down in the chair nearest to the door, rain running off his slicker to puddle on the floor.

"Closed where?" the sheriff demanded. Jake was kinder, and knew from experience that he would have to prime the pump if they wanted Charlie to talk. He set a foaming mug in front of Charlie, who mumbled his thanks, and drained half of it with one long pull and backhanded the foam from his mouth.

"Closed at the tunnel, or," he cackled, "what used to be a tunnel. It's down. Flat." He slammed his hand down on the table. "*Whap*, just like that. Flat." Charlie shifted his gaze from the sheriff to Jake, who picked up the empty mug and brought Charlie another one. Jake considered running a tab on the old coot, but what the hell, he had to carry Charlie half the month now when the social security check got thin.

"How do you know this?" Robinson asked evenly, with the certainty that the news about the tunnel was not the end of what had been a bunch of shitty surprises this month. It was probably going to get a lot worse. A hell of a lot.

"Well sir," Charlie began, buoyed up by the first of several free beers he was sure to get from Jake this wet night, "well sir, I know cause Lindsey told me. She . . ."

Robinson looked up at Deb, raising his eyebrows, and mouthed "Who?" as he listened to Charlie.

"She's a young girl of about twenty-two or so," Deb answered softly. "Been staying here in one of the old cabins over the winter. We sometimes have her watch the store for us."

". . . drove back and told me straight away," Charlie was saying, and took a long pull on his second free beer of the evening.

Oh, Lordy, I may have to close early tonight, Jake thought, but hell, he never did lock out a resident, especially during a storm, and they all knew it.

Robinson pulled the chair out from the other side of Charlie's table, reversed it, and sat with his arms folded on the back, facing the old man.

"So, where can I find this girl, Lindsey, now?" Robinson asked.

Charlie Heffner took another pull on his beer. Maybe he could get another one before he answered the question.

Then he would be three up on old Jake, and anything could happen after that.

"Hi, everybody." The cheerful voice came from the entryway. Robinson turned to see a girl in her early twenties, with long straight brown hair, standing in the doorway. She was wearing Levis, hiking boots, a man's wool shirt, and a big green raincoat. She had a haunted look, as if she had been through a whole lot on the dark side of life, Robinson thought.

"Hi, honey," Deb said. "Come on in and get warm." She turned to Robinson. "This old coot here is Sheriff Robinson."

"Nice to meet you, Miss." He rose to shake her hand.

"Lindsey Odom." She glanced at Charlie and then looked back at Robinson. "Old Charlie tell you about the tunnel?"

"Yeah, when did you see it?"

"About a half hour ago."

Deb signaled to Lindsey. "Can l get anything for you, honey?"

"Yeah, thanks, maybe a Coke."

Robinson got up and got a chair for her. Deb returned with the Coke.

"Uh, Sheriff, there's something else about the tunnel," Lindsey told him. "I was going down to Newharbor to maybe have a beer at this tavern where some of my friends go, that's why I was out in this storm. But when I got to the tunnel, I could see that part of the roof was, well, had fallen in, and there was a car—"

"In the tunnel?"

"Yeah, well partway, by this end. But I didn't see anybody or anything."

"Could you tell what kind of a car?" he asked, thinking of Meredith, Ellie, and her daughter.

"Just a regular one, I think. A small one."

Robinson got up.

"Jake, I'd appreciate it if you would go with me."

Jake nodded. He had already taken off his apron and was getting a raincoat. Robinson turned to the girl.

"Could the car have been a rental?"

"I don't know . . . but it . . ."

"Go on."

"I think that it may have had someone in it, but it was all smashed, with parts of the tunnel on it and all. I just saw it with my lights when I turned back . . ."

"See anyone around?"

"No, no one."

Jake was waiting outside on the porch when the sheriff got there.

"Think it's them, the cop and the woman?" Jake asked, somber.

"Don't know."

They left the porch, bending against the rain, walking to Robinson's Blazer. They got in and both turned to look at the store as they drove past, the lights looking lonely in the rain.

"Think that fella who's doing all the killing is here?" Jake asked as they left town, following the boiling Altona River.

"Don't know," Robinson grunted. "He hasn't had the time to get here yet, but it sure as hell wouldn't surprise me."

"I mean here in Cassville."

"Why here, Jake?"

"Well, this is the closest place to where the bodies were found."

"There are other places that he could stay," Robinson said. "There are a lot of cabins on the Altona River, between Cassville and the tunnel, maybe thirty or more in all. Besides, if he ever stayed here in Cassville, you would know the killer."

Robinson drove slowly, the storm bending the tops of the firs, a hundred feet above the road, twisting branches, the forest alive with movement. The road was littered with fir boughs.

"Tell me, Jake, does Deb know how to shoot?"

"Better'n us, John, much better than us."

Robinson stopped the Blazer and Jake ran out into the rain to move a large branch from the road, then got back in the car.

"Looks like the storm in '64," Jake said. "All of the coast and most of the valleys were a lake for weeks. It's no wonder that the damn tunnel caved in. That old mountain will stay put for only so long."

Robinson nodded, working his pipe and the steering wheel.

On their right, the Altona River ran over its banks in some places, and getting through the tunnel was going to be a moot point, the sheriff thought. The damn river was going to wash the road out from here to Cassville.

He slowed, and approached the last turn before the tunnel, slow, cautious. There had been enough surprises in his county and he didn't need any more. He parked at the entrance, and they walked through to the smashed car.

Robinson shined his light through the broken window, and the corpse's face leapt up at him. He jumped back, the blood pounding in his stomach.

Quiet.

He didn't know her . . . maybe she was one of the reporters. He blew out his cheeks, realizing then that he had been holding his breath. The tunnel was a mess, and looked to be completely blocked. They were standing just inside the north entrance, out of the worst of the storm. He glanced up nervously at the ceiling of the tunnel, or at least what was left of the cement casing that covered the basalt. Water was dripping off the rocks, splattering on the roof of the car.

There was no way to get into the car now, and they were exposed to more falling cement and rock.

"Spooky in here, Sheriff," Jake said as he glanced around at the tunnel with the dripping ceiling, echoing the sheriff's thoughts. They walked quickly back to the Blazer, Robinson holding his aching stomach, thinking that he had seen just about enough bullshit in the past few days to last his entire career. On the trip back, Robinson told himself he should have retired last year. But the past years had been good to him, nothing like this to deal with, anyway. He sure wished to hell that he could get out now. Couldn't do it, though . . . not in the middle of this shit. As they parked in front of the store, Robinson thought he saw a flash high on the mountain above the town.

Couldn't be. Couldn't see that far in the rain anyway. It would take a huge fire to show that much light. It wasn't exactly fire season yet, with all the rain. He looked again and it was gone. He didn't say anything to Jake, and followed him into the store.

The Cabin
CHAPTER
44

The soft light of the kerosene lamp gave the loft a glowing, warm feel as Meredith and Ellie looked at Stacey's sleeping form. The beds had massive, handmade log frames, with colorful quilts covering the mattresses. A hooked rug was on the wooden floor, giving the loft a cozy, homey feeling.

Stacey had fallen asleep almost before their dinner of canned stew and biscuits was finished. Meredith completed a quick check of the outside area, and made the broken window more secure with the picnic table, while Ellie got Stacey ready for bed.

When he came back in, he had carefully unwrapped Ellie's hands, and washed them, wincing at the scarred fingers. Ellie made him pull his jeans down and she wrapped his knee in cold towels until the swelling appeared to go down somewhat. By the time they were finished, Stacey had fallen asleep on the couch.

Meredith had carried the sleeping child up the ladder. She was now sleeping on her stomach, with her knees drawn in a little, hands and arms sprawled out to her sides;hair falling across her face.

"She's slept like that since she was a baby," Ellie whispered. She carefully brushed the hair away from her daughter's face, letting her hand linger, caressing Stacey's cheek.

"She's a gorgeous little girl," Meredith whispered back. His voice wavered. God, he was nervous! They stayed there, bent over Stacey, not looking at each other, with their heads inches apart. Ellie grabbed his arm, and turned into him, still not looking. She pushed Meredith playfully backward, until his legs hit the other bed.

"Don't you think that it's time for us to go to sleep?" she asked.

"Do you think that we will—"

"Will what?"

"Sleep," he finished.

"Oh, eventually," Ellie said with a laugh, and pushed Meredith over onto the bed, and fell on top of him.

She began kissing him, and started to unbutton his shirt, the bandages causing her to fumble. She pulled it off his shoulders, keeping the kiss, and he shrugged out of it, feeling himself grow hard

220

in an instant. All the feelings that he had reserved, that he had denied, seemed to flow from him, and he knew that this was right, that Ellie was right, and he wanted her.

Ellie reached for his belt, opened the buckle, and tugged at his zipper. Meredith kicked off his boots; Ellie broke the kiss and pulled on Meredith's pants, and he arched his back to help her. He lay across the bed, and began fumbling with the buttons on Ellie's shirt as she leaned over to kiss him again, her breasts swaying over his chest.

Meredith pulled the shirt from her jeans; she moved her arms to help him take it off, and he pulled her bra off, opening the catch the first time.

"You're pretty handy with that, mister," she breathed.

"One-hand Meredith," he murmured.

She groaned as he slid his hands up and cupped her breasts, both nipples going hard, so hard they began to ache.

Meredith let go of her beautifully curved, small but firm breasts, and slid his hands down to work on her jeans. Ellie moved up away from him, and shucked her jeans off, pulling her panties with them, and opened the covers of the bed, all before Meredith could rise up. She slid into bed, under the blankets and sheet, with Meredith still on top of the comforter.

Ellie couldn't control her emotions. She was shaking and consumed with desire, with love for this tender man, and knew that it would be right. She held the blankets up as he slid off the bed, and slipped in under the covers on top of her.

They both groaned at once, as Meredith lay full-length on Ellie, both shaking, trembling.

He took her face in his hands and kissed her softly.

"Meredith, I . . ."

"Sssssh."

". . . love you."

He slid down and began kissing her throat, holding her breasts in his hands, softly circling her nipples with his fingers, and then took first one, then the other nipple into his mouth, sucking gently.

Ellie arched her back, and moaned loudly.

Meredith began kissing her stomach, and slid slowly down between her thighs. Ellie began shaking harder, wanting him inside her but not wanting him to stop. As his mouth began searching, she grabbed his head and pushed it down, feeling her cheeks burning, not caring.

If he touches me with his tongue, I'll come, she thought.

His tongue slid into her and Ellie released a gush of wetness. Her body was on fire, she was consumed, she could stand it no more.

"Oh God, Patrick," she whispered harshly, wanting to scream. "Patrick, my God." She wanted him in her and pulled him up.

As Meredith withdrew his tongue, he fought for control, then slid into her wetness.

She was so wonderful, so alive, and so full of love for him. He wanted her so much. Ellie gripped his back, pushing him into her, both panting as she reached down with both hands and cupped his buttocks, thrusting him deeper.

"Ellie!" he cried hoarsely. "Ellie, I'm—" He spurted into her, hot and long, feeling as if all of his body, his soul, was going into this woman, and she climaxed again, shattering, powerful, crying out his name. How long they stayed that way, holding each other as tight as they could, neither of them knew. They dozed, and when Meredith came awake, the lamp had burned low, a soft glow on the stand. He felt as if he were crushing Ellie.

"I'm too heavy," he said, and pushed up on his arms.

"Never," she said, pulling him back down on her. Meredith rolled over, holding Ellie in his arms, until she was on top. She sighed and laid her head on his chest, exhausted. Neither of them wanted to talk, just to hold each other, to keep out the dark, to keep the bogeyman away.

Ellie rose up a few inches, saw her daughter sleeping, and put her head back down on Meredith's chest. She dozed, her arms flung on his shoulders, her legs wrapped around his.

Meredith held her loosely, and drew the covers up around them. He felt warm, loved. He had never had someone love him with such abandon before, with such fierceness, with nothing held back.

Suddenly he wanted Ellie and Stacey away from this place. He wanted to protect them, wanted to protect their relationship, however new and fragile it might be. He didn't want them here with this madness.

The cabin had seemed like a good idea at the time, but he felt— no, knew—that somehow the killer hadn't screwed up.

They were being led again. He had to get them out. They would walk to Cassville in the morning. He was not going to put them at risk anymore. The sheriff could find a way out, even with the tunnel blocked. Meredith was sure that the old guy would know of a way and probably had a search team coming in on a back road, a logging road of some kind.

They weren't staying. That was that. Reflexively he held Ellie tighter. She moved slightly, and pushed a foot out from under the covers. She sighed, and was still.

He looked at Stacey and Ellie in the soft light of the lamp, and was afraid. More scared than he had ever been for himself.

Carefully sliding halfway out from under Ellie, he blew out the light, then lay back and listened to the rain hitting the roof, trying to pick out any other sounds.

He didn't hear any.

The trunk of the fir tree was dry, even with the tremendous amount of rain that had fallen in the mountains. The boughs came down almost to the ground. Thomas Brunson pushed the branches apart, and stepped out into the rain. He tipped his face up and let the drops hit his face, blinking when they hit his eyes. He looked toward the cabin, just twenty feet in front of him, and saw the lamp go out.

Sleep well, my dears. You will sleep on my mountain.
Soon.

He smiled.

The cop was different. He would be dead long before the lovely and her daughter got to the mountain.

Brunson turned and moved down the path to the highway. It was still early, and he had more to do, and the night was his time.

223

Above Cassville
CHAPTER
45

Dawn broke on the mountain, the air heavy with the falling rain and the ever-present mist that shrouded the trees. It was quiet; the only sound that reached Thomas Brunson was the rustling of the brush and fir trees. He had just crawled through the passageway in the rocks and was standing looking down on the plateau, looking at his lovelies and the remnants of the fire he had started the evening before.

He turned his face upward, and stared unblinking at the raindrops.

He smiled.

His breathing slowed and he stood transfixed, a sentinel to the grisly scene that he had arranged below him.

The rain washed his face, and for a moment cooled the desires that raged. The upward-tilting face mirrored those arranged below. They were also staring up, unblinking in the rain, being cleansed.

His lovelies.

Suddenly he was eight years old again, standing in the rain, waiting for Cherry to be through. He put his hand out to touch the side of the trailer, her trailer, his fingers brushing the rocks beside him instead of cold metal. Thomas jerked his head down, and brought his hand up slowly to examine it, as if it might not be there.

The trailer was gone.

Cherry was gone.

She was here with his lovelies. After all, they were for her. He went down and sat with his lovelies, watching the rain with them. After a time, they spoke to him, his moss-covered skulls, teeth clicking like reptilian mandibles, telling him of dark things to come.

THURSDAY
JULY
6

The Cabin
CHAPTER
46

A sudden gust of wind blew a shutter against the cabin, and Meredith came awake with a start. He couldn't tell what time it was in the dim light of the loft, but it was dawn outside, grey, wet. The storm hadn't diminished, only gotten stronger, with more rain.

The small single bed in the corner of the loft that Stacey had been in was empty. He rose halfway up and heard her humming; the sound was coming from below, on the ground floor of the cabin. Ellie was curled, up, her back to Meredith, her arms around her pillow.

He looked at her sleeping form, and his feelings for her were no longer to be denied. He could tell her now. The shutter banged again, wind-driven into the side of the cabin, and he relaxed, and slid down deeper into the bed, under the comforter. Meredith turned on his side, and pulled his knees up behind Ellie's, and held her, warm with sleep, as she came awake. Her eyes opened slightly, and she gave Meredith a sleepy smile, rolled over, and put her arms around his neck. She pulled him down on top of her, snuggling against him, moving slowly.

"Your daughter, mmph."

Ellie kissed him, and he pulled his face up.

"Your daughter, she's up."

"That's nice," Ellie whispered. "C'mere."

"Love to. Let's check on her."

"Stacey," Ellie called. "What are you doing, Hon?"

The humming stopped. "Looking at the fish poles—is it okay, Mom?"

"Sure, Hon, we'll be down in a minute . . . okay?" Ellie barely managed the last few words, with Meredith moving on top of her. They heard the rattle of a pole in the rack.

"What's this?" Ellie asked softly, and slid her hand down Meredith's stomach until she touched him. Meredith squeezed her breasts with his free hand, propping himself up above her.

"Stacey!" he whispered.

"She's fine," Ellie whispered back, lips kissing his ear, as she pushed him down by his shoulders. She opened her legs for him, and he slid into her.

226

They quietly made love, carefully, tenderly, exploring each other's body, and chased away the demons.

After a while the voice from below brought them back to where they were.

"Hey you guys, anybody hungry?"

They stood in the driveway and looked back at the place where they'd spent the night so cozily. Meredith had left a note and some money for the owner of the cabin.

Ellie looked radiant in her hooded raincoat and jeans. Meredith would always remember her that way, the expectant yet wistful look on her face, the weak light shining through the clouds a welcome relief from the darkness and pouring rain of the early morning.

The rain had stopped, but the wind had picked up, and as Meredith looked at the overcast sky, he knew that they were in for the worst part of the storm before the day was out. But they should be able to get to Cassville before then.

"Meredith," Ellie said as she turned away from the cabin, "let's find the owner and see if we can come back here again."

"Sure."

They started off, with Meredith holding Stacey's hand, and Ellie walking alongside, and in spite of the reasons for being here, their spirits adventuresome. Meredith had decided to leave the bags, thinking that he could come back for them with Sheriff Robinson's Blazer when they got to Cassville. He kept the Sig Sauer .45 in a belt holster, concealed under his coat. When they reached the road, the blacktop was covered with windblown needles and branches from the fir trees that were close in. The trees, some of them over 100 feet tall, had branches that in some places almost touched overhead, making the road a blowing, creaking tunnel. They walked down the center, letting the wind blow them when they were going directly west. It was ten thirty when they left, and Meredith thought that it would take them two hours to reach Cassville.

They walked into Cassville at one o'clock, with Meredith limping badly, getting worried looks from Ellie. Meredith had carried Stacey most of the way. They found the sheriff at the store, helping Jake with some kerosene lamps. Deb made a fuss over Ellie and Stacey, taking them upstairs to the living quarters above the store, leaving Meredith with Sheriff Robinson and her husband.

"Hell, I thought you might be in the tunnel," Robinson said, relief showing in his face as he led Meredith to a chair. Meredith sat down and gingerly put his leg up on another chair. An old man and a young woman watched him from the bar. When he was settled, he told the men of their journey, and somehow felt better to be in the company of Robinson, this kind and good man who was sheriff and friend.

As Meredith talked, Robinson thought bitterly that he had been right all along. Things were going to get worse before they got better, and he could have retired last year.

As it was, he had only hours to live.

Sky Harbor Airport, Phoenix
CHAPTER
47

The General Dynamics Fl 6B Fighting Falcon jet fighter roared smoothly into the air, Detective Sergeant Dennis Patterson wishing from the back seat that he could have had more time with the instructions. The pilot, Lt. Col. Victor Rand, was based in Tucson with the Arizona Air National Guard. He called to Patterson from the front seat,

"You all right back there?"

"Yeah." Patterson found his voice a little shaky, although, unlike Meredith, he loved to fly. The Governor s office had come through with the promised assistance. Patterson's flight with the air guard was a result of the cooperation the National Guard had extended to the Phoenix Police Department in the kidnapping cases.

They went airborne at one-thirty, and only a few minutes later, with the ground falling away at an astonishing rate, the Falcon was already four miles high and still climbing. They would be at Travis AFB, north of San Francisco, in less than half the time it would take a commercial airliner to fly the distance.

"Hey, Colonel," Patterson spoke through his oxygen mask into the intercom.

"Forget the Colonel, call me Vic."

"Okay, Vic it is. Will you be doing any scary stuff, like rolls and fast turns?"

"Not cleared for it on this flight, but look me up when you get back and we'll go for another ride. My orders are to get you to Portland as quick as I can without burning up this old crate."

"Thanks, but I'll pass," Patterson told him. There wasn't much to do now but wait for the flight to end. He looked over the electronic gadgetry used by the weapons-systems operator, and then out at the wings, wincing at the harsh sun on the canopy. He knew that he would have enjoyed the flight a hell of a lot more had they found the Cochran girl alive.

A Maricopa County Sheriff's Deputy had found the van in mid-morning, left in a dry wash gully fifteen miles southeast of the airport. Patricia Cochran's body was in it, and word of her death reached

Patterson about an hour after he had told her family that they had a good chance of finding her abductor before he reached Oregon.

Phoenix was once again in a state of panic. As the lab techs began to process the van, it was clear to Patterson that the son-of-a-bitch had set them up again. He had attempted to reach Meredith and the sheriff up in Oregon, and learned that the sheriff's own office had been unable to contact anyone in Cassville since the evening before. A tunnel cave-in? Bullshit! Patterson thought. He didn't believe in coincidence. He had been on his way to the crime scene when he was recalled to the office and told to get his large ass to the airport and north.

He was more worried about that little girl and her mother than he was willing to admit.

They landed at Travis Air Force Base for fuel and then flew on to Portland. Colonel Rand gave Patterson a couple of quick turns and a smooth landing. They followed a jeep to a parking area, and Rand helped Patterson out of his seat and led him down from the plane. They walked quickly to a locker room, where Rand-helped Patterson change out of the g-suit he had been wearing.

"You get that bastard for us, Sergeant Patterson," Rand said quietly, "and you can ride with me as many times as you want."

A blue and white twin-engine was waiting for Patterson. He strapped himself into the seat beside the pilot as the plane started to roll. The pilot introduced himself.

"We're gonna try to land at a tight-assed little airport down the coast in Newharbor in a little while," he said. "And there's a hell of a storm coming in off the coast."

"We'll make it though, right?" Patterson said.

"Like I said, it's a tight-assed airport in the best of times. I don't even know if I can find the damned thing in a storm. We might have to turn back."

"We'll find the airport," Patterson said grimly. He felt more than ever that he would be needed in Cassville.

Soon.

Cassville

CHAPTER
48

Ellie and Stacey inspected the store, with Ellie remembering little from her earlier trip here. She took Deb up on her offer of a hot shower, and she and Stacey clambered up the stairs, with Deb following.

Jake lit a fire in the stove, seeming out of place for July, but it felt good. Meredith edged his chair closer to the stove. The old man, Charlie Heffner, sat a table away, slurping a beer. The girl, Lindsey, was making sandwiches at the end of the bar. Robinson came in, shaking water from his raincoat. He'd left almost immediately for the cabin to get their suitcases. Jake followed.

"Now tell us what really happened," Robinson said. He pulled a chair up next to Meredith's table; Jake stood at his side.

"There was a car in the tunnel," Meredith said, "with a dead woman in it."

"Yeah, we saw the same woman," Robinson said.

"We're supposed to sit tight here," the sheriff told them. "The Oregon State Police and the FBI are going to put up roadblocks—more than we've ever seen before—and they tell me that the bastard will never get past the tunnel."

"Hell," Jake said. "Nobody will get to us for a week. The whole damned mountain is slippin' and slidin', moving roads and creek beds. We have plenty of food and booze and gas for the generator." At the mention of booze, Charlie Heffner raised his glass in a salute, and drained it. "Me and Deb weren't planning on going anywhere this time of year anyway."

"That tunnel collapse is gonna screw up our search," Robinson said. Lindsey brought three bottles of beer over to the table.

"Maybe," Meredith said. He grunted with pain as he reached for a bottle and took a drink. "Ellie might be able to locate, to remember where she was taken . . . and save us a lot of time."

Robinson nodded. He glanced at Jake, who had walked behind his bar.

"Why here, Sheriff, why? What did we ever do to have these girls end up here?" Jake polished the bar vigorously with his rag, anger showing in his face. Lindsey nodded her agreement from the end of the bar. She had been at the store since morning, with nothing else to do. She looked scared.

They spent the afternoon and early evening in the bar. Meredith and Ellie put ice on his swollen knee. Stacey made friends.

Charlie Heffner suddenly stood and knocked his chair over with a crash. "Let's go get them mothers!" he yelled. It came out more like, "Lesh go get them mushhherrrs," but by then everyone in the little tavern had heard him long enough that they could understand him.

"Charlie, you want some help?" Jake asked, as he came around the bar.

"Nope, can do 'er myself." Charlie staggered and put out his hand to steady himself against the table. He struggled into his rain slicker and waved to the two of them at the bar.

"Hey, what's everybody doing?" Stacey interrupted, as she ran into the room, and launched herself at Meredith. He lifted her up, grinning, put a. kiss on her forehead, and sat her on the table, facing the room. "Well, we're waiting for you to come in and tell us what you've been up to." He gave her an affectionate hug, and she hugged him back. She was wearing a light blue flannel nightgown, her blond hair wet on her shoulders.

"They can tell you, Meredith!" Stacey yelled, pointing to the doorway at Deb and Ellie.

"We've been finding a place for Stacey to sleep," Deb said.

"And I have my own little room," Stacey said excitedly, "with a bed and a doll, and my own dresser, and—"

"Speaking of sleep, it's time for bed. Say goodnight, Stacey," Ellie told her daughter. She gave Meredith a concerned look, glancing at his propped-up knee.

"No, Mom!" Stacey wailed. She turned to Meredith. "Tell her no. Meredith . . . help me," she pleaded.

"I can't, Honey," he said with a smile. "Your mom, she's bigger than me."

Ellie plucked her daughter from the table.

"No! Mom! Mer'dith! Help!"

Ellie turned and planted a kiss on Meredith's mouth before he could move, and then took Stacey out the door and into the store. A declaration, Meredith thought, as Robinson gave him a curious look.

"Help! Somebody!" came Stacey's voice.

They heard Ellie say sternly, "Stacey, that's enough, now!"

Charlie wobbled to the doorway, and braced himself against the door frame.

"Hey, bub, take it easy," Lindsey called quietly from the bar, where she was sipping coffee. The kinship of outcasts, Meredith thought, hearing the warmth in her voice for the old man.

Charlie stopped, and came back to the bar, grinning at the girl. Lindsey suddenly walked behind the bar and drew a beer for Charlie, looking at Jake for approval. Jake looked at her and groaned. Charlie was drunk, no, he was staggering. But what the hell, these were strange times. He nodded his head at Lindsey, and stood at the end of the bar. Lindsey put the beer mug in front of Charlie and put her hand on his, looking into his veined eyes, and said quietly, "So how's it with you today, bub?"

"I'm fine darlin'. I jus' need another beer." He leaned forward, and brought his beer-flushed face up close to Lindsey's, and whispered, "If I was even ten years younger, I'd be taking you out of here to an easy life." He took a pull on the mug, draining the top half effortlessly.

"Sure you would, bub," Lindsey said, patting his hand, "but you wouldn't have to be ten years younger." It was a gracious lie, and they both knew it. Hell, they all knew it, but it warmed him. He grinned at her, face flushed, and jerked the mug to his mouth.

"Lindsey." He pronounced it `indsey' but it was close enough for them. "Lindsey," he began again, "if you ever need anything, anything at all, money, a shoulder, whatever . . . from this old . . . drunk . . . you know where to come." He finished the words with a rush and a wet belch.

"Don't you think I know that, bub? Finish your beer." She leaned over and kissed the top of his head. Jake turned on some more lights, causing the generator out back to take on a deeper rumble. It was getting very dark outside. Charlie loudly said his goodbyes as Ellie came back into the bar. He weaved his way out to the front door, and opened it against the rain.

They heard the door close, and listened to his steps leave the wooden porch.

"Think he'll be all right, Jake?" Deb asked. "I really think that all of us should stay here in the store, with that nut around, maybe close by." She shivered, and moved nearer to her husband.

"He should be fine," Jake said. "I'll go over to his cabin and check on him later. Anyway, from what Mr. Meredith says, the earliest the killer could be here is tonight . . . and the tunnel has been out since yesterday. We should be fine . . . right?"

Charlie Heffner stumbled, caught himself, and moved carefully around the post on the porch of the store. He hunched over as he met the wind-driven rain, and stopped as he came to the blacktop, fifteen feet in front of the store. He looked cautiously both ways for traffic, forgetting that there could be no traffic with the tunnel down and all.

Lindsey cleaned off the bar with a towel, anxious to do something. She suddenly decided to go home, and went into the back room to get her coat. If she told them that she was going home, they would insist on going with her. But she could do it alone.

She found a flashlight at the back door, and put on her raincoat and slipped out. The rain hit her, and since the lights from the bar did not come through the back windows, the darkness was total. For a moment she was disoriented. She put her hand on the side of the building, and followed it around the corner, trying not to think about what they were saying inside, about what that man was doing to women. He couldn't be here, they said, and she wanted to (wanted to, shit—needed to) get to her shack and take a few bomber puffs of some righteous (can you gimme hallelujah) home-grown that could lift her soul like the best Maui bud.

Something to calm her nerves.

She didn't particularly like strangers, and wasn't at all that keen about staying in the store, but she knew that she wouldn't be able to sleep in her little shack until the asshole was caught.

She got to the front of the store, and the lights from the windows lit up the road partway.

A shadow suddenly moved in front of her, and the sudden jolt was enough for her heart to stop beating. She gave a little cry.

Run!

Have to run!

Get out of here, girl, get back inside, she thought, and then she realized that it must be just Charlie, old Charlie. Boy would she give him hell for scaring her like that, and she relaxed to the point that she almost fainted. She felt a trickle of urine in her pants and chuckled. Nothing like pissing in your panties, Lindsey.

She started to move on, breathing out slowly, her heart hammering now, and a hand suddenly clamped around her mouth, and then her bladder did let go, and she couldn't breathe . . . she . . . couldn't scream. . . .

Charlie Heffner waited and watched the darkened, silent road. He decided at last that there were no cars coming, and started off with a lurch, like someone had just popped the clutch on an old pickup truck, and zigzagged diagonally across the highway, taking a bearing on the other side of the road. Halfway across, he staggered backwards and caught his balance, only to lose it completely a second later. He fell in slow motion, with a kind of loosening of his joints, a liquid fall that only drunks can achieve. He looked up for the light. He usually took a bearing on the white mercury light down at the corner where Moffitt's Union Station used to be. When the mill had shut down, Moffitt's closed, too, but the light had remained, with Jake paying for the electricity so he could light up the corner where he had some old trailers parked.

The light was out, the electricity a victim of the storm..

Well, to hell with it, Charlie thought. He didn't need the shit anyway. He had stumbled home to his little cabin often enough to get there blind. Or blind drunk.

"Wouldn't do to let old Sheriff Robinson catch me laying here, tits up in the middle of the damn highway," Charlie muttered to himself, the soft sounds barely audible in the falling rain. Charlie talked to himself no more or no less than anyone who spends too much time alone. He sometimes reminded himself that soliloquy was natural, and if it wasn't, who gave a damn anyway. After all, he was seventy.

He had a single goal now—to get home under his own power to a bottle of Jack Daniels he'd stashed away. All that talk in the bar about people missing. They don't pay much attention to old Charlie, he thought. They don't think that old Charlie listens, but he does. We sure don't need this kind of goings-on here. All we want to do, partner, is fish a little, screw a little—for those who still can, he laughed at the thought—and collect your social security—if those turds in Washington don't cut it off.

Not far to the old J.D., Charlie told himself. Yessir, that old bottle of Jack Daniels smooth Kentucky bourbon is going to go down mighty nice . . .

These thoughts took him to the back of the closed gas station, near where Jake had four old trailers parked, the eight-foot-wide ones that he rented to hunters and fishermen in season. Charlie had an old cabin on the river, about a hundred yards from the trailers.

Coming up on Lindsey's house. Not really her house, but an old shack that Jake let her stay in probably rent-free, Charlie thought, knowing Jake for the softie that he was.

Goddamn it was dark. He looked back the way he had come, and could see the lights flickering in the windows of the store, a long way off now, looking more lonely than homey. The rain continued to come down softly. Charlie didn't mind, it wasn't that cold, and was comforting in a way, and it cleared his head a little for the task at hand—getting to the bottle of J.D.

Hell, you couldn't live in the Coast Range, at least not on the windward side, without an appreciation of that liquid sunshine. A slow trickle had started down his back, but he shuffled resolutely on.

Not far now.

He continued across the weed-filled lot behind the old service station.

What the hell was that up ahead? Charlie peered into the darkness, trying to push the fog from his brain, trying to see what that was.

He stopped. He definitely saw something up ahead, next to Lindsey's shack.

Someone moving.

Something weaving.

"Nah, bullshit," he said, aloud this time.

The image was gone. Charlie moved forward, legs weaker now, shaking with fear and years of booze.

He saw it again, this time out of the corner of his left eye. He turned quickly, and lost the precarious balance that he had maintained since his fall on the road.

He fell in the wet gravel, the practiced fall of someone who's spent a lifetime falling.

Someone out there, Charlie. Nope!

Get outa this puddle, he thought. He pulled himself up into a sitting position, then rocked forward, and slowly, the years of practice paying off, got to his feet. He stood there, swaying, uncertain, and thought that maybe he should go back to the store, and maybe Jake would have some whiskey that he would part with.

Hell, old Charlie'd even pay for it.

The sounds of the Altona River reached him, somewhere close to his right, sounds ominous to him in the dark, sounds of the water as it swept over rocks and in some places the bank, pulling on trees and brush in its way . . . scary sounds . . . sounds that chilled an old man's bones.

Charlie stood swaying. He thought that he saw something down by his front porch. He turned, his mind made up. He would tell Jake and the others that he couldn't get his oil lamp to burning. He walked faster now, the thought of the Jack Daniels at home pushing away the fear, warming him the way a woman would have twenty years ago. Or fifty years ago, when he was in the barracks. "Right face!" he shouted, and executed the turn as if he were on the parade ground at Scofield Barracks. A near-perfect execution of the turn brought Charlie within sight of the store, the lamps still going.

He began to trot. He could see someone, that Meredith fella, he thought, walk up to the window of the store and peer out at the darkness.

"Shit."

Charlie fell down, hard. He sat up, bewildered, and began to feel his way around the gravel, looking for a purchase on the wet ground, just across the highway from the store. He slipped, and rolled on his side, and saw a blurry something just inches from his face.

Too close.

Couldn't focus.

The rain rolled down his back now, a river instead of a trickle. Charlie shivered. He started to get up again, and his eyes came into focus on the object on the ground.

He stared into the lifeless eyes of Lindsey Odom, or what was left of her eyes.

He put his hand out, slipping in her blood. She was lying on the gravel, on her back, with her feet pointed down the slope of the highway shoulder, head pointed toward the store. If it was daylight, you would have been able to see her from the bar. Charlie moaned, not heard by anyone in the store, a high, keening sound lost in the wind and rain. He got up, his vision blurred by the fall and the enormous amounts of booze he had consumed on this day, his last.

Thomas Brunson walked up behind Charlie, grabbed his shoulder, and spun him around, peering into the fogged eyes of the old man.

Brunson was grinning, rain running off his face like slobber, with the dim, flickering light from the store giving him a hideous, evil face, a face that reeked of death. He had traveled a lot of shadowland roads to be here, to fulfill his desires, to tend his garden.

Fear struck Charlie like a plunge in the nearby Altona River— cold . . . icy.

You've seen death before, he thought. Yes you have, old Charlie, and you are looking at the horned old son-of-a-bitch right now. He was as sober as he would ever be again. The fog was gone now, and he risked a glance at the store, and saw that they were all at the bar, just across the road, with their backs to him, all except Jake, and he couldn't see out in the dark. Brunson followed his glance, and shook his head from side to side, the grin getting bigger. It reminded Charlie of a story he had read about climbers who were lost on Mount Hood. The climbers were camped on an icy ledge, near death, watching the lights of Timberline Lodge far below, imagining the laughter in the lounge, almost hearing the clink of ice in the cocktail glasses.

So close.

Too far.

Like the lights of the store across the street.

Yeah, I've seen old death, Charlie thought. Hell, I saw enough on the seventh of December to last me a . . . Brunson brought the knife up fast and caught him in the throat, grabbing the hair at the back of Charlie's head with his other hand to hold him upright.

Charlie tried to scream, to warn them, and all he wanted was a sip of old Jake's bottle of fine Kaintuck sipping whiskey, old Jack Daniels hisself, and . . .

The knife slammed into his neck again and again, his blood gushing out, pouring on the ground, mixing with the uncaring Lindsey's.

Brunson grabbed Charlie by the shoulders and spun him around, giving him a violent push, Charlie then a grotesque walking dead man, a staggering dead man, discarded.

Brunson was already walking across the road with his eyes on the window as Charlie fell in the dark.

238

He absently wiped his knife on his leg and placed it in a sheath. He touched the Beretta in his coat pocket as he waited by the corner of the store.

Newharbor Airport
CHAPTER 49

"I'll settle for a dirt road if we can find the damned thing!" Williams shouted. Patterson looked out of his rain-streaked side window at the fog, fog so thick that he wouldn't even want to drive a car in it. Eight-thirty at night and where'd the fog come from—in Phoenix the temperatures would be over one hundred, he thought. They had been circling out over the Pacific Ocean, catching an occasional glimpse of the town of Newharbor, and then Williams would shoot inland, up the hill, attempting to find the airport. They were still shaken over that last attempt, an attempt that ended with Patterson screaming Lookout, lookout! Shapes of trees came through the fog at them, with no airport in sight.

His mission forgotten, the Phoenix detective strained to see through the window, looking for anything but fog. Williams must have his eyes punched back into his head, Patterson thought. The pilot had the throttle back and flaps down, drifting over fir trees that they must be clearing by just inches.

"There!" Williams yelled, pointing down to his left. He punched the throttle halfway forward and pulled the wheel back, climbing into a turn to the left, a turn that would bring them out over the town.

Patterson grabbed his seat belt and pulled it even tighter, like a weight lifter cinching up his kidney belt for a record attempt.

Williams circled around and dropped down again, flying by experience alone. He couldn't see a damn thing. He gave it a little more throttle, and dropped onto the paved runway. He stepped on the brakes, throwing up a shroud of spray behind them.

Patterson had expected to be met by a Deputy Sheriff of Adams County, but there were no patrol cars at the airport, only an ambulance. He shook his head at Williams and grinned, and then trotted through a downpour of rain. The medic was waiting in the office.

"I'm Reggie Stewart," he said as he extended his large brown hand. "I'll take you to the courthouse, and we got no time to waste if we want to save those folks."

They ran to the ambulance as the twin-engine Cessna began its takeoff roll.

Cassville

CHAPTER 50

Thomas Brunson shifted his position by the corner of the store, occasionally glancing at the dark shapes in the street. He shifted and pulled the slicker around his head. The people in the store—they thought they were so safe.

He had watched hundreds of times before, since he was eight years old, and no one had ever caught him.

Watching people from the outside.

Warm inside.

Cold out here.

He knew that he could bring them outside at any time, outside to be cold with him, to meet the lovelies, and he would bring them out very soon now.

He had been waiting for over two hours to see one very special person, a little girl.

Where was she?

Her mother, the lovely who knew him, was there, sitting on a table, laughing.

The pain hit him right up on the top of his forehead. Mother and daughter would like his lovelies. In fact, he would give them a special spot, and then—

Hey Thomas, whyncha sit on yer fist . . .

The voice slammed into his forehead, just behind the pain.

Hey Thomas, bend over, I'm drivin ' . . .

The laughter came up behind him and he whirled around, his fists clenched, to find no one in the alley, just him and the rain and wind.

He watched as inside the tavern the federal cop said something to a little girl, and she laughed, looking as if she had a long time to live.

Laugh, you little whore, he thought. You laugh, too, Cherry/Ellie, you mother cunt. I'll bring you out into the rain where the lovelies are.

With us. Then laugh.

Or scream.

Make all the noise you want. The lovelies are a good audience. Then you watch as I bring your mom. (*Cherry/Ellie?*) up to the mountain. The cops, the old fat sheriff, the federal cop . . . they'll all be gone.

Hey Thom—

He shut the voices out. He was more powerful now. He left the alley, less than a shadow. Someone could have walked by on the sidewalk and not noticed him.

He was good in the night.

He was invisible in the rain.

"Where's Lindsey?" Jake asked suddenly, cutting off the conversation between the sheriff and Meredith.

"Haven't seen her for the last half hour or so," Meredith said, and looked over at the table where Deb and Ellie were seated, looking at a Sears catalogue, sipping on some of Deb's Irish coffee.

Jake moved out from behind the counter, and walked back to the storeroom. "Her coat's gone," he called out to the others.

"Shit," Robinson swore under his breath. Jake came back into the bar. He looked at Deb. "She say anything to you about going home?"

"No, nothing. She probably just went to get some more clothes."

Meredith and the sheriff were already off their stools, putting on their raincoats. Jake joined them with a large square lantern. "She's been staying at the old Burke house, the one just past the old Moffitt Union Station."

Robinson nodded.

"I'm staying here," Jake said, and they noticed that he held an army Colt .45 automatic in his right hand.

Meredith and the sheriff walked through the darkened store to the front door, where they stood looking out at the darkness.

"I don't mind telling you, Pat, I don't like this one little bit," Robinson said softly. Ellie came up behind them.

"What's that light?"

Meredith saw it then, looking through the rain. There it was again! A flicker off to the right—no, more than that, it was a high flame, dying out, then leaping. Sheriff Robinson pulled open the door and they stepped out onto the porch, with Ellie, Deb, and finally Jake, crowding out behind them.

The flame spurted up, a block away and across the highway, casting an ethereal shadow over the drenched landscape, and it reminded Meredith of a dark occult ceremony, with black-robed figures dancing around flames.

242

A flickering strobe light from hell.

"It's the old Moffitt Union Station," Jake shouted at them, the wind and rain sweeping onto the porch, throwing the words at them in snatches. The sheriff and Meredith left the security of the porch, bending over against the wind and rain that hit them instantly. Meredith gasped as the rain hit his face. He didn't see the explosion until Robinson caught his arm. They both stopped then, and watched as a large flame flared up from the old pump island, lighting up the entire block. They were now less than 100 yards from the old station, and Meredith could see in detail the small orange "Union 76" globes that had been the trademark for years.

Ellie ran up to stand beside him , a small figure in a hooded coat, silent, watching. It suddenly occurred to Meredith—and, he imagined, the sheriff, too—that they were standing close to a burning gas station, too close, and the fire could, hell, probably would, burn down Jake's store as well.

"Can't be any gas in those tanks down there," Jake said as he came up behind the men, putting to rest Meredith's immediate fear. "The fire musta been started by someone."

"How do you know?" Meredith shouted.

"Because I filled them with water after old man Moffitt died and Union Oil pulled out. I didn't like the thought of all that gas down there, even a few gallons." Jake started forward, stopped, and put his arms out, signaling for the others to stay back. He walked backwards until he bumped into Meredith, keeping his eyes focused on something across the street and in front of the old pump block. Meredith walked around Jake and saw a body, the light dancing over the twisted form as if it were a greeting to the group from the store.

Ellie walked around Meredith's right side, and he put his arm out, too late to keep her from seeing.

Meredith heard her gasp.

It was the girl. Lindsey.

A chill came over Meredith and he felt frozen, more than the two minutes in the rain could account for. He glanced at Ellie, and saw her pinched, white face.

Of course! The feeling that the killer was in control had been with him all day. *Your instincts have been screaming, Meredith, old son, that he's here. And you didn't listen.* How could he have been so stupid, so blind to what was happening? He thought that he could protect them, and he was leading Ellie and Stacey to more horror; leading them to death.

The killer was here! And he had been since before they left Arizona. He was still running the show, playing with them at his will.

The body lying before them reminded Meredith of the ones he'd seen on the road where Ellie had been found. The killer's games were deadly games.

They moved forward in single file: Robinson and Meredith, followed by Ellie, Jake, and Deb. The fire, Meredith saw, was mostly inside the old lube bay and office. Something was burning on the cement floor. The service station was constructed of metal and glass.

Robinson held up his hand and yelled, "Wait here!" He motioned for Meredith to follow him. Ellie, Jake, and Deb huddled together, watching. Meredith started after the sheriff, then stopped, looking back at Ellie. Years later, he would remember her like this; so small standing next to Jake; her face a pasty white, with lines of fear etched into it, making her look older, harsher, her blond hair wet and matted, streaming down her face. But she was still so stunningly beautiful.

Robinson was kneeling by Lindsey, not touching anything, just looking, when Meredith came up. Her throat was cut, Meredith saw, and she was lying on her back.

He looked at the blood covering the body, and suddenly he knew what the killer did with it.

The blood was alive, dancing, flickering black, then red, then black again, in the undulating light of the fire.

Something was on the ground about twenty feet from the girl. Something small and round. A hat. Meredith picked up the wet, brown felt hat and held it up for the sheriff to see. Blood on the brim.

"Charlie's," Robinson said.

Other things were bothering Meredith, more than the obvious mistakes he had made by coming here, being trapped on this mountain with a killer, more than finding the body of a girl who had just been killed. He was the clinician now, the investigator; he could detach himself. Something that he should know, something that should be obvious to even the most disinterested onlooker.

Think!

He knew it was something important. Something bad.

Diversion!

That's what the gas fire was, a goddamn diversion. It sure as shit wasn't spontaneous combustion that started the fire, or dumped a body here for that matter.

A diversion! For what reason?

All the fires did was tell them that there was a body out here. But for what purpose? They were all present, except for Charlie, and where the hell was the old man? Meredith straightened, and looked back at Jake and the women. They had walked closer, but they were all here, Jake, Ellie, Deb.

He suddenly began running back toward the group, tugging at the gun in his waistband as he ran, seeing the shock in their faces as he ran by, hearing the sheriff's yell.

His grip was so hard on the handle of the Sig Sauer .45 auto that his hand was numb. He heard screaming behind him now, and he hit the porch dragging his useless leg. He realized later that it was Ellie, running just behind him. He slammed his shoulder against the front door, twisting the knob at the same time, then flew into the darkened grocery store and ran toward the stairs to the living quarters without slowing.

Stacey!

How could I have been so stupid!

He took the stairs two at a time, jamming his foot down, ignoring the pain, not caring about the noise, aware of his position, aware that a stairway in a shootout is a deathtrap, a kill-zone, knowing that he could be dead in a second, not caring, he had to get to Stacey!

At the top of the stairs he fumbled for a light switch, and Ellie caught up with him and ran past him before he could reach out and stop her. She ran in through the open doorway and into her daughter's room.

"Stay-cee!"

She screamed, a high, wavering sound, and it came back to Meredith as he felt his knee go out. He limped the fifteen feet down the hallway and burst into the room.

He stopped just inside the doorway, and stood there, holding onto the .45 with his right hand, hanging on to the door with the left. Ellie was kneeling before Stacey's bed, rocking, clutching her daughter's threadbare stuffed dog.

Moaning (*hey . . . ho . . . off to dig we go*). She flinched as Meredith walked over to her. He knelt beside her and held her, wrapping his arms around her with his gun still in his hand.

245

"Motherfuckers!"

Ellie's shout brought his head up and she shouted again, reaching for his right hand. She clawed at the hand, and he was too slow by half, and she jerked the large automatic from his grasp. She gripped the .45 and pulled it to her, and fell backwards, cradling the Sig in her lap.

Meredith didn't try to take it from her.

The bed was empty.

Stacey was missing.

Even with modern radio equipment, the ability to communicate was determined in part by atmospheric conditions. Smaller police agencies were not funded to the point where they could afford state-of-the-art satellite systems. Adams County was no exception, and Sheriff Robinson had to make do with an antiquated radio system with aging repeaters that relayed radio signals from mountaintops to the courthouse in Newharbor. The nearest repeater to Cassville was on the peak of Snow Mountain, about ten air-miles away.

Robinson thought that the repeater must have been damaged in the storm, as he should have been able to activate the repeater and talk to the dispatcher in the courthouse as if she were five miles away instead of thirty.

It was worth another try.

Without outside help, there was every possibility that they would all be dead by morning.

"This is Sheriff Robinson to County. Do you read?" As soon as he released the microphone button, the static came crackling over the speaker.

Nothing.

Dammit! Outside the car, the storm swirled and raged, and if anything, had gained in intensity. Robinson was sitting in his car in front of the store. Meredith, Jake, and Deb were inside, trying to control a frantic Ellie.

". . . county . . . Robinson . . ." The static in the speaker was replaced with his dispatcher Martha's voice! It was broken, and hard to understand, but he might be able to get through!

"Martha, this is Sheriff Robinson," he said, unable to suppress his anxiety and excitement, radio procedure forgotten now. The reply came back instantly: "Go ahead, go ahead, Sheriff." And so did the interference, sounding as if the speaker were under a waterfall, a roar drowning out the words. He continued to talk anyway, not knowing if she could hear him.

"Martha, we need help in Cassville. We have one dead and two missing. Repeating, we have one dead and two missing. We need help in Cassville." The static continued. Robinson thumbed the mike button again, and added, "The tunnel is completely blocked."

He stared out at the storm, unseeing. No reply from Martha. The static was worse than ever. He must have activated the repeater, at least once, and it was entirely possible that she could hear him quite clearly at the courthouse, although he wouldn't be able to hear any reply on his car radio. Keep trying, he thought.

"Martha, we need help in Cassville, one dead, two missing. Killer here somewhere, tunnel is out."

Robinson waited and listened to the static, and tried one last time. Nothing. He turned the radio off and pulled his large frame up and out of the car. He stood on the porch of the store, looking out into the darkness, the wind and rain bringing sounds to him that he didn't want to hear. As he entered the store, he had a sudden urge to get a half-gallon of Black Velvet and throw the cap away. He'd never wanted a drink in his life as much as he did right now.

CHAPTER
51

Patterson followed Reggie Stewart into the tiny dispatch room, where Martha was seated at the console. She held up her hand as they came in. "Here's the tape of the sheriff's last transmission." She punched a button and Patterson heard the hissing static. He listened with Stewart for more than a minute, straining to hear something. Nothing but static and garbled voices. The static suddenly cleared, and the speaker, sounding as if he were in a hurry, as if he were lost and far away, came through clearly.

". . . Cassville . . . we have one dead and two missing . . ."

"Sheriff John Robinson," Stewart muttered. He left the dispatch center at a run. Patterson stayed long enough to learn that there were no deputies available—Robinson had only four during the best of times—and help from the state police was more than an hour away.

They decided to take the ambulance rather than a patrol car. From the looks of it, anyone left alive in the town was going to need a medic, Stewart reasoned.

They loaded up quietly, with Follette, the other medic who worked for Stewart's Ambulance Service, in the driver's seat. Stewart handed a pump-action twelve-gauge shotgun to Patterson and they got in.

Martha stopped them as they were taking off.

"You'll need this," she said, handing a sack of sandwiches and two thermos bottles up to the cab. "I'll be by the radio until you get back," she called to Patterson, with tears starting down her cheeks. She raised her hand in a salute as the red and white ambulance disappeared into the swirling wet blackness.

"Keep Sheriff John safe," she whispered, and walked slowly back to her console.

The Mountain

CHAPTER 52

"Muh . . . muh muh Mommy!" Stacey sobbed and her breath caught. She struggled and fought for air, the arm clamped around her chest adding to her panic. She drew a breath, a great asthmatic whoop. She had awakened to a nightmare of grabbing hands, hands around her waist and mouth.

Wet branches hit her as she was carried quickly through the woods, branches that she couldn't see in the blackness. She was being carried up the mountainside on a trail. The man holding her slipped and said bad words a lot. When her mommy was gone with the *bad man,* Stacey would lie trembling in her bed and listen to Maria talk about the *bad men* and the *bad things* they did.

She shivered in her soaked nightgown, her movements becoming sluggish, her body finally giving way to the cold.

She dozed, the first stages of hypothermia a blessing.

She heard the clicking noises as they started down onto the plateau. It was too dark for Stacey to see, but Brunson walked as surely as if it were daylight.

There they were again.

Chitinous sounds, like thousands of tiny mandibles clicking together.

Clicking.

Brunson stopped. He raised his arms and held them slightly forward, as if all before him were his.

"Lovelies," he whispered, talking as it were alone on the plateau. "I've brought something for you."

Clicking. Growing louder as the wind picked up. To Stacey it looked as if the entire floor of the plateau, as much as she could see in the dark, was moving.

Squirming.

She closed her eyes tight and felt herself falling, and she cried out as she was dropped to the ground.

Brunson glanced at the lovely at his feet, irritation at this mild distraction working on his face. The clicking sound began again, and the floor of the plateau seemed to crawl.

He tilted his face up and stared into the large raindrops that were becoming more frequent. He grinned darkly, holding his arms up, standing there immobile. He looked out over the plateau, and from this height, he could see a little grey in the west, the dim light highlighting the shapes of the small fir trees that struggled at the top of the basalt column—some of them near the edge were bent, almost horizontal when a hard gust of wind hit.

Brunson felt the bundle at his feet moving, crawling. He wanted to show her to his lovelies, and he would have her before that happened. And the other one.

He walked to the center of the plateau and stood at the edge of a large brush pile—the loggers called it a slash pile, a mound of tree limbs and branches. Brunson removed a plastic tarp that held most of the rain from the brush. He pulled two large metal cans from the brush, cans that contained a mixture of diesel and gasoline.

He looked at the little lovely as he walked to the opening. She would be well-guarded, and he had to meet the others.

Phoenix

Ward was amazed at the heat that remained in the late evening, hours after the sun had gone down. He pushed his way in through the front doors of the Phoenix Police Department Crime Lab and felt the instant coolness. Thank God for air conditioning, he thought. Gardiner had called him less than twenty minutes ago, and said that it was urgent. In fact his exact words were, "Get your lazy ass down here. I'm at the lab—Meredith's in deep shit, like he might be dead already!" and he'd promptly disconnected.

Some bureaucrats wouldn't have put up with Gardiner's bullshit and jabs at their authority. Ward was glad to have Gardiner—this brilliant maverick could be making much more working for private enterprise. Ward could hire other programmers, but most of them worried more about GS ratings than they did about catching killers . . . or protecting people in the field.

Ward located the lab and found Gardiner huddled near a massive worktable with three Phoenix technicians. Gardiner cleared off the table with a sweep of his arm, and began to lay files on the desk. He pulled up a stool for Ward and handed him a file—Gardiner's profile of the killer.

Ward read the first paragraph and glanced up at Gardiner. After he read the first few lines, Ward felt very old, and very scared.

State Highway 32

Patterson was quiet in the swaying ambulance; he looked over at Stewart when they slowed.

"End of the line, at least for this truck," the medic said. "We're at the tunnel, and boy, is it ever blocked." The rain blew into the ambulance as Stewart got out.

They assembled the packs at the back door of the ambulance and carried them to the mouth of the tunnel. Follette was going to wait with the ambulance and attempt to keep radio contact with Patterson and Stewart, who had a small field radio. The radio should reach the short distance to Cassville and the surrounding hills.

"You ever in a war, Sergeant?" Stewart asked the short detective. Patterson was looking into the blackness of the tunnel.

"No . . . and if it was constantly green like this, I don't think that I would have liked it. I'm a desert person. You in a war?"

"Yeah," the large medic answered. "There was a lot of heat, not rain like this, a desert, and there were people out there at night trying to kill me."

Stewart picked up the short-barrelled twelve-gauge shotgun in his massive hand, and it reminded Patterson of a toy gun. "Only this time"—Stewart waved the gun—"this time this medic's gonna have something to say to those people trying to kill me."

Stewart started into the tunnel, and stopped just inside the mouth. He switched on a flashlight, and played the light around, looking at the jagged chunks of concrete that were on the roadway. The rubble made the place look as if it had been shelled. Water ran in streams and dripped from the ceiling. As they stood there, they could hear what sounded like rocks or cement fall from the ceiling onto the road, making them jump.

Missus Stewart's little boy Reggie was always too big to go into them little hidey-holes, the medic said to himself, and started into the tunnel.

"Stay at least ten feet behind me," Stewart said over his shoulder, as Patterson started to walk abreast of him.

Patterson looked up at the ceiling, waiting for the roof to fall on their heads. They picked their way around some of the larger rocks and pieces of cement. As they got to the curve, he could see Stewart ahead, stopped by a large slide.

The medic waved Patterson forward. They stood and looked at the rented Ford that Meredith and Ellie had wrecked at the slide.

"Empty," Patterson said. He shined his light on the debris, and found the path that Meredith, Ellie, and Stacey had taken to the top. He started to climb, picking out his handholds as he went up, his weight sending down small rivers of mud and gravel.

They found the other car near the mouth of the tunnel.

"We don't have time," Patterson reminded Stewart, as he started to pull dirt and rock from the car. The Altona River fell away to their left, roaring past unseen, dark and muddy. "How far to Cassville?"

"Five or six miles."

Patterson started out into the rain, with Stewart following, holding the shotgun with a grim readiness. It was eleven at night, and Stewart wondered just what the hell he was doing out here. But he knew that he had to help these people, and with a sickening feeling, he knew that they were much too late, even with the fast pace the fat little detective from Phoenix was setting. Stewart shifted the large medical pack on his back. He had become a medic because of the killing he had seen when he was a kid in the army.

But if that man harmed Ellie and her little girl, there would be a lot more killing before Stewart was through.

Cassville

CHAPTER
53

Ellie ran down the stairs and out the front door of the store, carrying Meredith's .45 automatic in her bandaged right hand.

The wind threw a wall of rain up behind her. Meredith ran after her, the pain in his knee causing him to yell as he got to the porch. If she kept going, he didn't think that he could catch her. He saw movement to his left, and looked through the blackness. Nothing. He started off that way, limping badly, wanting her to stop, wishing Stacey safe. Robinson had been ready to go, but they needed Ellie to tell them the location.

He could hear her moving up ahead on the road.

Running.

Screaming her daughter's name.

To find Stacey they had to move fast. But they had to figure out where she was first. Meredith knew that Ellie might remember the horror of her kidnapping; the locations, the mountain where she was taken—during times of great stress. Or she could have blocked it out so completely that she would never remember. He came up to her suddenly, a small shadow in the middle of the road, shaking.

"She's afraid of the dark," Ellie sobbed. Her right hand still held the pistol, wet bandages trailing down over the handle; her left hand twisted in her hair. Like Stacey, when she's upset, Meredith thought.

"She wanted to be a big girl and not let me know." Ellie sobbed in her hands, the bandages falling down, soggy, bloody, the gun sticking up at an angle above her face.

"It's so . . . dark . . . out here."

Meredith held her as she cried.

"We'll . . . never find her."

"Let me take you back," Meredith said gently, starting to turn her around.

"Nooo!"

Despair turned to anger.

She ran.

Meredith followed, his knee a raw mass of nerve endings.

He ran after her, more a tortured hobble than a run, the rain closing in on him, soaking him. They ran out of the light created by the store windows, and down the highway, in the darkness. He couldn't see the road, and ran trusting the flat paved surface.

He closed the distance and caught up with Ellie as they reached the last of the buildings in Cassville. He looked at her with her hair plastered down over her cheeks, her breath coming in ragged jerks, trying to talk.

". . . leave me . . ." she gasped, crying and trying to breathe and run at once, "alone."

Meredith struggled to match her stride, and put his right arm around her shoulder. She tried to break away, no match for his strength, and he slowed them down to a walk, with his arm clamped tightly around her.

They stopped.

The storm slowed to a drizzle, unnoticed by Ellie and Meredith.

Since she'd run from the store, Ellie held one thought—to get her baby back. Her mind screamed with revulsion at what Stacey might he going through. Her mind twisted with hatred.

"Shoot him!" she screamed, holding onto Meredith with one arm, and holding her stomach with the other, shaking with violent cramps. "Kill him!" she shrieked, lifting her face into the rain. She shook, and opened her mouth to scream again, and the vision of upturned faces flashed into her mind with a jolt.

The silhouette of a man flashed before her, her memory as sharp as if he were in front of her. He stood with his face turned up into the rain—the killer! Ellie shivered, her panic for her daughter momentarily forgotten as she relived the horror of the mountain, the plateau where she'd been taken. The faces! Turned into the rain, like his. Jesus. She saw him again with his face turned up, on the trail, and on the road. In the vision she saw landmarks, a milepost marker, with a 1 and a 6 on it. Meredith eased his grip on her shoulder.

She saw death, with wings . . . and a sing-song voice came to her, her own voice, she thought.

Hey!

Ho! It's off to dig we go!! Lights came up behind them from town. Meredith heard the growl of the sheriff's Blazer.

"Sixteen!" Ellie shouted.

Sheriff Robinson drove up beside them.

"A milepost marker, number sixteen—where is it?" she yelled at Meredith and Robinson.

They looked at her.

"Where is it?" she demanded, her voice going shrill.

"What are you talking about?" Robinson said. "Where's milepost sixteen? It's just out of town, toward the tunnel, about half a mile. Maybe less."

Ellie stood there, seeing the narrow, steep trail they would have to go over to find her baby girl.

Meredith pulled her into the Blazer, holding her on the front seat on his uninjured knee, and Robinson started the car forward.

Less than a minute later, the sheriff brought the Blazer to a stop in the middle of the road. Ellie pushed her way out of the Blazer and ran in front of the headlights, crossing the road, her slight figure melting into the darkness.

Meredith, aching and cold, hobbled after her with a flashlight. He thought how pitiful they must look: a small—"diminutive" came to his mind, cold, tired mother who was trying to save her little girl, a cripple, and an overweight sheriff who was still in shock from all of the events of the past week. He knew from experience the great truth of life-and-death emergencies: The cop on the street, rookie or veteran, has to do the saving . . . the fighting . . . the dying. The Emergency Teams, the SWAT Teams, are always at least an hour away from helping anyone. He told himself that it didn't matter how beat-up and ill-equipped their little group was—they were all Stacey had. Robinson joined them by the roadside, lighting up the brush and trees with a powerful flashlight.

There! A break in the bracken fern that filled the ditches showed a trail leading to the trees.

Ellie plunged into the fern and disappeared between two trees. Meredith lurched behind, with Robinson following. Ellie's small size and quickness saved her.

As Robinson entered the trees, the bullet caught him high up in the chest, and he staggered back and collapsed. Meredith dropped down beside him, feeling rather than hearing a bullet go by his face.

Ellie!

She was up in front of Meredith. Robinson's flashlight was on the ground, the beam pointing off to the left. The sheriff was making gurgling noises as Meredith dove over him and grabbed the light. He hit the switch and they were in total darkness.

More bullets streamed past Meredith.

The explosions came from in front of him, about thirty feet, he thought, the muzzle flashes lighting up a hand and arm for an instant. Meredith suddenly jumped up, switched on the flash and held it up high, trying to draw fire away from Ellie and toward himself. "Ellie! Get down!"

Meredith thrust the light forward, toward the shooter, hoping Ellie was off the trail staying low. A figure was in front of them, his back to a tree, holding a gun, and Meredith saw Ellie then, running at the gun, running right at the man, her bandages trailing like bloody streamers.

Shoot him! Meredith screamed soundlessly, his scream a dry gargle, and then he did scream.

"Shoot him! Shoot, Ellleee . . . shoot the . . ." And he saw her gun come up, her yellow raincoat flashing in the light, her arm coming down as she ran.

She didn't shoot. She ran at the attacker, looking for Stacey, not seeing her, and the man's arm came up toward her as Meredith watched, still holding the light, immobile, and she shot, standing in front of the attacker, shooting him at a distance of ten feet, her arm jerking with the recoil of the .45, the assailant's body jumping with each slug, the impact throwing a mist of blood in an arc, a brilliant heliograph in the beam of the powerful light. Must've killed him, Meredith thought, and watched as the body slumped on the trail.

Ellie stood above the body, swaying, holding the .45 down by her leg.

Robinson groaned and stirred. Meredith tried to kneel beside the sheriff, and found that his knee just wouldn't do it. He lowered himself down and sat, taking a quick look at Ellie. He got a faint pulse from Robinson, but he looked bad, very bad. We might be able to help him now, he thought. Ellie shot the man on the trail. The killer? But where was Stacey?

They had to continue on.

He straightened Robinson's head as gently as he could, and reached down and took the sheriff's revolver. He pulled the sheriff's raincoat tighter and stood, hobbling to Ellie. She was on her knees in front of the dead man. The blood on her raincoat was starting to run down in streaks.

"Not him," Ellie hissed. "Not him."

"What?"

"Not the man who got me," Ellie said coldly. "Not the man who got my baby."

She peered into the dead man's face.

With a sudden horror Meredith saw that the man at the tree was Charlie, the old man from the tavern. Meredith saw the rope then, in the light. Charlie had been tied to the tree, his throat cut. But how—?

The arm had come from around the tree. The killer had been right here.

Ellie had shot a dead man.

"Sheriff dead?" she asked absently, still looking at the man she believed had attacked them. She got up, rubbing her right hand on her jeans.

"Don't know. Not much we can do for him now. With both of us working at it, we might be able to get him into his car."

Ellie had already started up the trail. Meredith looked back at the sheriff, and then down at Charlie.

He had already seen more horror in this case than any human should ever have to, and he was suddenly cold, icy.

Meredith followed Ellie up the trail as well as he could, the knee betraying him with each step, he cursing the betrayal, the pain constant, seeking to stop him, as though his knee were part of the evil that waited for them on the mountain.

Ellie. The woman he cared for, loved. Somewhere up above him on the mountainside. From high above him came a sudden bright light, a great gout of flame, lighting up the forest in a surreal flash.

Meredith stopped, holding onto a tree, watching as the fire died down, its location marked by a glow against the backdrop of trees.

He judged it to be about three hundred feet above them, up a steep slope.

Their destination. And probably our damnation, Meredith thought bitterly. He pulled himself forward, grabbing onto trees, brush, trying to catch up with Ellie, wondering how many more times they would have to combat this evil.

Before the night was over, they found out.

CHAPTER
54

Reggie Stewart stopped and stared into the dark, straining to see. He waited for the detective from Arizona to catch up. The fat little cop was a good one—he had humped hard, and he understood the rules: You forget personal hurt when people need help. Stewart put his massive hand on Patterson's shoulder, and pointed.

"There, about fifty yards in front of us, a car."

"Yeah." Patterson followed his hand and saw the dark shape. "Can you tell what it is?"

"The sheriff's Blazer, I think, but just in case . . ."

Patterson had already moved to the left side, the river side of the road. They moved forward cautiously, with Stewart in the brush on the other side. The car was, Patterson saw, parked in the middle of the road, lights out. He held his gun on the car. They got within ten feet, and Stewart moved up, smoothly for a big man, and looked in, holding his shotgun with one hand, the barrel leading the way.

"Engine's still warm," Patterson said.

"Trail here," Stewart said. The big medic was looking at the brush, and a muddy track leading up the hill. "They're up the trail, probably Meredith and the sheriff, and they sure as hell wouldn't be up there this time of day if they didn't have to." He looked at the car and then up the darkened trail. The drizzle had stopped, but the wind remained, blowing trees and brush and raincoats.

"How far is the town from here?" Patterson asked.

"Less than a mile, maybe less than a half mile. We're pretty close."

Patterson followed Stewart to the trail head, and watched as the big man walked in a few feet.

"What the hell! Patterson, hey man, come here, fast!" Stewart yelled and disappeared farther up the trail.

Patterson turned on his flashlight, and saw Stewart hunched over a figure lying on the trail. He came up and saw the uniform and the blood.

"He dead?"

Stewart was pulling the raincoat off and checking for vitals.

"Not yet, but he probably will be soon. He needs to be on a table, like yesterday." He cut the clothing away swiftly, looking at the hole the bullet made in the upper chest. "I got a real messed-up thready pulse and not much ventilation. We got to get him down the mountain now. The little store won't do it. He'll probably be dead in a few minutes no matter what we do."

Patterson walked up the trail.

"Hey, Stu, check this out." The medic walked up the trail, glancing over his shoulder at the sheriff, unwilling to leave him for any time at all. He might go into cardiac arrest at any minute from loss of blood. He looked over the shoulder of the Phoenix detective.

"Fuck me," he said quietly. "Somebody cut the shit outta old Charlie." Patterson watched. Stewart reached down and pulled back a blood-encrusted eyelid. He looked at the holes in the raincoat. "And shot him," he muttered.

Patterson shut off the light and peered down the trail, feeling his skin crawl, as if someone were watching them.

They loaded the sheriff into the back seat of the Blazer, Stewart carrying most of the weight, his muscles popping. He found keys to the car hooked on Robinson's belt. He turned the heater on high, trying to combat the shock, feeling scared for his old friend, thinking that Robinson was a dead man.

"What about Cassville?" Patterson asked.

"No good," Stewart yelled above the blowing wind. "I've got to get him back to the ambulance as fast as I can." He grabbed the microphone.

"Follette, goddamn it, wake your ass up, we got one coming," Stewart growled. He reached the medic and told him to meet them on the Cassville side of the tunnel with a stretcher.

Robinson moaned, his first sign of life, and feebly moved his arm. Stewart reached in back and put his hand on his friend's face. Patterson watched from the driver's door.

"You know I have to try and save him," Stewart said, "and—"

Patterson held up his hand. "I know."

"Up to you now to save that lady and her little girl."

They stared at each other, their faces close in the dark.

"I know," Patterson said softly, "now get out of here."

He waved a silent goodbye as the Blazer shot forward, wishing that he were in Phoenix . . . and wishing that the little girl and Meredith and all the rest were all right.

But he knew that it was not so.

In fact, he might not be in time to save anyone.

He hurried to the beginning of the trail, and looked up into the blackness.

Detective Sergeant Dennis Patterson, of the Phoenix Police Department, started up the mountain.

He lived to retire and have three grandchildren, and died at the ripe old age of eighty-eight, which was an amazing age for a retired cop, and the horror he saw in the next thirty minutes stayed with him every day for the rest of his life.

He never forgot it.

Never.

He saw a light, somewhere up above him, and turned on his flashlight. His chest tightened with the thought that someone could be holding a gun on him right now, ready to pull the trigger.

To hell with it, Patterson. You can't live forever. Besides—shit happens.

Thomas Brunson walked from the opening to look at his new lovely. He didn't hear her whimper, or even know that she might be cold. They were on the southernmost end of the plateau, just above the drop-off with the vertical columns of basalt. The wind gusted up the rock face, bringing a stinging rain with it.

The large fire in the center of the plateau was burning fiercely, growing larger as the wood dried.

Light skittered over skulls and dancing lovelies, helping them come alive for the one who was invisible.

They were coming for the girl, as he knew they would. He was ready for them. He knew what he would leave here for the world to see would make him powerful. Those people in their cozy houses would fear him. He would be bigger than all the others . . . gun sales would go out of sight . . . and the fear would make old ladies sit up all night and young ones jump at every sound.

They have to know that I can be anywhere. Everywhere.

I will be a teacher for others like me.

The girl stirred at his feet. Her nightgown was soaked and muddy and torn, and stuck to her body, providing no heat. She was numb with cold, well along in the stages of hypothermia. She didn't see the lovelies.

He knew he would stop some of them, as he had at the tunnel and the trail down by the road. He could go anywhere.

Brunson picked up the girl as one might a suitcase and carried her under his arm. He walked carefully around the lovelies to the opening leading to the plateau to look for the ones who would save her.

He took the girl back down with him and absently dropped her near the fire. Stacey mumbled and drew up into a ball. In a while, her nightgown started to steam from the heat.

The light flickered on the lovelies' empty eye sockets, the once-pretty faces glaring their hatred.

He left his new lovely then, to go back and wait for the others who might help her.

Ellie held the gun out in front of her in her right hand, holding on to a scraggly fir with her left. Meredith was behind her, and his light bounced around, hitting the trail enough to let her see her way up. The trail, if you could call it that, was almost vertical for the last fifty feet. She pulled the raincoat back, stuck the gun in her waistband and grabbed brush and rocks to pull herself along.

Her left hand came away with some crumbling lava rock, and she gasped as the nail from her index finger ripped from the nail bed and stayed behind, blood streaming in the rain.

Gotta find Stacey.

Can't cry. Gotta find Stacey.

Meredith was somewhere behind her. She could hear him. He caught up as she got to the vertical part.

Gonna kill him. Even if Stacey's all right, gonna kill him. Not going through this again. Never. No.

She began to climb again, not aware of the fingernail now, or of the occasional rain, the cold, the wind.

She was aware of the darkness. *How can I find my baby?*

She clawed at the rock, at the scraggly fir trees, other fingernails giving way as she closed on the opening.

Meredith had been following her as well as he could. She was slipping and falling and getting up like a machine. As Ellie started up the vertical column, he yelled.

"Ellie!"

She gave no sign that she heard him, and continued up. He started after her as she disappeared into an opening in the basalt, moving resolutely now, with a certainty. She remembered! She knew where she was going.

Flashes of light came from in front of her. Fire!

The killer wants us to come!

They didn't have any choice. And they both knew it.

Meredith crawled up beside Ellie in the opening that overlooked the plateau, the brightness of the fire blinding him. He pushed himself up and the sheriff's revolver he had been carrying slipped away, falling into the darkness below. He numbly watched it go.

Ellie was panting. A strange hurt sound escaped her, a sound that Meredith was sure she was unaware of. She doesn't know I'm here, he thought.

He looked down at the plateau. Someone was screaming. It wasn't until Ellie moved that he realized it was him.

Stewart drove with one hand reaching back holding the sheriff's wrist, one on the steering wheel. I can't feel a pulse, he thought as he slid around the last turn, he saw the backdrop of the tunnel, the glistening highway, nothing!

Follette was not there.

Stewart got out and looked hard at the tunnel. Anger flushed his cheeks as he yelled for his employee. He felt it before he heard it—a rumbling deep in the tunnel, the roof falling in all along its length. If Follette was in there, he was a dead man.

Stewart walked back to the Blazer, and got in behind the wheel. He turned his head to check on Robinson.

The sheriff was dead.

Stewart threw the lever into reverse, whipped the wheel, hit the brake, and the front end of the Blazer slid around, pointing back toward the trail.

He gripped the wheel in his left hand, the shotgun in his right.

He slid off the rain-slick road twice on the way back to the mountain trail.

The fire was ringed with dozens of smooth stones, arranged as if they were seats in an amphitheater, waiting for the magician to begin his show.

Ellie gave out a cry as she saw the crumpled figure by the fire.

Stacey!

The fire was getting bigger as they watched. Some of the small fir trees nearby were beginning to smolder, and as they watched, a four-foot tree suddenly exploded and was engulfed in flames.

Ellie began stumbling down the slope, running and falling and running again, toward her daughter 100 yards away.

Meredith stood watching the scene below him. It was as if he were on a movie set, a movie that took place on a remote native island, the exploding trees reminding him of burning grass huts.

Why was that woman running to the fire?

He shook it off and started down the slope, carefully picking his way around the larger chunks of basalt that had fallen from the column that rose above him, absently picking himself up when his knee collapsed. There was something about the stones, the shape.

Meredith watched the fire and saw Ellie cradling Stacey as he came closer. Ellie had turned her back to the flames, and steam was corning from her clothes. Meredith could feel the heat now, from fifty feet away. He walked closer to the blaze. He would have to pull Ellie and Stacey out before they were incinerated.

The stones looked like bowling balls, smooth, fairly round, with holes.

Eyeholes!

They moved in the night. The rocks were skulls. Jesus! He made a quick mental calculation of what he had seen from above the plateau, and figured there must be—the thought staggered him, dozens of skulls here, in one place . . . probably killed by the same man, by one man.

Circle. Ellie's words came back to him now. Of course! he thought. The killer had his own audience.

Faces!

Sorrow!

Meredith stepped through the circle, stepping on twigs and branches—please God, he thought, let them be twigs—but he knew they were not, and a tremor went up his legs, and the hair on his back and arms stood out, even with the soaked clothes on his body. He began shaking, the crunching under his boots making his stomach ache.

I have to get to Ellie!

Five feet away. She had her head down, her hair covering Stacey's face, and was rocking her.

She was muttering.

He shielded his eyes with his hand, walking around a five-foot fir that was blazing away to beat hell.

"Hey, ho . . ." she said, and rocked. Slowly forward. Slowly backward.

He had to move them back, fast! The edges of Ellie's raincoat were smoldering. And her hair was smoldering. He reached down for her.

"Ellie . . . look at me . . . Meredith," he said more evenly than he felt.

Her eyes snapped up, unseeing. She's gone, he thought. Back to the first time that she was here. Or maybe even before she got here.

"It's off to dig we . . . we . . ."

Meredith grabbed her coat, searing his hands on the hot material. He jerked Ellie to her feet, bringing Stacey with her, and began to pull her toward him, taking a step backwards, and yanking her along, half carrying her, anything to get her away before she burned.

He moved her away, taking crunching steps, not able to look at the ground, holding both of them up.

At twenty feet away, he could feel the rain again; he was half dragging, half carrying Ellie, and she still had her daughter pulled tightly to her chest. Meredith had his arms under Ellie's, jerking them now, moving further away, and he grunted as something snapped in his knee and they went down, hard, with Ellie and Stacey on top of him.

They were thirty feet from the fire.

Faces.

The fire glowed and the faces reflected the light . . . mossy faces, faces brown from the wind and rain. Not faces. Skulls.

Meredith was staring into the lifeless eyeholes of a skull, eyeholes from inches away. He pulled back involuntarily.

The terror and waste and horror and extreme sadness, the sorrow of the clifftop, engulfed him.

These remains were once living, happy, vital women, with families, lovers, husbands, children. Josh. The thought came to him that Josh was going to once again have a parent killed, taken away, a desertion. How unfair it was. He wanted more than ever at that moment to be a father to his adopted son. He cried for him.

Why are we any different . . . ?

They would not get off the mountain. He was sure of it. The killer was playing with them, much as he'd played with those who were already here. Like he's been playing with us for a week, Meredith thought. Ellie trusted me. Stacey trusted me, and I've failed them.

Ellie stirred on top of him, her raincoat still steaming. Stacey's eyes were closed, but Meredith thought that she was breathing.

He tried to pull himself into a sitting position while holding onto Ellie with Stacey between them. *Got to get them down the mountain.* He didn't know where the madman was, but he sure wasn't going to try to take him on by himself when he couldn't walk and had Ellie and Stacey to take care of. Sheriff Robinson was going to need help, too. The fire was spreading to other trees and brush and getting bigger instead of burning out as he thought it must with all the moisture the mountain held.

Ellie's hair was singed, burned in spots, and her forehead had a piece of blistered skin that flapped down into her face. Stacey, protected by her mother's body, didn't appear to be burned at all.

Ellie stared at Meredith as he sat them up.

"Ellie," he said hoarsely, his voice just above a whisper.

She sat staring out over the plateau, giving no indication that he was there or that she heard him. Using his good leg for leverage, he managed to pull Ellie to her feet. They stood there, swaying, leaning against each other for support. He placed his hands under Stacey and held onto her as well.

"Ellie, we've got to get out of here, get Stacey to a hospital." Meredith looked away from her, and glanced at the fire, and behind it. He picked out dozens of skulls, with the mounds of bones that lay next to them, attendants to their agony. He shivered.

Get it outta your mind, Patrick, my boy.

"Circles," Stacey whined, bringing both their heads down to, look at her.

"Faces."

Ellie looked at Meredith, and he saw that she was here with him after all.

"Patrick . . . can you walk?" she asked, and looked down at his leg, which he was holding off the ground. He hopped for balance and thought absurdly that Ellie had called him by his first name only when they spent the night together in each other's arms.

"Yeah, and I can crawl if that doesn't work." He stood looking back at the fire and the edge of the plateau, with the entire area as bright as noonday. He gently pulled the gun from her hand and stuck it in his belt.

He felt Ellie stiffen and heard her moan, and then the tremors began *(Hey! Ho! It's off to dig we go)*.

Meredith twisted his head around to look at the path behind him and *(Oh Dear God Dear Jesus)* the horror made his guts run cold and his good knee buckled.

The entrance to the plateau was blocked.

He knew then what the blood was for.

CHAPTER 55

While Meredith was dragging Ellie and her daughter from the fire, Detective Sergeant Dennis Patterson was wondering why the hell he was in Oregon in the first place.

It was wet.

It was cold.

Someone was trying to kill him. Someone had killed a lot of people and then dumped the bodies here.

He was very cold.

He was soaked.

And he had to find Ellie and her baby. There was no one else.

He had to use the flashlight. The trail was steep and muddy, between trees that often were so close together he had to slide his ample body sideways to get through.

He ducked under a branch and caught it with his arm and the water dumped on him. His breath was coming in jagged spurts, and he was sure his heart was pumping at over twice its normal rate.

Something was gonna blow.

He came around the tree and leaned his back into it. Just rest a minute, he thought, thirty seconds or so. And turn off the flash, dipshit. He saw the fire then. To his right, maybe another hundred yards up. It looked as if there was a large flat area up there, with the fire suspended in the air.

Gotta be some bad shit up there.

He pushed away from the tree, and pulled his way up the trail, grabbing whatever was there, small trees, rocks. My heart, he thought. It's beating way too fast anyway. It was probably pissed because he'd left the desert. Wanted a cigarette.

He kept the light off, stuck it in his belt and tried to stay on the trail by pulling himself up with the brush. He came up to the basalt column, and followed it around to his left, blindly, cautiously, stumbling over boulders and other shit. At least in the desert, he complained to himself, you can walk around at night and not run into this crap, not to mention the rain.

He stopped, gripped by a sense of foreboding that made his throat close. He could feel the evilness of this place. Slowly, carefully, trying not to move, Patterson eased the flashlight from his belt. His hair bristled, and he was suddenly freezing.

He began to shake, uncontrollably.

Something was breathing its fetid breath down on him, close, oh so close that he knew that any second he would be ripped up, his flesh fed to the fire.

He brought the light up and hit the switch, the 20,000-candlepower beam making him wince before he saw what was illuminated.

A man, a horrible caricature of a man, partially hidden by the mouth of what looked to be a cave, the light showing a ghastly pallor and eyes that were feral and inhuman. He had a large knife raised above his head.

A man, and not a man. A man painted with what was once living. Ready to kill him, to throw himself down on him.

The worst part of it was the silence. Patterson had faced many killers in twenty-five years of police work, and it was usually with the noise of the street, with yelling, with the sounds of dying.

Brunson launched himself down on top of Patterson. The detective screamed and rolled to his left, and as he rolled he knew that it was not quick enough, and he slammed into the basalt wall. The flashlight dropped over the edge and was gone, the path again in darkness. He felt rather than saw the knife looping down, and screamed again as he tried to flatten himself against the wall. The killer stabbed at his shoulder blade, the knife glancing off and slicing up the muscle of his back, ripping him, the steel searing his body, and he stood up, throwing Brunson off his back and down the hill.

Patterson was not thinking now, only reacting, and he clawed at his raincoat with his right hand—his left hand didn't seem to work anymore—and rolled on his left side, his body facing uphill, his feet digging in to keep him on the path.

"Nooo!" the detective screamed. He heard the killer stop his roll down the path and charge back up at him again. Patterson rolled over onto his back and pulled the Magnum clear and jerked the trigger, the blast like a grenade going off, the muzzle flash lighting up the killer— and he missed!

"Back off, you fucking asshole!" he screamed, his voice breaking.

He moved the muzzle slightly, and fired again, and again. The killer was on him with the knife coming down, finding his chest, cutting deep.

Patterson slid into a blackness as Brunson disappeared. The detective fired three more times, pulling the trigger again and again, firing into shadows.

After what seemed like a long time, he pushed himself to his feet, his chest screaming and wet, the useless revolver still an extension of his arm, dizziness and nausea threatening to buckle his legs. He slid down onto a rock and stared into the darkness where the killer had gone, and sat by the trail, each breath a tearing pain.

"Stabbed . . . the mother stabbed me."

Detective Sergeant Dennis Patterson of the Phoenix Police Department began his slow struggle up the trail.

Cassville Highway
CHAPTER
56

"Ohhhh shit . . . gonna hit the tree!" Stewart yelled, as the Blazer bounded out of the ditch, missing a large fir by inches; he somehow got the car back on the road without letting up on the gas pedal. He pounded his fist on the steering wheel, demanding more speed out of the worn-out Blazer, swerving on the rain-slick road as he did so.

He saw the fire then, and it looked as if the entire forest up on the hillside was ablaze. You could probably see the light from Cassville. Stewart rounded the last corner and hit the brakes, ending the slide sideways in the road.

He jumped out with the shotgun and started around the front, not taking time to turn off the engine. He stopped, thought better of it, and removed the keys. The big medic ran to the trailhead, and removed a flashlight from his belt.

Stewart stepped around Charlie's body, a bloody sentinel guarding the trail, the mud around him turning to a blackish shroud.

Stacey grabbed weakly for Meredith, a compulsive jerk that feebly grasped his jacket. He turned as Ellie stared silently at the figure on the rise above them, near the entrance of the cave.

It's him! Oh God The horror of the place, the bones, the bodies, the dead girls . . . oh God—no please. Meredith heard Ellie whimper, and Stacey stirred against him, and blinked.

The killer started down.

Brunson was naked to the waist, his skin glistening in the firelight, twisting over muscles that seemed bunched, mutated, and covered with blackness.

Covered with blood.

He was carrying a long, heavy-bladed knife.

Machete.

He was thirty feet away.

"I've come to get you, bitch. To join these lovelies," he called down to them. "And you, cop, you can watch them burn." He laughed, his teeth showing more than the sound. He was twenty feet away.

Fear made Meredith's legs turn leaden, icy, his stomach a mass of twisting sour gel.

Fear. Stacey stirred again, and whimpered. Fear. Ellie's little girl. Meredith's little girl.

"Nooo!"

Ellie screamed, and suddenly pushed against Meredith, clawing at his belt, dropping Stacey against him, and finding the gun with both hands, she pulled it out, bringing it around Meredith, raising the barrel.

Meredith set Stacey on the ground and reached for the gun. Stacey walked away from her mother and Meredith, trance-like, up the hill, toward the killer. Meredith grabbed her and pulled her behind him.

The explosion startled Meredith. He watched as Ellie's hand jerked up, the heavy automatic settling back down as she started to run past him toward the man above them. She fired again.

Missed!

She held the gun with both hands, pointing it up toward Brunson.

"Ellie!"

She pulled the trigger again.

Nothing!

Meredith pulled Stacey up into his arms, and backed away from Brunson, back toward the flames.

He reached out and grabbed Ellie, pulling her with him.

Brunson started down the hill, swinging the machete, his face cold death. The fire made his sweaty, bloody face shine, an ugly, twisting mirror of madness.

"Get you," the face hissed. Meredith could hear the swish of the blade as Brunson swung it in a powerful arc. They backed toward the fire.

"Cut you up!" The face contorted, cheek muscles bound with energy, the eyes showing icy hatred.

The fire grew hot. on Meredith's back. He dropped Stacey lightly to her feet, his eyes not leaving the blade.

"Run," he whispered. He gave her a small shove to his left. "Stacey, run!" Meredith yelled, and pushed Ellie to his right.

He ran toward the machete.

In the opening, Patterson stopped his tortured slide through the cave and wiped his hand across his forehead. It came away wet, with sweat or blood, he didn't know. The light from the fire cast surreal shadows on the rock walls, and he thought that he would rest just a bit longer. He was here for some reason, something important, but he just couldn't remember what it was.

His back was wet, like his forehead.

His consciousness flickered on and off like an old crystal set . . . one moment he was in a dark place, like a cave, and didn't know why, the next second he was ten years old, in his older brother's room, looking at Spiderman comics and sipping on a Pepsi.

Explosions jolted him back to the cave, and he looked around wildly for a few seconds, the firelight flipping him back and forth from the cave to his brother's room.

(*Holy geez, Spiderman is trapped by a giant sea creature!*)

Another shot now, the .45 sounding like a Howitzer. Must be Meredith's, he thought.

He pushed up into the cave farther, his shoulder a burning hell of pain, and he thought insanely that this was bad shit, like maybe you could die, Patterson. He stopped, just before the lip of the cave, and dropped to his hands and knees on the rocks.

Patterson pushed his way out to the edge of the opening and saw the plateau. From where he was he could see the entire area, the fire and the figures below. It seemed to him later like he had been watching a few minutes of a silent home movie, one of the early 8mm jobs, the film with no sound. Bright. The fire was very bright. He leaned against the mouth of the cave, half in the light, half in darkness. The fire he had seen from below was burning on some trees down near the far end, by the cliff. Meredith and Stacey and Ellie were backing toward the fire and a near naked monster was swinging a sword at Meredith.

Hey! Patterson yelled, but nothing came out. He worked his mouth again. Meredith! He tried to get up. The explosion of pain in his back made his stomach roll, and he threw up, his plan to yell abandoned. He watched with horror as Meredith stumbled backward on what looked to be a human skull.

Patterson made one more attempt to yell, and mercifully passed out, face-down, as Stacey and Ellie split away from Meredith.

The machete blade caught the energy of the fire, projecting a field of light to Meredith, a supernatural, evil heliograph. The heat from the fire pushed Meredith toward his death, as he tried to run toward the killer.

Buy some time, Meredith. He had only one leg to use. "Run, Ellie! Stacey. Run!" Meredith yelled hoarsely, and he risked a glance to his left.

Stacey had stopped, with her thumb in her mouth, watching.

Meredith took a step and his knee snapped, his leg going under him at an odd angle, and he fell, the pain coming over him in waves.

Ellie ran by him, screaming. Running for Stacey. "Leave us alone, you rotten bastard, leeeeeve usssss alone!"

Brunson advanced, swinging the machete, stepping carefully over bones and skulls, his feet guided by their own antennae, intent on Ellie and her daughter.

"Bitch, I'm going to hand your head to your daughter!" Ellie reached Stacey and scooped her up into her arms, and retreated, edging around the fire to the cliff. She whined, the fear for her daughter making her gag. Stacey! *My baby. Gotta save her. My dear, poor, sweet baby.* She had a sudden vision of her daughter at nine months, a happy, round baby, so content, trusting, loving. Ellie looked at her four-year-old now, and saw that she'd become catatonic, eyes unblinking, unseeing. Tears ran down Ellie's cheeks, washing the soot and grime away in two distinct lines. *Her baby dirty, scorched.*

"Momma's sorry, baby," she whispered. She continued to back up on the left side of the fire, the heat burning her flesh.

She began to sob, shaking.

Brunson approached Meredith, who was struggling to get his legs working, trying to draw them under him so he could stand.

Brunson stopped and swung the machete downward at Meredith. Meredith rolled, blocking the blow with his left arm, the blood spraying out at the contact, and he fell down again, and rolled.

Brunson followed, swinging. Ellie ran toward them, still holding Stacey, not thinking . . . just running.

She didn't yell this time. She shifted Stacey's weight into her left arm and looked wildly for a weapon, survival instincts thousands of years old taking over.

Anything!

A piece of basalt!

She grabbed a porous rock at her feet, a rock with sharp edges and fused by fire, and came up behind Brunson as he was bringing the machete up above his head to strike Meredith with a blow, and she drove the rock into the middle of Brunson's back, between the shoulder blades.

Brunson bellowed with rage, and fell to his knees. Meredith rolled out of the way, and watched as the killer got up with the machete and walked purposefully after Ellie and Stacey, the only evidence of the blow a small spot of blood that was leaking from his back.

"Lovelies," he grunted. "My lovelies."

Brunson held the machete in front of him, swaying, forcing Ellie and Stacey back to the edge of the cliff.

Meredith followed, refusing to let his body give up now. He held his right knee with both hands, clamping hard, refusing the pain, walking on the twigs, not looking down, knowing that he had to reach Brunson before the killer reached Ellie and Stacey.

"Lovelies, come to me!" Brunson screamed, and swung the machete at Ellie's head, her back to the cliff.

Meredith began his run, a hop on one foot, jamming the right down as he would a crutch. His only hope was to tackle the killer and take him over the cliff.

At ten feet away, the machete began to descend.

At five feet, Meredith launched himself at Brunson, holding his arms out wide, yelling.

He took him up high, the blade cutting the air above Ellie's head, Brunson grunting as he was thrown off balance. Meredith hung on, his arms wrapped around Brunson, pinning the killer's arms to his side, Brunson trying to swing the machete against Meredith's leg.

Meredith was looking into darkness, with the killer's head dangling below him into space, his shoulders wedged on a rock at the very edge of the basalt column.

Meredith was losing the battle. Brunson was heavier, stronger, and it was impossible to hold onto the upper body, which was drenched in blood. Meredith dug in with his feet and pushed, trying to move the killer over the cliff, but he was losing his grip. Brunson grabbed Meredith and pulled him toward the edge. The killer screamed, his face twisted with hatred.

Take him with you! Meredith thought.

Take him over with you!

Brunson wrenched his arm free and pulled Meredith back to the edge. He got to his knees and gave Meredith a savage blow with the machete, hitting him in the ribs with the handle, knocking the wind out of him; Meredith doubled up, waves of grey breaking over his vision. Meredith tried to scream. *Run! Ellie!* He couldn't breathe. Brunson hit him again, pushed him down, and brought the blade up.

And suddenly Ellie was there! Through the haze Meredith could see her on her knees, beside him, beside the killer.

Ellie!

Leave me! He gasped, tried to yell at her to save Stacey, to run . . . take Stacey and *run!* Brunson twisted beside him, turning to face Ellie, rising. His body jerked and he sprawled flat, and rose again.

Ellie struck Brunson's head with a rock and he dropped down, making a crablike motion, crawling, clawing at the rocks in an effort to get away.

The rock came down again, the porous basalt shining black with blood, the wound spraying a red arc from Brunson's head to the rock. He made a whimpering sound, dropped the machete, and put his hand up to protect himself. The next blow smashed his hand to his skull, the sharp basalt cutting off his little finger.

The rock came down again, mashing the skull, splattering blood and brains over Meredith.

Ellie struck with the rock again.

And again.

The body started to slide.

Ellie swung again; the body shuddered with the blow, and dropped over the edge, trailing blood.

Quiet.

Meredith never did hear the body hit. He closed his eyes.

Stewart found Ellie there, holding the rock, swinging the rock at nothing, looking into the darkness. He was carrying her daughter.

The medic carried the little girl and Ellie down first, the mother and daughter cradled in his arms, his muscles tight with fatigue. He had dropped the shotgun on the plateau, but no one who challenged him would live.

As the medic struggled through the cave, Patterson was lying on his back. The blood foamed around his mouth as he asked about Meredith.

Stewart could only shrug. He carried the Phoenix detective next, holding him in his arms as one might carry an infant, the detective for once silent.

The fed had lost a lot of blood, Stewart thought. He took Meredith off the mountain as gently as he could.

Too many good people died here . . . he wasn't going to lose one more.

Sunday, July 9
Portland
EPILOGUE

"Mr. Meredith, open your eyes."

Meredith heard the voice through pain and fog, and tried to continue the drifting ride he was on. The voice persisted. He slowly tried his left eye and saw grey hair and a stethoscope.

"Can you hear me?"

"Yeah." It came out as a croak.

"I'm Dr. Winder. You're in Good Samaritan Hospital in Portland."

Good Sam. Been here before, he thought. Meredith looked past the doctor and saw Josh sprawled in a chair, his eyes shut, his head cocked at an impossible angle. Winder followed his gaze.

"Been here since they brought you in. Haven't been able to get him to leave."

Winder left. Josh came over for hugs, with Meredith's good arm holding tight. "I ain't leaving this room, Dad." Meredith nodded.

"Ellie and Stacey . . . they here?"

"Outside the door. There's a bunch of other people here, too. Some guy from Washington."

"Old guy, with silver hair?"

"Nope . . . a young guy . . . looks like a nerd."

Gardiner. "Get him for me, okay, son?"

Gardiner came in wearing his usual worn-out corduroy jacket, sporting a new "Love a Nurse" button. Another campaign.

"Nice vacation you're having here while the rest of us work, buddy."

Meredith grunted, looking at his left arm. It was encased from shoulder to hand in a plaster cast. He tried to move it, the pain coming over him in a wash.

"What happened, where'd we screw up?"

Gardiner told him about Brunson's flight from Arizona to Oregon. And he told Meredith how they all got off the mountain. Meredith had a fuzzy memory of parts of the wild trip . . . Stewart loading them into the Blazer, carrying them one at a time through the collapsed tunnel, and a wild ride to Newharbor to meet a life flight to Portland.

"Patterson?"

"Next floor down, ICU. Gonna be all right, though."

A nurse came in to give Meredith a shot. Gardiner followed her out with a grin.

Ellie entered, carrying Stacey, mother and daughter both wearing new blouses and slacks. Stacey had her thumb in her mouth, her finger curled around her nose.

Both so beautiful, Meredith thought.

Josh was polite . . . wary. He held onto his dad's hand. "I'm pretty beat up," Meredith said, trying to see behind Ellie's blue eyes. "Not worth much—"

"You'll do," Ellie said, smiling, and leaned over and kissed him, pushing Stacey into Josh. She pulled up from Meredith's face a few inches and peered intently in his eyes, the kiss still warm on his lips.

"Josh have a sister?" she asked.

Meredith shook his head, no.

"He does now." She kissed him again.

Friday, November 10
Newharbor

It was 4 P.M., and the sun was far over the ocean, giving the beach a golden tone, the air still and warm for November. A black Lab ran in the surf, a little too fat to go fast, but acting like a puppy, all the same. A five-year-old girl with blond pigtails chased him, laughing, screaming his name.

"Mac! Mac!"

Josh ran after her, not letting her get too far away. Meredith sat on the sand, watching, stretching his leg out, the new knee brace feeling better. Stewart handed Meredith a beer, ice dripping off the can.

"They gonna wear that old dog out," Stewart said, chuckling as Mac chased both kids. He turned to Meredith. "Nice family you have, my man."

Meredith felt his eyes water, not trusting himself to speak. He nodded, thinking, *yeah, nice family I have, thanks to a certain ambulance jockey.*

Ellie walked on the beach to their left, near the jetty. She waved to them. Stewart raised his arm and wiggled his beer can. The doctor said that she should walk. Meredith thought that he could see her swollen tummy from where he sat. Josh and Stacey would have a baby to grow with. To love.

Meredith turned to Stewart, able to speak now. "Don't you mean, my man, nice family we have?"

* * *

Over a mountain, miles from the ocean, a bird circled, effortlessly riding the air current that came off the bluff. It caught movement below, and turned the tip of its large wing toward the trees, waiting for the movement to stop.

ABOUT THE AUTHOR

Enes Smith relied upon his experience as a homicide detective to write his first novel, *Fatal Flowers* (Berkley, 1992). Crime author Ann Rule wrote, "*Fatal Flowers* is a chillingly authentic look into the blackest depths of a psychopath's fantasies. Not for the fainthearted . . . Smith is a cop who's been there and a writer on his way straight up. Read this on a night when you don't need to sleep, you won't . . ."

Fatal Flowers was followed by *Dear Departed* (Berkley, 1994). "You might want to lock the doors before starting this one," author Ken Goddard wrote, "Enes Smith possesses a gut-level understanding of the word 'evil,' and it shows." Ken Goddard is the author of *The Alchemist*, *Prey*, and *Outer Perimeter*, and Director of the National Wildlife Forensic Laboratory.

Smith's work as a Tribal Police Chief for the Confederated Tribes of the Warm Springs Indians of Oregon led to his first novel in Indian Country, *Cold River Rising. Cold River Resurrection* is the second novel in the Cold River series. He has been one of the few Šiyápu to hold that position in Indian Country. He worked as police chief in 1994 and 1995, and even though he is a Šiyápu, he was asked back as tribal police chief in 2005.

He has been a college instructor and adjunct professor, teaching a vast array of courses including Criminology, Sociology, Social Deviance, and Race, Class, and Ethnicity. He trains casino employees in the art of nonverbal cues to deception. He is a frequent keynote speaker at regional and national events, and has been a panelist at The Bouchercon, the World Mystery Convention.